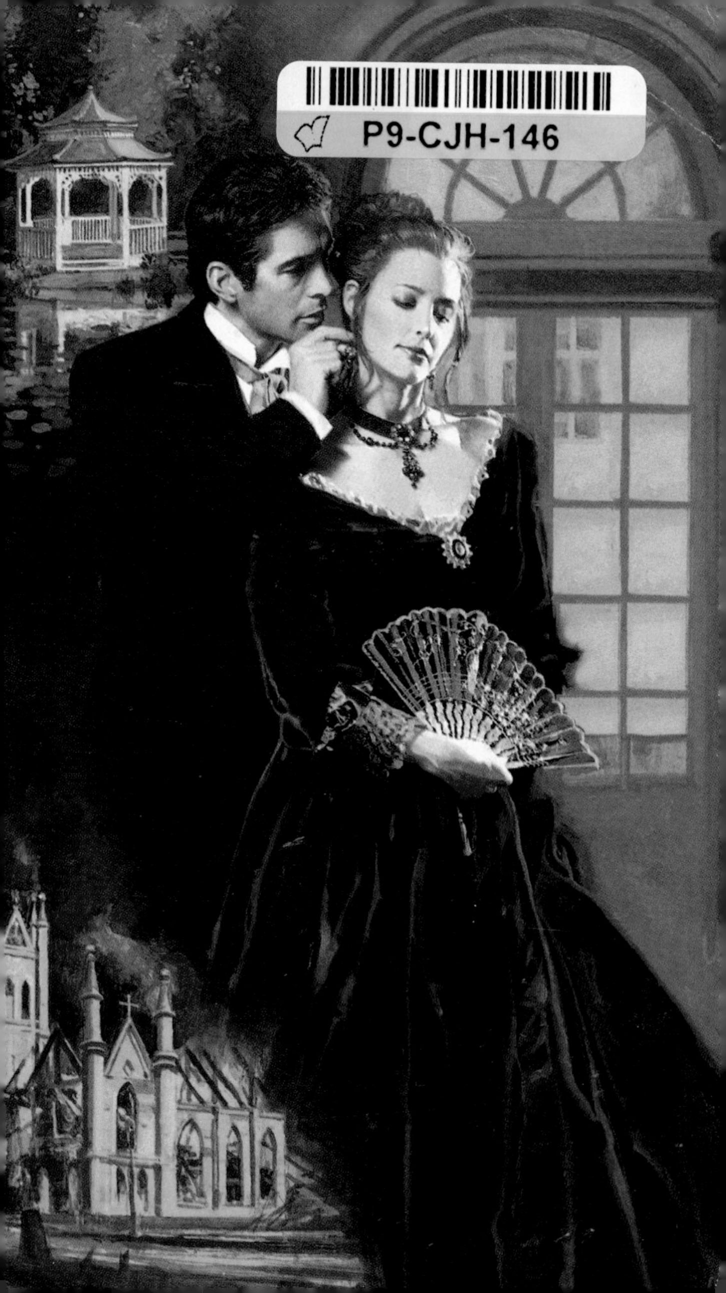

# SUSAN WIGGS

# THE MISTRESS

MIRA

ISBN 1-55166-610-3

THE MISTRESS

Copyright © 2000 by Susan Wiggs.

Visit us at www.mirabooks.com

Printed in U.S.A.

## ACKNOWLEDGMENT

Thanks to Joyce, Betty and Barb, for favors too numerous to count; to friends near and far, including Jamie for brainstorming a trading scam, and Jodi for therapeutic e-mail conversations; thanks to Jill for the Bunco book, and to the wonderful Martha Keenan, who always edits above and beyond the call of duty.

Special thanks to the Chicago Historical Society, one of the richest resources ever to make itself available to a writer.

To my third grade teacher, Mrs. Marge Green, who taught me cursive writing and told me the story of Mrs. O'Leary's cow.

One dark night,
when people were in bed,
Old Mrs. Leary lit a lantern in her shed;
The cow kicked it over, winked its eye
and said, "There'll be a hot time
in the old town tonight."

—Anon.,
quoted in the *Chicago Evening Post*

# *Prologue*

She looked older than her years from a lifetime of toil. The routine struggles of making her way in the world wore on her like the fading dye of her dimity dress. Up at dawn for the milking, feeding the hungry mouths that depended on her for every breath they took, keeping house, seeing to the livestock and navigating the unseen reefs and rocky shoals of everyday living had stolen her youth.

On a hot October night following a hot October day, Catherine O'Leary put the children down early. She washed up after supper, plunging her chapped and chafed hands into the tepid water. A high prairie wind roared through the shantytown that comprised her small world, across the river from the quiet, stately mansions of the grain barons and merchant princes. Her children had learned to sleep despite the boisterous, frequent celebrations of the McLaughlins next door. The neighbors were welcoming a cousin newly arrived from Ireland, and the thin, lively whine of fiddle music flooded through the open windows, causing the walls to vibrate. As she washed, Catherine

tapped her sore, bare foot to match the rhythm of
hobnail boots on plank floors emanating from the adjacent cottage.

Shadows deepened across the beaten-earth yard
leading to the cow barn that housed the source of the
family's livelihood. Her husband was out back now,
feeding and watering the animals. The dry, blowing
heat caused brown leaves to erupt in restless swirls
through the air. The wind picked up, sounding like
the chug of a locomotive coming on fast.

Catherine dried her hands on her apron as Patrick
returned from the barn, his shoulders bowed with ex-
haustion. She saw a flicker in the sky, a star winking
its eye perhaps, but her attention was all for her husband. This week he had worked hard, laying in supplies for the winter—three tons of timothy hay, another two tons of coal, wood shavings for kindling
from Bateham's Planing Mill. Baking in the arid heat,
the shavings curled and rustled when the aggressive
wind stirred them. In this heat it was hard to imagine
that winter was only weeks away.

She gave Patrick his supper of potatoes and pickled
cabbage, wishing he'd had time to eat with her and
the children. But families like the O'Learys did not
have that luxury. Imagine, sitting down like the Quality, with enough room for everyone around the same
table.

She took off her apron and kerchief. Pumping fresh
water into the sink, she bathed her face and neck, and
finally her sore foot; a cow had stepped on it that
morning and she had been limping around all day.
She drew the curtains and peeled her bodice to the
waist, giving herself a more thorough washing. She
braided her thick red hair, then went to check on the

children. Scattered like puppies in the restless heat, the little ones lay uncovered on rough sheets she had sprinkled with water to keep them cool. There was another daughter, Kathleen, firstborn and first to leave the reluctant arms of her parents to work as a lady's maid at Chicago's finest school for young ladies. Perhaps in the turreted stone building by the lake, Kathleen suffered less from the heat than they did here in the West Division.

Ah, Kathleen, there was a fine young article, Catherine thought fondly. By hook or by crook, she'd make good. The Lord in his wisdom had given her the brains and the looks to do it. She wouldn't turn out like her mother, overworked, tired, old before her time.

The sounds of revelry next door swelled, then quieted, mingling with the howl of the wind. Through the coarse weave of the sackcloth curtains, Catherine noticed a flash of light in the window.

"Let us to bed, Mother," her husband said softly. Patrick kissed her and put out the lamp. Settling her weary head on the pillow, she listened to the rustling and breathing of her children. Then she nestled into the strong soft cradle of her husband's arms, sighed and thought that maybe this was what all the toil was for. This one sweet moment of inexpressible bliss.

A knock at the door drew Catherine O'Leary back from the comfortable edge of sleep. The McLaughlins' fiddle wailed on and the bodhran thumped out an ancient tribal rhythm. Two of the children awakened and started whispering. Frowning, she propped herself up on one elbow and prodded Patrick. "Are you awake, then?" she asked.

"Aye, just. I'll see who it is."

She lay still, hearing the low murmur of masculine voices followed by the sound of the door swishing shut. Her sore foot throbbed heatedly under the thin sheet.

"It was Daniel Sullivan with Father Campbell, come to call," Patrick said, returning. "I told them we were already abed, and not in a state for entertaining company."

"God preserve us for turning away a priest," Catherine said, "but 'tisn't he who has to do the milking at dawn." Feeling guilty for criticizing a priest, she drew aside a corner of the curtain to see the two men leaving.

Daniel often took an evening walk to escape the stifling heat of his cottage, even smaller and more cramped than the O'Leary place. He had one wooden leg, and as he walked along the pine plank sidewalk, his gait had the curious cadence of a heartbeat. He kept his head down, for his wooden leg tended to wedge itself into the cracks between the boards if he wasn't careful.

She was about to settle back down for the night when she noticed a sweeping gust of wind lifting the priest's long black cassock, revealing skinny white legs and drawers of a startling green hue. "Now there's a sight you don't see every day," she muttered.

Outside the wooden cottage, high in the hot night sky, a spark from someone's stove chimney looped and whirled, pushed along by the wind gusting in from the broad and empty Illinois prairie. The spark entered the O'Learys' barn, where the milk cows and a horse stood tethered with their heads lowered, and a calf slept on a bed of straw.

The glowing ember dropped onto the hay, and the wind fanned it until it bloomed, then burned in a hot, steady circle of orange. The flames spread like spilled kerosene, rushing down and over the bales of hay and lighting the crisp, dry wood shavings. Within moments, a river of fire flowed across the barn floor.

It was full dark the next time Catherine awakened, once again by a knock at the door. More visitors? No, this knocking had the rapid tattoo of alarm. Patrick hurried to answer. Catherine drew aside the tattered curtain divider to look in on the children. Over their sweet, slumbering faces, an eerie glow of light glimmered.

"Sweet Jesus," she whispered, racing to the window and tearing back the curtain.

A column of flame roared up the side of the barn. Firelight streamed across the yard between house and shed.

Catherine O'Leary opened the cottage door to an inferno. Her husband ran toward her, his face stark in the flame-lit night.

He said what she already knew, voicing the fear that made her heart sink like a stone in her chest: "See to the children. The barn's afire."

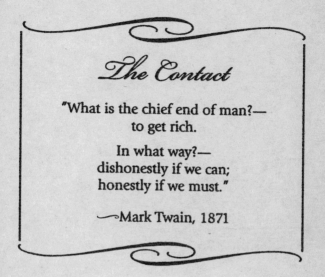

# The Contact

"What is the chief end of man?—
to get rich.

In what way?—
dishonestly if we can;
honestly if we must."

—Mark Twain, 1871

# *One*

Under a French gown of emerald silk, Kathleen O'Leary wore homespun bloomers that had seen better days. She told herself not to worry about what lay beneath her sumptuous costume. It was what the world saw on the surface that mattered, particularly tonight.

Next Friday, she would go down on her knees and admit the ruse to Father Campbell in the confessional, but Friday was far away. At the present moment, she meant to enjoy herself entirely, for it was a night of deceptions and she was at its heart.

The mechanical gilt elevator speeding them up to the third-floor salon of the Hotel Royale was only partially responsible for the swift rush of anticipation that tingled along her nerves. She clasped hands with her two companions, Phoebe Palmer and Lucy Hathaway, and gave them a squeeze. "Think we'll get away with it?" she whispered.

Lucy sent her a dark-eyed wink. "With looks like that, you could get away with robbing the Board of Trade."

Kathleen would have pinched herself if she hadn't been holding on so tightly to her friends' hands. She couldn't believe she was actually committing such an audacious act. Going to a social affair to which she wasn't invited. In a dress from Paris that didn't belong to her. Wearing jewels worth a king's ransom. To meet people who, if they knew who she really was, would not consider her fit to black their boots.

The bellman pushed up the brake lever and cranked open the door. With only a swift glance, Kathleen recognized him as an Irishman. He had the sturdy features and mild, deferential demeanor of a recent immigrant. Phoebe swept past him, not even seeing the small man.

"Mayor Mason will not be seeking another term," Phoebe was saying in a breathless voice that seemed fashioned solely for gossip. "Mrs. Wendover is having a flaming love affair with a student at Rush Medical College." She enumerated the tidbits on her fingers, intent on bringing Kathleen up to date with the guests she was about to meet. "And Mr. Dylan Kennedy is just back from the Continent."

"Remind me again. Who is Dylan Kennedy?" Lucy asked in a bored voice. She had never been one to be overly impressed by the upper classes—probably because she came from one of the oldest families of the city, and she understood their foibles and flaws.

"Don't you know?" Phoebe patted a brown curl into place. "He's only the richest, most handsome man in Chicago. It's said he came back to look for a wife." She led the way down the carpeted hall. "He might even begin courting someone in earnest this very night. Isn't that deliciously romantic?"

"It's not deliciously *anything*," Lucy Hathaway said with a skeptical sniff. "If he needs to pick something, he should go to the cattle auction over at the Union Stockyards."

Kathleen said nothing, but privately she agreed

with Phoebe for once. Dylan Francis Kennedy *was* delicious. She had glimpsed him a week earlier at a garden party at the Sinclair mansion, where her mistress, Miss Deborah Sinclair, lived when not away at finishing school. Kathleen had stolen a few moments from tending to her duties to look out across the long, groomed garden, and there, by an ornate gazebo, had stood the most wonderful-looking man she had ever seen. In perfectly tailored trousers that hugged his narrow hips, and a charcoal-black frock coat that accentuated the breadth of his shoulders, he had resembled a prince in a romantic story. Of course, it was a glimpse from afar. Up close, he probably wasn't nearly as…delicious.

She spied a door painted with the words Ladies' Powder Room and gave Lucy's hand a tug. "Could we, please?" she said. "I think I need a moment to compose myself." She spoke very carefully, disguising the soft brogue of her everyday speech.

Phoebe tapped an ivory-ribbed fan smartly on the palm of her gloved hand. "Chickening out?"

"In a pig's eye," Kathleen said, a shade of the dreaded brogue slipping out. She was always provoked and challenged by Phoebe Palmer, who belonged to one of Chicago's leading families. Phoebe, in turn, thought Kathleen far too cheeky and familiar with her betters and did her best to put the maid in her place.

That, in fact, was part of the challenge tonight. Lucy swore Kathleen could pass for a member of the upper crust. Phoebe didn't believe anyone would be fooled by the daughter of Irish immigrants. Lucy asserted that it would be an interesting social experiment. They had even made a wager on the outcome.

Tomorrow night, Crosby's Opera House was sched-
uled to open, and the cream of Chicago society would
be in attendance. If Kathleen managed to get herself
invited, Phoebe would donate one hundred dollars to
Lucy's dearest cause—suffrage for women.

"You can gild that lily all you like," Phoebe had
said to Lucy as they were getting ready for the evening. "But anyone with half a brain will know she's
just a common weed."

"Half a brain," Lucy had laughed and whispered
in Kathleen's ear, which burned with a blush. "That
leaves out most of the people at the soiree."

They stepped into the powder room decked with
gilt-framed mirrors and softly lit by the whitish glow
of gaslight sconces. The three young ladies stood together in front of the tall center mirror—Lucy, with
her black hair and merry eyes, Phoebe, haughty and
sure of herself, and Kathleen, regarding her reflection
anxiously, wondering if the vivid red of her hair and
the scattering of freckles over her cheeks and nose
would be a dead giveaway. Her long bright ringlets
spilled from a set of sterling combs, and the flush of
nervousness in her cheeks was not unbecoming. Perhaps she could pull this off after all.

"Lord, but I wish Miss Deborah had come," she
said, leaning forward and turning her head to one side
to examine her diamond-and-emerald drop earrings.
The costly baubles swayed with an unfamiliar tug.
Other than girlish games of dress-up, which she had
played with Deborah when she'd first gone to work
as a maid at the age of twelve, Kathleen had never
worn jewelry in her life. The eldest of five, she had
never even received the traditional cross at her First

Communion. Her parents simply hadn't had the money.

"Deborah wasn't well," Phoebe reminded her. "Besides, if she had come, then you wouldn't have had her fabulous gown to wear, or her Tiffany jewels, and you'd be sitting at the school all alone tonight."

"Cinderella sifting through the ashes," Kathleen said tartly. "You'd have loved that."

"Not really," Phoebe said, and just for a moment her haughty mask fell away. "I do wish you well, Kathleen. Please know that."

Kathleen was startled by the moment of candor. Perhaps, she thought, there were some things about the upper classes she would never understand. But that had not stopped her from wanting desperately to be one of them. And tonight was the perfect opportunity.

The well-tended young ladies of Miss Emma Wade Boylan's School received scores of invitations to social events in Chicago. Miss Boylan had a reputation for finishing a young woman with charm and panache, and charging her patrons dearly for the privilege. In return, Miss Boylan transformed raw, wealthy girls into perfect wives and hostesses. A bride from Boylan's was known to be the ideal ornament to a successful man.

The gathering tonight was special, and well attended by members of the elite group informally known as the Old Settlers. As it was a Sunday, there would be no dancing ball, so it was dubbed an evangelical evening, featuring a famous preacher, the Reverend Mr. Dwight L. Moody.

Proper Catholics were supposed to turn a deaf ear to evangelists, but Kathleen had always been challenged by the notion of being proper. Besides, the lecture was nothing more than an excuse for people to get together and gossip and flirt on a Sunday night. Everyone—except perhaps the Reverend himself—knew that. It was all part of the elaborate mating ritual of the upper class, and it fascinated Kathleen. Many a night she had stayed back at the school, paging through *Godey's Lady's Book,* studying the color fashion plates and wondering what it would be like to join the rare, privileged company of the elite.

Tonight, fate or simple happenstance held out the opportunity. Miss Deborah had taken ill and had gone home to her father. As a lark, Phoebe and Lucy had decided to try what Lucy termed a "social experiment."

Lucy swore that people were easily led and swayed by appearances, and there was no real distinction between the classes. A poor girl dressed as a princess would be as warmly received as royalty. Phoebe, on the other hand, believed that class was something a person was born with, like straight teeth or brown hair, and that people of distinction could spot an imposter every time.

Kathleen was their willing subject for the experiment. She had always been intrigued by rich people, having lived outside their charmed circle, looking in, for most of her life. At last she would join their midst, if only for a few hours.

"Are you hoping for a private moment with Mr. Kennedy?" Lucy asked Phoebe teasingly.

"He will surely be the handsomest man in attendance tonight," Phoebe said. "But you're welcome to him. I have a different ambition."

"What is wrong with him?" Kathleen asked, remembering the godlike creature she had watched in the gazebo. She knew that if Phoebe had wanted Dylan Kennedy for herself, she would have had him by now. "What aren't you telling us?"

"The fault is not with Mr. Kennedy, but with our dearest Phoebe," Lucy said, her voice both chiding and affectionate. "She has set a standard no mortal man can possibly meet."

"What is it that you want?" Kathleen asked.

"A duke," Phoebe whispered, nearly swooning with the admission.

Kathleen burst out laughing. "And where do you suppose you'll be finding one of those? Beneath a toadstool?" She feigned a mincing walk and stuck her nose in the air. "You may call me 'your highness' and be sure you scrape the floor when you bow."

Lucy swallowed an outburst of laughter. "Isn't a royal title against the law?"

"In *this* country," Phoebe said with an offended sniff. "And it's 'Your Grace.'"

"You mean you would leave the States in your quest for a title?"

Phoebe stared at her as if she had gone daft. "I would leave the *planet* in order to marry a title."

"But why?" Kathleen demanded.

"I wouldn't expect you to understand. Honestly, you've never known your place, Kathleen O'Leary. Deborah spoiled you from the start."

"That's because Deborah is smart enough to see that divisions of class are artificial," Lucy said. "As I intend to prove to you tonight."

"Let's not quarrel." No matter how hard-pressed, Kathleen always found it easier to tolerate Phoebe's snobbishness than to try to reason with her.

She checked inside her beaded silken reticule. As ornate as the crown jewels, the evening bag was anchored by a tasseled cord to her waist, the crystal beads catching the light each time she moved. As a lady's maid, she knew the contents of a proper reticule: calling cards, a tiny vial of smelling salts in case she felt faint, a lace-edged handkerchief, a comb and hairpin, a coin or two.

Because she was Irish, she could not deny a superstitious streak in herself. Before leaving the school tonight, she had snatched up a talisman to carry her through the evening. It was a mass card from St. Brendan's Church, printed in honor of her grandmother, Bridget Cavanaugh. The sturdy old woman had died three months earlier, and Kathleen ached with missing her. It seemed appropriate and oddly comforting to slip the holy card into her reticule, as if Gran were a little cardboard saint carried in her pocket. She lifted her chin and squared her shoulders. "I am as ready as a sinner on Fat Tuesday."

She and her friends slowly approached the salon, their footfalls silent on the carpet patterned with swirling ferns. Kathleen savored every moment, every sensation, knowing that memories of this night would sustain her through all the long years to come. She tried to memorize the plush feel of the thick carpet beneath her feet, which were clad in silk slippers made to match the Worth gown. She felt the rich, heavy weight of the emerald-and-diamond collar around her neck, and the tug of the matching earrings. She listened to the polite, cultured burble of conversation in the grand salon. To her, the mingling voices sounded like a chorus of angels. Everything even *smelled* rich, she reflected fancifully. French perfume, Havana cigars, fine brandy, Macassar hair oil.

They reached the arched doorway flanked by tall potted plants. The breeze through an open window let in a hot gust of air, causing the ferns to nod as if in obeisance. The uncertain luster of the moon polished the spires and dome of the courthouse in the next block. Far to the west, the sky flickered and glowed with heat lightning. It was a night made for magic. Of that, Kathleen felt certain.

She paused between Phoebe and Lucy. Under her breath, she said the word *prism* and left her mouth pursed. Miss Boylan taught that *prism* was the most becoming word a young lady could utter, for it caused the mouth to shape itself into a perfect bow, so attractive in company.

The trouble was, Phoebe and Lucy, rigorously trained by Miss Boylan, also said *prism,* and the three of them made the mistake of looking at one another.

Lucy burst out laughing first and Phoebe stayed sober the longest, but eventually they all erupted into gales of mirth. Trapped and exposed beneath the archway, they were unable to hide from the disapproval of long-nosed society matrons and haughty gentlemen peering at them through gold-rimmed lorgnettes.

"Oh, *that* went well," Phoebe said, hiccuping away the last of her laughter.

"A most discreet entrée," Lucy agreed. She linked arms with Kathleen. "We must proceed as if nothing has happened."

"Welcome, ladies, welcome!" A jovial man in a beautifully tailored claw-hammer coat came forward, acting the host. "And your happiness is most welcome indeed." He made a gallant bow from the waist.

"I was afraid the evening was going to get stodgy on me, but you've rescued us from that."

"Thank you ever so kindly, Mr. Pullman," Phoebe replied with an effortless curtsy. "We're honored to be included in tonight's affair."

"Everyone's welcome." He spread his arms to show off an impressively heavy watch chain anchored to a solid gold fob. "Do come in, come in."

"Mr. Pullman," Lucy said, "I'd like you to meet my friend Kate O'Leary from Baltimore." She winked and dropped her voice to a whisper. "You know, *the* Learys of Baltimore. They have just recently arrived in town for an extended visit."

George Pullman, famed entrepreneur whose palatial rail cars were described as "wonders of the age," fixed a keen, assessing eye on Kathleen.

Her mouth went dry. Her bones stiffened to cold stone and her cheeks were touched with the fire of humiliation. What a fool she was, to think she could pull this off. She was about to be found out and publicly unveiled by one of the most famous men in Chicago. She wanted to turn and run, but she could not seem to move her feet. She did the only thing she could think of. Summoning her best smile, she sank into an oft-practiced curtsy.

"How do you do, Mr. Pullman," she said with soft, precise diction. Not a trace of the Irish brogue that rolled unabashed through the cottage where she'd grown up. Not a flat, coarse vowel to be heard. Not a single waver of movement in the curtsy.

"Of the Baltimore Learys," he said at last, clearly fooled by Lucy's ruse. "My dear, you quite take my breath away." He seemed sincere. Then, remembering himself, he added, "You all do. My compliments to Miss Boylan." He moved on to greet someone else.

Kathleen didn't realize she had been holding her breath until she nearly burst, letting out a sigh of relief.

"I told you we'd fool everyone," Lucy said, gritting her teeth in a smile.

"Humph." Phoebe moved into the midst of the gathering like a ship under full sail. "George Pullman's money is as new as the Sinclair fortune. It takes generations of refinement to hone one's taste."

Phoebe Palmer never missed a chance to remind anyone who would listen that "old" money was far superior to "new." She considered it gauche for a family to get rich all in one lifetime rather than accumulating wealth over generations. Such things mattered to people like the Palmers.

Phoebe spent a moment scanning the crowd, her nose lifted high in the air. A hound on the scent, she sought out the most prestigious guests in the salon: Mr. Randolph Higgins, Mr. Robert Todd Lincoln, Miss Consuelo Ybarra, Mrs. Arabella Field. Then she focused on her quarry—Kim, Lord de Vere, son of the duke of Kilbride. A circle of fawning, fascinated Americans surrounded the carelessly, almost effeminately, toothsome young lord. Phoebe sought out Mr. Pullman to request a formal introduction.

Kathleen and Lucy exchanged a glance and had to struggle against another attack of the giggles. "Her great dream is to be a penny princess," Lucy explained. "British peers with bankrupt dukedoms and such often come to the States looking for a rich girl to marry. Then they use the girl's fortune to rebuild their estates."

"And she *allows* this?" Kathleen could see no benefit in the deal for a young woman.

"See for yourself."

Phoebe had turned herself into a simpering, self-ingratiating creature, begging for scraps at the skinny, chinless lord's side.

"What is wrong with a nice red-blooded American millionaire?" Kathleen asked.

"The fact that he's male," Lucy said with a grin, always quick to air her views. In favor of universal suffrage, birth control, free love and equal rights for women, she made no secret of her radical ideas. Try as she might, Miss Boylan had not been able to lecture such notions out of Lucy Hathaway's head.

"One day you'll meet a man who will make you beg forgiveness for saying that," Kathleen warned her.

"One day hell will ice over, too," Lucy said. "But I don't expect either event to occur in my lifetime. However, I was hoping to meet an interesting man tonight." Her scrutiny fixed itself on Mr. Randolph Higgins. A newcomer to Chicago, he was tall, broad and almost inhumanly attractive. "I've been thinking of taking a lover. Just to see what the fuss is all about."

Kathleen sucked in a shocked breath. "Really, Miss—"

Lucy clutched at Kathleen's arm. "Heavenly days," she said.

A chill of nervousness curled in Kathleen's gut. "What?"

"It's Philip Ascot."

"What the devil's *he* doing here?" Instinctively Kathleen hunched her shoulders, wishing she could hide. Philip Ascot IV was the fiancé of her mistress, Deborah Sinclair. Since Deborah was unwell tonight, Kathleen certainly hadn't expected him to attend. She peered at the young man suspiciously. Not a single blond hair nor a thread of clothing was out of place. He smiled politely while greeting Reverend Moody, a white-mustached, bombastic man, the only one present who believed his purpose this night was to save souls.

"I'll be found out for certain," Kathleen said, deflating in her beautiful dress.

"Will you?" Lucy lifted one dark eyebrow. "Are you sure he'd recognize you?"

"I've worked for his fiancée for years," she said. "He has seen me a hundred times or more."

"Then we'll simply have to brazen it out," said Lucy. "Come on. Just act as if you own the place."

Somehow, Kathleen found the poise to cross the room with a smooth, proprietary grace. Judging by the polite greetings drifting toward her and Lucy, she began to realize that she was carrying off the ruse. Mimicry had always been a gift of hers, helping her to absorb the same lessons in elocution, dancing, French and flower arranging her mistress had suffered through.

The difference was, Kathleen didn't consider the lessons a punishment. She loved every moment of them. She loved knowing which fork to use, which foot to put forward in a curtsy, learning how to say *pas de quoi* and shaping her mouth around the word *prism* before entering a room. It all seemed so lovely and refined to Kathleen. She couldn't fathom why Deborah detested her lessons so much. But then, her mistress had always been a quiet, circumspect young woman, overshadowed by her domineering father and, increasingly, by her high-society fiancé.

"Philip Ascot, as I live and breathe," Lucy said, approaching the fair-haired man and holding out her hand.

"Miss Lucy," he said, gallantly lifting her hand to his mouth. "You look fetching, as always."

"This is my dear friend Kate from Baltimore." Lucy took back her hand and presented Kathleen, pushing lightly but insistently at the small of her back.

Though she kept a social smile on her face, Kathleen felt sick. This was it. The moment of truth. Philip had only to take one look at her and he would recognize his fiancée's maid. He would expose her right down to her homespun bloomers and the calluses on her gloved hands. Too late, Kathleen remembered that he had given Deborah the diamond-and-emerald earrings last Christmas.

Sweet Jesus and the bald apostles. She was in for it now.

Philip made a formal bow and took her hand. Through her peau de soie glove, she felt the brief touch of his lips. Then he lifted his gaze to hers. "Enchanted, Miss Kate. What a pleasure indeed to meet you." He stared at her intently, a dashing smile on his face. But to Kathleen's shock, there was not a flicker of recognition in that stare. Only...an interest that was just a shade shy of polite. As quickly as she could, she freed herself from his touch.

"We are quite surprised to see you here, since Deborah is ill," Lucy commented. She had always been a plain-speaking sort; she got away with it because she was descended from a famous, blue-blooded family and was worth a fortune.

"Ill, you say?" He lifted an eyebrow. "This is the first I've heard of it." He shrugged, dismissing the mention of the woman he was soon to marry. "Another fit of melancholia, I presume. I'll look in on her tomorrow, perhaps." With a broad, cold grin he turned his attention to Kathleen. "So how long are you with us?"

Kathleen wondered why she had never recognized the vaguely predatory air that lurked just beneath the surface of this man's polished exterior. Perhaps, she realized with mild amazement, it was because she had never been the object of his interest before. When she was merely a maid, he paid her no more attention than a piece of furniture.

"Only a short while, Mr. Ascot," she said evasively. "Now you must excuse us." Without waiting for a reply, she took Lucy's arm and steered her away. As they moved toward the refreshment table, her cheeks felt as if they were on fire.

"You're trembling," said Lucy. "Are you all right?"

"I've just had a rather rude awakening. I've been in the company of that man dozens of times, because of Miss Deborah. But he's never even seen me before. He didn't recognize these earrings, even though he picked them out. Not that I would want his attention, but it's a wee bit disconcerting to know I attracted all the notice of a potted palm."

"He's an insufferable snob," Lucy said, curling her lip. "I have never been fond of him."

Neither had Kathleen, but she felt strange and hollow inside to know her existence was so insignificant to people like Philip Ascot. And he wasn't the only one. Earlier, Phoebe had ignored the elevator operator. Lucy had accepted a glass of lemonade from the tray of a passing waiter with the same lack of regard. Lucy, who hadn't a mean bone in her body, blandly smiled her thanks, but didn't actually *see* the neatly dressed waiter, didn't wonder what his name was, where he came from, whether his shiny shoes pinched his feet, or if he had a sweetheart or a wife.

To the upper crust, people like the waiter—even personal maids like Kathleen O'Leary—were ignored. Not out of malice, but out of sheer obliviousness.

Imagine going through life being invisible. As if she didn't exist at all. The very thought chilled and horrified her. It was more than vanity that made Kathleen want to be noticed. It was a keen sense of survival. If she was invisible, how could her life possibly matter? She wished she could march through her days with the conviction of Lucy, or the self-importance of Phoebe, or even the quiet gentility of Deborah.

Instead, she found herself at an unhappy crossroads. Because of her education, stolen from the tutors and governesses hired for her mistress, Kathleen no longer fit in with the working classes. Yet due to the circumstances of her birth, she didn't fit in with the privileged set, either.

Tonight, she decided, casting away the chilly shadows of doubt, tonight she would be a true lady, no one would be the wiser and Lucy would win her bet with Phoebe. Bolstered by that conviction, she resolved to set aside her doubts once and for all, and enjoy the evening.

She gave herself over to the experience, laughing and flirting with surprising ease and enjoyment. She met Mr. Cyrus McCormick, whose reaper works had made an even bigger fortune than Pullman's Palace

Cars. She exchanged pleasantries with Mrs. Asgarth, pretended to follow a lengthy gossip session delivered by Mrs. Cornelia Wendover and traded a promising smile with Andrew Ames, a slender, timid gentleman who owned a seat on the Chicago Board of Trade.

Even though it was the Sabbath, and the purpose of the evening involved the salvation of the soul, no one seemed to remember that. Helping herself to a flute of champagne, she took a drink, thrilled by the bubbly texture and tart flavor of it. Relaxing more by the moment, she began to feel truly accepted in the rare company of Old Settlers, estate tycoons, captains of industry and transportation moguls. She loved their power, their confidence, their unabashed flaunting of the fine things they owned. She admired the women in their Parisian gowns and Russian jewels. She envied the patina of culture that lingered on those who had spent time traveling abroad.

What a contrast this made with the society of her old neighborhood. In the West Division, there would be Mass on Sunday night, and afterward, perhaps a ceili with a fiddle band, plenty of cheap drink and dancing until everyone ran with sweat. As a small girl, she used to love a good ceili, but as she was drawn more and more into the orbit of the very rich, she had come to see the wild, Celtic celebrations as somewhat…barbaric.

Conscience-stricken by the disloyal thought, she plunged her hand into her reticule and secretly drew out her grandmother's mass card. The painting of Saint Bridget, her face bright with a martyr's glow, glared up at her accusingly. *And what manner of colleen are ye, then, ashamed of yer own flesh and blood?* Gran's voice seemed as close as a whisper in her ear. With a start, Kathleen dropped the card on the carpeted floor.

Before she could retrieve it, the heel of a large foot, clad in a shining leather shoe with a gleaming white spat, came down on a corner of the card, pinning it in place.

Sweet Mary, she would burn in hell for certain, letting some tycoon trample her poor Gran.

The owner of the foot didn't seem to know he was snuffing out a saint.

Kathleen wondered if she could slip the card out from under the foot without attracting his notice. Feigning a casual pose, she put out a dainty toe and attempted to drag the card toward her. No luck; the larger male foot held it pinned in place. She would have to stoop to pick it up.

Working as discreetly as a pickpocket, she unscrewed one of her earrings and dropped it on the floor.

"Oh, dear," she murmured. "I've lost—"

The gentleman turned.

"—my earring—" She broke off and stared. It was *him.*

Black-haired, blue-eyed and utterly captivating, Dylan Francis Kennedy had the sort of face Kathleen pictured when she and Deborah stayed up late to read forbidden, romantic tales of chivalry and daring. A wealth of curling, glossy hair set off the chiseled masculine jawline. The artful curves of his cheekbones and gently cleft chin were echoed by the shape of a mouth that made Kathleen remember Phoebe's description of him: *delicious.*

Unfortunately, at the moment, the delicious Dylan

Kennedy stooped and picked up both the diamond earring and Gran's holy card.

"Yours?" he asked, lifting an eyebrow.

"Thank you kindly, sir." Brazen it out, she told herself. In one swift movement she slid the card into the reticule, not bothering to secure the drawstring. But before she could take back the earring, he held it away from her.

With a smile that struck her absolutely speechless, Mr. Kennedy said, "Allow me."

# *Two*

"Absolutely not," Kathleen whispered after a long, awkward silence. She was aghast that this person would even consider such a thing. Letting a man put an earring on her, in a roomful of the best people in Chicago, would expose her as a fraud entirely. No proper lady would ever allow such a liberty. "Thank you for retrieving my earring. I shall retire to the powder room to put it back on." She held out her gloved hand.

His smile, and the merry gleam in his eyes, should have warned her. "My dear young lady," he said, "where is the fun in that?"

"Fun?" she squeaked.

"Isn't that why you're here?" He lifted an eyebrow, a dark curve that made him look more intriguing than ever. "For fun?"

Kathleen tried to gather her composure. In her fondest imaginings, she'd had clever conversations with dozens of men, had bantered and matched wits with people of breeding and quality. When no one was looking, she had practiced smiling, flirting, laughing, offering quips and amusing anecdotes. For the life of her, she could not think of one clever thing to say at this moment. But she was not about to let herself be struck dumb by a handsome man.

"I thought saving souls was on the agenda to-night," she said. "That should be fun enough for you."

"I'm a Catholic," he said smoothly. "Not a sober, pinch-mouthed Protestant. They don't believe in having fun. Not in this life, anyway."

His admission stunned her. The highest ranks of society normally looked down upon those of the Catholic faith. Only a certain privileged few could admit to it and still keep their place in society. That was one reason Lucy had picked Baltimore as Kathleen's fictional hometown. There, some of the oldest families were descended from venerable Catholic clans from centuries ago, which made them acceptable to socialites.

"Do I shock you?" he asked.

"Certainly not. *Sir.*" She deliberately emphasized the formal address. She knew that in this society, a person kept certain things secret. What could his blunt admission mean? That he knew the mass card for what it was and saw through her ruse? Or that he felt a genuine affinity for her because they had something in common?

His laughter was low and rich, a sound she thought she would never tire of hearing. "I beg your pardon. It's unforgivable for me to indulge in an intimate conversation with you before I've even introduced myself." His bow was perfectly correct. As if posing for a photograph, he leaned forward from the waist, one hand behind his back and the other held out palm up, as if in supplication. "Dylan Francis Kennedy, at your service."

She wondered if it was better to pretend ignorance or to admit she had known who he was all along. No, she couldn't do that. He'd ask where she had seen him before and she'd be forced to admit that she had been spying on him at the Sinclair mansion. "How do you do," she said. "I am—"

"Kate." He winked at her. "Your friend Miss Hathaway gave me permission to call you Kate. She said you were far too modest to demand a formal address."

She narrowed her eyes, skeptical of his dashing charm. "For all the gossip I've heard about you, I would expect informality."

"Now I am intrigued. What gossip?"

"That you are heir to a Boston shipping fortune, just back from a lengthy tour of the Continent," she said.

"You must have seen that in the *Tribune.*"

"And that you are looking for a wife," she added.

He laughed. "Ever since that nonsense was published, I've been inundated by ambitious matrons trotting out their rich daughters. Not that I wouldn't enjoy a parade of maidens, mind you—" he winked at her "—but I think I've narrowed the scope of my search."

She sniffed. "Then I shan't tell you the rest. You'll get a head swelled full of pride."

He chuckled. "Did your gossips say what manner of wife I'm seeking?"

"No, but I heard you've left a trail of broken hearts scattered across half the continent."

"Patently untrue. I am the one who is broken-hearted. In all my travels, I have been asking for the unattainable." He smiled sadly. "A woman of rare accomplishment and depth," he said. "One who has red hair, flashing eyes and knows all the words to the *Ave Maria*."

"You are an unforgivable tease, sir," she choked out, thoroughly intrigued.

He touched her elbow, leaning forward and lowering his voice. "I never tease. But don't worry. Your secret is safe with me."

"Which secret?" she blurted out. She was usually in control of her tongue, but his touch, even the light cradle of his hand at her elbow, disconcerted her.

"There's more than one?" He had the most alluring manner.

She bit her lip, thinking fast. Then she gave him the most dazzling smile she could muster. "Every woman has secrets," she said. "The more, the better."

He constantly seemed as if he were on the verge of laughter. "My dear Kate, I was speaking of your true identity."

She gasped. "If you know my true identity, why do you still deign to speak to me?"

"Because I want to put this earring on you. And if there's any *deigning* to be done, then it is you who has to deign because it's clear to everyone in this room that you outrank me."

"Outrank?"

"I knew you'd be too modest," he gently chided her. "Lucy warned me."

"She did?"

"Yes. She said you'd never flaunt your family tree nor the wealth that shakes from its branches like autumn leaves." He chuckled. "You see? I am insufferably vulgar, mentioning bloodlines and money in the same sentence."

"This is America," she said, hoping her relief didn't show. "We're free to talk of anything we like."

"And we do, don't we?" Still seeming to hover on the brink of laughter, he gestured at the exalted company in the room. The men wore custom-tailored suits and boiled collars so crisp that the edges seemed to cut their necks, and the women progressed through the conversation groups as if in the midst of a competitive sport.

Dylan Kennedy's suit, Kathleen observed, had the distinguished gentility of several seasons of age and wear, which made him look far more comfortable and natural in his role as lord of the manor. Not for him the spit shine and polish of new money, but the honored ease of generations of wealth. Next to him, even the English lord appeared bourgeois.

Then he did a most unexpected thing. Placing his hand under her elbow in a proprietary fashion, he guided her through an archway of the big salon to a smaller room with French windows flanked by garish faux marble pillars.

"Where are we going?" she asked.

"Sightseeing."

"But I—" She broke off as he opened one of the tall, hinged windows, revealing a view that stopped her in her tracks. "Oh, my," she said when she could breathe again. "That *is* quite a sight." She took a step out onto the small, curved balcony. The windstorm that had been chasing through the city all evening blew even stronger now, howling between the tall downtown buildings and whipping up the surface of the lake like buckwheat batter.

From this perspective, facing south and east, she

could see the curve of the river as it widened to join the vast, churning lake. Only a block or two distant, she noticed the dome and spires of the ornate court-house, and beyond that, the gothic steeple of St. Brendan's, the church of her girlhood. There, in a pious, sincere whisper, she had taken her first communion, accepted her confirmation and confessed her weekly sins. She expected that one day she would be married there under the gazebo in the little prayer garden, and buried there as well.

Tearing her mind from the moribund notion, she examined the perfect parallel lines of the streetlamps along Lake, Water and Randolph Streets. At the mouth of the river, giant grain elevators made ghostly silhouettes against the night sky. Every few seconds, the lighthouse at Government Pier lazily blinked its beam in her direction. And far to the south and west, the day seemed to linger, as if the sun had forgotten to set.

She smiled at the fanciful notion, thinking of her family in the West Division. Her mother would probably use the extra daylight to do chores. She was that industrious.

"Why do you smile?" Dylan Kennedy asked, his voice low and intimate.

"It's a beautiful sight, Mr. Kennedy. No wonder Chicagoans are so proud of their city."

"It's called the Queen of the Prairie," he said. "And you must call me Dylan."

A shiver of the forbidden passed over her. "I mustn't."

"Why not?"

"I scarcely know you."

"You can't be so formal with me after I do this."

"Do what?"

"This." Without further warning, he stepped very close to her, moving in so that she was trapped between a marble balustrade and his tall form. "Hold very still," he whispered.

"But—"

"Sh. Be still."

Her senses filled with the nearness of him. He had the most delicate touch of any man she could imagine. With the finesse of a gifted musician, the light fingering of a master violinist on the neck of his instrument, Dylan Kennedy placed one hand under her chin, turning her face to one side. She didn't know if it was her imagination, or if it was real, but she felt the fine brush of that delicate finger across her jaw as she turned her head.

"I confess I don't have much practice applying jewelry to a lady," he whispered, "but I am a willing pupil."

"Mr....Dylan, please. If you would hand me the earring, I could—"

"And spoil my chance to be near the most beautiful woman in Chicago?" His mouth was very close to her ear. She could feel the warm eddy of his breath over her skin. The sensation was so pleasant that, just for a moment, she closed her eyes. Then she felt his fingers gently manipulating her earlobe. Sweet Mary, what was happening to her? A man was touching her earlobe and she could do nothing but let her insides turn to melted butter. She held perfectly still, in a state of rapture, as he worked the tiny screw of the earring so that the teardrop-shaped jewel hung once again from her ear.

Then, all too soon, he stepped back. "Beautiful," he said, his bluer-than-sky eyes shining.

"You," said Kathleen in her haughtiest voice, "are a wicked man."

"True," he said. "That's why you find me so interesting."

"What makes you believe I find you interesting?"

"Let me think." He stroked his chin, pretending great concentration. "You followed me to this private balcony, as if for an assignation."

"I most certainly did not. You—you commandeered me as if I were a prisoner of war."

He laughed. "A prisoner of love, my dear."

"You've proved nothing except that you're even more wicked than I thought."

"Sweet Kate, you are fascinated."

She couldn't help herself. She laughed. "You are the most arrogant, conceited—"

"But I'm right about you."

"You have not the first idea about me." She left the balcony, edging back toward the carpeted room.

He took her arm to stop her retreat. "My first idea was that you blushed the moment you met me."

"I didn't."

"Oh, Kate. It wasn't just a blush." Bolder than ever, he touched the neckline of her gown, tracing the wide, U-shaped décolletage with a slow, deliberate caress. "You were seashell pink from here—" he traced his finger over the tops of her breasts and then upward, mapping the rise of her collarbone, the dip at the base of her throat, and then the side of her neck, up to the crest of her cheek and temple "—to here," he concluded with a low, liquid laugh. "I swear, I never saw a woman blush like that." He leaned forward and blew the whispered words into her ear. "Do you blush all over, Miss Kate? Do you blush with your whole body?"

Finally, finally, he had pushed her over the edge. Forgetting the drawing room manners she had donned along with the Worth gown, Kathleen drew back her arm and walloped him one. It was not an openhanded, ladylike slap designed to put him in his place, but a full-fisted roundhouse punch of the sort used in saloon brawls in Conley's Patch.

He went down like a heap of unmortared brick. The thud of his body brought several people rushing over from the main salon.

"What happened?" Mr. McCormick asked, his walrus mustache twitching as he sank down beside Dylan Kennedy.

Kathleen braced herself. Now Dylan would reveal her for exactly what she was—a lowborn immigrant's daughter, with crude manners, no sense of humor and a wicked punch. A fraud.

But he surprised her. Shaking his head and running an exploratory hand along the length of his jaw, he stared straight at Kathleen and said, "I fell."

McCormick stepped back. "So I see."

Dylan took his proffered hand and stood up. "I swear, I never fell so hard in my life." As he spoke, his gaze never left Kathleen.

And to her mortification, she felt herself heat with an uncontrollable blush. She didn't speak, and neither did Dylan Kennedy, but her thoughts rang loudly through her head: *He's right. I do blush with my whole body.*

* * *

"Can you believe it?" Lucy Hathaway said excitedly, later in the powder room. "It's *you*."

"What's me?" asked Kathleen.

"The woman Dylan Kennedy is interested in."

"Fiddlesticks." Kathleen took a clean linen towel from the brass serving tray on the counter and dabbed at her overheated face.

"She's right." Phoebe spoke with grudging admiration. "It *is* you. Dylan Kennedy wants *you*."

"How can you know that?"

Phoebe gave her a tight smile. "I have made a careful study of him since he arrived in Chicago."

Lucy laughed. "You mean you inspected his pedigree to see if he'd be a suitable husband for you."

"I most certainly did. Is there something wrong with that?"

"Well, is he a suitable husband?" Kathleen demanded. Discreetly, she studied the hand that had just socked Dylan Kennedy. The knuckles were bright red. She put her one glove back on before the others noticed.

Phoebe fussed with the organza rosettes on her gown, then turned and fluffed out her bustle. "He is certainly rich enough. They say he has two million from his family's shipping fortune. And he is stunningly handsome. I suppose you noticed that right off."

He is a god that walks the earth, thought Kathleen. She bit her lip to keep from saying it aloud.

Phoebe ticked off his attributes on her fingers. "He comes from the East Coast, attended Harvard, traveled abroad. People say he is involved in shipping down the Saint Lawrence to Chicago. One of the most lucrative trade routes there is. No wonder he's such a catch.''

"So *you* marry him,'' Kathleen suggested.

Lucy shook her head. "She's holding out for a duke, though Lord only knows why.''

"Then *you* marry him,'' Kathleen said, amazed to be having this conversation.

"I shan't be marrying anyone,'' Lucy said. "I intend to devote my life to the cause of equal rights for women.'' She grinned at Kathleen. "You're elected.''

Kathleen laughed to cover a sudden jolt of ungovernable yearning. "I'm a maid,'' she reminded her friends. "I hang Miss Sinclair's clothes in closets and do her hair for a living. My mother milks cows.'' She spoke flippantly, but underneath it all she felt a familiar mortification. She had always harbored the secret belief that she'd been born into the wrong life. Being in the company of Chicago's best people tonight was a delight beyond compare, yet at the same time it held the razor sharp edge of frustration. The night gave her a taste of a life she could never have. Meeting a man like Dylan Kennedy merely twisted the knife.

"Not tonight,'' Phoebe insisted. "Tonight you are a privileged young lady from Baltimore. Your ancestors were the founding fathers of the colony of Maryland.'' Lacking her customary meanness, Phoebe took both of Kathleen's hands in hers. "I didn't think this would work, but so far you've made people believe our story. Initially I wanted to win my bet with Lucy, but I've changed my mind.''

"You have?'' Kathleen was amazed. This was a side to Phoebe she had rarely seen. She wasn't sure she trusted it.

"Tonight, Kate, I want to see *you* win. Don't tell me you forgot about the invitation to the opera. That was the wager, or have you forgotten?"

*He made me forget my own name,* Kathleen thought wistfully.

The door to the powder room swished inward. Mrs. Lincoln, whose father-in-law had been the Great Emancipator, bustled in. A maid followed behind her, eyes cast down to the floor.

Phoebe pretended to be helping Kathleen on with her other elbow-length glove. "These are simply too cunning," she said loudly. "Did they come from Paris as well? I've heard you get all your gowns and gloves from the Salon de Lumière."

Before Kathleen could answer, Mrs. Lincoln put out her plump arms like a pair of wings. "My wrap," she said to the maid. "And do hurry."

"Is something amiss, Mrs. Lincoln?" Lucy asked.

"We've been hearing rumors of a great fire all evening. Robert wishes to go home early and secure the house."

Kathleen felt no alarm about the report. Fires were a common occurrence, especially during the current drought. The city engineers always managed to contain them eventually. She and the others wished Mrs. Lincoln a good evening, then returned to the party.

"Remember your goal," Lucy whispered to Kathleen. "You must get yourself invited to the opening of the opera house tomorrow night. If you do that, we'll never be plagued by Phoebe's snobbery again." She hastened away to the main salon to hear the lecture, finding a seat that was suspiciously close to Mr. Higgins.

Time was running out, Kathleen realized, edging

into the back of the room. While it was perfectly true that everyone here was cordial to her, she had yet to secure the invitation that would prove... She frowned, taking a seat on a divan across the room from where Reverend Moody was preparing to hold forth. Just what *would* it prove?

That she looked becoming in an expensive gown?

That Chicago society lacked a discriminating sense of who was worthy and who was not?

That the entire social structure upon which America was founded was a lie?

She smiled privately at the thought. Lucy would certainly love that conclusion. The truth was probably closer to her first thought, which was fine with Kathleen. Invitation or not, she intended to enjoy the rest of the evening. Tomorrow—and reality—would come soon enough.

She observed a group of men discussing the effect of the current drought on grain futures, and wished she could join in the speculation. Matters of commerce fascinated her, and she knew plenty from her shameless eavesdropping on her employer's financial advisors. It was yet another way she had turned herself into a misfit, for the world didn't need a woman from the labor classes who understood high finance. Yet she couldn't simply stifle her interest or quiet her mind.

Reverend Moody spoke in a loud voice, and his words discomfited her. He preached of humility and honesty, and here she was, the greatest of liars.

Pretending to need a breath of fresh air, she slipped through the archway to the smaller salon. In one corner, a group of men stood smoking cigars and speaking in low tones. They didn't notice her. The door to the balcony where Dylan Kennedy had practically seduced her stood ajar. She stepped out, and was struck by two impressions.

First, the wind had picked up strength and a curious heat, while moonlight imbued the scene with pearly blue magic.

And second, she was not alone.

"I just knew you couldn't stay away," Dylan Kennedy crowed.

She stepped back toward the door. "I had no idea you were out here."

"Of course you didn't," he said teasingly, blocking her retreat. "But now that you're here, I'm ready for you."

She blinked. "Whatever do you mean?"

"I've been waiting for your apology."

She flexed her hand unconsciously. "I am sorry you gave me cause to hit you."

"Is that as close as you'll come to apologizing?"

"It's more than you deserve."

"Then I accept."

A gust of wind lifted her skirts, causing the green silk to bell out like a hot air balloon. Kathleen pressed her arms to her sides, not so much out of modesty as fear that he would catch a glimpse of her rough muslin bloomers. She did not want to explain why an heiress would wear such a thing under a Worth original. The strong draft tampered with the twisted silk cord of her reticule, and she felt it slip down her shoulder.

"I am going inside now," she informed him, intending to escape before he addled her head by touching her as he had done before. She didn't trust him.

She didn't trust herself with him. Never had she felt so strong an attraction for a man.

She considered herself to be a woman of some experience, for she did not lack for suitors. Expressmen, railroad workers, lumberjacks and day laborers often came to call. Some of them, like Barry Lynch, a dock-yard clerk, were quite nice. But she had never felt the magic of true attraction...until now.

It wasn't just that he was handsome—though he most certainly was.

It wasn't just that he was amusing—though he was that as well.

Maybe it was because he was rich. Although, now that she thought about it, so were the other young men in the grand salon. And she didn't feel this hugely magnetic and thoroughly confusing attraction to any of them. Just Dylan Kennedy.

He pressed the French door shut with the palm of his hand. His arm reached across her line of vision. He smelled faintly of bay rum and wood smoke.

Wood smoke? That was unexpected. Most men smelled of cigars or cheroots, but—

"Something's burning," she said suddenly, swinging her gaze out across Chicago.

"I call it desire," he quipped.

"Please, stop joking. There is a fire somewhere. People were talking about it earlier."

The wind crescendoed to a truly frightful howl, and even in the protected shelter of the balcony, Kathleen felt its power plucking at her skirts and carefully coiffed hair. Scattered sparks streamed past, tossing and flickering like live snowflakes.

"Look at that," she said. "There *is* a fire."

"Those are probably just embers from someone's

chimney pot," Dylan said dismissively. "Even if it's a fire, the engine crews will have it under control before you know it." He pressed close to her, and the intimate heat that passed between them thrilled her. He seemed determined to pick up where they had left off before she had hit him.

And to be honest, Kathleen was interested, too. For the first time in her life, she had the feeling that she "fit" with this man. She felt at ease with him, even though he was a tycoon, rich and sophisticated beyond anything she could imagine. But he didn't know that. He would never know that. For after tonight she would never see him again. There was no harm in this flirtation, she told herself. No harm at all.

He seemed to sense her growing acceptance of him. "Is it true your family owns a controlling interest in Hibernia Securities?"

She caught her breath, but tried to act unsurprised. "You've been gossiping behind my back."

"I wouldn't call it gossiping. I'm interested in you, Miss Kate. I find you completely enchanting, even if you do wield a mean right hook."

At his words, shivers coursed over her. "I'm not sure you should be speaking to me in such a frank and familiar fashion," she said.

"Are you offended?"

"No." She allowed herself a small, speculative smile. "Intrigued." She dared to push at the boundaries a little more. "The gossip about you is that you are in need of a wife."

"Desire," he said softly, stepping close. He spoke the word with silken precision.

Inside her, something seemed to melt. "What?"

"Desire," he repeated. "I *desire* a wife. I'm not sure that is the same as need."

"I see." How had he wound up standing so close to her? She could smell the clean starchy scent of his shirt, could see the precision with which his valet had shaved his cheeks and jaw.

"Don't you want to know why?" he asked, practically whispering.

"Why what?" Her mouth felt cottony and dry.

"Why I desire a wife."

She cleared her throat, trying to make sense of the moment, of the sweet, compelling feelings flowing through her as she looked up at him. "Very well. Why do you desire a wife?" She couldn't help the spark of devilment that made her suggest, "Did your mother finally put you out of her house?"

He caught her against him and laughed heartily. "My dear Miss Kate, you are a caution. It is a privilege to know you."

Now, she thought, moving in for the kill. "Do you truly feel that way?"

"From the bottom of my heart."

"Then I wonder—" She stopped. "Oh, I am too bold."

"Go on. What were you going to say?"

"I was hoping you would invite me to the opening of Crosby's Opera House," she said. "I was hoping you would be the one."

"I will, Kate. I'll be the one. I am, after all, looking for a wife. Escorting you to the opera seems a good way to begin the hunt."

For a moment, Kathleen felt dizzy with her victory. She had won. She had proven she could fool a society gentleman into escorting her to the opera. But the moment came to a cruel and swift end. She wanted to take pride in her cleverness, but instead, she felt empty. Deceitful. Here was this perfectly nice man, innocently offering her an evening's entertainment, and she thought only of the wager. An apology hovered on her lips, but something—the expression dancing in his blue eyes—held her silent. In the matter of his quest for a wife, she couldn't tell whether he was joking or not. She speculated about the real reason for his interest in matrimony. Family alliances, convenience, sometimes even appearances. Occasional expedience, for accidents did happen even in the best of families.

"We have managed to have an entire conversation, and neither has revealed the least little thing about the other," she commented, stepping back.

"You find my air of mystery alluring," he said.

"What—" She swallowed. She had to raise her voice to be heard over the howl of the dry, blowing wind. "What gives you the idea that you are so alluring?"

"Ah, but I didn't say that. I said that *you* find me fascinating. It's not my fault, but you do."

"I certainly do not."

"Sweet Kate, when you punched me in the jaw with such ardor, I could only conclude that I arouse a strong passion in you. And then when you sneaked out here to be with me, I felt even more certain of your feelings."

"You are insolent," she said, grateful for the many hours she had spent studying with Deborah. She could stand up to this clever, clever man, just see if she couldn't. Long after her mistress had lost interest in her studies, Kathleen had absorbed all the lessons of the best tutors money could buy. "You are arrogant," she said to Dylan. "You are manipulative, sly and completely wrong about me."

He had a swift and elegant way of moving, and he employed it now, pressing her against the figured stone balustrade. He filled her field of vision—snowy white shirt and a white silk cravat framed by the beautifully tailored, slightly worn lapels of a dark frock coat.

"We like each other, Kate. We both felt the attraction."

She tossed her head, trying to appear unintimidated by his nearness. "I don't know what you're talking about."

"Of course you do, and it matters not at all." Very lightly, shockingly, he put his finger at the base of her throat, brushing the emeralds and diamonds of her necklace. "I know your game, Kate."

"And pray, what is that?" She spoke playfully, enjoying this far too much.

"I know what's under your dress," he said.

Saints alive. He knew about her muslin under-clothes.

"Beneath this gorgeous milk-white breast beats the heart of a guilty woman—"

"Sir, you forget yourself." Letting a man speak of one's breasts was absolutely taboo. It was so taboo that no one had even told her such talk was forbidden. She just knew.

"Tell me, what would your family think if they knew you were here?" he went on as if she hadn't spoken.

Heavens, but he was right about the guilt. She pictured her simple, loving family and felt like the ingrate of the world for pretending to be something she was not. They would see it as a rejection of their way of life, their values, when in fact, it had nothing to do with them and everything to do with Kathleen and a dream inside her that refused to die. But for the moment she was more concerned with fending off this man who seemed to see right through her.

"My family loves and supports me in all I do."

He lifted an eyebrow. "Sounds promising. And unusual for the heiress to a fortune. So they would not worry that you had come to hear an evangelist, a good Catholic girl like you?"

She tried not to show her relief. "Sir, my family would be far more worried about *your* attentions."

"Don't you want to know how I guessed your secret?"

"How?" she asked cautiously, though she knew it was the holy card.

"Because I am just like you, my sweet."

She nearly laughed at how wrong he was. How shocked he would be if he understood what that truly meant—that she came from a poor family with no property, no prospects. "Catholic, you mean? You've already said so."

"I am anything you want me to be. What do you want, Kate? What do you want?"

Every word dried, unspoken, on her tongue. Every thought flickered and disappeared like the sparks flying through the night sky. It was extraordinary. In all her life, no one had ever asked Kathleen O'Leary what she wanted. She was told with great frequency what she should do or must accomplish. But never had anyone posed the simple, straightforward question to her. No one waited so avidly to hear her answer.

And she discovered, in the long breathless moments that stretched between them, that she did not know the answer.

Until now, her life had been about what she didn't want. She didn't want the hardscrabble workaday life her parents endured. She didn't want to marry a dockyard clerk and crank out baby after baby, year after year. She did not want—and saints in heaven preserve her—to be ordinary.

Now here was this extraordinary man, promising her anything.

"You haven't answered me, Kate," he reminded her, gently prodding. "What do you want?"

"For this night to go on forever," she blurted out, and even as she spoke, she realized it was the most honest thing she could have said. From the moment she had donned the Worth gown, she had felt like a different person. Someone better, more important. Of course, it was all an illusion. She knew that. But the magic was as strong and seductive as Dylan Kennedy himself.

"I like that answer." He whispered the words into the shell of her ear.

He was going to kiss her, she realized. He moved slowly, deliberately. Not with the clumsy urgent hunger of other men who had tried to kiss her. He knew what he wanted and took his time getting it. He placed his knuckles softly beneath her chin and directed her gaze to his. Then he bent from the waist, almost formally as if making an elegant bow. His lips touched hers lightly, so lightly she wasn't sure she had felt it at all. She sensed the subtle warmth of his breath, scented with brandy, and an exquisite intimacy thrummed between them, so poignant that all of their lighthearted banter could not mask the fact that she grew suddenly thick-throated with yearning.

He kissed her as though nothing existed but her. As though she were the only other living soul on earth. As though he existed for the sole purpose of kissing her.

She had never believed she could be moved by a man's touch, or even by his kiss. Certainly on rare occasions there might have been a flash of excitement when a suitor stole a peck on the mouth, but what she experienced in Dylan Kennedy's arms went far beyond mere titillation. Her heart was engaged by this man, and he roused emotions more poignant and moving than anything she had ever felt. A longing seared her, and even as she reveled in his kiss, she knew why this experience was so overwhelming.

He was showing her, in this single, perfect crystal of a moment, all that she wanted, and all she could never have.

She surrendered to him utterly, softening and growing pliant in his arms. Here was a man who had probably held royal princesses in his embrace, handled blooded horses and business deals worth a staggering fortune.

In one single moment she wanted it all. She wanted to experience his life of bold, glittering excess. She imagined awakening in an airy, light-filled chamber with a gentle swish of organdy curtains. Breakfast would be served on bone china by white-gloved servants, and they would spend the day surveying their beautiful estate. In the evening they would attend a musicale, visiting with friends who laughed easily, made lighthearted conversation and admired the famous Mr. and Mrs. Kennedy.

Long after he stopped kissing her, she kept her eyes closed and her face angled toward his. Only the silken rustle of his laughter startled her back to reality. She blinked like a dreamer, awakening to find him laughing down at her.

"Where the devil are you, Kate?" he asked.

"Why should I tell you?"

"Because I want to go there."

Feeling sheepish, she stepped away from him. He tilted his head, peering shamelessly down her bodice. She smacked him on the shoulder.

"Sorry," he said, though he didn't sound at all contrite. "I was just checking."

"Checking what?"

"To see where that blush of yours starts. I'm having all sorts of ideas."

This was how wealthy, privileged people behaved. This delicious flirtation with an edge of the forbidden. And she wanted it. Oh, how she wanted it.

A spark drifted past, alighting on her bare arm, and she brushed away the hot sting. A frisson of fear touched her like the ember. "I don't think that strayed from a chimney pot," she said.

"Could be a leftover from last night's blaze at Conley's Patch," he remarked.

She frowned. Conley's Patch was known as the devil's acre, a lowly ramshackle neighborhood of saloons and brothels on the south side. How would a man like Dylan Kennedy know the first thing about the Patch?

Disconcerted, she turned to look out at the city. The

sun had set hours before, but an orange glow painted the sky to the west.

"I think the fire's spreading fast," she said, worried.

At that same moment, the French door banged open. The wind slapped it against the building and one of the panes shattered. Lucy blustered forward and grabbed Kathleen's arm.

"We've got to go," she said. "We must get back to Miss Boylan's before the bridges get too clogged with traffic."

Kathleen pulled her arm away, and the cord of her reticule slid off her shoulder. "But—"

"There are rumors of a fire."

"The fires aren't just rumors," Dylan said calmly. "There've been six a day and more because of the drought."

Lucy regarded Dylan with narrowed eyes.

"Don't worry, Miss Hathaway," he said smoothly. "I was not behaving offensively."

"Why not?" she asked. "All men do."

Kathleen guessed she'd had a run-in with Mr. Higgins. "We really must go," she said, reluctantly agreeing with Lucy.

"Yes, we must be getting back. Miss Boylan was quite insistent," Lucy said. "Our curfew is ten o'clock."

Even Cinderella had her midnight, Kathleen thought. But Cinderella was nothing but a story in a book, a dream of a magical evening that could never come true. Kathleen lived in Chicago, fires were troubling the city and it was foolish to cling to the masquerade any longer.

But she did have her private fantasies. She wanted

Dylan Kennedy to think back on this night and remember the mysterious, sophisticated young woman
who had kissed him with forbidden intimacy.

And so, in full view of Lucy, she wound her arms
around his neck and planted a long, impassioned kiss
on his mouth.

# Three

Just like that, she was gone.

But Dylan could still taste the phantom sweetness of her, lingering on his lips. He could still detect the pliant warmth of her mouth pressed to his.

He could still feel the hard heat of the passion she inspired, and he was compelled to wait out on the balcony until he was fit for mixed company. Blowing out a breath of exasperation, he ran his finger around his collar, yearning to loosen his cravat. He couldn't, of course. A gentleman never appeared with a less than perfectly tied cravat.

It was a great burden, being the most eligible bachelor in Chicago. If he'd realized the ruse was going to be this much trouble, he might have chosen something else—a divine prophet, perhaps, or a blind man. The guises had worked for him before.

Dylan Francis Kennedy, known in various other venues as the marquis de Bontemps, Sir Percival Blake, the Prophet Jephtha, and Dirk Steele—Man of the Comstock, used to consider himself the luckiest fellow in the whole U.S. of A. He breezed through life, donning different identities with the same ease as trying on a new chapeau. With his affable grin, his unusual physical abilities and his flamboyant style, he had fleeced a living from the smug, the self-satisfied, the richer-than-God, and he made no apologies for it.

But unfortunately, he'd arrived in Chicago with the notorious Vincent Costello dogging his heels. Under normal circumstances, Dylan would have the means to dodge his former partner. The smell of money never failed to put Vince off the scent. But this time, things were complicated.

This time, Dylan was flat broke.

Worse, Costello was flat broke, too. That made him cranky and unpredictable.

Dylan had arrived "from the Continent"—that always impressed the right people—with less than two bits to his name. The very notion grated. There had been times when he had stood poised just inches from total success, only to have a deal go bad or a mark wise up. He usually had a knack for salvaging something from the ashes.

Not this time. This time, escape had cost him everything, including the clothes on his back. He had wanted a change from the life of burlesque performing and carnival tricks that had kept him and Costello in the money. He'd grown tired of thrilling the crowds with his daredevil tricks while Vince picked pockets and collected wager markers from the onlookers. Most of all, he'd needed to escape Costello's daughter Faith, who had imprisoned him with the mistaken belief that he would marry her.

During a stint in Buffalo, Dylan decided the time had come to disappear. He had to get away from them, for they were getting too close in ways that made him hot under the collar. He didn't know how to be close to people, and he didn't want to know.

And so, on a bet, the famous marquis de Bontemps

was to walk a tightrope over Niagara Falls. Dylan had done the stunt several times, curiously unperturbed by the violence of the raging cataract that lured so many tourists and daredevils from around the world. He studied the odds, chose his spot, measured his chances and then, while hundreds watched one evening, he had done the unthinkable. He had fallen. He'd gone over Niagara Falls. The horrified people who had watched him plunge to his death, who had wept to see a fine young man cut down in his prime, had forgotten all about the wager. And Dylan, who had carefully practiced the maneuver of falling, clinging to the underside of a boulder, then pulling himself along a cable to the Canadian side, had fought his way to shore in the dark. He had stolen away to the west, leaving his partner behind.

Or so he had thought. Costello probably grew suspicious when no body was recovered. Dylan should have known Costello would hunt him down like a bloodhound. Bleed him dry like a stuck pig. Or worse, make him marry Faith like a decent man.

Dylan needed a big touch, and he needed it soon.

Pressing his fist on the carved concrete rail of the balcony, he cursed the timing of the fire. And here of all places. He and all his aliases were unknown in Chicago, so he'd considered the city fertile ground for reinventing himself. He had finagled a spot on every elite guest list in town, but the masquerade would be over if someone discovered his serious cash flow problems. He didn't know how much longer he'd be able to keep up the illusion of being the man of the hour.

The woman in the green silk gown had fluttered into his life like a petal on a breeze. No, he corrected himself, like a guardian angel. When he had met the heiress, who let him address her by the delightful nickname "Kate," he thought his prayers had been answered. Her gown was Worth, her diamonds were genuine and her looks and personality enchanting.

She was clearly loaded with a fortune that needed a bit of lightening—preferably by Dylan. Pushing his face into the swirling hot tempest, he rotated his shoulders and glared out at the distant horizon, shimmering now with a fire in the west. It was going to be a long night.

"Damn," he said, letting the howling wind snatch the curse away. And again, "Damn."

He had been so close to winning her over. Even when he thought he'd have to work to earn her kisses, she had simply given him one. Given him a kiss and left, a spark on the wind.

If only he'd had a little more time, he would have succeeded with her. He could sense the opening bud of her interest. He almost dared to think he'd actually enjoy stealing from her. Generally, spoiled heiresses were a tough lot. They required a great deal of maintenance: cosseting, flattery, heartfelt pronouncements of utter devotion, promises from the bottom of his heart. Not this one. She was beautiful and merry. He would have had fun taking a fortune from her. She would have loved being taken by him.

Sadly for him, she had disappeared before he could learn more about her, capture her heart and steal her money. Perhaps he could track her down at…whose house were they going to? Miss Boylan? Who the hell was Miss Boylan?

A hail of flying embers suddenly blew through the area. With another curse, Dylan jumped back, brushing at his sleeves. The silk frock coat, from Savile Row via an unwary gentleman's closet, was the last decent thing he owned, and he'd best not burn a hole in it.

As he turned to reenter the salon, he heard a crunching sound under his heel. With a frown, he stooped and picked up some forgotten object, bringing it inside with him. It was a green silk evening bag, crusted with beads that perfectly matched his lady-love's dress.

With rising hope, Dylan parted the opening of the bag and looked inside. A burning whiff of ammonia nearly knocked him on his ass. Damned smelling salts. He had broken the bottle when he'd stepped on the bag. Within seconds, tears were running down his face. He was about to cast aside the silk bag when he noticed something else secreted within the emerald folds, under a soaked handkerchief.

A card of some sort? Frowning, he extracted it, hoping it was a calling card. If it was, then his task would be far easier.

But it was not a calling card. It was…a holy card, the one she had dropped when she'd lost her earring.

Odd. He hadn't seen one of those in years, not since he had shown up at Gerry Carmichael's funeral in Boston, claiming to be his sole heir.

This one depicted Saint Bridget looking both very Irish and very virtuous. The overly sentimental artwork touched a chord in Dylan, and for a fleeting moment, a wave of sadness surged through him. As it often did, his heart kept trying to remember a past he had vowed to forget. Memories strained to break into his consciousness, but he resisted them, knowing they held nothing but darkness for him. He had spent a lifetime fleeing the past, and he wasn't about to lose the race now. Through sheer force of will, he banished the phantom feeling, convincing himself that he had only imagined the sudden, searing pain.

Impatient with himself, he turned the card over and read the printed prayer. And there, at the very bottom, was the name of the deceased being honored: Bridget Cavanaugh. Beloved wife, mother, grandmother. The sponsor of the card was St. Brendan's, just a few blocks away, according to the address given.

Dylan palmed the card and slid it into the flat front pocket of his trousers—appropriately enough, next to the part of him that wanted Kate the most. He grinned at his own crude wit. Suddenly his luck was about to change.

But first, of course, he had to figure out where she had gone. Donning his best smile, he breezed into the main salon. The crowd had thinned somewhat. Apparently others were also worried about the fire that had sent Lucy and Kate speeding on their way.

Dylan found a tray of champagne glasses and helped himself to two, lifting them in the direction of Mr. Pullman in a salute. Then, when Pullman turned away, he knocked them back like water.

Lately Dylan had a new sense of weariness, an ennui. The exhilaration of a narrow escape had lacked its former heady sweetness. Running for his life was becoming too routine, and for the first time ever, Dylan began to wonder what it would be like to settle down, go straight.

With a rueful half grin into his champagne glass, he drained the last drop. How on earth would he know? His earliest memory, one he couldn't forget no matter how hard he tried, had been of a deception.

*Just wait right there, my boy, and Mam will come back for you.* He had tried to sit very still and quiet, hoping his good behavior would bring her back sooner. The steamy train station had seemed as big as a witch's castle to him, with its gleaming marble floors, soaring ceilings, gritty air and skylights glittering high overhead. Mam had once told him that the plump naked creatures were supposed to be cherubs—little babies with wings—but to him they looked evil, their carved stone mouths puckered, their fat hands clutching at clouds and clusters of grapes, their curling hair frozen in stone.

The smells of steam and cinders had choked him as he watched passengers hurrying zigzag across the marble, heels clicking, black-faced porters whistling smartly and wheeling groaning carts of baggage out to the trains. Destinations were shouted down the terminals: *Philadelphia. Saratoga. Buffalo. New Haven. Boston.* He encountered a boy his own age who had boasted, "We have a first-class berth all the way to Boston," before a governess grabbed him by the upper arm and hauled him off with a whack to the backside and the warning, *Don't consort with riffraff. You'll catch a disease.*

Much later, a man dressed in a black gown had taken him by the hand and brought him to a church that echoed with whispers and eerie songs. He had dug in his heels, not wanting to face what the priest had brought him to see—a plain pine box, candles burning low. *Look at her, boy. Tell us her name.* He had run away as quick as ever he could, slipping out the door and passing crooked headstones in the churchyard. He skirted a freshly dug grave that reeked of damp earth and broken lilies, and the dewy grass wet the toes of his scuffed shoes as he ran.

He returned to the steamy, oily train station, because his mam had told him to wait there. The black-gowned man came looking for him again, but he'd huddled under a bench in the waiting room until the man left. Hours or maybe days later, a kindly porter had asked him if he was lost. He had shaken his head and mimicked the well-dressed boy's voice: *I have a first-class berth all the way to Boston.*

That had been the beginning. He had been nine years old, and he'd learned his lesson well. People didn't keep their promises. And more important, folks believed what they wanted to believe.

Dylan was tempted to drink away the bitter taste of the unwelcome memory, but he couldn't afford the indulgence. Things were looking bad for him and he had work to do.

"Shame on you, Mr. Kennedy," scolded an annoying voice. "You've been hiding yourself from us."

He put on a smile designed to disarm and turned to greet Alice and Mabel Moss, nieces of the mayor of Chicago. The smile worked. They giggled and put up fans to hide their prominent teeth.

"Ouch," he said, "that accusation stings even worse coming from your beautiful mouth." While they giggled even harder, he said, "I was out watching the progress of the fire. Looks to be a bad one."

Mabel waved her fan with nonchalant grace. "Oh, dear, yes," she said. "Uncle has gone to the courthouse to see that the alarm system is alerting the West Division."

"But never worry," Alice enjoined. "Chicago has

a perfectly grand fire department. Steam engines, hose carts, alarms everywhere you'd care to look.''

''I do hope the fire's not in the vicinity of Field and Leiter's store,'' Mabel said with a worried pout. ''I'm expecting an order of silk from Bombay. I declare, it's impossible to hire a decent dressmaker these days. The city's positively overrun by—'' she shuddered visibly ''—immigrants and foreigners.''

''Can't abide them myself,'' Dylan said earnestly. ''Especially the Visigoths.''

She frowned in confusion, completely unaware that while she'd spoken, Dylan had relieved her of her little reticule. He hoped it contained something more useful than Kate's smelling salts.

He palmed the small bag as he bowed to the young ladies. ''It has been a distinct privilege,'' he assured them. ''And now I must be going. Perhaps I'll make myself useful in battling the fire.''

As he walked away, he heard one of them whisper, ''He's *so* brave.''

He resisted the urge to add a swagger to his step. He wasn't being brave at all, but practical. Fires could be useful in appropriating a bit of short-term gain. He considered looting to be the sport of commoners, beneath him, but the occasional snatched jewelry or cash would not come amiss.

He stopped at the cloak room and sweetly convinced the matron in charge that the Italian silk opera cape and sleek Canadian beaver top hat belonged to him. Then he went outside and stood beneath the awning, studying the terrain. The edge of the canvas flapped in a high wind, though no evidence of fire had reached the area. He pressed down the new hat to keep it in place.

"I ordered my phaeton half an hour ago," snapped an angry voice. "Why the devil hasn't it been brought round?"

Recognizing Philip Ascot IV, Dylan tipped his hat. He had always disliked the type: bland, vacuous, with just enough education from the right places to give him the sense that anything he wanted was his for the taking. Ascot possessed nothing but a venerable family name to recommend him. Sadly, in some circles that was more than enough. It was said that Ascot was engaged to marry Arthur Sinclair's beauteous daughter, Deborah, who came with a dowry in excess of a million.

If Dylan needed another reason to dislike Ascot, there it was. He had gotten to the wealthy Deborah first.

No matter, he decided, pacing the pine block sidewalk, trying to make up his mind where to go. The red-haired heiress would do just fine for his purposes. He might even marry her if need be. It wouldn't be the first time he had wed out of financial necessity.

But he didn't want to think about past mistakes now. Regrets were always so inconvenient.

Instead, he thought about Kate some more. God, that hair, those lips. The swiftest route to her dowry would be to seduce her so she'd be forced to marry him. He found himself wishing for the luxury of time with a woman like that. Time to coax laughter and sighs from her, time to learn what her favorite color was and what she liked to eat for breakfast. Under the circumstances, however, he had to act fast. He considered the holy card in his pocket and wondered if it would provide some clue so he could find her again.

Lord de Vere and his entourage exited the Hotel Royale. Their inbred, aristocratic faces were pale and pinched. Lord Kim's bewigged attendants sniffed the air like hounds on the scent. Dylan decided a bit of ingratiation was in order.

He flung back the edge of his cloak and tipped his new hat. "My lord," he said, mimicking the courtly manners he had observed while gambling aboard a French steamship one year. "I thought you were a guest at the hotel."

"Ah, Kennedy. So I was. We deemed it prudent to *ficher le camp,* what with this fire and the winds so unpredictable."

"So where will you be *ficher*-ing to?" Dylan asked, trying his best not to mock the mincing attitude. But he couldn't help himself. The English lord was a two-legged joke.

"Mr. Cornelius King was kind enough to offer his summer house on the north shore."

"Indeed." Dylan winked. "And did he offer anything else? His eldest daughter, perhaps?" Everyone knew the weak-chinned Englishman was in the States to find a rich wife. An admirable pursuit, thought Dylan. Though they'd never speak of it, they had something in common.

Lord Kim worked his mouth, fishlike, in soundless outrage. He sputtered, then found his voice. "I'm sure I don't have the slightest interest in the young lady."

Clearly the man had no sense of humor. Dylan laughed to show he meant no offense. "Then it's a pity about your plan to marry money," he quipped.

Again the codfish look from the Englishman.

"Well, the fortune generally comes with a woman attached," Dylan concluded.

De Vere's face froze. Then, while his attendants braced themselves for a flood of fury, he surprised them all by flinging back his head and braying with laughter. "You are a caution, sir. I should not like you at all, yet I find that I do. Ah, here is the coach." A boxy coach and four came around from the livery. The team was spirited, probably jumpy from the heavy, smoky smell of the air and the occasional flying spark.

"Join us, Mr. Kennedy?" Lord Kim offered.

It was on the tip of Dylan's tongue to accept. Then the oddest thing happened. The courthouse alarm bell, a couple of blocks distant, drowned out his "Yes, thank you."

"Eh? Sorry, dear chap, I didn't hear what you said," the Englishman prompted.

"I said," Dylan heard a stranger's voice intone, "I had best stay in the city and lend a hand fighting the fire."

"We'll leave the heroics to you Yanks," said the Englishman. "They say fools rush in..." Laughing at his own wit, he entered the coach.

As he watched the big, roomy vehicle roll away up Clark Street, Dylan gritted his teeth and cursed. What kind of fool stayed in the city, after all? What was he thinking? Within an hour he could be at some millionaire's country place in Lake View, sipping sherry and making up stories about his Harvard days.

The courthouse alarm sounded again. Dylan ducked his head into the wind, held his tall hat in place and started walking. People milled about in the streets. No one seemed unduly alarmed, and neither was Dylan. Fires had been a nightly event of late because the weather was so unseasonably dry. He decided to make an early night of it, then begin his hunt for the delectable Miss Kate in the morning.

Though no one in Chicago knew it, his *pied-à-terre* was actually a *pied-à-l'eau*—a broken-down cabin boat moored under the Rush Street Bridge. He had found the leaky, listing vessel moldering in the river, and had claimed squatter's rights. It was cramped, smelly and depressing, but he endured the conditions because he knew they were only temporary. He just had to figure out a new angle and he'd be back in the game.

Things grew more chaotic as he headed toward the lake. Crowds surged along the Van Buren Street rail line, fleeing from the West Division. Dylan hurried, his long strides putting ten city blocks behind him as he made for the bridge that spanned the mouth of the river near Lake Michigan.

On the sloping bank under the bridge, he stood still for a few moments, reluctant to seek shelter in the miserable boat. The wind held the shrieking promise of a tornado, somewhere out on the prairie beyond the stockyards. Horses in the roadway shied as their drivers laid into them with whips.

Dylan tried to decide whether or not he was afraid, and realized with no surprise that he was not. Things like firestorms and waterfalls didn't scare him. Never had, which was probably why he had done a brisk business performing daredevil acts. He had a knack for learning tricks and a flare for the dramatic. His first stunt had taken place right in the train station where his mother had abandoned him.

With nothing left to lose, he had climbed to a steel girder in the terminal. He had no thought but that he wanted to be up high, like a bird, where nothing could touch him. He still remembered the faces of the on-lookers. No one dared move or look away. Their riveted expressions of awe and dread had given him a keen sense of power. So long as they watched, he held them in the palm of his hand. Their attention went wherever he commanded it. With a heady feeling of complete control, he could make them gasp, cause their hearts to pound, force them to weep or sweat with worry for him. When he leaped down and stood unscathed on the platform, coins had showered him and he knew he was made for this life.

Not long afterward, he had apprenticed himself to a saloon owner in the bowery where he had performed stunts of increasing complexity. He quickly graduated to confidence games, tricking people out of their money by convincing them that a painted brick was solid gold, or that his Colombian parrot could tell the future, or that he was a direct descendant of an Egyptian king. In his lonely search for a place in the world, he had donned every persona except his own. He didn't even know who he was anymore, and didn't much care.

Hoping he'd left a bottle of spirits in the boat, he decided to seek shelter instead of standing around watching the chaos. The wind whipped viciously at the opera cloak he had helped himself to, temporarily covering his face with the expensive fabric. At the same moment, someone—a very large someone—jostled him, and he found himself shoved back against a timber bridge support.

"You move pretty fast for a dead man," growled a deep, unpleasant voice.

The cloak was pulled out of his face. "Nice threads, Dylan," said the voice, rich with sarcasm.

"But you weren't wearing it the last time I saw you. Seems I recall you were wearing ten thousand dollars in bank notes strapped around you."

Damn it. He was hoping to avoid this. What a fiasco. He thought his daredevil escape over the falls meant he'd seen the last of Costello. Within hours of fleeing Niagara Falls, he had donned a new identity and hopped a train, knowing his former partner was likely to track him down in due time. As smart as Dylan and even less scrupulous, Costello had a special gift for getting what he was after.

"Vince," he said, staring down at Costello's meaty fingers, which clutched the cloak at his throat. "How did you find me?"

"I followed the smell, you low-bellied slug."

"Very funny."

"Yeah, I was tickled pink when I read in the papers how a certain Mr. Kennedy just got back from hobnobbing with the Vanderbilts all over the Continent. The bit about your being granted the Studleigh Prize by Queen Victoria was a dead giveaway." He snorted. "Studleigh was the name you took for card-sharping in Albany."

Dylan didn't bother playing dumb. "How have you been?" he asked, and since Costello had not killed him yet, he dared to add, "How's Faith?"

Vincent Costello dropped his hands. His face, which resembled a very healthy russet potato, with interesting knobs and creases, closed in a furious scowl. "You broke her heart, Dylan. She thought you were going to marry her. Even though I just about spent my last breath trying to convince her you're no damned good, she's got it in her head that she wants to marry you."

"Well," he lied, "the feeling was mutual."

"Then do you mind explaining why you simply disappeared? With, I might add, our entire capital strapped to your waist."

"Oh," said Dylan, tensing to flee. "That."

"Yes," said Costello, pulling a gun. "That."

"What's blocking the roadway ahead?" Lucy Hathaway asked the driver. Their coach, a bulky rockaway with an extended front and the school crest painted on the doors, had rolled to a halt. She had to lean out the window to speak to him. Kathleen could see the roaring wind snatch at Lucy's jet-black hair.

"A horse car," the driver yelled. "Someone cut the horse loose and took the fare box. I can see the thief heading on foot for the river."

"Oh, for heaven's sake." Lucy pulled her head back in and flopped against the leather seat. "At this rate it'll take half the night to get back to Miss Boylan's."

Phoebe used the speaking tube rather than risk mussing her hair. "Driver, go around the horse car. We really must be getting back."

Kathleen cast a worried glance at the Randolph Street Bridge behind them. The railed span overflowed with people, livestock, horses and mules hitched to all manner of conveyance.

"Saints and crooked angels. The fire must be even worse than it looks," she said. In all the excitement and traffic she had not even told them her news—that Lucy had won the bet. Dylan Francis Kennedy had invited her to Crosby's tomorrow night. She said nothing, though, for the victory seemed a trivial matter now.

Phoebe impatiently rapped her fan at the speaking tube. "Driver, did you not hear what I said? Go around the horse car at once."

They could feel the coach swaying as the team strained in the traces. But there was no forward movement. Kathleen looked out at the crowded street. With a cold clutch of nervousness she saw the reason they had made no progress.

"Our driver has fled," she told the others. She dropped her cultured manner of speaking and unknowingly echoed the thick brogue of her mother. "Sweet heaven, preserve us, we have no driver."

"Don't be ridicu—" Phoebe half stood, her hand on the door handle.

At the same moment, an explosion split the air. The fire had reached a store of gunpowder somewhere. The coach jerked forward with such force that Phoebe was slammed against the seat. With a scream, she plopped down. Kathleen felt her head snap back with the motion. The driverless horses scrambled ahead in full panic. Not only did they draw the coach around the abandoned horse car, they headed in a new direction entirely.

"We are going directly toward the fire," Lucy said. Her voice was thick with fear.

"We're going to die," Phoebe wailed. "Dear God, we're going to die and I never even had the chance to marry a duke. And I never saw Pompeii. And I've never eaten an oyster. And I'm still a virgin—"

"Can you shut her up?" Kathleen asked Lucy.

Lucy clutched at Phoebe's shoulders and shouted *"Shut up!"* in her face.

Kathleen battled the rocking, lurching motion of the uncontrolled coach as she yanked the expensive silk skirts up between her legs and tied the fabric to fit like bulky trousers.

"Do be careful," Lucy shouted, realizing her intent. "Please, be careful."

Kathleen nodded grimly. She unhooked the stiff leather windshield of the coach. Immediately smoke and blowing sparks streaked into the interior. Phoebe started to scream again, but Kathleen ignored her and climbed. She was able to grasp the underside of the high seat where the cowardly driver had perched.

The hot wind roared over her face, carrying the scent of the terrified, sweating horses. By the age of eight, Kathleen had learned to drive her mother's milk wagon and she was determined to control these beasts. "Ho there," she shouted, hoping they would respond to a verbal command. "Ho!" Then she yelled, "Please, ho!" and finally, *"Ho, damn it!"*

The team ignored her. They churned along a broad avenue flanked by burning buildings. Their long manes streaked out behind them. Straining every muscle in her body, Kathleen managed to hoist herself through the windshield to the driver's perch. The speed was dizzying, terrifying. So was the knowledge that the crazed horses were drawing them deeper and deeper into the heart of the fire.

The reins. She had to get hold of the reins. The trouble was, the driver had dropped them and they now snaked uselessly along the street.

She kept shouting *Ho* and they kept ignoring her. She spied a length of leather that had not come entirely loose, but had become fouled around part of the undercarriage. Perhaps she could reach that. Holding the seat with one hand, she stretched down and forward with the other.

A groan came from her throat. She couldn't reach. Kathleen wanted to sob in frustration, but she had never been one to cry and saw no point in starting now. She kept reaching. Stretching. The leather slapped tantalizingly against her hand again and again. She finally grabbed hold and gave a shout of triumph. With all her might she hauled back on the single rein.

At first the horses fought her control, but eventually responded to the desperate tugging.

Another explosion sounded. It was terrifyingly close, the heat of it sucking the air from her lungs. With the force of a blow, the blast knocked Kathleen from her seat. She was slammed against the pine block roadway, stunned, unable to draw a breath. People rushing toward the lakefront veered to avoid the racing coach. The horses turned sharply in the middle of the street. The tongue of the coach unbalanced the vehicle and it went over on its side. While she watched in helpless horror, the horses reared, protesting the resistance, struggling to free themselves.

The impact of her fall reverberated through Kathleen's teeth and bones. With slow determination she hauled herself to her feet and hurried over to the coach. The straining horses were dragging it on its side, but the big rockaway barely moved. Kathleen grabbed for the half door just as it banged open.

"We're all right," Lucy said, hiking back her skirts to clamber out.

"Thank God." Kathleen took her hand, helping her, then reached for Phoebe. White-faced and clearly shaken, Phoebe was battling tears. "Hurry," Kathleen said. "The whole neighborhood is burning around us."

Phoebe's beaded gown tore on the door latch as she scrambled out. "Help," she shrieked to a man and woman hurrying past. "You must help us!" The passersby clutched their bundles closer and ignored her. She exhorted a man on a horse for assistance, and shouted to a hose cart driver, but no one stopped.

"Help me free the horses," Kathleen said.

"No, we must get the coach up. It's our only hope of escaping," Phoebe wailed. "Sir," she yelled at a huge man in fringed buckskins. "We need help with the coach—"

He said nothing but took out a gleaming knife. Phoebe shrank back as he pushed past her. With two easy slices, he cut the traces. Then he slapped the horses on the rumps and they raced away.

"He...he...the horses!" Phoebe yelled.

"At least they have a chance now," Lucy said.

Kathleen fixed her gaze on the hose cart crew. On the side of the conveyance she could make out the number 342. Her blood chilled, for that was the fire district that encompassed her parents' home. Suddenly the rushing crowd, the blinding heat, the bellowing roar of the fire all faded away. She stumbled on the broken pavement and lurched around a light post, approaching the crew.

"Have you come from the West Division?" she shouted.

One of the men kept the hose stream aimed at the building that had exploded. "You bet. Nothing left there to save, miss."

A whistle sounded and the hose cart crew drew away. Sick with fear, Kathleen stumbled back to rejoin her friends.

Lucy grabbed Phoebe's hand. "This way. We'll go on foot."

"I'll do nothing of the sort," Phoebe objected.

"We've wasted enough time squabbling already. Come along, Kathleen."

As it turned out, Phoebe had her way. By trading a ruby brooch, Lucy found seats for the three of them on the back of an express wagon. The vehicle, laden with rugs and furnishings from a law firm, lumbered along Washington Street, heading toward the Sands at the edge of the lake. Kathleen felt dazed, unable to think or speak. Her legs dangled off the back of the wagon, and she realized she was facing west.

*Nothing left there to save.*

She wondered dully how long the area had been burning. Had flames consumed her parents' house while she was laughing and flirting with Dylan Kennedy? Had her little sister Mary and baby brother James fled in terror while she was drinking champagne at the Hotel Royale?

The knot of guilt in her stomach tightened. She clutched at her middle, only vaguely aware of her friends' anxious discourse as they sifted through the rumors that sped through the night. Field and Leiter's six-storey retail emporium was in flames. The gasworks and numerous substations stood directly in the path of the fire. The waterworks was threatened. If it failed, there would be no water for the hose crews.

None of it mattered to Kathleen. She couldn't bear to think of anything but her family and what might have become of them.

And then she acted without thinking, doing exactly what instinct told her to do. Without looking left or right, she jumped off the back of the cart. Through the steady roar of the fire and the howl of the wind, she could hear her friends calling her name but she didn't turn, didn't pause, didn't flag in her determination. In seconds, a wall of smoke and flame swallowed the retreating express wagon. It occurred to her that she might never see her friends again.

Between her and the West Division lay a fiery maze only a fool would try to cross. But she had to go anyway. She had to find out what had become of her family.

# Four

"Can't go that way, miss," yelled a passing merchant who staggered along, weighted by a stack of goods from his shop. "It's burning worse'n hell."

Kathleen acknowledged him with a nod, but ignored his advice and continued along Van Buren Street toward the bridge. She had gone this way a thousand times over the years, making the journey from the opulent prosperity of the North Side to the chaotic neighborhoods of the West Division. She always knew, once she reached the river, that the bridge was more than a way to cross the water. It seemed to span two worlds—the world that she'd come from, and the world she yearned to inhabit.

Tonight, for a cruelly short period of time, she had been there, in that world where she desperately wanted to be. Her brother Frank often teased her about her longing and ambition, and he swore that once she sampled the good life, she would find it as stale and artificial as faded silk flowers.

Frank was wrong. Her first taste of high society had been…delicious. Dylan Kennedy had made it so. Imagine, Dylan Kennedy singling her out for his attention, flattering and kissing her as if she were the most desirable woman on earth.

She wanted to savor the memories, but at present

it was all she could do to survive the night. There was no use pretending she wasn't afraid. She was. Everything she could see on the other side of the river was in flames. Wind and fire were one and the same, turning buildings and trees to dizzying towers of fire. The heat reached across the water, searing her cheeks.

Struggling against the crowd, jostled and buffeted like a leaf on the wind, Kathleen tried to pick her way to the bridge. The very sky itself rained flaming brands down on the twin arch supports of the span. In the river, boat whistles shrieked for the bridge to be opened on its pivoting pier, but the walkway was crammed with frantic people, every one of them fleeing directly toward Kathleen. They came on in a solid wall of humanity, and the fire behind them roared like a live thing, a dragon.

She fell back at the bridgetender's house. She'd never get across here. Choked by frustration, she turned north, praying the Madison Street Bridge would be less crowded. In order to get there she would have to pass the gasworks, a frightening prospect given the rain of fire.

But not nearly as frightening as the situation she discovered in the middle of the street. A hail of cinders spattered her, and she cringed within her cloak. She stopped and stared at a police paddy wagon lurching along the roadway. A red-faced driver, his cheeks puffed out around a whistle, stood high on the box, his whistle shrieking. They came to an impasse, where the macadam road was blocked by stacks of crates and trunks someone had abandoned.

The driver and a man on the back had a hurried conversation, then unhitched the horse. People passing by took one look at what was happening and picked up their pace.

Blessed be, thought Kathleen. They're freeing the jailbirds.

The lieutenant opened the back of the wagon, then joined the crowd rushing toward the north and east. Men poured out into the middle of the street. She recognized their striped garb, but even more, she recognized the harsh, deep lines in even the youngest faces. Their eyes were hard and darting, even when they looked up at the flaming sky and, suddenly aware of their freedom, dispersed like sparks in the air.

She did not know any of these men, but the look of them was familiar to her. These were the faces of men who had grown up as poor as she, but rather than toiling for a wage at the stockyards or a lumber mill or a varnishing factory, they had taken to crime. Some of the men had the very look of violence in their gleaming eyes and badly healed broken noses, while others might have been altar boys in church in their younger years. A body just couldn't tell, she thought, keeping to the side of the street, away from all the commotion.

Appearances could be so deceiving.

She concentrated on forging a path through the smoldering debris to the nearest bridge, and tried praying through her gritted teeth. But the words to even the simplest prayer simply would not come. She did not know how to ask for all that she wanted—for her family to be safe, their home to be standing. Forgiveness for seeking beyond her means for a life not meant to be hers. Safety for her friends, whom she had abandoned in order to make the desperate dash across the city.

Some of the newly freed convicts started looting
the shops and businesses that lined the street. They
helped themselves to jugs of liquor, lamps, bolts of
cloth, anything that wasn't nailed down. Despite her
understanding of these men, the pillaging shocked
her, and she hurried faster. Even so, she was not quick
enough to elude a heavyset, mean-eyed convict who
shoved himself up against her on the walkway. He
was a black man with a sculpted mouth, a bald head
and a thin, raised scar under one eye.

"Let's have a look at those jewels now, sister," he
said, his meaty paw reaching for her borrowed necklace.

There was no time for fear or hysteria. Kathleen
had been raised in the rough West Division, and she
didn't hesitate. "Over my dead body, boyo," she
said, and at the same time, she brought up her knee.
The mean eyes bugged out, and she felt the rush of
his hot breath as he doubled over, wheezing, leaning
against the concrete base of the bank building. Kathleen knew she had only seconds before he recovered,
angrier than ever, so she darted down a side alley.

Away from the bridge. But there was nothing else
for it. Too many of the convicts overran the vicinity.
She preferred the unknown perils of the fire to the
very familiar dangers of newly freed prisoners. She
hoped the narrow, smoke-shrouded alley would lead
to another westbound street, but instead found herself
in a maze of walled-off mews. After a few sharp turns
to the right, she became disoriented. She passed no
one; the area had been evacuated. Stable doors hung
open to empty stalls, the stores of hay fueling the
conflagration. Only the occasional rat streaked past,
seemingly as lost as she.

Suddenly a crashing sound ripped through the air. Looking back the way she had come, she saw that the walls on either side of the alley had caved in on themselves. A fountain of dust and ash rose from the sky. But out of the ashes came something…someone. A man. Staggering, wounded. She blinked and squinted against the stinging smoke.

There was another crash, and she lost sight of the man. Then the wind screamed through the alley, scouring the air so that, for a few seconds, she could see clearly.

He wore prison stripes and a look of hideous fury. He had a bald head and a scar under one eye.

And he was hopelessly pinned by a fallen roof beam.

Kathleen wheeled around and started to run away, for the first time truly afraid for her life. After a few yards, she dared to turn and look. He fought with the charred, smoking beam, desperately trying to drag himself out from under its weight. With one arm, he reached toward a shadowy doorway. Bright embers and sheets of tarred roofing wafted down, setting fire to all they touched.

Kathleen hurried away, expecting to feel a rush of relief.

Instead, she kept thinking of the way the Negro man struggled, the twist of his open mouth. She imagined his bellows of pain and rage, drowned by the roar of the storm. She wondered if he knew how to pray.

And against all common sense, she stopped running and turned back. He was a convict, a thief and possibly a murderer, but was it for her to condemn him to the flames of eternity?

She trembled as she returned to his side, crouching down and tugging at the huge beam. Tears of hot sap spurted from the wood, burning her hand. She flinched, but kept pulling at the beam.

"Best get on out of this place," the man said in a low voice.

She didn't pause. "You can't stay here," she said. "You'll burn like Saint Joan if you do."

He managed to push one leg out from under the beam. His foot was clad in a cheap China canvas shoe with holes cut for his toes. His arms were still pressed to the ground.

"Can't move," he said with a rough sneer. "An' that ought to make her ladyship happy."

She swallowed hard, tasting a dry grittiness in her throat. "Hush up. I'm trying to help you."

He eyed her with suspicion. "Help me what? Burn like the sinner I am? You done enough already, thank you very kindly."

Realizing that she lacked the strength in her arms, Kathleen sat down in the roadway and pressed her feet to the beam. "Look, I don't have time to argue with you. Push from below, and I'll push with my feet until we move this thing off you. Unless you prefer to sit here and caterwaul like a bleedin' infant until you suffocate."

He seemed to respond to her sharpness more than her compassion. With a nod, he indicated that it was time to push. With him heaving from below and Kathleen pushing with both legs, the beam finally moved. Crawling inch by inch, the convict freed himself. Kathleen jumped up with a shout of triumph. Then, seeing that he might be injured, she stuck out her hand.

He closed his soot-blackened hand around hers, nearly pulling her down as he levered himself to a standing position.

"There now," she said, "I'll help you walk. But keep your greedy mitts off the necklace."

"You're no bigger'n a minute," he said. "How you going to help me?"

She angled a glare up at him. "Didn't I just? It's not the size that matters," she reminded him. "Come, and be as quick as you can."

He settled a big, heavy arm across her shoulders and they started along the smoke-filled alley. Kathleen could feel him wince each time he put weight on his injured ankle. His bald head, shining with sweat, had a gash across the right side. Still, he drove himself to match her pace.

"Why?" he rasped, wheezing with the rhythm of their hurried footsteps.

She knew what he meant. "You're a bully and a thief, but so are most men. That doesn't mean they should all be burned alive."

He coughed out a laugh. "I can name a dame or two who'd disagree."

The injured man smelled, and he weighed heavy against her, but Kathleen just wanted to get the two of them to a place of safety. The fire pursued them like a deadly enemy with a mind of its own. The wind drove the flames to lick at their heels. They needed to find a place of relative quiet, where the air was at least breathable. They walked for what seemed like hours, encountering dead ends and blocked passageways. Sometimes the smoke blinded them utterly.

"Do you know where we are?" she asked the convict.

"Not a blamed notion." He grunted as his foot struck a stray brick in the road. "My name's Eugene, by the way. Eugene Waxman. Friends call me Bull."

She didn't have to ask why. He was as big as an untrimmed side of beef, and just as muscular. Her back and shoulders ached under the weight of him even though she sensed his effort to support himself as much as possible.

"Kathleen O'Leary," she replied.

"It's good we should know each other's names," he said.

Somewhere overhead, a window exploded outward. He tucked her head under his arm to shield her from the falling glass. When she looked up at him, she could see flecks of blood on his head where he'd been hit.

"Why?" she asked, chilled despite the heat of the fire.

"So we don't die among strangers."

But they didn't die. They fought and struggled through the maze of streets and faintly, between the bellow of the flames and the howl of the wind, they heard bells. The courthouse alarm or a church bell, perhaps. They followed the sound, and finally emerged at an intersection overrun by people racing to and fro, encountering barriers everywhere they turned.

Kathleen didn't know whether to laugh or weep. After all her struggles, she had wound up in Courthouse Square, not four blocks from the salon where the evening had begun so pleasantly.

"Shit," said Bull, drawing out the syllable in disgust. The huge, gothic building housed the jail in its basement. "I just left this place."

"I'll save you from that monster, miss!" hollered an earnest-looking man. He raised a tasseled horse-whip high overhead, aiming it at Bull.

Kathleen realized that the man assumed she was being mauled or abducted by the convict.

"Stop!" she yelled. "Leave him alone!"

The earnest man retreated, shaking his head.

"Take off your shirt," she ordered Bull. At the look on his face, she gave a harsh laugh. "Modesty is no virtue on a night like tonight," she added. "I'd best find you something to wear that doesn't make people so suspicious."

He looked mortified as he peeled off the horizontally striped shirt. In the heated glow of the fire, she saw that his back was marked with a furious cross-hatching of scars. He might have been a slave at one time, she realized.

Half a block farther, a flatbed wagon, overloaded with salvaged goods, rumbled by. She made no apology as she helped herself to a wicker laundry basket. Rifling through a jumble of clothes and linens, she found what appeared to be a man's nightshirt.

"Put this on," she said, tossing it to him.

She caught his look of wary gratitude as he tugged on the stolen shirt. It stretched taut across his massive shoulders but was far less conspicuous than the prison stripes.

Kathleen scanned the area, craning her neck toward the west. "I need to get across the river," she said, thinking aloud.

"Best get to the lakeshore, miss. Nowhere else is safe—"

"My family's in the West Division. I have to find them."

"Be like finding a needle in a haystack tonight."
He gestured at the press of humanity surging through
the streets.

She felt a twinge of exasperation. "I won't be arguing over it with the likes of you." She took a deep
breath, wincing at the harsh, sooty flavor of the air,
and started up the street toward the bridge.

But tonight, the world was clearly against her. She
could not take two steps forward without being
shoved three steps back. A hose cart crew rushed past,
forcing her to plaster herself against a stone wall in
order to avoid being trampled. An open tar tank from
a roofing plant had caught, and the whole area was
wreathed in flame.

A marshal in a peaked hat and long coat put a brass
speaking trumpet to his mouth. "Clear the area," he
boomed. "We can't save the gasworks. Clear the
area."

Kathleen looked fearfully at the gasworks complex.
At least one huge gasholder blazed with eye-smarting
brightness. Men with buckets climbed to its top, while
others led horses away from the company barn.

"Why can't you stop the fire, for pity's sake?"
Kathleen demanded. She recalled Lucy Hathaway's
politician friends, promising that the new waterworks
could pump the whole of Lake Michigan over a fire
if need be.

He halted, just for a moment, while the false light
of the fire played over his grimy, sweating face.
"Don't you see, miss?" He was panting in ragged
gasps. "We'd sooner stop the wind."

She forced herself to accept what she had not dared
to see until this moment. The very sky itself roared
with flame. Windblown sparks rained down in a

deadly storm. This was different from the other fires that had plagued the city throughout the dry season. In the summer, a good neighborhood blaze might attract spectators like a baseball match at the White Stockings stadium.

Tonight, curiosity had turned to terror.

"Move along, miss," the fire marshal said, his brass buttons flashing importantly. "You don't want to be around when the gasworks blow. See if you can flag down a hack."

She moved out of the way so he could direct his crew toward the blazing Hinkler's Stage and Omnibus Company. With a deepening sense of dread, she headed north to the Lake Street Bridge, ever aware that her options were running out.

She felt a tingling at the back of her neck, a presence, and she whirled around. The man called Bull loomed like a shadow over her.

"Why are you following me?" Kathleen demanded.

"You all alone and the city's going crazy. Somebody might take a notion to grab you. Rob you, maybe."

"A shocking idea," she said, leveling a look of accusation at him. But she could not cling to her anger. She was too desperate to find her family. "You're right about the robbing," she conceded. Without slowing her pace, she unclasped the precious Tiffany necklace and removed the matching earrings and bracelet. She had a fleeting memory of Dylan Kennedy putting the earring on her. Even now, in the middle of mayhem, she felt a sweet, melting sensation deep inside her. She wondered why she hadn't thought to hide away the valuables before. She simply wasn't used to wearing anything of value. She would have put the jewels in her reticule, but she had managed to lose that somewhere. A bad sign, losing Gran's mass card. It was supposed to have been her good luck token.

"Don't look," she said to Bull, and turned away.

"You just a skinny little thing, anyway," he grumbled.

She stuffed the jewels down her bodice, grimacing at the sharp feel of the priceless stones next to her skin. He was a convict, guilty of Lord-knew-what heinous offenses. He had tried to rob her. Yet now, with him limping along beside her, bleeding from the head, she felt unaccountably safe.

The next bridge was impassable. Seeing it, she had a sinking sensation in her stomach. Carts, buggies, wagons and pedestrians poured across the span.

Bull said nothing, but she could feel his "I told you so" emanating from him as if he had spoken it aloud. Shouts and the clatter of wheels filled the air and she had to jump back to make way for the fleeing populace. In their arms, people carried the things they could not bear to leave for the fire to devour.

Some looked grateful to escape with the clothes on their backs. Others wore layer upon layer of clothing despite the heat. There was one old lady in a fur coat and hat with so many layers beneath that she appeared as swollen as a tick. One nervous, suspicious woman grasped at her valuables, looking over her shoulder and hovering over her treasures like a hen with a clutch of eggs. In contrast there was a man wearing nothing but a nightshirt and a silk top hat. In one hand he held a bottle of brandy, in the other a cigar. He sat calmly in a crowded hack, watching the mountain of fire beyond the bridge. A woman hurried past on foot, pushing a baby carriage. From the expression on her face, it was clear that everything important to her lay within the carriage.

Kathleen wondered what she would save if she stood to lose everything. And she discovered, with a flash of resentment, that the answer eluded her. She had nothing of her own, nothing worth saving. Unlike the woman with the pram, she had no idea how to cherish what she had rather than wishing for something different.

Her gaze fixed on a man clinging to the tailgate of a stout insurance patrol wagon. She squinted through the smoke and—

"Pegleg!" she yelled, pushing toward the street. "Daniel! Mr. Sullivan!"

Daniel Sullivan, known to all as Pegleg for his wooden prosthesis, lived in her family's neighborhood. At the sound of her voice, he glanced around, craning his neck.

"It's me, Mr. Sullivan," she cried. "Kathleen O'Leary!"

"Lord bless you, child, so it is." The man shifted on the cart. Crammed with too many passengers and driven by Commissioner Benjamin Bullwinkle himself, the wagon lumbered along at a snail's pace. "Can you climb aboard, then?"

She shook her head, refusing the invitation. She was able-bodied and did not need to take a seat from someone who might need it more. "My family," she shouted, walking alongside the cart. "Have you seen them?"

"Indeed I did, not an hour before the fire started."

"Was anyone hurt?" she forced herself to ask.

"By the grace of God, nary a soul," he said, "though the Lord only knows what's left of the old neighborhood now."

Her knees wobbled. She was so close to weeping with relief that she could taste the tears in her throat. Suddenly she knew exactly what was important to her. "Do you know where they've gone?"

"To the vacant lot behind Shults's saloon to wait out the fire. You'll not be seeing them tonight by the looks of things. You'd best get yourself to safety."

She cast a dubious glance to the west. The glare of the fire made her squint.

"My girl, keeping yourself safe is all they would want in the world. You know it's so. Don't even think about trying to get over to the West Side." He jerked his thumb toward the lake. "Get yourself to safety, colleen. You'll find them when this is all over."

In the flickering light, she studied his face. Pegleg had small kindly eyes and a mouth that always found a smile for his neighbors. He'd never lie to her on a matter like this. If he said the O'Learys were all right, then they were all right.

The wagon lurched through a gap in the crowd. Before she could speak again, the vehicle rolled away. A drunken man reeled forward, detaching himself from the throng. He put his arm around Kathleen, his hands taking unspeakable liberties with her person. "Come along, lovely, I'll rescue y—"

A very large fist grabbed the man by the scruff of the neck and pitched him away like a thrown cat.

"Best step out of the road, miss," Bull said. "Lot of traffic coming from the West Side."

He stood like a boulder in the roadway, his massive shoulders straining at the seams of the ill-fitting shirt.

He seemed to have appointed himself her personal bodyguard. She wondered what his motive was. Hope for a reward? Gratitude that she had helped him out of the burning alley? Or did he intend to try stealing her jewels again?

"Thank you," she said, scowling after the drunken man. "I was about to kick him in the—"

"I reckon I could guess," Bull said quickly.

A galloping team bore a cart straight toward them. She backed up against a figured stone building and Bull did the same, narrowly escaping being run down. "Have you a family of your own, Mr. Waxman?" she asked him. "Is there someone you're trying to find tonight?"

"Got no family," he said bluntly. "No home or place of my own."

She studied him in the flickering light. He looked very tall and forbidding. His head had been shaved recently, for lice, she supposed. The job had been carelessly done, and in addition to the large gash from the collapsing timber, there were small cuts here and there from falling glass. He reminded her of the bloodthirsty pirates in some of the forbidden stories she and Miss Deborah used to read together in secret, late at night.

They followed the seething crowd, Bull reluctantly leaning on her and gritting his teeth every step of the way. Squinting against a storm of flying sparks, she recognized the slender, handsome spire of St. Brendan's in the distance. Against the unnaturally bright sky, it glowed like a beacon.

St. Brendan's might be safe, she thought. It was as if the very hand of her own dear gran were guiding her toward sanctuary. The old woman had found sol-

ace there, and its yard, with a wrought iron gazebo
and a little prayer garden, was her final resting place.
That had to mean something. But how to get there?
She would have to go north to the river and then
double back south in order to avoid the conflagration.

She was shouting her plan to Bull when, at the
corner of Monroe and Market Streets, the world split
apart. A huge explosion, fueled by someone's abandoned supply of gunpowder or kerosene, brought
down buildings like dominoes. Fireballs whooshed
through the alleys, sucking away every bit of fresh
air. For a few terrifying moments, Kathleen could find
nothing to breathe. People and wagons and animals
lurched and tumbled along the road like leaves before
a storm.

Kathleen clutched Bull's hand and held on tight,
ducking her head to avoid flying debris. He dragged
her into the shelter of a brick doorway, where broken
glass crunched underfoot and the firestorm howled
past with the fury of a prairie tornado.

Just for a moment, everything went eerily still. It
was as if the storm were gathering its breath for another assault. Kathleen heard the swish of her own
heartbeat pounding in her ears, and she gripped Bull's
hand with all her might. In the terrible lull, a voice
sounded, shrieking through the unnatural silence with
an unearthly resonance that made Kathleen's scalp
tingle. "My baby! My baby!"

Her cry summoned a crowd. The panicked mother
rushed toward a burning building shrouded in smoke
and flame. High in a broken-out window, a pair of
small hands clung to the concrete sill. "My baby!"
the woman screamed a third time.

Seconds later, the wind shifted and the fire took

hold again. Flames rode the swirling gale through the ruined street, feasting on the doomed buildings and trees, swallowing up the building with the stranded child.

Two people restrained the hysterical woman. She fought them, calling for her baby, trying to claw her way free. Kathleen knew for certain that the woman would plunge straight into the fire to rescue her missing child. Everyone watching shared the excruciating pain of hopelessness.

Then, out of the smoke, a man strode forward, backlit by the flames. An opera cape billowed from his shoulders like a pair of dark wings, and he didn't even hesitate as he walked into the inferno.

More spectators gathered, wide-eyed with terror and mute with wonder. Kathleen held her breath and beside her, Bull stood as still as a hitch post. The mother kept screaming as she tried to escape those who held her back. The stranger leaped toward an exterior iron stairway. He reached for the bottom rung of the ladder, pulling himself up with lithe, graceful movements. Finding a foothold on the stair, he climbed swiftly to the second storey. Balancing on the window ledge, he teetered wildly, hair and cape blown by powerful gusts of wind.

"God save the ee-jit," an onlooker said. "He's going to get himself killed."

Someone else hushed the speaker, though he'd only said aloud what everyone was thinking.

The reaching flames swallowed up the man on the ledge. There was no sign of the child, either. Kathleen squinted, desperate to see through the curtain of fire, but for endless moments, no one could tell what was happening.

The distraught mother wailed, making the most terrible sound Kathleen had ever heard. People turned away, covering their faces. Kathleen shut her eyes and sagged against the doorway, drained and defeated from witnessing the tragedy.

Then a collective gasp compelled her to look again. The tall man had reappeared through the smoke and flames. He descended the ladder with fluid haste.

In his arms he carried a small, screaming child. In a hail of sparks and ash, the man dropped to the ground and raced away from the fire. He surrendered the child to the weeping, grateful mother and then turned away. The firelight fell over curling black hair and a face that struck Kathleen mute with recognition.

Dylan Kennedy.

# Five

Of all the misbegotten luck, Dylan thought, brushing impatiently at a spark that had settled on his silk-lined cape. And he'd been doing so well up till now. Costello had him dead to rights, but a timely surge of traffic on the bridge had provided a distraction. More nimble than the older man, Dylan had climbed up under the bridge, heaved himself over the top and melted into the crowd.

At the Omnibus Stables he'd commandeered an express wagon, and had done a brisk business in the wealthy Lowry Block, offering to transport valuables to safety. He'd collected some fenceable fine art, a bit of cash and jewelry, and some decent clothes, including a set of Italian shirts a gentleman would be proud to own. Now he found himself empty-handed and forced to rescue useless toddlers from the flames. He'd had to abandon the well-provisioned cart in order to go after the child and give it back to its blubbering mother.

The feat was no more hazardous than the firewalk he used to perform for audiences in Buffalo. But while he had been occupied with the rescue, the wagon had been taken by the flames, all the booty ruined beneath tons of incinerating rubble. People watching the rescue had looked to him as a hero, a role that fit him about as well as a hair shirt.

The night was still young, he told himself, staving off a wave of weary frustration. And deep down, he acknowledged that no fortune was worth the life of a child.

He wiped the sweat and ash from his face, squeezed his stinging eyes shut and pinched the bridge of his nose. When he opened his eyes, he noticed a woman in a green dress hurrying toward him. Her face glowed with wonder and admiration, and he realized she had witnessed the rescue.

For the first time in hours, a grin broke over his face. Maybe his luck was about to change.

He performed a graceful bow as if he stood in the middle of a formal ballroom rather than a burning street. "Shall we dance?" he asked.

Her smile of pride and relief made him feel ten feet tall. "I can't believe you did that," she said. "You were truly wonderful."

"All in a night's work." He sounded perfectly modest, but inside, his heart sang. For once, his timing had been impeccable. He had found his heiress again, and he had impressed her. That was something, at least.

An African giant loomed over her abruptly, and Dylan felt a clutch of fear in his gut. Shit. If he had to defend her from this brute—

"This fellow bothering you, miss?" the giant asked.

"Not at the moment," she said. "Mr. Kennedy, this is Eugene Waxman. Also known as Bull."

Bull wore prison trousers and a threatening scowl.

Dylan recognized the implacable look of unquestioning loyalty in the huge man's face. For some reason, the giant had given his large self, and his allegiance, to the small and beautiful heiress. Maybe he hoped for a reward for rescuing her.

Not if Dylan had anything to say about the matter. *He* would rescue her. If people of quality wondered what he would do with the reward money, he'd promise to donate it to his favorite charitable cause. Himself.

Hot light flashed over her as flames shot skyward. She was beautiful still, despite a decided undoing of her red hair and some wear and tear on the ruby cloak and green dress.

And her jewels were missing.

He wanted to ask what she had done with the diamonds but didn't want to be too obvious. Nor did he want the huge person called Bull to get any ideas.

Dylan did not let his concern show, but cocked out his arm. "We had best *ficher le camp*," he suggested. "I'm not fond of hot weather."

She hesitated only a moment, then took his arm. "Bull needs help walking," she said. "He has a head injury, and I think he hurt his ankle. I'm sure you won't mind supporting him."

Dylan and Bull stared at one another. Suspicion flashed between them, followed by a rapid succession of dislike, distrust, perhaps even recognition. Dylan had a sixth sense about people. He could pick out a chiseler in any crowd; it was like looking into a mirror.

Bull wasn't a chiseler but a brute criminal. The

moment passed and Bull shook his head. "I reckon I can walk on my own now."

Kate looked exasperated, but she started forward. Bull limped along beside her. Dylan kept sneaking glances at her unadorned ears, bosom, wrists. Had someone stolen the jewels? Had she hidden them away somewhere? He felt a sinking disappointment. She was one of the most charming creatures he had ever met. But she was even more charming with her jewels.

A speeding cart, minus its driver, stampeded down the middle of the road. Dylan had no time to think, only to act. He grabbed the tailgate of the cart and hoisted himself up. The jolts over the ruined roadway nearly flung him off, but he took hold of one long leather ribbon. It was an amateur's rig but he could still control the horse. Hauling back with gradual pressure, he managed to stop the cart at the curb beside the river.

Kate and Bull came toward him as he jettisoned the few items that remained in the cart. A crate of old quilts and a box of family photographs and papers hit the water with a splash, then sank out of sight.

"Those are someone's treasures," Kathleen objected.

"Now they'll always know where to find them." As his passengers climbed in, Dylan urged the tired, nervous horse forward. "I thought you'd be off to the suburbs, waiting out the fire in safety with the other society fribbles," he said.

She stared straight ahead as she answered, "I was unfortunately separated from my friends. Our coach crashed."

"Was anyone hurt?"

"No, but all was chaos."

"What was your destination?" He hoped like hell she didn't expect him to provide accommodations.

She didn't answer, and he thought she had not heard. As they passed the *Chicago Tribune* building at Dearborn and Madison, he noticed men on the roof, frantically and futilely wetting it down in order to fend off the approaching blaze.

A building across the way exploded, and the horse bolted. Even straining to hold the beast in, Dylan began feeling decidedly more optimistic about things. His red-haired passenger clutched the sides of the cart and regarded the fire as if it were a dragon pursuing them. Fear did not diminish her looks; perhaps it even enhanced them by lending her a vulnerability that made him want to keep her safe. No wonder the jailbird stuck to her like a large tick.

They were nearing a branch of the river when he heard the shouts.

At first he could see nothing through the murky veil of smoke. Then a gust of wind cleared the area and he saw a family by the roadside. A prosperous-looking man and woman struggled to help an elderly invalid toward the lake. Burdened with a strongbox and a swaddled baby, his wife followed behind.

"They need help," Kate declared. "Stop the cart."

Capital, thought Dylan, pulling back on the reins. A bleeding heart.

*"Meine mutter,"* the man said, then stammered out in German-accented English. "She cannot walk. I have nothing to give you in exchange for the cart—"

His wife rapped out something in German and indicated the heavy box. The man nodded and opened it, igniting Dylan's interest. Perhaps there was a deal to be made after all.

The German extracted a dog-eared document. "I am the owner of the Hotel St. George," he said. "Here is the deed. I give it to you in exchange for your cart."

Dylan eyed him skeptically. "You're giving me a hotel?"

"*Ja,* the deed is all I have left after this unholy night."

"The hotel has burned to the ground, hasn't it?"

The man spread his hands. "You never know, eh?" A scribbled receipt was drawn up, signed and witnessed using the charred end of a stick for a pencil. The proprietor handed over the papers.

Dylan felt his optimism slipping, but he took the worthless document and thrust it inside his shirt. "Let's get her into the cart, then," he said.

He and the German made a seat of their clasped hands. The old woman was surprisingly hefty and quite vocal as they lifted her. She shrieked and babbled the whole time, clutching, with absurd protectiveness, a live chicken in her arms. The German's wife hovered nearby, cradling the baby to her chest.

Dylan knew the horse couldn't handle all of them even if the cart were large enough—which it wasn't. Kate and Bull had already assessed the situation and climbed out of the wagon.

"Isn't he just the sweetest thing?" Kate cooed over the squalling infant.

Dylan heaved a long-suffering sigh. He spoke briefly to the German, pointing out what he hoped was the most expeditious route to the lakeshore. The crammed cart rolled away.

Dylan patted the deed. "I sold him the cart in exchange for the Hotel St. George." He laughed at her confusion. "Don't worry. It's probably a pile of ash and rubble, but I've always been fond of gambling."

Bull held his bleeding head and started walking with slow, slogging steps. They managed to cover only half a block before the blaze hemmed them in on three sides. Flames roared down the alley like great, hot tongues, driving them back.

"Where are we?" asked Kate, clutching his arm in a way that gratified him. It was an unfortunate neighborhood of brothels and bunko houses. Ramrod Hall disgorged a small army of soiled doves in various states of undress, many of them clutching their valuables to their ample chests. Kate eyed them with frank fascination and possibly a little envy.

There was nowhere to go but south. The way to the river was choked off by buildings that had collapsed in a series of explosions. The route eastward, to the lake, consisted of one vast, burning wasteland. Kate held fast to his hand as he pulled her along with the crowd. Bull stayed obstinately at her other side.

Dylan wished the jailbird would go away. There was an unwelcome intelligence in Bull's dark eyes, a knowledge of the harsh ways of the world. A man like Bull was no easy dupe and Dylan preferred them easy.

He squeezed Kate's hand and smiled. "Courage, my dear," he said. "We'll find a way out of this, see if we don't."

As if to mock his words, flames lashed out of the building they were passing. The heat was so intense that at first it numbed him. Then came the hideous glaring pain, streaking over him like a lightning bolt. With an instinct he didn't know he possessed, he wrapped his entire self around Kate and shielded her from the worst of the roaring flames.

"This way," Bull bellowed, leading the way down a narrow, smoke-filled street. Using his massive shoulder, he butted open a thick, painted door and they scurried inside. Dylan slammed the door behind them. It was fully dark and clammy with the smells of earth and stone. Some years ago, all the buildings of Chicago had been raised to avoid flooding. Many of them had crawlspaces and forgotten places beneath them.

"Hold tight," Dylan said. "We'll figure out where we are." With one hand grasping Kate's and the other groping along the wall, he moved forward. In a few minutes his shin smacked up against a riser. Gritting his teeth to keep in an oath, he said, "I've found a staircase." They climbed blindly to another door and opened it. A high window somewhere let in the firelight. Thick pillars flanked a brick-and-stone chamber crowded with benches. Dylan stopped and turned.

"Where the hell are we?" he wondered aloud.

"St. Brendan's," said Kate, her voice thin with wonder and relief. "We've come full circle."

"What?"

"It's a church. St. Brendan's church."

St. Brendan's, the name on the mass card she'd dropped. This was what had led him to her. An eerie feeling passed through Dylan even though he didn't believe in the supernatural.

"Come in," called a brisk, pleasant voice. "Come in, and quickly. Be certain you close the door behind you. And here I thought I would be the last to leave." A youthful priest swept toward them as if borne on a wave of optimism.

"I am Father Michael McCoughy." Brisk and officious, he led them across a dim sanctuary, cavernously empty of humanity. At the end of the main aisle stood a huge font half-full of holy water. Colored windows depicting images of sweet-faced martyrs glowed with the light from outside.

An unexpected feeling came over Dylan. A certain…sentiment so filled with tenderness and awe that it made him catch his breath. His heart filled with the ache of yearning, and he stood speechless, staring.

*Remembering.*

But what was he remembering? He had no memory of being in this church. Truth be told, he had barred memories of his early life from his mind, no matter how much his heart wanted to remember. For him, life began in a train station in New York City where his mother had walked away from him and never looked back.

He had no idea why he felt such a warmth and affinity for this place.

The priest was speaking and gesticulating. Dylan forced himself to pay attention.

"We did all we could," the cleric said, "and the rest is in God's hands. This way, through the back of the sanctuary, was clear a few moments ago."

"Must we leave, Father?" asked Kate, her voice

keen with distress. "We've come so far, and Bull is injured."

"'Tisn't safe. We've soaked the carpets and doused the walls but the fire's only a block away. The steeple's made of wood, so it's bound to catch and torch the place altogether. If it leaves this place standing it'll be a miracle entirely. We must leave here, much as I hate to do it. The closest safe haven is the courthouse. You can rest there."

"I won't go to no courthouse." Bull sank to a pew, holding his head.

"'Tis said the building is fireproof," the priest reminded him.

Dylan had seen several fireproof buildings this night. Their steel structures had not burned, but they *had* melted, bringing a brimstone of rubble down, every bit as deadly as burning timber. But he said nothing. Already the temperature in the church had risen. Bull sat down on the pew and closed his eyes.

"So why are you still here, Father?" Dylan asked.

He patted the front of his robe. "I have to safeguard some of the church papers. We've a special place for such things." He hastened behind the high altar, moving a grate from the stones of the presbytery. "I won't be a minute," he called over his shoulder.

"And how is he going to keep them from burning?" Dylan asked in a whisper. "Divine intervention?"

Kate caught her breath in outrage. By the golden light of the fire, she looked utterly magnificent. And offended by his joke. He sent her an intimate smile and touched her hand. "Surely we can make light of it."

Propped up on a pew, Bull snored, hauling in a breath like a steam engine. Dylan could see her trying to cling to indignation, but she lost the battle and smiled up at him.

Dylan eschewed the usual rush of gratification that he felt when a mark swallowed his bait. Women like Kate weren't used to being lied to. They never expected it. Deceiving her on this small matter was no great achievement.

"Don't be put off by my irreverence," he said, offering fair warning. "Maybe I'm simply trying to cover up my deeper feelings for you."

She smacked his arm. "Stop being a tease in church."

He gazed down at her, using that soft look women loved. "Kate, I am not teasing. All my life I've waited for a woman like you. I stopped believing she existed. Until tonight. When I met you, I learned to believe in miracles again." The fact that he sat at the altar of a church, lying through his teeth, did not faze him in the least. "May the Almighty strike me dead if I lie," he added defiantly.

When the shell over the upper choir collapsed, he got a little superstitious. Grabbing Kate's hand, he hauled her toward the principal doorway.

Father Michael came rushing back from the presbytery. "We're out of time," he said, calm but clearly worried. "Help me get Mr. Bull on his feet. We'd best hurry to the courthouse." He and Dylan grabbed the big man by the arms. Bull moaned and protested, dazed from his head wound.

"This way," the priest said, pushing and pulling the man down the aisle to the main door. He paused at the deep stone font. "Wait," he said. Scooping with both hands, he liberally doused Bull with holy water, soaking him from head to toe. "For the run to the courthouse," the priest said as Dylan and Kate followed suit.

"I ain't Catholic," Bull said, sputtering.

"You are now, my son," Father Michael told him with a wink.

In the churchyard, they encountered a group of men with an artillery cart. Led by a city alderman, they intended to use explosives to destroy the whole church to keep the fire from spreading to the adjacent neighborhood.

"The only wooden part of the building is the steeple, sir," Father Michael shouted.

"And already a corner of it's in flames," the officer shouted back. "It'll be a torch to ignite the rest of the neighborhood. To get the steeple down, we've got to dynamite the whole structure."

"You can't dynamite a church." Kate regarded the priest in alarm. "It's a desperate mortal sin, surely," she said. "Isn't it?"

Dylan read the genuine distress on her face, smudged with ash, yet beautiful still in the eerie, flickering firelight. He was amazed a woman like this hadn't been spoken for. She had the sort of soft, lovely face that made a man want to promise her the moon and the stars.

"Suppose," he said, calling himself a fool even as he spoke, "the steeple alone were to come down. Would that satisfy you?"

"It would indeed. But how——"

"Give me all the rope you have, and ten minutes. And unhitch those draft horses from your artillery." Dylan felt disgusted with himself. It wasn't like him to risk his life saving children and churches, yet in the past hour, he had unwittingly devoted himself to doing just that. But something in the bewhiskered man's skepticism, and in Kate's worshipful gaze, inspired him. With a showman's flourish, he shed his cloak and frock coat, hefted several coils of rope, then went up the side of the building, using corbels in the masonry as handholds.

He knew the stunt looked more dangerous than it was, particularly for him. In his varied careers, he had performed many feats of gymnastics, but when he reached the ridge of the roof some seventy feet above the ground, he began to question his own sanity. Sparks hissed at his wet clothing, and roof tiles came loose under his feet. Balancing with arms outstretched, he grimly traversed the roof. By the time he crossed to the steeple, the wooden spire roared with flames. Smoke spewed from the louvered sides, choking him and enshrouding him so that he knew he wasn't visible to the onlookers far below. With the sting of embers raining on his back, he managed to loop the rope around each corner of the spire.

He lowered himself with the ropes, hearing a huge cheer go up when he appeared below the billows of smoke. Remembering his showman's style, he took a bow and tried not to cough. Then he set to work quickly, securing the ropes to the base of the burning steeple. A crew of men on the ground cleared the area. The straining horses brought down the ruined steeple, its remains breaking into searing embers in the churchyard.

Dizzy from the smoke, Dylan used the last rope to rappel down the side of the building.

"Bless you," said Father Michael, his eyes shining as he offered a jug of water. "Bless you for what you have done."

Dylan drank greedily from the jug, battling a fit of coughing.

Like an angel of mercy, Kate used a cloth dampened in the baptismal font to wash his face.

"Save that cloth," Dylan said with a grin. "It could become a holy relic."

She shook her head in exasperation, then turned her attention to Father Michael. "It's a shame altogether to lose the steeple," she said.

"Indeed it is."

The smoke must have addled his brain, for Dylan felt the urge to make a grand gesture. Before he could stop himself, he blurted out, "The steeple will be replaced once this is all over. If it takes the last copper penny of my fortune, I'll see it rebuilt." It was almost worth the insincere promise to watch the expression on Kate's face.

"You're one hell of a fool," Bull muttered.

Under the arched central portal of the church, they prepared to evacuate. The lovely gardens had become a wasteland of scorched earth. The men of the explosives crew hastened away to their next target, leaving the four of them to make their way to safety. Supported by the young priest, Bull pushed at the wrought iron gate, snatching his hand back as the hot metal seared him.

"It is a vision of purgatory," Father Michael said, kicking the gate open with his thick leather brogan. He and Bull started out, the priest reciting Psalm 23 in ringing tones: "The Lord is my shepherd…"

"Wait a moment," Kate said with sudden urgency.

"Now what? Did you spy a cat caught in a tree or something?" Dylan had already had his fill of foolish heroics for the night.

"…maketh me to lie down in green pastures…" The priest's voice grew fainter as he walked away.

"It's not that. But as we were standing here I—" She clutched his arm. "A feeling came over me, and I suddenly realized that it's now or never."

"Now or never for what?"

"I think perhaps you should kiss me." Her long-lashed eyes worshiped him.

Few things caught Dylan off guard, but this did. "Kiss you."

"Yes, please."

"I'm more than happy to oblige," he said. Under the dripstone archway of the church, he took her in his arms, amazed that even after the night's ordeal, she retained an exquisite female scent that drove him mad. He slowly bent his head and kissed her.

"Yea, though I walk through the valley of the shadow of death," called Father Michael, "I shall fear no evil, for thou art with me…"

Kissing Kate was like taking a holiday from the real world. She transported him utterly, took him away from the troubles that deviled him. He had always known he loved wealthy heiresses. What surprised him was that she made that love feel like a form of adoration. She tasted like heaven and, when he drew back to gaze down at her, she looked like an angel. Perhaps he would marry this one. Yes, that would do nicely. Her fortune would see him through the hard times. If Costello found out, he would hit the roof, but her money would calm him down. Dylan would find a way to make it work.

The roar and lash of the flames reminded him that they had best be going.

"I just have one question," he said as they plunged across the churchyard toward Courthouse Square. "Not that I'm complaining, but why did you feel the need to kiss me just then?"

She clung to his hand as they confronted a wall of flame racing in from the west. "In case it's the last thing I do."

# *Six*

Kathleen didn't know who to thank for getting them to the courthouse intact—God, the Blessed Virgin or Dylan Kennedy. Certainly Dylan deserved much of the credit, navigating the way through a burning tunnel of fire from the church to the courthouse. They had skirted a roaring pit of debris and arrived filthy and singed, but unharmed.

She was still in awe of his climb to the steeple. When he'd disappeared into the smoke, she had refused to move or breathe until she saw him again. He was the most marvelous man she had ever met, and she never wanted to leave his side.

He seemed to possess a special gift for finding a way to escape danger. And the remarkable thing was, he seemed to enjoy a sense of mortal peril, laughing and cheering the others on when their energy flagged.

The courthouse rose like a splendid medieval castle above the rubble and ruin. The massive fortress bore a tall cupola that towered above the surrounding buildings of the business district. It was Chicago's showpiece, a monument to civic pride and decorative excess. Its rounded windows, lacy stonework and figured wrought iron gave it a solid permanence that had attracted many refugees from the fire.

The lifeblood of the city pulsed through the heart

of the marble monstrosity. It contained the offices of the mayor, the Board of Police, the chief marshal, the county courtrooms and the jail in the basement. The main fire alarm telegraph had been, for hours, drumming out warnings in every direction.

Kathleen shaded her eyes to take in the soaring spires and turrets, the fantastic bell tower. She had passed it many a time over the years, traveling from the Sinclair mansion to her parents' rustic home.

Turning away from the courthouse, she stared adoringly at the sweaty, smudged, handsome face of Dylan Kennedy. When he kissed her, it felt like a benediction. When he smiled, she forgot who she was. When he held her close, she stopped being afraid.

Since the destruction of the gasworks, the lights had gone out. Other refugees in the courthouse carried lanterns or simply stood at the windows, staring in mute amazement at the fire that burned brighter than the sun. The iron picket fence around the yard actually glowed red in places from the heat. The ornamental maples on the lawn flamed like giant torches.

On one side of the building, men worked a hose attached to a fire plug. They stood in a line in the windy gloom, aiming the stream at the limestone walls. A marshal, in a long canvas coat pocked with black holes from falling sparks, strode through the foyer shouting orders. A few men, armed with buckets and brooms, headed to the roof to fend off the flames. A line of clerks and couriers scurried up from the basement with boxes of court and county records. They were loading them into carts at the rear of the building.

"Where do you suppose they think they're going?'' asked Kathleen. ''Don't they know there's no way to get clear of the fire from here?''

''They'll find out soon enough.''

''Our friend here needs to sit down,'' said Father Michael, sweating and wheezing as he propped up Bull.

Kathleen wanted to tell the priest that a miracle had brought her to the church. He was a young man, new to St. Brendan's. That was why he hadn't recognized her as one of the parishioners. But if she survived this night, she would have quite a confession to make.

Dylan glanced around the swarming foyer. ''To the courtrooms,'' he suggested, leading the way to the wide marble stairs.

The largest room had been set up as a makeshift infirmary. Most of the wooden furniture had been cleared out. The sight of suffering, wounded people lying on pallets or coats or even the bare floor touched Kathleen's heart with pity and fear. She thanked God her family was safe, but the burned and broken people in this room reminded her that not everyone had been so lucky.

''*Kathleen?*'' A tentative voice spoke her name.

She whirled to confront a tall, lanky man whose face was smudged with soot. It was Barry Lynch, a clerk who had been trying to court her for a year. She immediately glanced around to see if Dylan had heard. He was preoccupied with helping Bull, she saw with relief. ''Barry,'' she said, her hands closing around the back of a witness box rail. ''I didn't expect to see you here.''

His arms, long and gangling past a shirt several sizes too small, reached for her. She took a step back. ''I'm glad to know you're all right.''

"And you. But what is that you're wearing? You look like a fine lady."

"I, uh, I made some new friends," she said, unable to think of a better explanation. She felt so awkward around him. He believed he was wooing her, but the courting was entirely one-sided. The sincere, hard-working dockyard clerk had admired her since they were children playing along the banks of the ditch behind the O'Learys' cow barn. He was a decent, God-fearing man and the idea of pledging her life to him gave Kathleen a case of the shivers.

"Is everything all right, Kate?" Dylan asked, coming to her side. With a nonchalance she found slightly thrilling, he slid his hand around her waist in proprietary fashion.

Barry scowled. "Who are you?"

"Barry, over here! Give me a hand with these buckets," someone shouted.

Still scowling, he stalked away.

"Who was that?" Dylan asked negligently.

"Oh, just some clerk or other, I imagine," she replied. Then, as Barry and his companion went to rejoin the firefighting, she felt appalled at herself. Just because she didn't want him as a suitor did not mean she should dismiss his very existence like Peter denying Jesus. She made a vow to add that to her ever-lengthening confession next Friday.

An agitated man stood in the marble hall, shouting incoherently. Kathleen and Dylan exchanged a glance. If he had lost his mind, he would not be the first this night. But this particular man, gesticulating at the parade of records clerks, looked familiar. She thought she had seen him somewhere before.

"Good God," she said to Dylan as recognition dawned on her. "That is the mayor of Chicago."

"Your Honor," Dylan said with the same steely calm he had shown at the church. "Please, come and rest in the courtroom. I'll find you something to drink."

"I cannot leave my post, sir," Mayor Mason insisted.

"You're needed in there, by the citizens who elected you, Your Honor." Dylan shepherded him to the door.

The dazed mayor wandered in and sat on the jury bench, holding his head in his hands. But only for a moment. He seemed to draw strength from the worried people gathered there. He drank water from a jar someone handed him, then stood. "I must go to the bell tower to check the progress of the fire."

"We'll go with you," Kathleen declared.

"We will?" Dylan asked.

"Of course. We mustn't let him go alone." Judging by all her escapades this night, she should be bone weary, but instead she felt curiously manic, invigorated, her nerves tingling. Without looking to see if Dylan followed, she and the mayor went out into the marble hall and hurried to the top storey, where they climbed a narrow, winding utility stair. The bell, being rung in alarm, filled the narrow shaft with earsplitting noise.

Between the bongs of the bell, the mayor and Dylan spoke like old cronies. And they probably were, she reflected. What a wondrous thing, to be so important that you were on a first-name basis with the mayor himself. Dylan inhabited an exclusive world and tonight, for the briefest of times, she belonged to that world. The trouble was, she wanted to stay, and she knew that would be impossible.

They emerged from the stair into the smoky air high above the city. The soaring cupola, the four-faced clock and the massive bell overwhelmed Kathleen with their huge proportions. She felt like a tiny doll on the fire watchman's platform, clinging to a rail as a horrific wind whipped over her.

The tall flagpole made an eerie swishing sound as the storm wind bent it like a bow. The watchmen stationed on the tower signaled to acknowledge the mayor. Kathleen gripped the rail and looked down.

"Mother Mary and Joseph," she said under her breath. From this vantage point, she could see the fire and all the devastation in its wake. Streets paved in glowing coals. A blackened swatch of scorched earth. A hellish roil of smoke. At the leading edge of the band of destruction blazed the long hungry tongues of the wind-driven flames, lapping up everything in their path. She faced the West Division, trying to make out her parents' neighborhood, but the area lay in distant blackness. The river, regarded as an unbreachable barrier earlier in the evening, formed an insignificant ditch crammed with flaming vessels, burning bridges, tugs screaming to get the spans to rotate. Explosions blinded her. Every store of gunpowder and kerosene in the city fell victim to the devouring flames.

A few blocks from the courthouse, a blazing raft of shingles dropped into an open tar tank on the roof of another gasworks substation. A large gasholder flared up, roaring like the breath of a monster. Kathleen shrank against Dylan, grateful for the solid feel of his arms around her. When she dared to look again, the firelight played over the mayor's face, which seemed frozen in unspeaking dread.

Finally Dylan said the words that made it all real. "My God. The whole city is doomed."

And he was right. There was not a single safe place except those areas the fire had already taken, feeding upon them until there was nothing left to burn. Looking out across the helpless grid of streets and buildings was like watching a great ship sink. Tragic, inevitable, painful to witness. People were dying down there, she thought with a clutch of horror. Without really thinking about it she wrapped her arms around Dylan and set her cheek against his chest.

"Tell me that's the brewery, not the waterworks," Mayor Mason said, pointing toward the lake.

The tall, slender spire, with its rococo trim, rose up from a sea of flame. Dylan shook his head. "It's the waterworks. Once that goes, we'll have no more hoses."

Mayor Mason ran a shaking hand along the stone wall of the tower. Now that the danger was at its worst, he seemed to gather himself up. "This courthouse is considered fireproof." He smiled sadly, shaking his head. "But the cornices, and God knows what else, are made of wood. This building will go, along with everything else."

"Yes," Dylan said. He looked down at a wagon laden with crates of records pulling away from the curb. The hose cart's stream, which had been spattering the periphery of the building, lost its pressure. The crew simply boarded the cart and left. Four more of the ornamental trees on the lawn went up simultaneously. Branches tore off like severed limbs and the wind blew the flaming brands at the building.

"Time to go, sir." Dylan pried his rigid hands from the ledge. "Those wagons should be carrying evacuees, not paper files."

The statement jolted the mayor into action. "Exactly so," he agreed, needing nothing more than the word from Dylan to reclaim his nerve. He rushed down the stairs. "There's not a moment to lose."

Within a short while, he was ordering wires to be sent out to neighboring cities, appealing for more engines. He dispatched men to organize the evacuation of everyone in the courthouse. He granted permission for explosives to be used to destroy buildings in the path of the fire. Dylan returned to the tower to pull more alarms. Kathleen didn't think twice, but hitched up her skirts and followed him up the stairs.

"Oh, no," he said. "You're staying below."

"Says you." She pushed past him and clambered up the stairs.

The watchmen had been forced to leave their posts. Dylan had time to pull only one more alarm when a burning glob of pitch blew in from the roof through an open window. Kathleen screamed and jumped back. The flames instantly lit a pile of shavings left by a workman who had been repairing the clock. The fire mushroomed with breathtaking speed.

"Let's go!" Dylan grabbed her hand and they raced for safety. Smoke and flame blocked the iron stairway. "Damn it," he yelled. "If it was me alone, I'd get out of this mess, but—"

"Just show me how it's done," she said, remembering his precarious descent from the steeple of St. Brendan's.

He made her sling one leg over the banister and she slid down, howling in pain as the hot metal burned her hands. She landed on the floor, just managing to scramble away before Dylan came down behind her. Flames licked through cracks in the ceiling. Plaster rained down thick and hard. They fled by way of the west wing, slamming fire doors shut behind them.

In the basement, a near riot was taking place. The remaining prisoners, finding the outer door to the jail still locked, were ramming it with a heavy plank. In the telegraph room, an Associated Press reporter pounded out his transmission, but stopped midsentence and fled.

For the next hour, the mayor occupied himself with the evacuation, aided by Dylan, a clerk named Kirby Lane and Father Michael. There were only two wagons. Women, children and the elderly went first, cramming into the carts until the men had to push from behind to help the straining horses. Someone tried to make the elderly Judge Roth climb aboard, but the old man resisted, insisting between hacking coughs that he could walk.

In the midst of the argument, a great crashing sound came from within the courthouse, followed by a bellow of pain. Father Michael rushed outside. "It's Mr. Lane," he told them. "I think the poor devil's buried."

"Well, get him out, and he can have my place in the cart," Kathleen said.

Father Michael caught Dylan's eye. "I can't," the priest said. "We've got to dig him free of the rubble."

Dylan pushed Kathleen toward the second cart. "Up you go, my love, and hold on tight."

She grasped the tailgate of the cart. "You're not coming?"

"There's no room."

Her chest froze when she thought of leaving him, leaving Bull and Father Michael, possibly losing them all. Their peril tonight had bonded them together, and she couldn't abide the thought of leaving them. She jumped back out. "Then I'm not going, either."

He swept her up in his arms, and the sensation left her breathless with excitement. But he bundled her up onto the cart again. Then he took her face between his hands and kissed her, briefly and hard.

In that moment Kathleen knew: she loved him. Against reason, pride, sanity, she loved this man. She had never told him anything but lies. This was the one truth she could admit.

"I love you," she said.

He blinked, startled. "And I adore you, sweet Kate." Then he kissed her one last time and pulled back. "Just in case," he said with a wink. "We'll be along on foot, after we dig out Mr. Lane."

A whip cracked and the wagon pulled away. Only Dylan and the mayor, Father Michael and Bull, Kirby Lane and the judge remained. Dylan came to the door and lifted his hand in farewell. Seeing him framed by the marble pillars, blown and buffeted in the fiery wind, finally brought home the terrible truth to Kathleen. These men were going to die. With no more horses, no wagon could convey them. With one man wounded and another buried in rubble, carrying them would be difficult if not impossible.

Dylan turned and disappeared inside the doomed building.

Kathleen did not consciously make a decision, but

she remembered the feel of Dylan's mouth on hers and his arms holding her fast. She felt love shower her like a plethora of unearned blessings. And she knew she didn't want to live a single moment without him.

She bolted out of the cart.

If anyone noticed, they raised no objection. Likely everyone's attention was fixed ahead at the lakeshore, not behind, where everything was dying. She raced back to the courthouse.

She didn't make a sound, but as she approached, Dylan came to the doorway as if alerted to her presence by some mystical awareness. A flash of elation crossed his face, but just as quickly it darkened to disapproval. He strode across the scorched lawn toward her.

"When you declared you loved me I thought I had never heard anything so foolish," he ranted. "But congratulations. You have surpassed your own foolishness."

Before she could defend herself, he hauled her into his arms and kissed her with passion and anger and something she couldn't identify. Something so wondrous and luminous that she wanted to cherish it forever.

"Get inside, and hurry," roared Bull from the doorway. "Bring that fool woman with you."

Dylan took her hand and they raced inside the courthouse. The judge regarded them with fond exasperation. "You are a most devoted pair," he remarked. "How long have you been married?"

Kathleen's cheeks reddened. "We aren't married, Your Honor."

He winked at her. "You kiss," he stated, "as if you are."

"You weren't supposed to see that."

"At such a time, it is a comfort to see a great love being born."

*At such a time...* The words disappeared, eaten up by the same hungry force that sucked the very air from their lungs. But the judge's meaning was stamped indelibly in Kathleen's mind. They fell to unearthing Kirby Lane, who lay beneath a broken marble pillar. His face was gray with shock, his expression only mildly puzzled. Had he been screaming in agony, she would have hoped he might survive, but he had a placid, almost beatific look on his face as he patiently watched the removal of the broken stone. Father Michael hid Lane's face from view, but not before Kathleen caught a glimpse of blood seeping from his nostrils.

Kirby Lane remained strangely calm, as if detached from his ruined leg and from the pain. His face was pale, his lips blue as he looked out at the burning street. "The wagon isn't coming back, is it?"

"I don't think so, son," the priest admitted.

"Leave us," said the judge. "There's no sense in all of us burning to death."

"We're not leaving," Dylan snapped. "Let's not waste time arguing about it."

From a marble-floored waiting room off the foyer, Bull dragged in several wet carpets. They used them to line the walls for what little protection they would offer.

"So we wait," said the judge.

No one said anything. They all knew the wagon would not return. Outside, the fire raged with an animal roar. Dylan drew Kathleen aside, bent low and said, "There's nothing more we can do for Mr. Lane."

Her stomach churned. She had never watched anyone die before. "Are you sure?"

"He doesn't even feel the pain anymore. We've tried to clear the debris away, but he's done for. His injuries are too grave."

A soft moan escaped her and she pressed herself against Dylan. "We are going to die here," she said, speaking everyone's thoughts aloud.

"You had your chance, fool," Bull said.

"Who are you calling a fool, boyo?" She could hear the brogue creeping into her voice but no one seemed to notice. They were all too defeated and too frightened to care. Yet when Kathleen looked at Kirby Lane, compassion pushed past her terror. Squaring her shoulders, she went and sat down beside him, taking his hand in hers. Her own hands were blistered and burned in places, but the injuries seemed minor now. His cold fingers twitched a little at her touch, and when he gazed up at her, he tried to smile.

"Is there anything I can do for you?" she asked quietly, aware that the others had gathered around.

"No, I'm...I'll be all right." He spoke so softly that she had to lean forward to hear. "There's not much...I've left undone. How about you, Miss Kate?"

"Ah, so much," she said with stark honesty.

"Then...do it." He coughed weakly. "What are you waiting for?"

Kathleen trembled, overwhelmed by the situation. The wounded man fell still, and she pulled her hand away, certain he had died. Fear rolled through her and she backed away.

Father Michael bent and turned his ear to the slack mouth. "He's fallen unconscious," he whispered. "But he's breathing still. 'Tis a blessing that he can sleep."

They all sat listening to the howl of the firestorm. The long, unbearable moments drew out. Judge Roth went to the window but turned away, shaking his head.

"We need a miracle," Mayor Mason said at length.

All eyes turned to the priest. Father Michael held up both hands in his own defense. "I'm a priest, not a magician. I can't conjure a rescue out of thin air." He raised his hands, palms up. "I can baptize you if you like. Perform last rites—" Seeing the expressions on their faces, he quickly added, "I can hear confession." He ticked off the options on his fingers. "Impose penance, offer absolution, perform the sacrament of marriage—"

Kathleen got up and paced the room, then simply stood watching out the window. Beyond Courthouse Square, the inferno resembled the inside of a steam engine boiler. She shut her eyes, thinking of Gran and her family, wondering if they would ever learn what had become of their daughter. Their daughter, who had grown far too proud, too fond of fine things and fancy ways. If not for that foolish pride, she wouldn't be here in the first place.

Dylan Kennedy's arm went around her shoulders. It felt so wonderful she almost believed she could die happy because she had known a man like him. But it wasn't enough. His tender touch reminded her, with the sharpness of a knife stab, of all she would never have—the pinkish beauty of the sky at dawn, the sound of a bird singing in springtime, a baby girl named after Gran....

"Please, sweet Kate," he said, "don't despair."

"These are our last hours on earth," she whispered.

"Then try not to spend them in misery."

She swallowed hard in order to find her voice. "And how do you suggest I spend them?"

His hand slipped to her waist. "I can think of a few better ways."

That made her sink deeper into despair, and she pulled away, joining the others who stood vigil by the wounded man. "Father," she said to the priest, "I should make a final confession, but I don't deserve absolution. I am a hopeless sinner to the end."

"What in heaven's name do you mean, child?"

"Look at me." She spread her arms.

They all looked. Glaring, she clasped together her tattered bodice. She didn't mean *that*. "Here I am, in the last hours of my life. I should be feeling an enormous religious ecstasy in preparation to meeting Him who made us all. But am I? No. I'm having the most silly, selfish regrets that ever crossed my mind. I am so disappointed in myself."

"Oh, Katie." Dylan stroked her hair. "We're all having regrets. If ever there was a time to feel selfish, then now is that time." He smiled, so kind, so compassionate. She looked into his face and saw all she had ever wanted. And all she could never have.

"What is it you regret?" the judge asked gently. "Surely you are too young to have made any serious mistakes."

"My mistake," she said, her throat aching, "is that

I dared to have dreams that don't belong in the heart of a person like me. And my greatest regret is that not a single one of those dreams will have a chance to come true. I shall die an old maid, never knowing a bride's joy or—''

"I think we can rule out the 'old' part," said a faint, ironic voice.

They crouched down to regard Kirby Lane in surprise. "You woke up," Kathleen said. Surely that must mean he was getting better. Yet a single glance at his gray face and blue lips told her otherwise. A trickle of blood seeped from his ear. He was weaker than ever. The simple sentence he had uttered seemed to take all his strength.

"These…long faces…aren't helping," he said haltingly. "Surely you can think of some better way…to pass the time."

Dylan held Kathleen at arm's length and gazed at her in a way that made her skin prickle with awareness. His eyes were like mirrors, silvery on the surface, reflecting the brightness of the fire. "Mr. Lane is right."

Father Michael pressed his hands together and nodded his head. Kirby's lips thinned in a valiant effort to smile.

Kathleen didn't understand. Should they pray? Sing hymns? Beg for mercy?

Before she could grasp his intent, Dylan sank down on one knee. "Marry me, Kate," he said with deep, abiding sincerity. "Make your last act on earth a gesture of affirmation. Bring me one final drop of joy that I may die a man fulfilled."

She nearly swooned with shock. Nearly melted with yearning. She was so enchanted by him that she forgot to breathe. She knew what he was doing, of course. He was trying to distract her from thoughts of their hopeless situation. Like a priest with a condemned prisoner, he was trying to fill her with hope rather than grief. At their darkest hour, he wanted to give her something new and bright to cling to.

"Do it," Kirby said, the words uttered urgently between chattering teeth. He lifted a cold, pale hand, holding it out to her. "We'll all be a part of something fine and good—" his voice trailed to a pain-filled whisper "—in our final hour."

The mayor touched his heart. "It would give us something to do besides brood upon our fate."

"But—" Everything was happening so fast. Her mind whirled with confusion. How could she possibly do this? How could she even consider it?

"Sweetheart, in a few hours none of this will matter," Dylan said softly.

"But what if we survive?"

"Then we live happily ever after. Unless you object to finding yourself wed to a man who adores you."

And she would have to tell him she was no heiress from Baltimore but a housemaid from the West Side. "There is something I must explain—"

The crash of a falling timber drowned out her words. They all huddled together, heads down, as plaster rained from the ceiling. Dylan shielded Kirby with his body. When the collapse was over, he wadded up his frock coat and propped it under the injured man's head.

Gran would have called the sudden destruction a sign from God. But the message wasn't clear to Kathleen. Was it time for the truth, or time to do something wild and foolish before the rest of the building caved in?

"I'm not who you think I am," she said, but the screech of the wind drowned her out. It was uncanny. Each time she tried to speak up, the noise of the storm roared louder. No one was listening, anyway. They all rushed through preparations, seizing upon the project with pitiful eagerness.

Kathleen held on to Kirby's hand, looked out at the burning night and stopped trying to protest. As her last act on earth, marrying Dylan Kennedy surpassed all her imaginings. If they lived through the ordeal, the marriage would be invalid, surely, conducted without a license under such unorthodox circumstances. When this was all over, she could simply vanish into obscurity. He would never know she was only a princess for a night, disappearing like Cinderella, but unlike Cinderella, never coming back.

Yet the proceedings felt tenderly, touchingly real as Kirby Lane, insistent that he was well enough to discharge his duties as court clerk, applied his tremulous signature to an ornate certificate. The mayor stamped it with an official seal, then handed it to the judge to sign and notarize. Dylan scrawled his name, and then the document was passed to Kathleen. Her hand shook. She forced herself to scratch out her whole name, Kathleen Bridget O'Leary, but no one else looked at what she had written.

Father Michael took a black bound missal from the pouch tied to the scourge around his waist. They all gathered around Kirby, and the pulsating light from the fire outside bathed everything in a surreal and eerily beautiful glow. Even the throaty roar of the consuming flames added to the atmosphere of inevitability and solemnity.

Dylan Kennedy closed his hand around hers, and Kathleen kept hold of Kirby. She was expected to marry. All women of her station were. She had been asked many times, by Ned Coombs at the Quimper shipyards, a joiner. And Rye Stokes, who was a tanner. And of course, Barry Lynch, she recalled with a pang of guilt. She had never given him any encouragement, she rationalized. So she was not *really* being disloyal, was she?

Kirby's fingers twitched, and she imagined he meant to reassure her. *Do it. What are you waiting for?*

Kathleen shut her eyes and made a heartfelt wish. In her most secret moments, she had dared to imagine a wedding like the one being planned for her mistress, with a caterer, flowers, a trousseau, a full symphony and a dozen attendants on each side, flights of doves to celebrate the moment of joining and everyone of importance in attendance.

Now here she was, a dazed and bedraggled refugee clinging to the hand of a man she had just met. Yet she felt as if her heart had always known him, and she couldn't have been prouder if a choir of angels and the Pope himself had presided over the union. In dreams, she had seen the laughing sky-blue eyes and the beautiful blue-black hair, the perfect, patrician features and the demeanor of Dylan Kennedy, a man who knew exactly who he was and where he belonged in the world.

And so, as the fire screamed and roared at the courthouse doors, she pledged her life to him.

# *Seven*

Dylan could not think of a more absurd end to his misbegotten life. Rarely impulsive, he had been half joking when he'd proposed to Kate. But the others had latched on to the fantasy, making it their quest to see the tragic young couple wed before they died.

Now it was over. They were wed. It was all a perfectly nice bit of theatrics. The priest, the mayor and the judge were true professionals, conducting the swift rite with appropriate solemnity.

"I never saw," whispered the beleaguered Kirby Lane, "a sweeter, more holy wedding." He smiled at them as if from a great distance. "The two of you...rob this night of its fury."

Dylan tried not to hear the earnestness and despair in the man's voice, but it haunted him. Good God, the man really was dying.

Chilled to the marrow, Dylan bent and kissed his new wife, only to be startled by the heat and ardor of her response. It was the kiss of a bride who was in love, exactly what she fancied herself to be. What she actually was, of course, was an insurance policy.

If he survived, he would be back in hot water. The beauteous Miss Kate's fortune would come in handy.

The fire had raged on through the brief ceremony,

and it was looking less and less likely they would make it to tomorrow.

He kept hold of her hand and smiled down at her, giving no inkling of his thoughts. "There," he said. "Now you are a married lady." He touched her cheek, feeling a curious lurch of sentiment in his chest. It might even be a genuine emotion, but he was such a master of pretense that he could not be sure. Yet something about her moved him. She was beyond beautiful, though her beauty alone didn't explain the effect she had on him. The honesty of her expression captivated him, and he could tell the others in the courtroom were affected by her as well. In a world of too little goodness, here was someone pure and sweet, untainted by the evils of mankind. And quite conveniently wealthy. He mustn't forget that.

"What are you thinking?" she asked softly.

"Just pondering your many virtues."

"Is that all?"

She didn't seem satisfied with lighthearted quips, so he dug deeper. "I was thinking that marrying you is one of the few good choices I've made in my life."

She bit her lip and lowered her head. When she looked back, she said, "I've never been anyone's good choice before."

"That," he said, "is impossible to believe."

The wounded Kirby Lane moaned, and Father Michael bent to comfort him. The others gathered around. Kirby's face was shockingly pale and glazed with moisture. He closed his eyes and his lips moved soundlessly.

"He is *in extremis,*" Father Michael whispered, drawing them away so Kirby wouldn't hear. "I don't know what to do."

"For the love of God, you're a priest," Dylan snapped. His fear for the dying man emerged as anger. "Of course you know what to do."

Father Michael pressed his hands together, then knelt beside the wounded man. He tried to offer water, but Lane could not drink. The priest whispered in Latin, and Dylan guessed that it was the prayer of extreme unction, uttered as a last-ditch effort to find grace in the next world. Dylan didn't think it did any good, but he had always believed in hedging his bets. Feeling as powerless as the others, he stalked to the door.

"I'm going for help," he said between his teeth. "This man needs a doctor."

"You won't find a doctor or anyone else out there," the mayor said.

"We've got to do something, goddamn it," Dylan burst out. "We can't just stand around while he—"

"Hush up," Bull interrupted. "Don't you be talking like a fool."

Father Michael beckoned them all with a silent gesture. Lane lay unmoving, except for his mouth. Dylan went down on his knees and strained to make out the words.

"...save all that passion for what matters," Kirby was saying, and he went on, but Dylan couldn't decipher the rest. They stood around in a frozen tableau, waiting and watching in shock and sadness.

After a while, Kirby Lane exhaled a woman's name, as if expelling his soul from his body. And then he breathed no more. Father Michael's shoulders slumped as he rolled up the marriage certificate and herded the others to a doorway where the ceiling was still intact. "Kirby Lane," he said in the most mournful voice Dylan had ever heard. *"Requiescat in pace."*

The slow, steady disintegration of the building continued. Plaster and debris pelted them, and a large iron fixture fell with a bang. No one could think of anything more to say. The priest covered the body with a fringed drapery panel. With a shuddering sigh, Kate pressed her cheek against Dylan's shirt.

She did not weep; he suspected that would come later, like sensation returning to a frozen limb.

They all watched the golden blizzard of the fire. From where they stood, they could see no escape route. Even several feet from the window Dylan could feel the heat of the blaze encroaching steadily, getting hotter by the minute. The huff and roar of the fire was almost rhythmical, like the tramp of footsteps of an invading army.

Yet unlike an army, this had the fierce uncontrollable power of the wind behind it. This was not a force that would respond to charm or fast talking. For the first time, Dylan found himself confronted by something he could not control or manipulate or talk his way out of.

Through the veil of flame, he saw…something. A movement.

He bolted for the main door. "Where are you going?" asked Kate.

He turned back briefly. In that second his heart constricted with wonder. His *wife*. He'd had them before, of course, but he had never been pleased by the prospect…until tonight.

"I just need to check something out, love. I'll be back."

"But—"

He raced outside into the red-hot maw of the dragon. So much had been destroyed that there was less and less to burn. He ran to where he had spied the movement. When he saw what it was, his heart sank.

Two goats, trotting willy-nilly in a panic, shied first one way and then another. They lifted their feet from the hot ground, bleating constantly. Dylan contemplated the improbable sight for a moment. Then he was amazed to see the goats disappear, seemingly into thin air. Following them, he saw that they had entered the LaSalle Street tunnel. He moved in to get a better view. Just then, flames sucked through the opening, and he pulled back to avoid getting burned.

The torrent of flames subsided. Shielding his face from flying sparks, he went to investigate. The air that wafted up from the dark tunnel was stale...but decidedly cooler. Though hope flickered like a beacon inside him, he reminded himself that he was bound to the courthouse by a wounded man, an elderly judge, the nervous mayor, a priest...and Kate.

His *wife*.

Yet into these thoughts slipped the automatic self-preserving instincts that had guided him all his life. He could slip away. On his own. Here, now, he could go underground and disappear. Unhampered by the others, he might make it to safety. Hop a train and see where it took him. He could resurrect the marquis de Bontemps in New Orleans, or don a new persona in San Francisco, or become Dirk Steele—Man of the Comstock, in Nevada. Perhaps that broken-down cabin on the shores of Lake Tahoe still stood unoccupied....

But something strange occurred to him. He didn't

want to go. He felt faintly disgusted with himself. He had always dived for safety before. Why not now?

Because he *liked* being Dylan Kennedy. He was comfortable in this skin. And he didn't want to give up on a chance to change his life.

Maybe that was what this fire was to a lot of folks. Some people's lives were burning down to nothing this night, and they would be compelled to start over from scratch.

He wanted to start again. He wanted to do it with Kate.

Discomfited by the unfamiliar sensation of considering the needs of another person, he went in search of some sort of cart or conveyance. He found nothing but hot, smoky rubble until, in what might have once been a toolshed of some sort, he spied a wheel that still seemed intact.

Using his cloak to keep his hands from burning, he excavated the object. A two-wheeled barrow. It had been recently used to transport horse manure, but it was sturdy enough to hold the weight of a man, maybe more.

He steered the barrow into the courthouse, bumping it up the steps with a great clatter. Father Michael came out to see what the commotion was about. He didn't need an explanation. "Bring the water can," he said over his shoulder. Then he jumped into action, shouting for the others to come, promising them that Dylan had found a way to escape. They all came out to the courthouse steps.

Trying to conceal an icy sense of doom, he executed a formal bow. "Your chariot awaits."

Father Michael shepherded them down the stairs, his shoulder propped under Bull's arm to steady him.

The mayor helped the elderly judge. Dylan didn't let a flicker of doubt show as he made the judge sit in the barrow and covered him with a water-soaked carpet. Then they all wet down their clothes with the last of the water. Father Michael whispered a prayer for Kirby Lane. Dylan caught Kate's eye, struck by the depth of her fright yet at the same time, moved by her unflinching courage. She had never once wept or panicked.

In the broad, barren square, they watched the courthouse in its death throes. The brownstone center section burned out of control, and oddly, the bell still clanged as flames feasted upon the tower. The limestone façade melted in the heat and ran down the sides like huge tears. Jets of smoke and flame escaped the windows and vents. The clock briefly read the true hour—2:12 in the morning—and then the great hands slid down the clock face. A moment later, the giant tower crashed into the basement. The earth shook with the impact as Dylan and Father Michael shepherded everyone away.

"There's a passageway through the horse car tunnel," he explained. "We can make it to the lakefront." He was such a good liar he almost believed himself. For all he knew, the passage led to a deadly furnace. "We can," he reiterated. "It'll be all right, Kate."

It was a wondrous phenomenon, seeing the trust and relief that flooded her face. "Let's go, then," she said.

Until that moment, Dylan had not realized what a powerful force her trust was. Though surely an emotion born of their extreme danger, the love she

claimed to feel for him made him want to slay drag-
ons, move mountains, walk across hot coals.

The opportunity presented itself the moment they
crossed the courthouse yard. The roadway, once con-
structed of pine blocks, flamed like a river of fire. He
led the way along its edge to a spot where the flames
had died down for lack of fuel. "We'll have to run,"
he shouted over the wind, catching Bull's arm. "Can
you make it?"

Bull flexed his bad ankle. "Don't have no choice
now, do I?"

Dylan pointed the way to the sloping passage he
had spied earlier. There was no sign of the goats, dead
or alive, which meant they had gone *some*where.

"Let's go," he said, feeling a surge of determination. As he spoke, he swept Kate up in his arms. She
gasped and tried to scold him, but he heard nothing
except the roar of the fire and the swish of blood in
his ears as he ran across the road. Father Michael and
the mayor pushed the judge in the wheelbarrow, and
Bull came limping along behind.

Dylan refused to put Kate down until he reached
the other side where the surface wasn't smoldering.
The road led to the shadowy underground passageway. They paused to make a torch out of a burning
wooden beam, then Dylan led the way. Ducking under a low, crumbling ceiling, they found themselves
in a crude tunnel with no end in sight. But anything
was preferable to the horror they had left behind
them.

"I keep thinking of poor Mr. Lane," Kate said.

"Believe me, he's not thinking of you." Dylan
grabbed her hand and forged ahead. The glowing
length of wood afforded very little light, but he could

see the passage narrowing up ahead. He said nothing. If they had to go single file, if they had to crawl, they would, dragging the judge behind them. Now that there was even a glimmer of hope, Dylan realized he would stop at nothing in order to survive. He bent lower, held the makeshift torch in front of him like a knight of old and pretended to be a man of honor. The man she believed him to be.

In the bowels of the dank tunnel, there was a silence he hadn't heard since the bellowing of the wind-driven fire that had raged all night. He could hear Bull's heavy breathing, the squeak and grind of the barrow and a scrabbling sound he suspected came from rats. He saw no point in talking, for there was nothing left to say. Either they would live through this, or they wouldn't. He trudged on, brandishing the red-tipped board, and inevitably, the thing went out. He swore between his teeth and then tensed, expecting a rebuke from Kate, but she surprised him by echoing his oath with the panache of a seasoned dockworker.

Dylan hoped he would live through this, because he was really growing fond of his wife. Of course, if they *did* survive and Costello found them, there would be trouble. But amidst all the mayhem, and with Kate's fortune, they might be able to quietly disappear. Perhaps they would visit Monte Carlo or Bolivia....

A patch of pale gray glimmered before his eyes. At first he thought it was a trick from staring so long at the glowing board, but as he continued forward, he saw that they had reached the end of the tunnel. "Hurry," he said, finally daring to offer hope. "I think I see the other side."

The lighted spot drew them and he picked up the pace. The uneven surface sloped upward. Bull added his strength to pushing the wheelbarrow, and they emerged into the gray half light.

People darted like wraiths through the smoke, most of them pushing steadily eastward, toward the lake. Shouts and whistles filled the air when Mayor Mason appeared, and he nearly broke down and wept as he was greeted by the sight of his sons. They had spent an hour trying to return to the courthouse and had nearly given up hope.

The mayor let out a cry and stumbled toward them. The overloaded cart lurched and sagged as he clambered aboard. "Hurry," he said to the others, "there's no time to lose."

Kathleen shook her head and latched on to Dylan's arm. "There isn't room," she said. "The mayor and Judge Roth must go."

By now, he knew her well enough not to argue. Ah, how he wished this could be real. A beautiful, wealthy woman worshiping him, refusing to abandon him. Though the two older men protested, she got her way. The mayor of the city paused to bow his head to Kate. "It has been a distinct pleasure, Mrs. Kennedy. A wedding I'll not soon forget."

She flushed, clearly confused and delighted by her new title.

"The rail yards in the South Division are clear," one of Mason's sons shouted. "Trains are pulling out to the safety of the suburbs."

"That's where we'll go, then," Dylan declared. The four of them would have to cross the river again, then double back to reach the lakefront terminal. It seemed a minor undertaking compared to the ordeal they had just endured.

After the cart bore the others to the north, he led the way on foot along a city block of gutted buildings and ruined carts, blackened trees and broken glass, pocked by still-flaming heaps of unrecognizable debris. Ruined walls and shattered masonry blocked the roadway, and they had to veer around it. No landmark remained to tell them where they were, but the weak shimmer of light on the horizon beckoned from the east, where the lake lay. After crossing the bridge, they came to an area of exclusive town houses the fire had not yet reached. The small patches of lawn were sere but not charred, the trees bare but not burned. An air of abandonment haunted the empty houses.

Kathleen grabbed his sleeve. "Dylan, look." She pointed to a decrepit residence, its broken shingle whipping in the wind.

"The Hotel St. George," he said, his hand straying to the deed inside his shirt. "Maybe my luck's about to change again."

"Don't be too sure of that," said Bull. The fire drew nearer with each heartbeat. They could hear the ominous crackle of timber not far away. A moment later, the roof took fire.

There was no time for regrets. They rushed down the block toward the lake. At least, he hoped it was the right direction for the lake. The capricious wind leaped and swirled, teasing flames to conflagrations on both sides of the avenue.

Ahead, the wagon disappeared into the smoke. Telegraph posts stood in the bluish light like branchless trees, the wires long gone. Iron beams, twisted and distorted by the raging heat, lay across the road. They walked on, weariness dragging at them, until Dylan recognized the rail yard of the Illinois Central and Michigan Central. "We're near the water's edge," he said. The grain elevators were mere skeletons, but a line of train cars appeared to be intact. A locomotive, huffing black billows from its smokestack, was coupled to a short line of cars. Rail workers ran to and fro, trying to organize the evacuation. "Let's go," he said, picking up the pace. "Maybe we can get clear of the city."

Bull groaned and Father Michael set his jaw, but they followed gamely enough. Dylan moved down the row of train cars, trying the doors.

"What in the name of Saint Dympna's drawers are you doing?" Father Michael asked as Dylan grasped the rail of one of the cars.

"Getting us the hell out of here." He pushed open the door to a passenger car, then grasped Kate by the waist and lifted her up. She squawked a little, in confusion but not in protest. He set her down and braced his hands against the sides of the door. "Let's go."

Bull didn't have to be told twice. He heaved his bulk aboard the train car and collapsed on a velveteen banquette. After an initial hesitation, Father Michael did the same, sitting across from Bull, who soon started to snore. Taking Kate by the hand, Dylan made a foray into the next car, finding it crammed full of refugees. The door to the car beyond that was locked, but his nimble fingers made short work of the mechanism.

"It's a Pullman Palace Car," he said. "And it's totally private." He locked the door behind him.

Kate gasped in wonder. "We don't belong here."

"Nonsense. On a night like this, it's every man for himself."

Thick Brussels carpeting, heavy velvet drapes, French plate mirrors, black walnut woodwork and oil chandeliers gave the car the look of an elegant parlor. Dylan suspected Kate probably rode in cars like this all the time, but she seemed genuinely enchanted by the etched windows and fringed furnishings, the screened lavatory area and most of all, by the bowl of apples and cherries on a round table, gleaming in the smoky, early morning light.

"How thoughtful of someone to serve us breakfast," Dylan said, helping himself to an apple. Kate laughed a little nervously, then fell upon the cherries with an appetite that matched his. They ate in exhausted silence until Kate got up to explore the rest of the car. Dylan gathered up some apples to take to Bull and Father Michael, but when he stood, a sudden lurch nearly made his knees buckle. He hurried to the door and saw, to his amazement, that the Pullman had been coupled to the line heading south. The car occupied by their companions stood still, disappearing into the smoke.

He and Kate shared a look. "We've been separated from them," she said quietly.

"Yes."

"Dear God. Will they be all right?"

"Those two?" Dylan spread his hands. "After tonight, do you doubt it?" He sat beside her on a tufted chaise and took her hand in his. "We'll find them again, once we figure out what's happening." He tried to move on to the next car, but found it locked. The side was stenciled with the rail company's initials. Looking down, he saw the track rolling past.

"We can't leave Chicago," Kate said urgently.

"I don't believe we have a choice. But don't worry, we'll come back," he assured her, wondering if it would be a promise he could keep. They were headed south, very slowly.

Kate got up and wandered through the car. It was a private vehicle, and it appeared to have been prepared for an excursion. Under the sleeping berth were drawers filled with articles of clothing, and fresh linens hung from a washstand behind a folding screen. "Oh," she said, a single syllable that made him think she had seen God. She lifted a thick china ewer. "There's fresh water."

He heard splashing sounds from behind the screen, and smiled. She was such a lady, humming as she scrubbed away the ashes and cinders of her ordeal. He did some more exploring, opening cupboards and storage benches to see what else he could discover. In a bank of built-in cupboards, he found two suitcases filled with more clothing. He tossed some things over the side of the screen.

"Here, you should put dry clothes on so you don't catch cold."

"But this doesn't belong to me."

"Love, do you really think that matters?"

She gave a small, nervous laugh. More splashing sounds and then more humming drifted through the room. He craned his neck, trying to see what she'd done with her jewels, knowing this was not the time to ask her about them.

When she emerged from behind the screen, a silly, beautiful smile lit her face. She wore a long white gown—a peignoir, he thought it might be called—

and had managed to put some semblance of order to her bright hair.

"I feel much better now," she said.

"You'll feel even better after this."

"After what?"

He held up a green glass bottle he had found in a cupboard, then went over to a pocket door and slid it aside. Turning, he gave her his most charming smile, one eyebrow lifted. "My dear," he said, "champagne...and our marriage bed."

# *Eight*

A sound escaped Kathleen—not quite a laugh, but not quite an offended huff, either. "I do admire you," she admitted, "for being able to joke after a night like we've had."

She watched, fascinated, as a slow, honeyed smile slid across Dylan's lips. It was like watching the sun rise—dazzling, mesmerizing. She tore her gaze away and went to the window. The slow motion of the train had ceased, and they seemed to be out in the middle of nowhere. Darkness haunted the edges of dawn, adding an atmosphere of deep intimacy. Dylan didn't speak, but selected a pair of glasses that hung by their stems in a cupboard. With the flourish of a skilled sommelier, he uncorked the champagne. The popping sound made her jump, and her heart beat even faster.

He filled the two glasses and crossed the room, holding one out. "Who says," he asked softly, "that I'm joking?"

The glass felt heavy, its cut facets sharp in her hand, and she knew it was real crystal, probably from Ireland. But not everything from Ireland was for the very rich, she thought wildly.

"Of course you're joking. We can't possibly—"

He interrupted her by closing his hand over hers and putting the glass to her lips. She was forced to choose between drinking, or dribbling champagne down the front of the finest embroidered peignoir she had ever worn.

She drank. Though barely chilled, the champagne tasted delicious. She had only sampled it a time or two before, enough to know she adored the taste. He held the glass while she took a deep swallow and closed her eyes.

"Much better," he said in that same soft, cultured voice. "You like champagne, don't you?"

"It is like drinking a magical potion," she whispered, and before she could open her eyes, he put his lips where the crystal glass had been.

His light, evocative kiss sipped the droplets of champagne from her mouth. "I agree," he said.

A powerful warmth raced through her, as if she had drunk the whole bottle instead of just one gulp. Shocking heat settled in her most secret places, and she felt it start—exactly the sort of blush he had teased her about...was it only last night? She prayed he would not notice. She would die of embarrassment if he noticed.

Resting his hands on her shoulders, he stood back and examined her in the strange light, a mingling of smoke-filtered morning and firelight from the burning city. "Ah, Kate, you're doing it," he said.

"Doing what?"

"Blushing with your whole body, just as I'd imagined."

Damn him. He had noticed. But she didn't want to die. She wanted to be rid of the gown and robe, wanted to feel their skin touching, as their lips had done. "We...can't," she forced out.

"Can't what?"

"Do...what I think you want to do." She couldn't believe she was having this conversation with a man she barely knew. A man who happened to be her husband.

"You want it, too," he said gently, almost as if he pitied her. "You want me to make love to you. There's no shame in that." His finger traced the curve of her lip. "I'll do a good job, Kate, I promise you that."

Not for a single second did she doubt him. She felt herself melting into nothingness, no strength or backbone to stand on her own. Reaching back, she clutched a brass rail for support and searched herself to find even the tiniest shred of willpower. *No.* Her mouth formed the word, but her voice deserted her. She cleared her throat, tasting the fire she had survived. "No," she said again, this time audibly.

He didn't seem in the least discouraged. "You don't mean that."

"I do."

"Sweetheart, you're my *wife*. Surely you've not forgotten that we were married last night."

She started to melt again. She would never forget the most magical night ever, when a real-life prince had made her his bride. "I could not possibly forget that," she admitted.

"So?" He let his hands slip down her arms. Almost by accident, his knuckles grazed her breasts. "What is the trouble? I realize it was a bit unorthodox, but that only makes this more special."

She gripped the railing harder. "We didn't expect to survive last night."

"But we did. Don't you see, Kate? It was a gift, and we would be making a mockery of that gift if we didn't celebrate our miraculous deliverance in the most elemental and life-affirming way possible.''

Oh, he was good. Persuasive. And achingly sincere. Her grip on the brass rail slackened somewhat, and she had to remind herself to hang on. ''We mustn't,'' she whispered, sounding weak and ineffectual in the face of his silky persuasion. ''We married in haste, assuming we would die, and there were no, er, contingency plans for what would happen if we lived. No…provisions.''

''I have a confession to make.'' He toyed with a ringlet of her hair, seemingly fascinated by the way the ruby lock curled around his finger. ''From the moment I saw you, I was making plans and provisions.''

''You were?''

''I was. You nearly broke my heart, running off like that, without saying goodbye.''

''That was because—'' *Tell him. Just say it.* Oh, she wanted to. She wanted to confess that she was no refined heiress from Baltimore, but a lowly maid whose parents still spoke in the brogue of their native Ireland.

He was a kind man, she told herself. More than kind. He was handsome and brave and brilliant, and so perfect she wanted to sink down and weep at his feet, begging forgiveness for having deceived him.

''Because what, Kate?'' he asked tenderly, arranging the lock of hair on her shoulder with the care of a museum curator.

Her mouth went dry. Her stare was riveted by his extraordinary eyes, eyes so blue they resembled mirrors, reflecting her image back at her. What she saw looking back was herself, helplessly in love with him.

"I...forgot what I was going to say."

She had lied to him so much this night that it felt strange, telling him the truth. But it was absolute gospel that she had forgotten what she wanted to confess. What she wanted...was her wedding night.

Never mind that it was aboard a strange train car where they clearly didn't belong. Never mind that the dawn was coming on. Never mind that several miles to the north, the city still burned out of control. None of that mattered. All that mattered was that Kathleen O'Leary had discovered a way to make all her dreams come true.

She made no conscious choice, but let her heart decide. Dylan Kennedy claimed he adored her. She *knew* she loved him. They would consummate their marriage, and it would be such a mystical, transporting experience that her small white lie would cease to matter. When she finally told him the truth, he would be so deeply in love with her, so inexorably joined to her, that her deception would cease to matter.

"Then don't say anything at all," he whispered in reply, and pulled her into his arms.

She surrendered her grip on the brass rail, needing nothing but Dylan now that she knew what she wanted. Still melting and helpless, she clung to him, aware of the smoke-infused state of his clothing. The reminder of their ordeal only made her more eager to fulfill the promise they had made at the courthouse. That they had sworn it before a priest, a judge and the mayor only increased the weight of the pledge. That a man had died after witnessing the union only underscored the solemnity of their vows.

The entire universe, she thought, when she was still

able to think, had lined up to enable them to be together in this way. It was fate. Her own dear gran would say so. Fate had brought her and Dylan together, and no small, insignificant mortal such as herself had the right to deny it.

He asked nothing of her, and he gave everything. With hands so gentle she barely felt his touch, he slipped the peignoir off her shoulders and down her arms. Sliding his fingers beneath the thin straps of her gown, he leaned down to kiss her. Just before his mouth touched hers, he said, "I want to see you, Kate. I want to see you blush."

"Yes." She breathed the word on an exhalation of surrender. She was glad she'd discarded her bloomers behind the screen. Seeing her much mended homespuns might cause him to ask questions she wasn't ready to answer.

With slow, tender movements he brushed the straps aside until there was nothing left to hold the gown on. The sheer fabric slid like a caress down the length of her body, unimpeded by shift or bloomers. She felt as wicked as a sinner, and twice as hot.

"Beautiful," he murmured, stepping back so that he wasn't touching her at all. "Beautiful," he said again.

And despite the sinful pose and the blush and everything else, she felt as beautiful as he claimed she was. He had the uncanny talent of making love to her with his eyes alone, nothing more. He wasn't even touching her, yet she felt the heat of his gaze skim over her breasts, belly, hips, legs. It was wonderful and frustrating and confusing, and she stood waiting, almost faint from wanting him.

"Let me take you to bed," he whispered. He took

her hand in a curiously formal manner, lifting it and leading her to the draped alcove bed. The Pullman car was a pure wonder, with its lush opulence and the way everything fit so perfectly in its place. The sleeping berth was made up with a feather bed and linens as fine as anything in the Sinclair mansion. The clean, sharp scent of lavender wafted up as he lifted the covers and gently pressed her down. She went willingly, reclining on the cloudlike softness.

He bent and kissed her. "Wait for me, love," he said.

His eyes never left her as he kicked off his shoes and peeled off his waistcoat and shirt. He had a fine broad chest and arms banded by muscles—which surprised her. She had expected the slender physique of a man of leisure. An involuntary gasp escaped her. She felt so wretchedly empty that she nearly sobbed, holding her arms out to him. He smiled. She didn't understand the sympathy that softened the edges of that smile, but it didn't matter. He was her prince, her dream come true.

He lifted the covers and lay down beside her, the comfortable mattress sighing beneath his weight. Holding himself propped on one elbow, he lowered his head to kiss her mouth. At the same time, he moved his free hand over her in a leisurely motion. He gave no particular attention to her most sensitive places, but seemed to encounter them almost by accident. It was maddening, wonderful and frustrating. She kept moving and lifting herself toward him, wanting more and more of him.

He made her shameless with need. She could no more govern her desire than she could control the moon or the stars, so she made no attempt to pretend she didn't want him. She wound her arms around his neck and kissed him with ravenous hunger, even daring to push her tongue against his lips, slipping it past them, as he had done to her.

He stopped kissing her for a moment. She froze, fearing she had done something unforgivably terrible. But before she could stammer out an apology, he smiled that magical smile and said, "You're a temptress, Katie Kennedy. You know how to make me wild for you."

From his tone, she deduced that this was a good thing, so she went back to kissing him. Being a temptress was even more fun than being an heiress, she discovered. She reveled in the complete freedom of running her hands over his bare shoulders and down to his hips, feeling the contours of him, the silky hard shape of him. He whispered things in her ear, things that made her more wild than he. Though she didn't understand everything he said, enlightenment came with the movements of his hands and mouth. He would whisper something and then touch her in a certain way, so that she understood the act he was describing.

There were kisses that made her burn, kisses that nipped and marked her as his and his alone. There were caresses that branded her with the heat of his passion, and caresses that made her cry out and lift herself toward him, a shameless offering, a plea.

This, she thought, floating in a crimson haze, this was what she had been born for. Yet until she had met Dylan, she had not even known.

He pressed apart her legs and put himself there, his muscular arms making a sturdy frame around her. She felt a stinging pressure, but rather than resisting, she rose toward it, welcoming the sensation. The moment of surrender had been discussed at exhaustive length, in awed whispers, by the ladies of Miss Boylan's. But when Dylan came to her, she knew the dormitory discussions were wrong. It was assumed to be painful, but Dylan made her understand why the term deflowering had been invented. With a sure but delicate touch he plucked away apprehension and inhibition. He made it seem the most natural thing in the world to kiss her in unexpected places, to touch her in ways she had never even imagined. She unfurled her entire self to him like a flower to the summer sun, entrusting him with her body, her heart, her life.

She was unprepared for the power of love's pleasures. His lovely intimate stroking and the motion of his body joining with hers transported her to a place of stars and perfumed magic. She heard herself cry out, and then Dylan kissed her, absorbing the ripples of her pleasure and joining their mouths as deeply as their bodies.

She told Dylan that she loved him, and heard him answer. She had not known it would be this way. No whispered warnings could have prepared her for the power and beauty of this experience. Turning her head to one side, she glimpsed the flickering fires outside the train window and—

"We're moving again," she said suddenly.

"Yes, my love," he said agreeably, with a suggestive motion of his hips.

"No, I mean we *are* moving." Much as she adored clinging to him, she forced herself to sit up, take notice. She drew on her robe and went to look out the window.

Sure enough, the smoky landscape was sliding by, slowly at first but even as she watched, it moved with gathering speed. Dylan pushed himself up beside her, resting his chin upon her shoulder as he looked out at the misted lake.

He got up and walked stark naked to one end of the car. She was amazed by how natural he seemed, walking about in the nude. With an elaborate lack of concern, he went over to the dark oak sideboard and poured two more glasses of champagne. She found that she could not take her eyes off him. He had a physique that captivated her entirely; he was long-limbed and muscular, yet not bulky. He had the body of a gifted athlete, and she wondered if it was a natural fitness or if the very rich followed some sort of regime to ensure physical perfection.

She told herself it was wicked to be staring at him so, even though he was her husband. "Where do you suppose this car is headed? And why?"

He returned to the bed, holding out a glass to her. "I imagine they're clearing the terminal for the relief trains to get through. Remember, the mayor wired for help last night, so they must be preparing for it. Who knows where we're headed? I've always had good luck with trains."

It was an odd thing to say, but she couldn't question him further, because he quite deliberately parted her robe, exposing her to his heated stare. Kathleen tugged her robe shut. She bit her lip, thinking of her family. "I must get back to Chicago," she said.

"Of course you must." He angled his head to

nip—dear God, he was *nipping* her again—at her neck. "You'll need your clothes...and jewels, of course." He misinterpreted her anxious expression. "Don't be bashful, darling, Phoebe Palmer told me all about your fortune. You needn't worry, the fire couldn't have reached the finishing school."

How sweet of him to be so concerned about her clothes and jewels. And how he would laugh when he learned she owned two dresses, both homemade, and her only jewel, her da often joked, was the emerald of her eyes. The silk gown she'd worn was all but ruined; at least the borrowed jewels, tucked now into the toes of her shoes, were fine. She would have to return them to Deborah Sinclair as soon as she could. The thought filled her with apprehension.

"What's wrong?" Dylan asked.

"I was just worried about my friends and family."

He seemed befuddled. "It must be strange to care about something that much."

"Why strange?"

"No reason. Look, they'll be fine. And so will we. You have to trust me on this, love."

Soothed by his reassurances and by another glass of champagne, Kathleen surrendered her fears. There seemed to be nothing else for it but to cling to Dylan and let him chase away thoughts of tomorrow. Meanwhile, the train kept moving slowly and inexorably away from the city. He began to make love to her again, and she welcomed him, unfolding for him and lying back with a sigh. For the second time, they consummated their unorthodox marriage, and for good measure, they consummated it again...and again. Watching the angry glow of the fire growing ever more distant as the train headed south, Kathleen knew a happiness so sweet that she nearly wept with it.

What had she ever done to deserve such a marvelous man, a man who worshiped and cherished her?

What had she ever done...except lie?

# *Nine*

Dylan lay on his side, propped on one elbow, the bedsheets bunched around his waist. He gazed down at his sleeping wife and listened to the soothing, lazy sound of the train. She lay like a fallen angel, her fire-colored hair spread out on the pillow, her lips slightly parted and almost imperceptibly swollen from kissing. He had made two very faint marks on her delicate white throat. Her fragile, silken skin bruised so easily beneath the sensual assault of his kisses.

She was such a lady, as finely made as a porcelain doll. She was by far the best one he had ever married, and this union, for once, might even be a legitimate one. What a strange notion, a marriage that could last. He had never before considered being with a woman long enough to watch her change with the years. He wondered what Kate would be like in ten years. Rounder, perhaps, her body shaped by childbearing. Twenty years? Threads of silver in her hair, maybe, and wispy laugh lines by her eyes. Forty? Her beauty was the sort that would endure, for it depended not on artifice or youth, but a handsome bone structure and strong, clear features he would never tire of studying. Her looks, he thought cheerfully, would last as long as her fortune. He was glad he had found her. This was one he wanted to keep.

Of course, he would have some explaining to do if his past ever overtook him, but in the wake of this disaster, what were the chances of that?

As the parlor car chugged slowly past autumn fields blanketed in mist, he began to hope that maybe those chances were growing slimmer by the mile.

Kate stirred, curling against him like a contented cat. Her ardent response in the marriage bed had been a surprise. More than a surprise. A revelation. Society women were trained from infancy to despise sex in every way, shape and form. They were made to truss themselves up in corsets and stays, to hide their bodies even from themselves. It was said no proper lady would ever dare to see herself naked. Yet Kate had discarded bashfulness along with her splendid French gown and welcomed everything he had given her. She had surrendered utterly, and somehow that had added to his pleasure.

Dylan considered himself to be a man of varied tastes and wide experience. He certainly hadn't expected to find something new and rare and startling with a high-society virgin. But he had. There was no denying it. There was no denying that his physical release had held an edge of sweetness so searing that it took his breath away. No denying that there was something supremely gratifying in simply holding her for hours afterward.

His newest wife was far more than he had bargained for. Far more than he deserved, truth be told. She was definitely a treasure.

No woman had ever affected him this way, not even that female contortionist in Buffalo who had kept him so entertained back in his burlesque days.

With a sigh of contentment, he lay back on the

pillows and wondered whose parlor car he had appropriated. It was said George Pullman spent no less than twenty-seven thousand dollars outfitting each of his premier train cars, and that the most important men across America commissioned their own private cars from him. Perhaps this one belonged to Cyrus McCormick or Arthur Sinclair. It was certainly well-appointed enough for men who could afford gaudy ostentation.

The etched glass, ornately carved furniture and lacy appointments were not to Dylan's taste, but he had only to consider the alternative—his leaky, rotting boat—and he no longer cared if the chicken-footed table started to squawk.

Folding his arms behind his head, he listened to the lazy rotation of the iron wheels and tried to make a plan for the future. First off, they would have to disappear. It was an easy enough feat. He used to do it on a regular basis. Billing himself as Bondo, the Escape Artist, he would pretend to rob audience members of their fine jewelry, watches and gold pieces, only to assure them that he would be locked up like a criminal in a four-sided cage with iron bars, his hands and feet cuffed and chained. Costello used to play the audience volunteer, and when the first gasps of amazement died down, others would come forward. When Dylan was pretty certain of a good haul, he would escape, never to return. The audience was left scratching their heads. You'd think, he mused, they would understand what two simple, tilted mirrors could do, but that was part of being an illusionist. People believed what you convinced them to believe.

Smiling, he touched Kate's silky hair. She was a prime example, she and the swells who moved in Chicago's exclusive circles. They were all convinced beyond question that he was from an old, wealthy family just a shade less than royal. It was all veneer, polished to a high sheen by constant vigilance and practice. He was so good at it that sometimes he convinced *himself* he was Dylan Francis Kennedy. In his most private moments, he sometimes felt a small, uncomfortable sensation of disquiet. He had worked so long and hard to become someone else that his true self now lay buried beneath layers of artifice. He had made up so many identities and histories for himself that he was no longer certain which was real and which was illusion.

Sometimes a slipping sense of loss panicked him. At such times, he calmed himself with the reminder that his former self—that lonely, frightened boy abandoned in a train station—was hardly an identity worth preserving.

But still. In the peculiar quiet moments, like now, when there was nothing to do but think, he felt a hollowness that should be filled with the real things of life. Friends and family and the permanence of being anchored to a particular place. A long time ago, he came to the conclusion that he was simply not meant to have those things. He wondered why he still brooded upon them. He should learn to be content with what he had for the time being—a beautiful rich wife, the use of a fine parlor car, a future that might prove to be quite interesting.

What a way to escape Chicago. He ought to stop questioning his good fortune.

Perhaps they could head east to Baltimore, where Kate would introduce him to her family. Fitting in with the wealthy Baltimore clan should be easy enough. For whatever reason, Dylan felt an affinity with these people he had never met, who were so beloved by Kate. He had no idea why, just as he had no idea why he'd felt something come over him in the church during the fire. Flickers of memory, but nothing he could hold on to.

Lulled by the slow sound of the train, he joined his wife in sleep.

The first thing Dylan did when he awakened was make love to Kate.

He didn't even really think about it or plan what he was going to do. It was full dark, and she was just...*there,* warm and pliant in his arms, and it was the most natural thing in the world to kiss her awake, to fit himself between her soft thighs and love her until her cries and sighs crescendoed.

"I think there is something wrong with me," she whispered afterward into his ear.

"What the devil do you mean by that? You're perfect, my love. Absolutely perfect."

"No, I'm afraid I am the worst sort of sinner."

"Why would you say a foolish thing like that?"

"Well, because I—I *like* this."

"Like what?"

She moved her hips. "This. Being with you like this."

"And how does that make you a sinner?"

"I'm not supposed to like it. You're a God-fearing man. You know this."

He fought back loud guffaws of laughter. "Ah, Kate. You're no sinner. You are a married lady, and some marriages, believe it or not, are meant to be happy. In every way."

She lay silent as he separated from her and gently held her in his arms. That was when he noticed what he should have noticed the very second he had awakened.

The train was no longer moving.

She really did make him foolish with lust. He had best learn to be more careful. He got out of the berth, smacking his head on the low alcove and gritting his teeth to keep in a curse.

"I'd best see where we are," he said. There was no light at all in the parlor car. He felt his way to the window and saw an orange glow. Monday's sunset? Tuesday's daybreak? The burning city? He couldn't tell, and the watch he had pickpocketed Sunday night had stopped because he had neglected to wind it. Out the opposite window, the fog-shrouded lake hid its secrets in a vast nothingness.

"Can you see anything?" Kate asked from the bed.

"Just the lake. And some flickering lights along the shore." Dylan felt ravenously hungry all of a sudden. He lit a lamp and went rummaging, finding a tin of soda biscuits and a jar of honey. When he brought them to the bed, Kate gave a cry of elation so heartfelt it sounded as if he had made love to her all over again.

"I'm starved," she declared.

In the dark, they made a feast of the biscuits and honey, washing the meal down with the rest of the champagne. It was warm and flat but they drank it anyway, laughing together, spilling crumbs in the bedclothes. When Kate claimed she could not eat another bite, he held a honey-dipped spoon high above her.

"Don't you dare," she said, half laughing, half horrified.

He held her pinned to the bed with one hand and watched the amber ribbon of honey spin downward like a spider's web. It pooled on her stomach, and she gave a little cry of shock and dismay.

"I'm hungry for something sweet," Dylan whispered, wiggling his eyebrows in exaggerated fashion.

Kate smacked him on the shoulder. For a rich girl, she packed quite a wallop, he thought.

"You're making a mess entirely," she said indignantly, in what he was beginning to think of as her bossy voice. It was sharper, brassier than her usual voice, with a curious lilt.

"I promise to clean it up," he vowed, moving the spoon so that the dribble of honey drew a curlicue on her stomach.

"Stop it. I don't want to be sticky all night long."

"You won't be," he said easily. "Look, I've drawn the shape of a heart."

She pushed herself up on her elbows. "I don't see it. You are wicked to the bone, Dylan Kennedy."

"But I've made you a heart. Here, if you can't see it, I'll show you." He put the spoon in the honey jar and set it aside. And then, while she gasped in shock, he traced the shape of the heart with his tongue. He worked slowly and methodically, making certain not a single drop of honey escaped his notice.

"Oh, dear heaven," she whispered.

"What's wrong?" he murmured against her silky skin.

"You had better stop this right now."

"Why? Don't you like it?"

"It's not a matter of liking." She gasped. "I can't even collect my thoughts when you do that."

"Then don't think." He licked a path from her navel to her breast. "Just lie still and let me get all this honey off you."

"But I—"

"Sh. I don't want to spend the night with a sticky wife."

She gave up protesting when he circled first one breast, then the other, then took each nipple in turn delicately between his teeth. He kissed and licked her where the honey was, and even where it wasn't. Within a very short time, she gave herself up to him entirely. She opened herself, even her soul to him, and when he sank down into her again, he had the strangest sensation that this was exactly where he belonged.

At daybreak they ventured outside into a chill, damp autumn day. Enjoying his role as lord of the manor, Dylan spoke with the railroad men, who confirmed that they had stopped at Eden Landing and were clearing the tracks for the relief trains. It took little skill to convince them that he was the owner of the Pullman car. An anxious-looking businessman wearing an ill-fitting suit shaded his eyes and regarded the lake. "There's a fortune in grain on the barge *Elyssa* out there," he said. "And no way to get it to the markets now. What with the wires down and the Board of Trade destroyed, they'll probably have to dump the entire harvest in the lake."

"Could you find a fleet of tugs to take it to Milwaukee?" asked Kate.

Dylan looked at her sharply. Each time she opened

her mouth, she surprised him. Did they teach her the grain trade in finishing school?

"That would take weeks," the man said. Lifting and then replacing his battered flat cap, he introduced himself as David Fraser.

"Dylan is a man of business," Kate said with a discomfiting wifely pride. "Perhaps he could figure out a way to get your grain to market." She batted her eyes. "Couldn't you, Dylan?"

"Of course," he lied. "Perhaps when the emergency's over, we might come to an agreement."

"You'd be a godsend, then," Fraser said. He and Kate fell to talking, of all things, about the price of a bushel of wheat and whether or not the Board of Trade would be able to reopen. Fraser seemed quite confident Dylan would find him a grain contract.

Restless, Dylan wandered off and idly picked up several stones from the ground. With the habit of long practice, he juggled them in a circle. After a few moments, Kate and Fraser noticed him, and he grinned at them through a wreath of spinning stones.

Kate gave a little laugh. "Where on earth did you learn to do that?"

He winked, catching the stones one by one. "Harvard." Before she could question him further, he said to Mr. Fraser, "Pardon me, sir, but there's something in your hat." With a flourish, he reached for it and held it out. The smallest stone from his juggling lay in the crown.

It was an old ruse, but it almost always worked. While the mark stood in confusion, he left his pockets untended. But when Dylan looked into the man's plain, worried face, he simply handed back the hat. No sense in adding to the poor sod's troubles.

The engine whistle shrieked, and as the cold evening descended, the few refugees were ordered aboard again. Kate seemed preoccupied, standing at the window and staring out at the lake, broad and endless as the sea.

"Do you find bargeloads of grain that fascinating?" Dylan asked teasingly.

Deadly serious, she turned to him. "I suppose so," she said, "when they are worth a fortune."

Kathleen came awake eyelash by eyelash. She was that sore, that tired. It took long moments of concerted effort to drag one eye open, then the other, and when she finally managed to focus on something, it was her husband's face.

Lord, but he was a handsome devil, she thought with a shiver of pure sinful lust. Even with his cheeks shadowed by the stubble of a beard, he looked as perfect as a god. She still couldn't believe she was married to him, that she had done the most unimaginable things in this bed with him. Was that what the rest of her life with him was to be, then?

She wanted it to be. She wanted it with all her heart. Yet each moment drew her closer to having to confess the truth about who she was and where she came from. Putting it off would serve nothing.

She slipped out of bed and went behind the screen. She ached in every muscle, bone and joint, and she ached in other places as well. She'd lost count of the number of times he had made love to her. In fact, she didn't know when one session ended and another began. It just seemed like one long magical night of love, interrupted here and there by sleep. With Dylan, even eating soda biscuits was a way of making love. She shivered just thinking about it.

She used a soft linen towel and water from the basin to bathe herself. She contemplated the formal gown and shoes she had worn Sunday night, and shuddered at the thought of putting on the smoky garments once more. In one of the traveling valises, she found a lady's shift and put it on, then a shirtwaist and skirt. She stuck the jewels inside the bodice of the shirtwaist.

She had one remaining comb left in her hair, and she used it to tidy her curling, smoky locks, making a simple braid down her back. Studying her image in the small pedestal hand mirror, she felt a small welling of disappointment. This was nothing like the elegant, gleaming style she had affected for Sunday night. She looked...ordinary. Never mind that she greatly resembled the person she truly was; she much preferred the rich mystery of the woman she had been that night. The woman Dylan Kennedy had fallen in love with.

A shiver of fear coursed through her. Exactly what did he love? A bold debutante in a Worth gown and diamonds, or the person underneath? In the very smallest corner of her heart, she was afraid to learn the answer.

When she emerged from behind the screen, Dylan was awake and gazing at her. His wonderful smile bathed his face in radiance, and she dared to relax a little.

"You look lovely," he announced.

She relaxed even more. He was a man of depth, bless him, able to see beneath the artifice of dress. "I was thinking I look quite plain."

"Clean and braided and fresh as a schoolgirl," he said. "You awaken my lecherous impulses."

Before she could scold him, her body reacted with a rush of warmth that flooded the places he had discovered last night, places that were sweetly sore from his tender attentions. And the all-over blush he alone had the power to ignite swept over her. "I'll just look out and see where we are now."

She went to the window and froze. "Jesus, Mary and Joseph," she whispered, her breath fogging the window.

He got out of the bed, bringing a sheet with him to wrap loosely around his waist. "What is it?"

"Look where we are."

A low whistle emerged from between his teeth. "I'll be damned." Standing behind her, he rested his hands on her shoulders.

"We've come back to Chicago," she said, baffled. "The train was on the move all night, and now we've come back."

He inspected each end of the car. "We're uncoupled," he reported. "I imagine they wanted this car out of the way so the freighters can come and go."

"We should try to find out what became of Father Michael and Bull Waxman," she said.

"Anything might have happened to them, with the city in flames. I hope they had the sense to stay put in that train car."

She bit her lip and made herself look out at the ruined city with its broken walls and crumbled chimneys. "It is like gazing upon a corpse," she said finally.

His arms slid around her, cradling her body to his, and she took comfort in his nearness. All the land-

marks were gone. The skeletons of once fine buildings were visible through the shifting veil of smoke
and mist. She shuddered, trying to get her bearings
amid the shattered masonry. Huge chunks of smoldering debris created the illusion of some awful tomb.
The long, straight roads stretching westward from the
lake still smoldered, their surfaces paved by live
coals. Nothing obstructed her view except the smoke,
but the lively wind playing across the river and lake
parted the curtain from time to time.

A sob caught in her throat.

"What is it, my love?" Dylan asked, turning her
in his arms.

She pressed her palms to his warm, smooth chest,
taking comfort in his nearness. "I was just…thinking
of my family."

"There, there. I'm certain they'll worry when they
hear of the fire, but when we find a telegraph station
that's operating, we'll send a wire to Baltimore in-
forming them that you're safe and sound." He lifted
her hand to his lips. "And married."

Her throat locked with fear. She had to swallow
several times before forcing out the words. "Dylan,
about my family—"

"They'll understand. They have to. Our marriage
was meant to be." He was so earnest, he broke her
heart. "What are the chances of us meeting on the
night of the worst fire in history? Things happen for
a reason, Kate. You have to believe that."

When he called her Kate, she wanted to wrap herself in his image of her and never come out. But
enough pretending. The train had returned to the station. The harsh light of day penetrated the smoky

gloom, revealing the wreck and ruin of the city. It was time to tell Dylan the truth, too.

"Please, just listen," she said softly. Even as she spoke, her hands moved over his bare chest and shoulders, as if to memorize the landscape of his body. And somewhere deep inside she knew why. After he was gone from her life she would have nothing but memories.

"My family is in Chicago," she said.

He grinned. "Excellent. Why didn't you say so before?"

She couldn't help smiling back. "I've been trying to." The smile faded. "They are—or were—in the West Division."

"Odd," he said. "I always thought the West Division to be a shantytown. Perhaps while I was overseas, some fashionable hotels were built."

"I wouldn't—"

"Look, sweetheart." He pressed a finger lightly to her lips. "The city is impassable. The streets are too clogged with rubble to navigate. Maybe we could take the river, but if the bridges are down, we won't get far. The heat and wreckage are too dangerous." He tucked her cheek against his chest. "We'll go when it's safe, and not a moment before. I won't risk losing you, Kate. God forbid that I should lose you."

She felt the slow, steady beat of his heart against her cheek, and she could hear the whisper of fabric as the sheet slid, unheeded, to the floor. Without quite knowing how it happened, she found herself undressed and pressed back onto the bed, transported once again to the dreamworld he created with his love. She nearly wept with the beauty of it, and she clung to him.

As the smoke slowly blew across the smoldering ruins of the city, she realized beyond doubt that they had survived. She was safe in the arms of Dylan Kennedy.

Her husband.

And in her heart, a dream came to life like the sudden, unseasonable bloom of a rose. She *could* have the genteel way of life she had always craved. The fire was an act of God. Of fate. Destiny. Dylan had said as much. Everything happened for a reason. Why shouldn't that reason be that she had been born into the wrong sort of life? Perhaps this was fate's way of fixing a mistake.

Ah, how often she had fantasized that she'd been born into the wrong family. When she was very young, she imagined that she had been born to an exotic foreign princess who had tearfully left her with compassionate nuns. The nuns had delivered the mysterious babe, wrapped in the sheerest veiling, to a kindly but impoverished family, who raised her as their own.

Though admittedly fanciful, the notion that the Lord must have meant for her to find Dylan eased her misgivings over the deception. He loved her. He'd proved it in so many ways, with his kisses and his caresses and the things he whispered in her ear. Of course he loved her. And when he learned the truth, his love would not change. When he met her family, his heart would melt with affection.

Sated by his lovemaking, she sighed contentedly and tucked herself against his shoulder. The magic of love, she now knew, was that it made anything, everything, possible. Being in love was far more wonderful than she had ever dared to imagine. She adored

him so insanely that when she lifted her head and saw
him smiling down at her, she knew in every bone of
her body that he would forgive her anything, just as
she would absolve him if there were anything to forgive. That was the true gift of love.

They slept some more, lightly, and a few hours
later were awakened by a prolonged grinding noise
from the rail yard. They got dressed and stepped outside, blinking through the smoke. A few strangers
milled about, some huddled together in groups, some
wandering lost, a few calling out the names of family
or friends. They resembled survivors of a great battle—disheveled, disoriented, displaced. Scorching
winds still howled in from the prairie, fanning the fire
to seek out new fuel.

Meanwhile, men discussed the disaster in hushed
whispers. A burning vessel had drifted into the Chicago Avenue Bridge, setting the span afire. People
had died screaming as the fire pursued them into
dead-end streets and trapped them there.

But the mayor's frantic predawn telegrams had
reached their destinations. Dylan spoke briefly with a
railroad man who said they were moving cars again
to make room for engines and firefighters from distant
cities. Milwaukee sent three engines. Others began to
arrive from Cincinnati, Louisville, Detroit, Port Hu-
ron, Springfield and Pittsburgh. Without horses to pull
the engines, men wheeled them by hand to battle the
still-menacing fire. Demolition crews attacked buildings that stood as fodder for the flames. Streams of
water, drawn by hoses from the lake and river, played
on bridges, lumber, coal piles, goods stacked by the
shore.

"I should join in the effort," Dylan said.

She grasped his hand, remembering his ordeal on the steeple of the church. "Don't," she said in a fearful whisper. "Dylan, I beg you. Stay with me." She put up her hand to cup his stubbled cheek. "You've given enough of yourself to this fire. Now *I* need you."

A shadow flickered over his face, but then he swept her up into his arms. A young girl tending a donkey nearby sighed with longing as he carried Kathleen back to the parlor car. People could tell they were in love, she thought.

"It's getting late," he whispered to her. "Time for bed…again." Within moments, the darkness consumed them, and they gave in to the passion that seemed to rule inside the confines of the train car. Before meeting Dylan, Kathleen had had no idea it was even possible for a man and a woman to spend so much time doing this, and the rest of the time thinking about it, dreaming of it. She realized that, at any moment, someone could open the parlor car and find the two of them, but she was too lovestruck to worry about it.

"What are you thinking?" Dylan asked her, toying with a lock of her hair as if it were a rare and precious artifact. She had lost count of the number of times he had kissed her and joined his body with hers, and the thought immediately made her want more.

"That if I have to be confined like this, there is no one I'd rather be with."

"You are incredibly sweet," he said. "I've never met anyone with your sweetness, your candor."

"I want to tell you all the secrets of my heart," she confessed, so moved that tears stung her eyes. *All but one.*

"Then tell me, Kate. Tell me, and I'll make them all come true."

She blinked away the tears and managed a laugh. "I'm afraid you're too late for some of them."

He looked crestfallen. "What do you mean?"

"Well." She sat up in bed and helped herself to a biscuit, wishing there was something else to eat. "I used to dream about my wedding, for one thing." She nibbled a corner of the biscuit. "And believe me, it was nothing like the courthouse wedding."

"Tell me what it was like," he asked softly.

She stared intently at him and wondered if that particular shade of blue had been invented just to adorn his eyes. With a single glance, the brush of a caress, he drew from her every possible emotion, and she found herself speaking with an ease she'd never felt with anyone. Not Deborah, not her mother. "I used to daydream about the grandest wedding imaginable. I would wear an ivory gown covered in seed pearls and a veil that flowed like the very mists of time." She paused and let go of the daydream. "Do you think me terribly shallow for dwelling so much on fashion?"

"No, Kate. Your dreams are a part of you. And I of all people know what lies beneath your fashionable surface." He reminded her of this by lowering his head to her naked breast.

She tucked the sheet up around her, fastening it beneath her arms. "Do you want to hear this or not?"

"Of course, my dear. I simply got carried away. Go on. Where were you? Ah yes. The grand wedding. And the ivory dress with beads—"

"Seed pearls," she corrected him, trying not to giggle with the absurdity of it. "There would be glo-

rious music playing.'' She shut her eyes and inhaled.
''We'd have a ceremony outside, of course, under a
garden gazebo all twined with flowers. The smell of
lilacs and lilies of the valley would perfume the
air...and after the speaking of the vows, white doves
would take flight.''

''Doves?''

''At least a dozen of them. Think how pretty they
would look against the blue sky.''

He grew quiet, his face unsmiling and pensive.

''I know it must seem silly to you,'' she said, discomfited.

''Not silly, Kate. Not in the least. You've survived
a terrible ordeal, and you deserve to have your dreams
come true. I wish this wasn't just a train car, but a
golden palace. I wish these soda biscuits were made
of butter, and the honey was caviar. I wish I could
have given you the wedding you dreamed about.''

With a cry of dismay she came up on her knees
and straddled him, pushing him mercilessly against
the pillow. ''Dylan Kennedy, don't you see what I
am trying to say?''

He thought for a moment as if trying to decide
which answer would satisfy her. ''Um, maybe you'd
better explain.''

''I was a foolish article of a girl,'' she declared. ''I
did not know the first thing about dreams—true ones
or otherwise. I dreamed of a beautiful ceremony, yes.
But I was too stupid to see that it's all just pomp and
illusion. It's what comes after that matters. And never
once did I dream about what comes after.'' She
smiled at his endearing male bafflement. ''Foolish,
foolish me. You've shown me that what comes after
is better than any daydream.''

He swallowed, his Adam's apple sliding enticingly. She bent and kissed it.

"Really?" he said.

"Really."

With wicked precision, he grasped her hips and positioned her just so. "Prove it," he challenged her.

And she did, finding within herself an unabashed sensuality that responded to his slightest provocation. In the hours she spent with Dylan in the parlor car, she felt as though they lived in a world unto themselves, where no one and nothing could touch them. He made it easy, she thought, so easy to lose herself in loving him. So easy to forget that she had yet to tell him the truth about herself.

"Extra, extra, read the story of the century," called a young, clear voice. "Extra, read it right here!"

Groggy, Dylan lifted his head from the pillow next to Kathleen and squinted out the train car window. It was dawn…Wednesday? Thursday? He couldn't recall.

The newsboy's call faded. Dylan hurried out of bed, pulling on pants, shirt and shoes even as he left the car. The reek of creosote and wood smoke nearly gagged him, but he followed the boy's voice. The urchin's face was smeared coal-black, and his eyes shone as Dylan whistled to get his attention.

"Paper, mister?" the kid asked. "First extra in the city, guaranteed." He proudly displayed a page, printed on one side. "It's the *Journal*."

Digging in his pocket, Dylan found some pennies and gave them to the boy, who seemed inclined to talk. "I'd best go," he said, walking away. He didn't like being around kids like this one. It always made him think of himself at that age, abandoned, all too eager to be whatever someone wanted him to be. At that age he had been as earnest as a puppy, one that would follow even the most abusive master anywhere in order to keep from being left behind again.

When Dylan was that age, he would have done anything to avoid being abandoned.

He *had* done anything, he thought with a shudder. Anything and everything.

Rolling up the small paper, he stalked back to the palace car, slamming the door hard enough to rattle the etched windows. Kathleen was awake, watching him anxiously from the bed.

"Is everything all right?" she asked. She bit her full lower lip, then added, "You don't look like yourself, Dylan. What is it?"

He almost laughed at her then, it was so damned ironic. He never looked like himself because he didn't have the first idea who the hell he was. But he guessed that she, who seemed to know him with more of her heart than anyone he'd ever met, saw a difference in the devil-may-care bridegroom who had left her sleeping in the berth. Perhaps she saw the disquiet that burned in his eyes. Perhaps she somehow heard echoes of the leftover thoughts of the past he couldn't quite force himself to forget. With a practiced will, he thrust the thoughts to the back of his mind and put on a dazzling smile.

Yet when he came to the bed, he noticed something interesting about Kate. She didn't seem dazzled. She gave him a sad, loving look, full of an intimate knowledge he didn't want her to have. What the hell was it about her, that she could see behind his careful façade and probe at him in places he didn't want her to wander?

"Here," he said, averting his eyes. "I found a kid selling papers."

"So soon? How on earth did a newspaper manage to go to press?"

"I didn't ask." He scanned the page, grateful to have something to focus on other than the chill darkness sweeping over him. "Says here they found a rotary press in Cincinnati and brought it back to town." He gave a short laugh. "I'll be damned. I wonder if that's where the train took us."

She shifted very close to him. She smelled of the fire and womanhood and sex, making him crazy with wanting her. She intoxicated him more deeply than the sweetest wine, and in a world gone mad, she was the only thing that made sense to him, the only thing he could believe in. If he had any idea how to love someone, he would love her.

"What does it say?" she asked, her breath warm on his shoulder.

He browsed through a story of frantic hyperbole, chuckling at the florid narrative predicting the end of civilization as they knew it. Some of the fulsome descriptions made him laugh aloud and Kate gasp.

"You mean there are lynchings? Public executions?"

"I doubt it. Just makes good copy. Look at that," Dylan said, angling the page toward her. "They blame the fire on a cow belonging to a Mrs. O'Leary."

*"Who?"*

"Says here, a Mrs. O'Leary of de Koven Street. It

seems the creature kicked over a lantern, sparked a barn and destroyed an entire city.'' He laughed. ''Can you believe an entire city was destroyed by a drunken milkmaid?''

# Ten

There was nothing left to say, so Kathleen said nothing. She knew the jig was up. In fact, the masquerade had gone on longer than she'd had any right to expect. But letting go hurt more than she'd ever thought possible.

With surprisingly steady hands, she took the paper from him. At first, she actually did try to explain. *Mrs. O'Leary is my mother.*

Yet when she looked into his face and saw all her dreams reflected back at her, she could not speak. She had to commit these last moments to memory, for as soon as she spoke up, the interlude in the train car would be over.

But she would have her memories, would always remember him like this. Forever noble, forever handsome, forever perfect. He would never grow old in her eyes. He would never develop habits to annoy her. He would never raise his voice, lose his temper or take her for granted. He would always be the lover in the train car who had shown her a glimpse of paradise.

She wanted it to be enough. She prayed she could live on these memories for the rest of her life.

"Kate, love, are you all right?" he asked.

She nodded and set the paper aside. "I am, but...I must leave this place."

"Maybe you're right," he said, going to the window. He propped his arm on the edge and faced away from her. Over his shoulder she could see refugees, dazed and confused, exiting the other train cars. "Did you ever consider that we could simply disappear?"

"What do you mean?"

"Well, now that we've lost track of Father Michael and Bull, no one knows where we are. What if we were to go away?"

"Go where?"

"That's the beauty of it. I don't know. We could follow the sun and wind up in California. Or we could go to Canada, or take ship somewhere, letting the winds direct us. No one would ever know."

She laughed briefly. "Whyever would we do a thing like that? It's impossible."

"Oh, it's possible. Believe me, it is. An event like this fire—that just makes everything easy. Willingly or not, people will change their whole lives because of this fire. We could do it willingly, make our own choices, go our own way."

"What would our families think? It would be beyond cruel to allow them to believe we had died."

He was silent for a long time, as if he had not thought of that. Finally he said, "Never mind, it was a fanciful notion. I like your company. You make me too damned happy. I could spend all my days with you and you alone."

He smiled, looking so appealing that suddenly, without thinking, she launched herself into his embrace. As his arms went around her and he pressed his lips to her temple, she shut her eyes against a burning regret. In just a few days, loving him and touching him had become as natural to her as breathing. It was said habits took years to develop, but in this case, the saying was wrong. She had learned to love Dylan in an instant, and now she could not remember what her life had been like before he became a part of it.

Yet she would have to learn to go on, as one learned to go on after the death of a loved one. She thought of poor Gran, whose misplaced mass card had been the catalyst for her meeting Dylan. It was almost as if Gran had brought them together, an angel of destiny. But why would she do a thing like that? Didn't she know a love between a society favorite and an Irish maid could never survive?

Gran always did have a sense of humor.

And Kathleen, for all the grief deep in her heart, had learned to go on without Gran. She would do the same in Dylan's case. In the years to come, she would try not to picture him marrying a proper lady from a proper family, holding another woman in his arms at night, fathering children with jet-black hair and merry blue eyes.

"We must go. Right away," she said, more loudly than she had intended. She pulled herself from his embrace. "I really must go."

He gestured at the car with a sweep of his arm. "Sweetheart, we have everything we need here. Not the daintiest of fare, I admit, but I suspect it's a sight better than the rations they're serving at Lincoln Park. What is your great hurry?"

According to the paper, some thirty thousand refugees lay encamped at the waterfront park. She wondered if her family had gone there. She had to find them—absolutely had to.

"It's my family," she said at last.

"The ones staying at an estate west of town."

She shut her eyes and prayed for patience. He seemed determined to make this difficult for her, by making it so easy to lie. "I never said that."

"You said the West Division. And I maintain the city is still impassable. We'd be taking a bad risk, going out so soon."

She stood up and folded the green evening gown as best she could, tying one of the black velvet ribbons around it to form a beggar's bundle. Then she fastened Deborah Sinclair's diamonds inside the waistband of her skirt, feeling Dylan's eyes on her like a fall of sunlight. He didn't question her concealment of the jewels, probably assuming she wanted to protect them from robbers. What Dylan didn't know—yet—was that the jewels might already be considered stolen. The disaster had made her a common thief. She had taken possession of her mistress's diamonds and silk dress. She had helped herself to the clothing and food and belongings of whoever owned this parlor car.

"God forgive me," she whispered. Then she turned to Dylan. "You have been good to me," she said, willing her voice not to waver and betray her. "You have been my savior, my protector...my husband, my lover. But everything happened under extraordinary circumstances. Soon things will return to normal."

"Kate, what are you saying?"

She wet her lips, wishing there were an easier way to get the words out. "That I won't hold you to promises you made when you thought we were going to die.''

For a moment, a sheen of ice seemed to glaze his clear blue eyes, and the look was so chilling that it frightened her. But then he laughed. ''Is that what you're worried about, darling? That I won't stand by you now that the fire is out?''

''I'm saying you don't *have* to—''

''What sort of man do you take me for?'' He stood to his full, impressive height, looking splendid despite the shadow of his beard and the burned holes in his shirt and waistcoat. ''Dylan Francis Kennedy is a man of his word. In the courthouse, I took you as my lawful wedded wife.'' He strode across the carpet to her, pulling her against him so that she felt his heat, his shape, filling her with reminders of their passion. ''And right here in this train car, I took you as my lover. Those are bonds that won't be broken, Kate.'' The strange chill flickered in his eyes again. ''Unless you want it that way.''

''Ah, Dylan. The last thing I want is to undo what we did at the courthouse and…here.'' Even the most fleeting thought of his intimate caresses produced a blushing warmth in her. ''But things don't always turn out the way we want—''

''Hush.'' He stopped her with a firm kiss. His hand at her waist mapped the small bulge where she'd concealed the diamond-and-emerald jewelry. ''If you insist on finding your family, then of course that is what we'll do. I'll be with you every step of the way, Kate. I swear I will. I'd never abandon you, no matter what.''

That was exactly what she feared. Every pledge he made, every promise, bound her to him more inexorably. Yet even as her mind framed a protest, her heart spoke for her. She adored him so insanely that, when she saw him smiling down at her, a new hope was born.

Perhaps he would forgive her deception. Perhaps he was as deeply in love as she. Seeing where she came from wouldn't change that.

"All right," she said. "And bless you for it, Dylan Kennedy."

A soft thoughtfulness came over his face.

"What is it?" she asked anxiously. "Why are you staring at me like that?"

He smiled. "No one's ever blessed me before."

Finding their way through the smoldering city proved to be a dangerous ordeal. Fallen buildings and warehouses forced them to take a meandering path across the city. They passed Terrace Row, its once fashionable, expensive town homes now reduced to eerie, silent tombs. Field and Leiter's marble palace, once a monument to prosperity, had been reduced to broken walls, the interior filled with unrecognizable debris fused solid by the tremendous heat. Everything looked so strange to Kathleen, from the sooty cornerstone of the *Tribune* building, to the jagged walls rearing up through the business district. An occasional naked tree or telegraph post pierced the horizon. The river moved sluggishly, littered to its banks with half-burned bridge timbers, ships blackened to the water-line and matter that exuded such a noxious odor she held her sleeve against her face and refused to look at it.

Plumbing pipes and iron stoves lay everywhere. A pile of timothy hay, half-consumed, still burned with occasional jets of fire spurting from its sides. Coal heaps glowed like the inside of a volcano.

All her life, she had lived in this city. Now she felt as if she walked the face of another planet. She did not recognize where she was. None of the familiar landmarks remained.

Shadows darted in and out of the ruins, survivors who, for reasons of their own, did not want to be found. She recalled the prisoners released from the courthouse jail and shivered, but then reminded herself she was every bit the deceiver.

A passing police patrolman hailed them. His breath reeked of alcohol, but he was helpful enough, directing them toward Madison Street where, he promised, the horse car was running.

"And if you need it," the officer added somberly, "they've set up a morgue in the livery stable on Milwaukee."

She felt Dylan's eyes on her and set her chin. "No," she said firmly. "No one we know died in the fire."

"The lady's right," Dylan said, tightening his arm around her.

"The homeless and hungry will be served down at a packing house at Eighteenth and the river," the officer said, eyeing their disheveled state. "The mayor has already issued a proclamation against sales of any liquor."

But not against drinking it, Kathleen thought wryly.

"That's sure to be a popular one." Dylan thanked the officer and they continued half walking, half climbing over the still-hot rubble. From passersby they obtained more snippets of news. Hastily printed broadsheets with screaming headlines appeared, distributed by eager newsboys.

And to Kathleen's dismay, some reports named Mrs. Catherine O'Leary as the cause of the holocaust. The *Tribune* called her parents "The worthy old couple who owned the cow stable" while the *Times* was full of vitriol, describing her mother as "an old hag and a pensioner of the county." Another report blamed "a tall, stout, Irish woman with no intelligence" and her husband, "a fast talker with a rich brogue, a stupid-looking sort of a man, who acknowledged himself that he could neither read nor write."

Each and every report darted painfully into Kathleen, though Dylan didn't seem to notice her sinking emotions. The papers were absurdly wrong, but that didn't seem to matter to the journalists bent on creating a sensation with words. She wanted to rip the accusing paper to shreds. Instead she decided to change the subject.

"What of your family?" she asked. "Will they be frantic when they hear of the fire?"

He hesitated, then said, "Of course. I'll send a wire as soon as I locate a telegraph office."

"You've not spoken of them," she pointed out, and suddenly the omission seemed odd.

"Isn't much to say." He grinned. "But I assure you, the news of our marriage is sure to be received with delight."

He hadn't really told her anything, she realized, but didn't pursue it. Soon enough, her own secret would be revealed. Still, she couldn't keep from imagining his wealthy parents. They probably lived very handsomely in a fine old Boston house. How proud they must be of their charming son. What would they think when they learned he had married a pauper?

They wended their way through the wreckage. In the smoky distance she saw a hulking silhouette of stone. As they drew closer, the shape took on the familiar profile of St. Brendan's church. Kathleen stared at it in astonishment. "It worked," she said breathlessly. "It's still standing." She grew dizzy looking up at the roof, remembering how Dylan had risked himself to wet down the building and keep the steeple from igniting the rest of it. "You saved it. All but the steeple."

"Not hardly." He seemed totally unimpressed with himself. "The thing's gutted. It'll probably have to be torn down."

"It could be rebuilt," she insisted. "The walls and roof look perfectly sound. Come spring, the gardens will grow again."

"Sometimes the damage is too great," he said gently but knowingly. "Some things aren't worth saving."

"But you prom—" She stopped herself and shrugged. In truth, she had no business reminding him of any promise he had made, even his expansive pledge to spend his own fortune to rebuild the church. As soon as he met her family, he would understand her deception and she would have no choice but to release him from all vows.

At McCormick's reaper factory across the river, cables, anchors and pig iron formed an evil-looking soup. Iron fences had melted, columns pulverized. The courthouse had literally collapsed in on itself, its limestone walls reduced to liquid.

A chill slid over Kathleen's skin. The holocaust

had decimated the place where she and Dylan had married. Surely that was a sign that they never should have gone through with it.

Yet for the life of her, she still held off explaining. Though she knew it was weak and infantile, she could not bring herself to tell Dylan in plain words that she was the daughter of the infamous Mrs. O'Leary, an Irish immigrant who milked cows for a living.

In a secret corner of her heart, she believed that taking him in person to her family would soften the blow. Perhaps when he met the O'Learys, he would take Lucy Hathaway's point of view that social divisions were artificial and easily crossed. Oh, please, thought Kathleen. Let it be so. Let him love me for the person I am rather than despise me for the place I come from.

She pushed aside her private misgivings over the deception. When he met her family, his heart would melt.

Aye, that was it. Let him see for himself that her mother was a kind, good woman, not the irresponsible, drunken harridan the papers depicted. Let him meet baby James and Mary, and Connor and Frank and her dear father who worked so hard. Then perhaps Dylan would understand why she could not go away with him, could not simply disappear from the middle of her own life.

And in an even smaller, more secretive part of her heart, she had another barely acknowledged hope. This was Dylan Kennedy. He was known not just for his charm, his looks and his family fortune. Last night, he had also proven his compassion and humanity. Hadn't she seen it with her own eyes? Hadn't she seen him pull a toddler from certain death and defend a church from the flames?

Those were not the actions of a man who would scorn people because they were poor. Perhaps he would take one look at her simple, hardworking family and see them for what they were—people who were worthy, though not lucky enough to be born in the right place to the right people with the right fortune.

Dylan would love them anyway, because he was a man with a loving heart.

Suddenly Kathleen felt sure of that. He would accept her family. He would use all his power and all his wealth to help them. Then Kathleen *would* have the genteel way of life she'd always craved. She trusted it as she had never trusted her instincts before. Yes, he would fall in love with the O'Learys as he had fallen in love with her. She should never have doubted him.

As they exited the Madison horse car, she pressed him into a broken doorway where no one could see them and kissed him hard on the mouth. When she drew back, he was grinning.

"What the devil was that for? This couldn't be another of your last-thing-I-do kisses, could it?"

She flushed, remembering her rash aggression the night of the fire. "No. I just wanted to show you that I'm sorry."

"Sorry for what?"

"For misjudging you. I was wrong to think you were like that, and I apologize."

"Like what?" he asked cautiously.

"A terrible snob who looks down on the poor and doesn't believe they are fit to mingle with."

"When did I say that?"

"You didn't. I just thought you believed it, and then I realized how wrong I was, and I'm sorry I thought it at all."

Laughing, he took her hand. "My love, you will never grow bored with yourself," he predicted. "You have the unique talent of conducting entire quarrels and conversations in your head, without even needing a second party to talk things over with."

His humor buoyed her along Clinton Street as they headed south. They had found the westernmost edge of the fire, a neighborhood of cottages and shanties. People were bringing lost children by the cartload to the Half-Orphan Asylum a few blocks north. To the east lay a wasteland of powdered embers. Every so often, they encountered a house or two that had managed to survive.

As they drew nearer and nearer to Number 137 de Koven Street, Kathleen felt her mood sinking by inches. It was one thing to romanticize their Romeo and Juliet affair, but quite another to make the rest of the world understand it.

"Kate, love, are you certain you know where you are?" Dylan asked. "This doesn't look like the sort of place your family would—"

"I know exactly where I am," she said faintly.

The next half block resembled an unhealthy set of teeth, with gaps where houses used to stand. Kathleen hardly dared to breathe for the suspense. She craned her neck to see if her family's home had been spared.

It had.

As she looked at it, with its charred wood siding and broken-out windows, a black scar of scorched earth where the cowshed used to be, she felt a lurch of her heart.

This was the lowliest hovel on the block, but it was the place where she had been raised, where she had learned to keep rhythm at the butter churn while her mother sang ballads and where her father's laughter rang to the rafters even when times were hard.

Sitting in front of the house, on the blackened steps, was a woman in a robe and kerchief. She sat with her head bent and her knees drawn up. The pose and the gray smoky air made her look older than her years.

Kathleen must have made some sound, half sob, half gasp, for Dylan sent her a questioning look. "Do you know this poor woman?"

At that moment, her mother looked up. Her face, which had been drawn in sorrow, suddenly bloomed with a smile of purest relief and thankfulness. Too moved to speak, she simply stood and opened her arms. Kathleen broke away from Dylan and went to her, feeling the strong, familiar embrace that had kept her feeling safe and loved all her life. Into the smoky, damp shoulder, she murmured, "Mam. Oh dear God, Mam, you're all right."

Her mother pulled back, her work-worn hands cradling Kathleen's face, stroking her hair. "Blessed be," she said. "Blessed, blessed be."

"The others...?"

"All fine, but we've nary a thing left except this broken old house." Her eyes shone as she kissed Kathleen's forehead. "And I've never been richer, colleen, never."

A masculine clearing of the throat reminded Kathleen of the less pleasant duty that lay before her. Now she had to untangle the web of lies that had brought her to this place. Trying to appear calm, she took both her mother's hands in hers. Feeling the calluses and creases of labor there, she had a brief, swift vision of herself at her mother's age—and the vision terrified her. God forgive her, but she didn't want the life Mam had endured, with all the hard work and babies and worries keeping her awake at night.

She squared her shoulders and drew her mother to the front boardwalk. "I've brought someone to meet you," she said simply, and turned to face Dylan.

He stood back, regarding the two of them with a puzzled expression. "One of your domestics?" he asked.

Her mother, who had inherited Gran's sense of humor, burst out laughing. "Sure and who is this fine gentleman, then?"

With the inborn grace that had captivated Kathleen in her first glimpse of him, Dylan bowed from the waist. "Dylan Francis Kennedy, ma'am."

"My, but you've the manners on you, sir. You must be one of the nobs from the North Side." She dipped her head and averted her eyes in deference.

Kathleen felt a deep and secret shame at her mother's servile attitude. You're just as good as anyone, Mam, she wanted to scream. She always wanted to scream when her mother dipped and scraped before the monied folk, but she never did.

Dylan's smile was charming, though still baffled. Kathleen took a deep breath, knowing she could put this off no longer. She held her mother's hand tightly.

"Mam," she said, "Dylan and I were married late Sunday night." Before either could react, she put her hand out to her husband. "Dylan, this is my mother, Mrs. Catherine O'Leary."

Nothing. No sound or movement. Even the autumn wind ceased to blow.

Kathleen could feel her mother's fingers chill. She could see the same arctic cold suddenly freeze in Dylan Kennedy's eyes.

Dropping her outstretched hand, she tried to pluck a bit of courage from the silence. Dylan loved *her*, she reminded herself, not her financial circumstances. It didn't matter one whit that her family had nothing. His own vast fortune would suffice for the two of them. And if he was any kind of a son-in-law at all, it would keep her family as well.

It was Dylan who spoke first. He drew himself to his full, impressive height, and gave her a smile that was as cold as a winter moon. Insolence, and a dark admiration, flickered in his face. "Brava, my dear. You gave a masterful performance. You actually had me—and all of society as well—believing you were an heiress."

"I never meant to—"

"Please." He held up one hand, palm out. She could scarcely believe it was the same hand that had caressed her so tenderly she had nearly wept. "Don't spoil the show with stammering explanations. Your maneuvering was utter perfection. Leave it at that, Kate."

"Kathleen," she said, scarcely able to speak as her insides shriveled up. "Kathleen Bridget O'Leary. I signed the marriage certificate in that way exactly."

"That will teach me to inspect signatures." He pointed his toe and bowed, right there in the middle of the road. A few neighbors had wandered out of the ruins to watch. "Kathleen Bridget O'Leary, if I had not lost my hat in the fire, I would doff it to you. I thought myself too wise in the ways of the world to fall for a trick like that, but you fooled me. You charmed and beguiled every soul you met that night. There should be some special prize for your performance."

He straightened and addressed her mother. "It was an honor to meet you, ma'am. You've a daughter of rare talents." The cold, silvery rage flashed in his eyes as he regarded Kathleen one last time. "Perhaps we'll meet again one day," he informed her, "when hell freezes over."

With that, he turned smartly and walked away, looking dignified, unapproachable and intimidating as he strode toward Madison and the horse car.

Kathleen had turned to stone. She was unable to think, to feel, to move as she watched him go. She stood like a statue, the burned and tattered Worth gown still tucked under her arm, all her dreams as cold as corpses inside her.

She never wanted to move again. Never wanted to breathe or speak or even blink. Because she knew that if she did, she would shatter.

Her stare stayed riveted on the tall, black-haired man walking away. At the end of the block, a mound of wheat still burned. When he walked past it, a plume of fire jetted out, followed by a black billow of smoke. And when the smoke cleared, he was gone, as if he had disappeared with the wave of a magician's wand. As if he had been a dream.

"Well, miss." Her mother's voice came to her as if from a vast distance. "And what is it you've got yourself into now?"

The words melted her strange, frozen state. It was a painful thawing, for Kathleen was forced to feel everything at its most intense. She had never experienced a broken heart before. Indeed, she had thought it a fiction invented by poets and singers. But now she knew. A broken heart hurt with a pain so sharp she could not even scream or rant or beat her breast— all those things she associated with heartbreak. All she could do was turn to her mother and feel the scalding tears press at the backs of her eyes. She held in her grief, unwilling to weep.

"There, there," her mother said, tucking a sturdy arm around Kathleen's waist. "Come inside, then, so the neighborhood snoops will find something else to spy on."

Kathleen allowed herself to be led into the dim little cottage, marveling that it still stood after the fire had swept through the neighborhood. She set her meager bundle on a stool. Little James and Mary ran to her on chubby legs, clinging to her and giggling until her mother swatted them off with an affectionate pat.

"Where are Da and the lads?" Kathleen finally managed to ask.

"Out scavenging for supplies, like everyone else. The place was left standing, but the barn's gone, my new wagon burnt and all the winter stores of hay and shavings are ash." She gestured at the plank table of pine, pale from all the years of scrubbing. "Sit down, colleen, and we'll have a chat."

Kathleen moved stiffly, like a mechanical doll. The way she felt inside, it was a wonder she was able to move or even think. Yet here she was, on a visit with her mam, just as if it were her half day off.

"Do you know, Mam, what they're saying in the papers?"

Infinite patience shone in her lined face. "Not that I've read it myself, but Mrs. McLaughlin's boy was by to show me a story or two. And some ee-jit reporter came to ask me if it was a rough night when the fires came."

Despite her world coming apart, Kathleen's lips twitched with a smile. "And how did you answer, Mam?"

"'Rough!' says I, 'Why my God, man, it was a terror to the world!'" She leaned back on the bench and sucked her teeth. Finally, she added, "It could've started here, colleen. I'd be seven times a liar if I denied it."

"Ah, Mam, there've been fires everywhere in this terrible drought. A spark from anyone's stove could have landed in any barn or mill."

"They say I'll be called to answer before the Board of Fire."

"Where you'll tell them the truth, and they'll know it for an act of God."

Her mother nodded, then fell silent for a time. Behind the curtain, the little ones tumbled about, giggling and stacking blocks of wood, then knocking them down. Kathleen knew her mother was waiting. She knew she would have to speak of what she had done. Better now, she told herself, than after Da and the boys returned.

"It's true, what I told you about Dylan Kennedy," she said. His name stuck in her throat like unshed tears. "I married him Sunday night. We were trapped in the courthouse and we thought we'd die for certain."

She remembered with utter clarity the emotions that had blazed through her. Terror, yes, that was to be expected. But she had felt a curious and rare exhilaration as well, clinging to Dylan, waiting for the end. In that moment she had thanked God, realizing that she would die in the grip of something many women would never discover in a lifetime—a perfect, all-consuming love.

Or so she had thought. Apparently she had not realized what was going through Dylan's head at the time. Speaking past a knot of shame in her throat, she explained the prank she and the young ladies of Miss Boylan's had played, and how the fire had turned the world inside out.

"I tried to come home, Mam, but there was no getting through the city," she said. "Near midnight, we took shelter in St. Brendan's, but we had to leave when the steeple burned." She recounted the terror and thrill of watching Dylan on the roof, the drama of racing for the safety of the courthouse.

"There was a priest," she continued. "A Father Michael McCoughy."

"Ah, the new young priest," her mother said. "I recognize the name though I've never seen him say Mass."

"There was a judge present as well." She went on to describe Kirby Lane, the clerk, and the escaped convict called Bull. Her mother gasped aloud when she admitted the mayor himself had attended her wedding.

"Think of it, then, the most important nobs in the city at my own daughter's wedding."

If things had been left at that, just the swift, terrifying ceremony and then they'd gone their separate ways, Kathleen could have endured. She might even have cherished the memory of the drama, told her grandchildren of it one day. But the story didn't end there.

"After we managed to escape," Kathleen said, leaning forward and lowering her voice so the little ones wouldn't hear, "we found shelter."

"Ah, that's lucky then, that is."

Kathleen swallowed and forced herself to go on. "It was a Pullman car, Mam, all tricked out like the finest room in the Hotel Royale."

Her mother made a lightning sign of the cross. "Jesus, Mary and Joseph, he tupped you."

*Repeatedly.*

Kathleen heated with a fever, remembering all the ways he had loved her, all the ways she had let him, all the ways she had learned to love him. She did not have to respond to her mother's statement. The truth was written all over her flushed face.

"Tell me this, colleen," her mother said. "Do you love him?"

Kathleen shut her eyes as her heart trembled. "You saw him, Mam."

"Aye, the angel Gabriel come to earth, he is. Ah, but I do admire those black Irish looks, I do." Her mother took her hands, and Kathleen opened her eyes. "Colleen," her mother persisted, "the face of an angel can't soothe the soul or soften the advancing years. Only love can do that. So I'll ask again. Do you love the man?"

"I thought he was everything I ever wanted. I thought what I was feeling was love."

"No wonder you—" She seemed to remember herself and shut her mouth.

Kathleen was proud of herself for not breaking down as she tried to explain. "When I went through with the wedding, it didn't matter whether I loved him or not. I thought I was going to die with him. I thought that served as reason enough. Later, after we survived, I truly did believe it was love. He made me feel— Ah, Mam, he made me feel like a born princess, he did."

"Just what you wanted all your life," her mother said quietly.

Filled with shame, Kathleen stood abruptly and went to the window, gazing out across the burned yard. A thick length of chain and part of the ruined wagon lay amid the ashes. Other than that, she did not recognize the place. She hung her head. "I didn't think you knew, Mam."

"A mother always knows. Always."

Kathleen despised herself in those black moments. What had it been like for her mother, working so hard every day just to get by, knowing that all her efforts would never give her eldest daughter what she yearned for?

"I'm so sorry," she whispered. "I should have known there was a penalty for reaching for something beyond my grasp."

"Sorry, is it?" her mother blustered. "Is that all you have to say?"

"I don't know what else—" Kathleen stopped and looked closely at her mother. Sure enough, she detected a gleam in her eye. "Mam?" she asked. "What are you thinking?"

"We're left with nary a thing. The roof over our head is all, but that won't keep our bellies full."

"I could never go back to work for Miss Sinclair,

not after all that's happened," Kathleen said. "She probably wouldn't trust me, anyway, nor would Miss Boylan. But I'll find work somewhere else."

"Whatever for, colleen? You're married to a rich nob of a fellow. Why in heaven's name would you do a servant's work?"

Kathleen realized her mother's intent. "Ah, no, Mam, you saw what happened just now. I dared to hope the same thing—that once he met you, he would be only too glad to look after the lot of us. I didn't believe such things would matter if the love was strong enough. I was wrong, though. He walked away from me. I'll never see him again."

"He's your husband, for pity's sake."

"I don't even know if the marriage was lawful."

"Sanctified by a priest." She clasped her hands. "Witnessed by the mayor himself and performed by a judge. If that ain't lawful, then what is?"

"I don't even think there's a record of it."

"No papers signed, sealed?"

"Well, yes, since we were in the courthouse, we had a document—"

"Where is it?" Her mother waited tensely.

Kathleen closed her eyes, trying to recall. "I can't remember. It was signed all around, and notarized, and then...Mr. Lane took a turn for the worse, and... I've no idea who took charge of the certificate."

"Then it might be found. Good. You'll need that."

"For what, Mam?"

"Why, for proof, you goose."

"Ah, no. I'll not go tearing after a man who can't abide the sight of me."

"Where is your pride, girl? Where is your pluck?" Her mother bustled around the cabin, seizing the green silk dress and shaking it out, critically eyeing the damage. "You were that close to having what you always wanted," she said, measuring an inch between thumb and forefinger.

"But Mam—" Even as she tried to frame a protest, a righteous indignation took hold of Kathleen's heart. She knew then that it wasn't broken at all, but strong with determination and resolve. "You're absolutely right, Mam. I've a duty to my family and myself. I must claim my place as Dylan Kennedy's lawfully wedded wife."

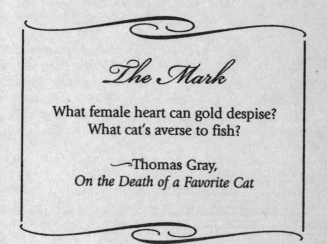

## The Mark

What female heart can gold despise?
What cat's averse to fish?

—Thomas Gray,
*On the Death of a Favorite Cat*

# *Eleven*

As Dylan loitered in the rail yard by the lake and drank from a stolen bottle of whiskey, he tried to remember how many times he had been married, and which of the unions had been legitimate. But for the moment, all he could think about was his latest wife.

"To Kathleen O'Leary." He lifted his bottle in mock salute. It still felt strange, saying her real name. Kate or even Katie had suited the bright, clever, beautiful young woman who had captivated him with a blink of her emerald eyes.

She had been all freshness and innocence, refinement and privilege. She'd possessed the sort of unconventional and unabashed sexuality men usually only dreamed about. She'd been everything he desired in a woman, neatly presented in one delectable package. A fantasy made of diamonds and silk, perfumed with a floral opiate that robbed him of his reason. Who could have known she concealed the cold, indifferent conscience of a con artist?

Dylan was furious—at himself, not her, though he could probably whip himself into a fury over her if he slowed down on the whiskey. He had spent his life creating illusions and should have seen right through her ruse. But she'd been so damned good. She'd given a flawless performance. Her accent and mannerisms had been dead-on in her portrayal of the perfect little heiress on an adventure.

At least he could take comfort in the fact that she had fallen for his trick as well. Although he had wanted to stick around to see her reaction when she learned she had not, in fact, married the toast of Chicago, he knew the time had come to disappear. He was broke, he was in trouble, and hanging around this smoldering wreck of a city wouldn't do him any good at all.

"Let's see," he said to his drinking partner. "I think the first one I married had it annulled when she found out my true age."

"Why'd she do a thing like that?" Eugene Waxman, better known as Bull, had returned to the rail yard to hop a freighter out of town. He had encountered Dylan, who convinced him to delay his departure, have a drink and listen to his tale of woe.

They sat leaning against a stack of crossties at the waterfront, surveying the activity in the Illinois and Michigan Central yard. The string of cars with the Pullman had been moved aside and presumably forgotten. Dylan figured he could probably make use of the car until he decided where to go next.

He used to find this peripatetic way of life exciting, but lately the thought of embarking on yet another journey wearied him. Kathleen had been far too entertaining. Her absence left a shadowy hole in him.

"Well," he said, thinking back to the chaotic years of his youth, "since the lady had two grown sons, she wasn't thrilled to find herself wed to a fourteen-year-old." He grinned crookedly at the expression on Bull's face. "I've always looked mature for my age. Could raise a beard by the time I was thirteen." The few days he had spent with that first wife—Mabel was her name—had been pleasant indeed. She had a decent income from her late husband's property, and big white breasts as soft and fragrant as bread dough.

When she had discovered that he wasn't twenty-one, as he'd claimed, she went off to puke into a chamber pot. She'd hired a discreet solicitor to quietly invalidate the marriage and then had engaged her largest son to send Dylan out of town wearing the livid stripes of a horsewhip on his back.

"Over the next few years I steered clear of marriage," he admitted, passing the bottle to Bull. "But not women. Christ, who could give up women?"

"I hear you." Nodding his great head, Bull took another swig.

"I promised to marry a couple of them, but I always escaped after I took what I needed."

"Money, jewels, that sort of thing," Bull said knowingly.

"Yeah." Dylan was starting to like Bull. Nothing shocked him. Considering his past—a slave in Missouri, a fugitive in Illinois, a Chicago convict freed by the fire—he had seen a lot worse than a confidence game. "But I always made sure I left them with blissful memories." Dylan was sincere in this. In the only way he knew how, he gave them what he could—physical pleasure, a few laughs, assurances that they were all stunningly beautiful. If they were hoping for anything more than that—and most women, annoyingly, were—they had to look elsewhere.

After that first fiasco, he should have stuck with married women and he should have worked alone—a bit of wisdom he'd learned the hard way. At the age of fifteen, he had fallen in with a gang run by a

ruthless boss in New York City. He'd learned unde-
tectable methods of picking pockets, all manner of
sales swindles and shady games from "Honest John"
to carnival roulette.

But he'd acquired the skills at a price. At the hands
of a man named Lyle Watts, Dylan had discovered
exactly how much torture the human spirit could endure. He had been pushed beyond his limit. He remembered Lyle's scent of bay rum, the iron strength
in his big hands and the suffocating quality of the
darkness in which he imprisoned his prey. In
exchange for the protection of his organization, the
gang boss had forced Dylan to do things that even
now, years later, made his guts twist and shrink with
revulsion. In freeing himself of the painful grip of
Lyle Watts, he had discovered his true talent. He was
a gifted escape artist.

It was a skill that would serve him well in later
years.

"Eventually, though, I did marry again," he explained, brushing aside the tainted memories of gang
life. "Twice. Three times, I guess, if you count Sunday night's phony heiress."

"Looked real enough to me," Bull said unhelp-
fully. In the rail yard, workers hurried to and fro,
switching tracks and getting ready for relief shipments
from other cities. Watching them, Bull stroked his
chin as if wishing for a shave. "Three times?"

"Yeah. The next was to a lady who died and left
me a bit of money." He could not say more, for he
had no idea how to explain Cecilia. Lyle Watts had
ordered him to woo and wed the delicate, consump-
tive woman who was doomed to die of her illness in
a matter of months. Hardened by the Watts gang, Dy-

lan figured Cecilia St. James for an easy mark. She lay bedridden, lacking a family and desperately lonely.

But she'd surprised him. Her huge eyes, staring out of her pale, wasted face, haunted him. At their very first meeting, she managed to break his heart. She inspired in him a fierce protectiveness that was as close to love as he had ever felt. He told Lyle he wanted to back out of the deal, but it was Cecilia who had been so insistent. And so, speaking vows in the shrouded silence of a sickroom, he had married her. A few months later, she died in his arms, whispering his name, never knowing the true reason he'd made her his wife.

He wished he had been more careful with her fortune. It was gone in six months, frittered away by failed schemes Lyle had cooked up.

Even the harsh lessons of gang life failed to wise him up, however, and he'd acquired another partner. In a saloon in the Bowery he had met Vincent Costello, the only mark ever to catch on to Dylan's special method of shortchanging. Rather than take revenge on Dylan, Costello had proposed a partnership. Dylan had agreed, for Vince had seemed a kind mentor in contrast to Lyle. He was as smart and ruthless as any good con artist, but somehow managed to retain his humanity underneath. Dylan could see it when he spoke of his wife and daughter, claiming in all sincerity that he would die for them.

Dylan had been intrigued by the concept. He couldn't imagine another person in his life being so important he would die for her.

"What about the next one?" Bull asked, clearly intrigued.

"Dinah." Dylan giggled and drank some more. "I used to recite couplets because her name rhymes with—"

A shrill whistle pierced the air, and with a grinding of machinery, a train rolled in, its cars marked with the colophon of Cincinnati. Crates stenciled *Relief Aid for Chicago* and *Catholic Relief* were stacked high on the flatbed cars.

"So what about Dinah?" Bull asked, raising his voice to be heard over the chuffing of the locomotive.

"Richer than Croesus."

"Who's he?"

Dylan shrugged. "Some rich fellow."

Dinah Galloway had treated him like a spoiled lapdog, lavishing him with attention, parading him out to social engagements so her friends could marvel at his dramatically handsome looks and fine manners. During this period, he had learned the ways of high society, quickly adopting the proper accent, mannerisms and sense of style exhibited by the old-money rich. He told people he had gone to Harvard, and they believed him because he knew the secret handshake of the Porcellian Club. He claimed ties to an old Boston family, inventing an impressive pedigree for himself. He effortlessly talked his way into the most exclusive men's clubs and high-class parties in the city.

He might have gone on indefinitely pretending to belong to a society that would despise him if they knew his true background. For a while, he'd enjoyed the power and privilege of his status, the fine food and stylish clothing, the pretty French maids who let him tumble them in the linen closets of the Galloway mansion.

But Dinah Galloway became a leech upon his soul.

Her demands and appetites challenged even his un-usually broad experience in sexual matters. Since his initiation by Mabel, he had developed a number of proficiencies, often out of necessity. But his rich mistress's craving for energetic, slightly violent sex always left him feeling odd and soiled. Her manic, ravenous needs drained him in ways he had never imagined, and he found himself facing each day with dread and weariness.

At the first opportunity he had left, taking a good share of her jewelry with him. The marriage hadn't been legal, anyway. Everything he had put on the marriage certificate had been a lie, including his name, his birthplace and where he'd been educated.

"She was too strange, even for me," he said to Bull, and decided against elaborating. It was almost a relief to hook up with his old crony, Costello, again. By that time, Costello was widowed, his daughter grown and just out of parochial school.

"After leaving Dinah, my partner and I joined a revue—burlesque acts, performing animals, that sort of thing—based in Buffalo. I was the best escape artist, contortionist and daredevil in the show."

"Best liar, too, I reckon." Bull took a swig from the bottle and made a blissful face.

"I'm an excellent liar," he admitted readily, "but not about the revue. Ever hear of the marquis de Bontemps?"

"Hell, yeah. Everybody's heard of him. Crazy French fellow who crossed Niagara Falls on a tightrope."

Dylan grabbed the bottle and raised it in salute. *"Le marquis, c'est moi,"* he declared.

"Huh?"

"I'm the marquis de Bontemps. Or was, until he retired."

Bull narrowed his eyes. "Horseshit. They say he fell in and was never seen again."

"Well, you're looking at him now."

Dylan vividly recalled the terror and bone-crushing ordeal of the most daring stunt of his career. It was supposed to have been his escape from Vincent Costello. The two of them had not been getting along, and Costello's daughter Faith had added an uncomfortable element to the partnership.

Faith, a quiet, pious girl who was the apple of her father's eye, had decided that she'd fallen in love with Dylan. He liked Faith and often felt a brotherly devotion to her, but love was something he neither understood nor believed in. When her thoughts turned to marriage, he had "fallen" into the churning rapids with most of their earnings wrapped in oilcloth and strapped to his belt, hoping he'd seen the last of Costello and Faith. The sweetness of freedom had been balm for the many wounds and bruises of the ordeal.

But on Sunday night, it had become clear that he'd misjudged his old partner, who was even more experienced and more unscrupulous than Dylan. Costello had tracked him down. Only the convenient timing of the fire had saved his skin.

Bull proved to be a pleasant and congenial drunk. He leaned back against the stack of beams and, within a few minutes, was snoring. In the distance, Dylan could see a group of patrolmen, hastily called up and deputized to guard the relief supplies. Despite the whiskey, he still had enough common sense to cover Bull with an old, half-burned saddle blanket he'd found somewhere, concealing the prison stripes. Then

Dylan stood up, swaying a little as the bright inner fire of the whiskey lit his head.

He studied the empty bottle in his hand and tossed it away. It didn't break on the sandy shore. Looking out across the rail yard, he spent a few blurry moments contemplating the Pullman where he and Kathleen had holed up to escape the fire.

The whiskey had failed to do its job, for a flood of inexcusably deep sentiments washed through him. That train car had been their hideaway, their private retreat from the world. For two days, his life had been more splendid than he had dared to believe life could be.

And like everything else, it was a sham. She was a counterfeit heiress who had wed a fraudulent bachelor under false pretenses. He wondered why he felt so betrayed, why he was taking it so hard. It wasn't as if he had never been abandoned before, had never fled a risky situation or had to start over again. It wasn't as if he hadn't committed similar betrayals of his own.

Perhaps, he reflected woozily, the sting of betrayal came from the fact that Kathleen had reminded him that dreams sometimes did come true. But not his dreams. He was a fool to even consider the possibility.

For a long time he stood looking out at the lake, a vast fresh sea stretching out to eternity. Behind him, he could hear the noises of the rail yard. From the shouts and clamor, he gathered that more relief had come in, as well as firefighters and engineers from other cities. Before the fires were even out, Chicago was already rebuilding itself.

It was a concept Dylan could relate to.

He nudged at Bull with the toe of his shoe. Vaguely he recalled helping himself to the good leather shoes at a cobbler's shop, blithely telling the proprietor to send a bill around to a false address. He wished all transactions could be so simple.

"Bull," he said. "Time to go."

Bull snorted in protest, but dragged his eyes open. At some point, and without much deliberation, Dylan had decided to travel with Bull for a while. The ex-convict was a man of few words, a trait Dylan deeply appreciated. Bull hadn't asked too many questions about the situation with Kathleen. He was also intimidatingly huge, another useful quality when traveling to unknown places. "We'd better see what's pulling out of here," he suggested.

Bull nodded and stretched his enormous body, looking like the strong man in Phineas Barnum's traveling revue. "Where to?" he asked.

"Let's go see if we can find something bound for St. Louis. That'll give us all the choices we need."

"I ain't going to the South," Bull said.

"But it's not—" Dylan stopped himself. He was wrong to expect Bull to return to a land that held such hellish memories for him, even if it was no longer legal to own slaves. Somewhere down in Missouri, on a farm, Eugene Waxman had lived in bondage to another man. Dylan didn't blame him for never wanting to return. He knew all about running from nightmares. "We'll head west, then. Maybe get ourselves all the way to California."

"California." Bull tasted the word, then nodded his head. "All right." He stared out across the churning lake. "I did like Chicago, though."

"So did I."

They went over to one of the trains, where the unloading had almost finished. A knot of people stood about. Dylan hung back. He and Bull would wait until the empty train pulled out, then hop into an untended car. Acrid smoke huffed into the air, and the smell of hot steel wafted from the tracks.

"Say farewell to Chicago, my friend," Dylan said.

Bull hesitated, studying the crowd. He stuck his hands in his pockets and rocked back on his heels. "Don't you think," he remarked, "that you should say goodbye to your wife first?"

Dylan frowned, turning to Bull. "What—ah, hell."

Moving through the crowd, like a ship with emerald-green sails unfurled, Kathleen O'Leary bore down on them.

The long trek through the ruins had put Kathleen in high dudgeon. Her family had not allowed her to wallow in misery for long. She knew better than to let something as trivial as a broken heart hold her back. A lively talk from her mother had filled her with determination to keep what was hers by right—Dylan Kennedy.

Her mother had hastily brushed the green silk gown and had mended the more obvious tears and holes, declaring that Kathleen should dress the part of the lady she had become by marrying him. No O'Leary would allow herself to be abandoned by a man, her mother had said.

Kathleen had embraced the notion and set out on her own. She had not expected to find him, but here he was, near the rail yard where she had become his wife in every sense of the word. By the time she found him, she was in a fury.

And he was reeling drunk. She could tell, even from a distance, for she was an Irishwoman with a sense about such things. She recognized the slack insolence of his grin, the negligent but unsteady grace with which he held himself.

She barely acknowledged Bull with a curt nod. He wisely stepped out of the way, seeming to guess she did not wish to be trifled with.

She made straight for Dylan. But the moment she stopped in front of him, all the angry words she'd stored up deserted her.

He doffed an imaginary hat. "Ah, my little fortune hunter is back. What is it you require? More compliments on your artful maneuvering? More applause for your finesse at deception?" Before she could duck away, he chucked her under the chin, his touch deceptively gentle. He smiled coldly down at her. "I was fooled from the very first moment I saw you, love. Did you know that?"

"You're drunk," she said uselessly.

"But that will pass." He walked down to the lakeshore as if taking a casual stroll along the beach. "Being a lying, cheating, gold-digging little swindler won't," he called over his shoulder.

She flinched, having no choice but to follow him. "Dylan." She swallowed, stung by the idea that he could so easily dismiss the past few days. She wanted to find the man who had shown her the world from a balcony, proposed to her on bended knee, married her in the midst of disaster, then taken her to bed where he had introduced her to wonders beyond imagining. "You must give me a chance to explain."

"Ah, no." Without slowing his pace, he held up a hand to stop her. "Don't be like the magician revealing his secrets. You'll spoil the elegance of your ruse.''

''It wasn't a ruse.'' She forced herself to step in front of him and look up into his cold, narrowed eyes. ''Not in the way you think. And, anyway, what started out as a prank became something…real.''

''As real as your banking fortune,'' he scoffed. ''Step aside. I wish to take a walk. *Alone*.''

She let him pass, but continued walking at his side. The chill gray water bit at the shore littered with charred debris from the fire. ''Didn't our whirlwind courtship, our wedding vows, our—'' she blushed to remind him ''—our um, honeymoon, mean a thing to you? Only yesterday, you swore you loved me.''

He fell silent, and just for a heartbeat, she dared to hope she had reached a core of decency inside him. ''Did I?'' he said. ''Fancy that.'' Then he burst out laughing, although his laughter had a bitter edge. ''Tell me, what was your game before? Were you an actress?''

''Certainly not.''

''You had to've been.'' He leaned forward, towering over her, insisting on an answer. ''How the hell did you learn to act like that?''

''Like what?''

''Like the breeder's best bitch at the state fair,'' he snapped. ''You had me believing you spoke French and—''

''I do speak French.''

''Something you learned at your mama's knee in your mansion on de Koven Street?'' he sneered.

''Leave my mother out of this. She has troubles enough of her own.'' She clenched her fist to keep from smacking him. "I learned French at Miss Boylan's finishing school, if you must know."

"Ah. So you swindled Miss Boylan, too?"

"No, I—" She took a deep breath. She might as well tell all. If she'd learned anything in the past few days, it was that her capacity for deception had its limits. It was an exhausting business, pretending to be something she wasn't. "I was a lady's maid to Miss Deborah Sinclair, who attends the school."

He stopped at an isolated stretch of beach south of the rail yard. Pulling a half-smoked cheroot from his pocket, he inspected it and then tossed it aside. "I'm acquainted with her father. Famously rich. Shamelessly ambitious." He winked. "He had good taste in hired help, though."

Kathleen clenched her other fist. "You would never understand. You probably treat your servants like trash. Miss Deborah was good to me." She hung her head, knowing she could never look her mistress in the eye again. She would have to find some way to return the Tiffany jewels and the Worth gown without encountering Deborah.

"Miss Deborah didn't want to attend the affair Sunday night, for she was unwell." Kathleen felt even lower. A proper maid would have stayed with her mistress. But Deborah had been just as insistent as the others in convincing Kathleen to go out that night.

"Some of the ladies made a bet," she continued, forcing herself to go on. "Miss Phoebe believes that good breeding is a detectable quality, and that I would be caught out, even wearing this gown." She plucked at the green silk skirt. "Miss Lucy maintains that anyone can be fooled by artifice if it's clever enough.

And so they wagered that if I could secure an invitation to the grand opening of the new opera house, Lucy's point would be proven." It sounded so absurd now, so frivolous. What on earth had she been thinking?

But she knew. All her life she had yearned to be included in the charmed circle of a rich girl's world. When the opportunity had been offered Sunday night, she had seized it with pathetic eagerness. Now she felt infinitely older than the foolish dreamer who had donned a fancy gown.

"Congratulations, love," Dylan said with quiet scorn. "I seem to recall inviting you to Crosby's, didn't I?"

"Yes."

"You should be proud of yourself. I've no doubt that everyone in attendance Sunday night was taken in by you." He applauded in exaggerated fashion.

"Dylan," she said, hating the pleading note in her voice. "I know you're disappointed in me, but couldn't we go on from here?"

"Out of the question."

"But—"

"Christ. I suppose there's only one way to get rid of you."

She felt a small flutter of confusion. "What do you mean?"

His fingers made a mocking exploration of her collarbone, caressing her in a way she had loved in the train car. "Next time you decide to entrap a husband," he said in an admonishing tone, "you really should check out his credentials. If not, you risk making a serious mistake."

She jerked away from him. "I don't understand."

"Ah, but you do. You've swindled a swindler."

The flutter of confusion buzzed a little louder in her head. "I still don't—"

"We're cut from the same cloth, you and I." He laughed again, and the sharp reek of whiskey poisoned the air. "I suppose I should make a clean breast of it. After all, there is nothing to be gained from you now."

Gained from her? Surely he didn't need to profit from marrying into wealth. "But your fortune is one of the largest in the country." A chilling thought seized her. What if he meant to use her as a broodmare, to get heirs? Unconsciously, she wrapped her arms around her midsection.

With false patience, he took her hands away and held them in his. "Dear heart, listen carefully. I don't often tell the truth, but I might as well now, so you'll see why we must forget we ever met."

She could more easily forget her own name, she thought, twisting her hands out of his grip. The terrible, soul-shriveling hurt inside her burned unbearably. Only a short while ago, she had believed with all her heart that he loved her. Now he seemed perfectly prepared to forget her.

"I'm listening," she said.

"I am as poor as you." He thought for a moment, rubbing his cheeks. Somehow during the day he had managed to shave, and even drunk, he was more handsome and groomed than anyone had a right to look. "Poorer," he added. "I don't even have a *family*."

The buzzing in her head crescendoed. Nothing made sense anymore. Dylan Kennedy, poor? "What do you mean?'' she asked. ''Did you lose your fortune in the fire?''

''I can't lose what I never had.'' The expression on her face seemed to amuse him no end, and he subjected her to that velvety laughter she would always associate with him. ''You still don't get it, do you? I am a fraud, too. A grifter, a confidence man, taking money from undeserving, gullible, wealthy fat cats.''

''No,'' she whispered, thinking this was some lie he'd concocted just to punish her for her deception. ''Not you. You're lying so I'll release you from our wedding vows.''

''Actually, this is probably the first time I've told you the truth.'' He struck a casual pose, leaning back against a broken dock support and crossing his ankles. ''I'm a bit relieved to be able to let down the pretense for a moment. The Dylan Kennedy you thought you tricked into marriage doesn't exist. Never did. He was someone I invented. I made up his life, his background, his pedigree, his family and his fortune.'' Reaching out, he gently lifted her chin to close her gaping mouth. ''Judging by the way you're gawking at me, I was damned successful. But alas, I was nothing more than a paper prince, a fiction made out of lies and wishes.''

She reeled in shock as a living legend died. Every young lady at Miss Boylan's had wanted him, believing him the catch of the season. He had found a welcome at every exclusive club and party in the city. The merchant princes of Chicago had bowed and scraped to him, eagerly bringing him into their circle of power and privilege.

When she finally found her voice, she asked, "Who in the name of the short saints are you, then?"

He turned both hands palms up. "Dylan Francis Kennedy is a legal identity for me. I liked the name so much I went to the trouble of bribing a judge. But it's not the name I was born with. I chose it from someone else's family tree."

"Why would you do such a thing?"

He smiled. "You can answer that yourself, sweetheart."

Her face burned with humiliation. She felt naked before him, exposed to his knowing scrutiny. He knew her deep secret yearnings, her absurd longings. She forced herself to look him straight in the eye. He knew these things because he had felt them himself. Still, she was skeptical. Why would he go to such lengths to deceive people? Did he really mean to snag a wealthy wife, as he claimed?

No wonder he was so bitter, she thought, searching his face for a trace of humanity but finding none. Look who he'd ended up with.

She believed him because his explanation had the ring of truth—but so had everything else he had ever told her, including the fact that he loved her.

He had been lying. Like her, he had pretended to be something he was not. Wealthy, educated, privileged, refined. Born into a "good" family. Perhaps that was what bothered her the most and shamed her so deeply. She *had* a good family, yet she had gone to the party Sunday night and behaved as if they hadn't existed.

Dylan smiled, his expression shaded with the slightest bit of pity as he read her thoughts. "We're alike, you and I. Too bad we must go our separate ways, because I enjoy certain things about you." His summer-blue gaze swept over her. "A lot."

Her humiliation burned hotter as she remembered all the times she had declared her love for him, all the wanton ways she had touched him and let him touch her. What a pitifully shallow creature she was, falling in love with a make-believe prince. She deserved the hurt she was feeling. She had earned it.

Yet even her pain was impure, if such a thing could be. It was anger, not shame, that filled the burning emptiness created by his betrayal.

Outrage gave her the strength to stand tall and proud before him rather than crumpling into a weeping mass of misery at his feet. Her mother had warned her of this while mending the green dress. "Always keep your pride. No matter what you're feeling inside, colleen, hold your head up and look him in the eye."

"You," she said, and her voice trembled with a righteous anger. "You low-bellied, opportunistic cheater." She didn't yell, but something in her tone wiped the smile off his face. "We are nothing alike. I will deny it to the last of my days."

"Come now," he said. "I always thought I knew my way about a confidence game, but you had even me fooled—"

"I am guilty of only one deception, for which I have the deepest regret," she snapped. "I acted on the spur of the moment. It was a lark, something the ladies at finishing school dreamed up. You seem to have made a career of this."

"Indeed I have, and you should consider doing the same, darling. You're awfully good."

She took a step back, wishing he looked like the devil he was. "How can you live with yourself year after year? What is the appeal of cheating people so remorselessly as you did the night we mar—Sunday night?''

He took a step closer, backing her against the timbers of the old, broken fishing dock so that she had nowhere to retreat. She felt the warmth of his body, and in spite of her indignation, she remembered the sensation of being held in his arms, remembered how it had made her feel as if she had finally found what she'd been seeking all her life.

''In that one night,'' he pointed out in a low, intimate whisper, ''you lived higher and better than you ever did in a whole lifetime of being hardworking and law-abiding.''

He had more lines than a traveling snake oil salesman, she thought. And sweet Mary help her, she had believed every single one. Her throat filled with words she could not speak. Pressing her lips together and praying she would show no emotion, she shook her head.

''That's no denial,'' he taunted. ''I can see it in your face, sweet Kathleen. Yes, I like that name better than Kate. I can look in your eyes and see that you loved what happened to you when you were with me. You can't stop thinking about it, can you?''

''Not with you bullying me about like this,'' she managed to say. ''Get out of my way.''

''Why? So you can run away from me?''

''I think you're the one who feels compelled to run,'' she said with sudden insight.

That brought on one of his mesmerizing smiles. ''Ah, you're quick, Kathleen, a gifted learner. But I've already seen evidence of that.''

''Tell me why,'' she said, suddenly needing to

know the answer. "Why do you live your life like this, lying and cheating people instead of making your own way, your own living? Why must you steal a living, even an identity, from someone else?"

"It's a dog-eat-dog world out there. Others are out to cheat you. I learned that at a very early age. So I just want to be the shrewdest cheater in a world of cheaters."

She laughed harshly. "How honorable of you. Fleecing innocent people is such a high calling."

"Ah, Kathleen, you've not been paying attention. I don't fleece the innocent. Those who fall victim to my games always have hearts filled with greed and larceny. Take yourself, for example. If you had kept your place, I never would have given you a second glance."

"It's such a comfort to know that."

"I don't care if you're comfortable or not. I'm just telling you, you can't swindle an honest man—or woman. You're the perfect example of that. My only regret is that you turned out to be a worthless mark."

Though offended, she conceded his point. "Can we stop quarreling about this? It does no good at all to accuse each other. We must decide what to do from here."

"Don't you get it? I've already decided. I'm hopping the next freighter out of town. In a few hours, you'll be no more than a big disappointment interspersed with some extremely pleasant memories."

*No.* Her mind screamed the word, though she made no sound. When she managed to gain command of herself, she said, "You are probably quite experienced at turning your back on your troubles. Walking out on them."

He laughed gently. "Oh, Kathleen. If you only knew."

"Well, you can't do that this time."

He grabbed her shoulders. Before she could say another word, he kissed her, so long and hard and suggestively that for a moment she forgot they were standing beneath a dock jutting out over the lake. For a moment she knew only the deep sweetness of intimacy, the sharp ache of yearning. He possessed some sort of dark magic that pushed aside her anger and resentment and made her shamelessly hungry for him. Then she remembered herself and pulled away.

*Why can't you be real?* she wanted to yell at him. Instead she said, "You can't simply walk away."

"Watch me." He relinquished his hold on her shoulders, turned on his heel and headed back toward the rail yard.

Hating herself, and hating him almost as much as she loved him, Kathleen followed. "We are married," she stated. "We haven't a penny between us, and I've a family to worry about."

"I'm not worried."

"You should be. As of Sunday night, they are your family, too."

He took a swift breath, and she suspected she had found his one vulnerable spot. *Family.*

Pressing her advantage, she said, "You are simply going to have to become an honest man, earn an honest wage and leave your wastrel ways behind."

He stopped in his tracks, then doubled over with guffaws that rang across the rail yard, mingling with the hiss of steam engines and the grind of steel wheels on the tracks. For a few moments, he could not speak or breathe. After a while his mirth subsided to the occasional chuckle. "Has hell frozen over?" He pressed his brows into an exaggerated scowl. "Funny, I don't feel a change in temperature."

"You can't joke this problem out of existence. You married me." To keep from weeping, she clung to indignation. "Or have you chosen to forget the way you went down on one knee, begged for my hand, swore it was the only way you could die happy?"

"Well, we didn't die, and happiness never lasts. You and I are proof of that. But it was a hell of a night, wasn't it?" He lifted one eyebrow and flicked out his tongue in blatant suggestion. "The day after was even better."

"And now you have responsibilities—"

"Tell me," he asked, pacing in an imitation of a lawyer in court, "did you really think you were the first?"

Her jaw dropped.

He tipped back his head and laughed.

Kathleen felt all the blood in her body drain to her feet. Her pallor must have disturbed even him, for he reached out a hand to steady her. "Actually, you needn't worry about Sunday night's charade. That's all it was. The courthouse burned. I have no idea where the marriage certificate went. Do you?"

"No."

"It's burned to ash, no doubt. So there's no record whatsoever of our little escapade."

No record, she thought, except his image, forever branded on her heart.

He seemed to have sobered up considerably as he found a jagged path back to the terminal. "As charming as you are, I really must be going," he said.

"We spoke vows before a priest," she reminded him.

"Which would probably move me deeply, were I a Catholic."

Ah. Yet another lie. She didn't even bother being surprised. "You are," she said simply. "You knew all the responses as only a Catholic can. You're just saying that in hopes of invalidating the marriage."

"There was no marriage," he snapped. "Just a bit of cheap theatrics to comfort a dying man." He let go of her arm. "So that," he concluded, "is that. Have a nice life, Kathleen O'Leary." Whistling, he turned his back and swaggered away.

At a loss, she stared after him, wondering what in heaven's name to do next. Weep? Wail? Scream? Scold? Or join him in laughter and self-mockery?

Before she could make up her mind, someone called out, "Dylan Kennedy! Stay where you are!"

She and Dylan both turned at once to find a tall, heavy man wearing a well-cut suit and a crooked handlebar mustache, stiff with wax. In one hand he held a bullwhip. In the other, a Colt's five-shooter, aimed straight at Dylan's heart.

# Twelve

Dylan let a friendly, guileless smile slide across his face even though all the whiskey he'd swallowed suddenly wanted to lurch back out into the open. He closed the distance between himself and Vincent Costello with a manly stride, politely ignoring the loaded gun.

"Well, Vince. Fancy finding you here," he said, making certain he stood between Kathleen and the gun. Shit, he thought. Of all the rotten luck. He could sense Kathleen behind him, breathing in and out like a beached trout, still angry and hurt by the way he had left her. What the devil did she expect, that he would simply concede she was right and go straight? Become a dairy farmer or coal man, for Christ's sake?

Costello glared at Dylan's outstretched hand. "Stay where you are," he ordered.

Kathleen's breathing accelerated. Maybe, thought Dylan, she had been telling the truth, that she'd never been in the game and Sunday night was her first. He wanted to tell her not to be scared, he'd handled Costello before.

She surprised them both by pushing out from behind Dylan. "Don't shoot!" she shrieked. "I beg you, don't shoot him." And she flung herself in front of him.

Dylan and Costello shared a moment of pure, flabbergasted confusion. Dylan thought fast. He'd have to explain her, but how? If he admitted he'd married her, Costello would shoot him down like a dog.

"That's just like you," Costello said with a sneer of contempt, "to use a woman as a shield. You haven't changed, Kennedy."

Dylan kept his best smile in place and swallowed hard, trying to keep the whiskey down, even though it burned at the back of his throat. Carefully he edged away from Kathleen, disengaging her hands from his lapels. "You'll have to excuse this poor creature," he said reasonably. "She's been clinging to me like a barnacle ever since the fire."

Costello eyed her keenly, his small sharp eyes taking in a face and figure Aphrodite would envy. "Why?" he demanded.

"Because she's distraught. Likely to do anything… Just a moment." As if leading her in a dance step, Dylan took her hand and brought her over to a flatbed pump car. He held her elbow in the clamp of his hand and prayed her horror at the gun would keep her quiet. "What did you do a fool thing like that for? Don't you know guns are dangerous?"

"Only to cheaters like you," she said. "That man wouldn't have shot me. He doesn't even know me."

Her naivete was stunning. "Wait here," he said between gritted teeth. "Don't move, and don't say a word."

Kathleen made a small squeak of protest. "I'll do nothing of the sort. I—"

He pressed her against the edge of the car and hid his lips in her hair. "Trust me on this," he implored her. "He means business. He'll shoot me."

"And that should concern me, after what you just said—"

He touched a finger to her full lips, wishing she wasn't so damned pretty and soft—she bit him. Swearing, he snatched his hand away.

"You just threw yourself in front of me," he said peevishly, shaking out his hand. "At least part of you is concerned."

"A reflex, that's all."

"Look, he's a dangerous man. We've had our problems in the past. I have to make him believe we can make amends."

She crossed her arms in front of her and glared straight ahead. "You have one minute, boyo."

"Just promise you won't say a word, no matter what I have to tell him. Let me sort this out on my own. I'll make it all right, Kathleen. I will. Trust me on this." He gave her a look that melted with sincerity, one that had worked on her in the past. He made his eyes go soft, his mouth slightly open, the way he might just before kissing her.

It failed to thaw her, but she didn't get angry. She did something worse. She bit her lip to keep it from trembling, and whispered, "I wish I could trust that look on your face."

Damn. She made him feel as if he'd just kicked a puppy. He turned quickly and went back to Vincent Costello, who had lowered the gun but kept it in his hand.

"Well?" he asked.

"She's my mistress," Dylan said on a wave of inspiration.

"Mistress!" Costello roared.

Dylan flinched and hoped Kathleen would hold her tongue.

"You scum! Jackal!" the older man said. "You promised to be true to Faith—"

"Exactly." Dylan lowered his voice to a conspiratorial, man-to-man whisper. "That is exactly why I had to take up with a lesser woman. Your daughter is as delicate as a snowflake, Vince, you know that."

His whole being seemed to soften at the mention of his beloved daughter. "True enough. Never understood why she's so smitten with you, but for once, you're right. Delicate, she is."

"Fragile," Dylan supplied.

"Fragile, too. That's my Faith."

"And as you know," he reminded Vince, "a man, with a man's needs, is far from delicate and gentle. In my enthusiasm for Faith, I feared she might think me too…aggressive. That is why I made the painful decision to take a mistress."

He sneaked a glance at Kathleen. Even from a distance, he could see her shoulders stiffen and her knuckles whiten. She was probably trying to decide whether or not to wallop him. There was nothing fragile or delicate about Kathleen.

"You see, I didn't want to inflict my, uh, needs on Faith. Without some avenue for relief, I might have brought those most unfortunate needs to your daughter. Sir."

Costello beaded his eyes. "You low-down—"

"Ask yourself, Vince," Dylan said calmly. "What man does without a mistress? You yourself had one even while you were married to Mrs. Costello, of sainted memory. And she thanked God on her knees every day that you took your coarse needs else-where."

"But my Faith—"

"Is her mother's daughter," Dylan assured him.

Vincent Costello's soft spot—his daughter, and the memory of his late wife—was the only vulnerability Dylan had ever found in him. His harsh, rough face went slack at the thought of the women he loved.

Dylan was curious about a love like that. How was it that a man as ruthless as Vincent Costello could feel such tenderness for a wife and child?

But that was a matter to ponder later. Now was the time to press his advantage, knowing he had to make his point quickly or risk Kathleen speaking up and ruining everything. "I don't want to hurt Faith," he said in a very low voice. "That's why I took off."

"You can start making amends by handing over the cash you made off with."

"I told you, Vince. It's gone." He thought of the moldering hulk of the boat he had been living on, a small fortune stashed in the bow. "Burned in the fire."

"A likely story. You—"

"Mr. Costello! Sir, you're needed over here." A railroad switchman waved his arm. "Got another re-lief train to unload."

Costello squared his shoulders. Dylan frowned. "You're working for the railroad now?"

"For the church." The older man smirked, the way he used to when he played the shill in the burlesque shows. "Mayor Mason's already declared martial law. He's been making appointments for the rebuild-ing, handing out policeman's stars like sugar candy." He tucked his thumbs in his armpits and rocked back on his heels. The gun dangled from one fingertip. "I'm in charge of the Catholic Relief Aid Fund."

Dylan shook his head. "Unbelievable."

"Someone's got to handle all the thousands of dollars pouring in." He squinted peevishly at Dylan. "You could probably secure some sort of post. Procurement's your specialty."

Just then, Faith showed up, as pale and earnest as a plaster saint, perched on the driver's seat of a cart full of homeless people. She wore a gray dress, lacking in all ornament except for the large crucifix around her neck. The black kerchief on her head resembled a nun's wimple. When she spied Dylan, her eyes sparkled with the fervor of a martyr in ecstasy.

"Mr. Kennedy!" she called, handing the reins of the cart to a boy. She climbed down with awkward haste and hurried over to him, her sturdy brogans marking the ashes on the surface of the yard. Clasping her hands in elation, she beamed at him. "Papa swore he would find you, and so he did. I'm so pleased that you're all right."

Burningly aware of Kathleen's scrutiny, he bowed from the waist. "By the grace of God, I am."

She didn't question him about his disappearance. Unlike Kathleen, she had never forced him to justify anything he'd done. Faith didn't need to be won over. She was already his. She had been for years, ever since she was a girl of thirteen, regarding him with worshipful eyes as he performed illusions for a carnival crowd.

"Thank you, Papa," she said, then gestured at the cart. "This is perfect timing. I need help with my relief project."

Faith always had a project. It was amazing that the

daughter of one of America's most artful criminals harbored nothing but pure charity in her heart. No matter where they traveled, she always managed to find some sort of benevolent work for the unfortunate. It was a trait Dylan admired, but not enough to give her the one thing she longed for—a firm date for their wedding.

He longingly watched a string of train cars uncouple and head south. With all of his heart, he wanted to be on one of those cars, alone, unfettered, headed straight into the night. He wondered if Bull had hopped a train yet. If he was smart, he'd get out now.

"You heard my daughter," Costello said. "She needs help." The railroad worker whistled for his attention. "As for myself, I must dedicate my efforts to the relief work."

"A model citizen," Dylan muttered under his breath. Letting Costello handle donations for the refugees was like putting the fox in charge of the henhouse. Dylan only wished he'd thought of it first.

Costello assured Faith he would be close at hand. When she had appeared, he'd smoothly concealed his gun. He had a gift for doing that. Surely she must know that her father was a notorious criminal, an occasionally violent man, but she regarded him with nothing less than love and respect. "Take care, Papa," she said as he walked toward the terminal. "I'll find you later." Then she turned to Dylan, beaming under her invisible halo. "My prayers are answered," she said. "I did so want to find you again, and now I have. Everything is going to be perfect." Grabbing his arm, she pulled him toward the cart.

"Actually," he said, "I was on my way to, uh, organize a soup kitchen for the hungry."

"Aren't you a dear?"

"Completely." It was awkward as hell, having Kathleen close by, dressed like Cinderella out past her curfew. She seemed to be waiting and watching. Maybe she would keep her distance.

Faith gestured at the wagon. "These good people must all be sent to hospitals out of town. I need help getting them to a train, for they're all wounded."

The ideal situation for Faith—helping the poor and the wounded. Dylan hoped for her sake there was an afterlife; Faith sure was racking up the rewards.

He craned his neck to see how Kathleen was taking it all in, but she was nowhere to be seen. The flatbed had been abandoned. Dylan scanned the area, and nearly swore aloud when he spied her with the cart Faith had driven by herself from the city.

Kathleen sat on the tailgate, a man's head in her lap, stroking his hair. She barely acknowledged Dylan as he approached.

"This is Barry Lynch," she said quietly, keeping her attention focused on the unconscious man.

"I'm so grateful you know his name," Faith said. "He was found near the courthouse."

At the sound of Faith's voice, Kathleen glanced up. "Who are you?"

"My name is Faith Costello," she said demurely.

Kathleen hesitated. Dylan held his breath. She sent Faith a cordial smile and said, "Kathleen O'Leary."

Dylan eased out a long, silent breath of relief. He pretended it was the most natural thing in the world to be in the company of the woman he'd promised to marry and the one who called herself his wife.

"Barry's a friend," Kathleen said, her hand trembling as she stroked the long-bodied young man's brow. "He was at the courthouse Sunday night." To Dylan's shock, heartfelt grief shimmered in her eyes. "I barely acknowledged him."

"There now," Faith said soothingly. "He'll be all right. His burns aren't terrible, like some, but he's had a bump on the head."

Kathleen took a bandana handkerchief from the pocket of the fallen man and gently dabbed at his brow. "Poor Barry."

"He's a fine-looking man, isn't he?" Faith commented.

"I—" Kathleen glanced up, blinking slowly. "Yes, I suppose he is."

Barry Lynch moaned softly and moved his head on Kathleen's soft thighs. Dylan wanted to knock him unconscious again, the blighter.

"Quickly," Faith said. "He needs water." Someone passed her a flask, and she held it to his lips. His eyes fluttered open and rolled back, unfocused. Then he drank a little, the water spilling out the sides of his mouth onto Kathleen's dress. He seemed to be staring at the crucifix on Faith's bosom. Kathleen very carefully eased out from under him and Faith stepped in, gently supporting his head with her hand.

"Where am I?" he asked.

"You're at the Michigan and Illinois terminal," Faith said.

He couldn't take his eyes off her. "Are you sure you're not an angel?"

She favored him with a dewy-eyed smile. "Heavens, no."

"I thought I'd die in that fire."

"You're going to be fine, Barry Lynch. I promise."

"How do you know my name?" he asked in a wavering voice. "You *are* an angel...."

Kathleen caught Dylan's eye. With a jerk of her head, she motioned him away from the wagon, heading for cover between two standing cars.

They were arguing almost before they were out of earshot.

"Now do you understand why I can't stick around Chicago?" Dylan demanded.

"Because you're not only a swindler, but a liar as well."

"You're one to talk."

"How dare you tell Mr. Costello I am your mistress?"

"Would you prefer I call you my illegitimate wife? Or better yet, the trollop I abandoned in a train yard?"

She hit him then. It was no ladylike slap but a decent right jab to the jaw that made him see stars. He didn't trust himself to speak, but held his jaw, working it from side to side to make sure she hadn't broken it. It knocked aside the last comforting effects of the whiskey. Fuming, he stalked away, scanning the train cars for a likely hideaway. He saw none, but remembered with searing clarity the Pullman car where he and Kathleen had celebrated their marriage. Whether or not the union was legal, the days they had spent between the sheets had been real, as vivid as a brand in his mind. How was it that this redheaded virago had been so sweet, so pliant, so passionate, only a day ago?

"It's no more than you deserve, Dylan Kennedy," she called, catching up with him. Her voice was calmer now, as if she had spent the tension of her anger in the punch.

"And less than I've endured before," he said, discovering his jaw to be in good working order, although it throbbed badly. "I wish you'd quit hitting me. I can't abide a woman who hits."

"I wouldn't have to hit you if you'd face up to your responsibilities."

"I've already told you," he said with exaggerated patience. "Our marriage was as real as a shell game. Smoke and mirrors, sleight of hand. I'm not responsible for you or your family."

"What about the other promises you made?"

"Like what?"

"Well, you promised to help Mr. Fraser with his grain shipment."

Dylan scratched his head. "Mr. who?"

"Mr. David Fraser. You promised him you would find a way to get his grain to market."

He finally remembered the earnest, desperate man out on the eastern shore. "There is no possible way I could concern myself less with him," he said stonily. "Or anyone else for that matter. Besides, there is no business to be done in the city. What does it matter, anyway?"

"It'll create a false shortage and the price will go through the roof," she explained. "Then it will plummet when that barge shows up."

"Correction. I *could* concern myself less than I did a moment ago," he said in a bored voice. "Besides, no barge can show up until a tug is dispatched. And no tug will depart because the port is still in a state of chaos and there are no wires getting through."

"The Board of Trade's burned and all records are gone," she said thoughtfully. "All the performance bonds and price discoveries. It will be a fine mess. Unscrupulous deals will abound.''

Dylan gave a mock shudder. "I can't stand unscrupulous men. Scoundrels, all of them.''

"There's no need for sarcasm. But I suppose I can't make you care about a promise you made if you won't even care about me.''

Her temper had the odd, unsettling effect of making her more attractive than ever. He had to drag out a sarcastic remark. "Now you're catching on.''

"Except," she said with a subtle lift of her eyebrow, "I think you *do* care about me.''

"You're dreaming," he snapped, and started to pace. Why was she so damned hard to dismiss?

On a platform a short distance away, Vincent ordered workmen about, setting up a desk with a ledger and strongbox. Dylan felt a hint of reluctant admiration. Leave it to Costello to get himself a post receiving money.

"How do you know Mr. Costello and his daughter?" she asked, following his gaze.

"He's a...commission merchant of some sort." Dylan didn't elaborate.

"Well, he is certainly doing his part for the city.''

"Indeed," he said wryly.

"You should consider joining the effort. Mayor Mason doesn't know you're a cad. He'd probably give you a job.''

"I don't take jobs. Not that sort, anyway.''

"All right. Then you must come this way," Kathleen said, grabbing his sleeve and giving it a tug. They climbed over the coupling between two cars and hurried down a rocky bank. There was, he discovered, at least one advantage to her true identity. She knew the streets of Chicago even with the landmarks burned away, and within a few minutes, she had led him from the terminal to the financial district.

But he knew her better now. She was up to something.

"Wait a minute," he said, stopping in his tracks. "Why am I following you?"

She poked her nose in the air. "You have no choice."

He laughed. "Just try holding on to me," he challenged her.

"I believe I could enlist Mr. Costello to help. He seems very good at…holding on to things."

Dylan spread his arms in frustration. "Why would you want to? I'm no good, Kathleen. You don't want a liar and a con artist for a husband—"

"You just said you weren't my husband."

In truth, he didn't know for sure. It just seemed safer to assume the marriage wasn't valid.

"Then what do you want with me?"

She smiled with a sweetness that almost fooled him. "The larceny in your heart."

Maybe it would amount to nothing, or maybe for once in her life she would get lucky. Kathleen hoped she could remember the way to the roofless building she had passed. She prayed it was the building she thought.

While marching across Chicago to reclaim her errant husband, she had encountered a still-burning building. From its location, she guessed that it was the Hotel St. George, the place Dylan had acquired just before the fire destroyed it. At the time, she had been enchanted by his whimsy in the midst of a disaster. But what she had seen today inside its gutted skeleton was far from whimsical.

"Three blocks south of the river," she murmured. "That would make it Randolph Street. And then four and a half blocks west of that. LaSalle Street."

Dylan had stopped protesting. He seemed resigned, though she suspected he'd bolt as soon as he could conveniently do so. However, she understood him well enough now to know he could not resist an illicit opportunity. He appeared to be the sort of man who thrived on such things. For the time being, he belonged to her.

She used anger and outrage to build a defensive wall around her more tender feelings and hoped it would work. She hoped she appeared as cold and clever as he, hoped that one day this terrible yearning would stop. Yet it walked with her every step of the way. He had been the perfect, storybook bridegroom. If she had drawn him straight from her dreams, he would have turned out the exact man she had married in the courthouse with the sky raining fire.

But like a dream, he faded away as reality intruded. And like a dream, he was too wonderful to be recaptured. She prayed one day she would be able to think of that night, and the days that followed, with fondness. For now, she could only feel the searing, empty hurt left by his betrayal.

Gran always used to say no good ever came of a lie. Kathleen wished she had listened. Instead, she had rashly dived into a world where she didn't belong. Within a matter of hours, she had destroyed her own life. God alone knew what would become of her now. She was a ruined woman, no longer fit to be anyone's virgin bride. Probably not fit to work as a lady's maid anymore, either, when people heard what she had done. Phoebe Palmer, who loved a ripe bit of gossip, would see to it that everyone knew the tale of the Irish maid who had crashed a society party. But that wasn't even the worst Kathleen imagined for herself. What if she found herself with child? No respectable household would take her then.

She caught herself thinking of the molls and saloon girls of Conley's Patch. Ruined women, all, suffering the uncertainty, abuse and diseases common to their profession. Mother Mary and Joseph. What if she became like them?

The thoughts only heated the hurt inside her, and she quickened her steps, reminding herself to be cold, calm. "What is your association with Mr. Costello?" she asked him. "The truth, please."

"We've been business partners off and on over the years. We put together a traveling stage act that did extremely well for us. Better, I found out, for Costello than for me. He was skimming the profits, right from the start, while I did all the work. Took all the risks."

"What sort of risks?"

"Nothing illegal at first. We had some Java sparrows trained to do card tricks, a learned pig that could spell, a pair of horses that could do sums. I lacked the patience for performing animals," he confessed, "and besides, they ate too much. So I stuck to my own feats of daring and illusion. I performed as an escapologist, a quick-change artist, a contortionist." He winked. "My most popular stunts were being a human frog and playing the fiddle with a bulldog suspended from my bowing arm."

"I don't believe you," she said.

"I don't blame you," he replied. "They were all

cheap illusions, but I gave people a good time, and they were willing to pay for it. Look, where is this place? We've been walking for half an hour and you've shown me nothing but smoke and rubble.''

She didn't address his question. She kept thinking back to the first night of the fire. He had moved like a gymnast, climbing up to the peak of the church. With a stunning lack of fear, he had mounted the steeple, showing no more concern for the height than a man going out to the morning milking. She remembered his almost comical bow after he had dispatched the wooden steeple. He _was_ a showman.

''Why was Mr. Costello so angry with you?''

He took her arm to help her avoid a deep crevice in the roadway. She wished she could recoil from his touch, but instead, she caught herself liking the evocative intimacy of it.

''I made off with the till,'' he said mildly. ''It annoyed him.''

In spite of herself, she felt a reluctant admiration for his audacity. ''I can see how it would.''

''He tracked me all the way from Buffalo. I thought I'd lost him, but he turned up Sunday night.'' He drew her tight against him as they squeezed through a narrow alley. ''Still annoyed.''

''Did you give him back his money?''

''It isn't—wasn't—his. He just thought it was.''

''Where is it now?''

''I don't know. It's…complicated.''

''So that's where you come from?'' she asked. ''Buffalo?''

''That's one of the places. We had an act at Niagara Falls.''

''What sort of act?''

"I walked a tightrope over the Falls."

"Oh," she said. An improbable story, yet it made a crazy kind of sense. She recalled a set of stereograph pictures she had seen of the majestic cataract. "Wasn't that dangerous?"

He laughed, still holding her although the road had widened. "Sweetheart, that's the whole point."

"How did you steal the money and elude Mr. Costello?"

"Well, one night just before the show, I strapped the cash to my chest and back, under my costume."

"You wore a costume?"

"Of course, ninny. Haven't you ever seen a daredevil act before?"

"No."

"My character was the marquis de Bontemps. I dressed like a French nobleman."

She couldn't help herself. The image made her giggle. "All right. So you're all tricked out like a peacock, with a fortune strapped to you."

"And then, in the middle of the tightrope, teetering above Niagara Falls, the unfortunate marquis fell to his death. His body was never found."

Kathleen stopped in her tracks. "You lie."

He shrugged. "I often do, but not about this."

They started walking again, and somehow, her hand found its way into his. As if to make up for the burned, hideous wasteland of Chicago, the sunset was spectacular, a fan of slanting pink fronds through the smoke-laden air. A feeling of isolation pervaded this section of the city. There was no one about, not even a watchman or fire patrol looking for new flare-ups.

She tried to picture Dylan falling in, struggling

against a raging current. What sort of man was he, to take a risk like that?

"Why were you so desperate to get away from Mr. Costello?"

"He's a cheat."

"I see. And that makes you his moral superior?"

He shrugged. "Let's just say I choose my marks more carefully than he does." He gave her a lingering look. "Most of the time. Anyway, I decided I could do better on my own. And then Faith—" He paused.

"What about Faith? She seems a fine and virtuous girl."

"She had this crazy idea that I would marry her."

She took her hand from his. She was beginning to understand. He regarded marriage as more dangerous than crossing Niagara Falls on a tightrope.

This man, she thought, was a walking disaster. And a bundle of contradictions. So why did she find him so fascinating?

At the corner of Randolph and State, she noticed a ruined building with ornate cornice work and beautiful gothic windows, empty as a huge ghost. She studied it for a moment, and then, despite her fury, fatigue and broken heart, she started to laugh, almost weeping with mirth.

Dylan stepped back, regarding her as if she had gone mad. "What the devil's wrong with you?"

"It's the opera house." She hiccuped her laughter away. "Crosby's. We were supposed to attend the opening night together, remember? I must tell Miss Lucy that she won the wager." She paused. "But perhaps the wager's not settled after all, for they did say I was to be invited by a *gentle*man."

"Then clearly I'm not your man," he said peevishly.

She caught his arm before he turned on his heel. "Wait," she said. "It's just another block or two." He grumbled, but she kept hold of him, and in a few moments found the fallen building she was looking for. She stopped and glanced from side to side, making sure they were alone. "There," she said, pointing.

He squinted through the smoldering murk. The remains of the interior lay in complete disarray, everything crashed into the basement. An iron stove lay on its side, and the outline of a fireplace marked the only wall that remained standing. Everything else was unrecognizable.

"What is it?" he asked.

"The Hotel St. George. Your property," she reminded him.

"Lucky me."

She was growing exasperated at his recalcitrance. "Come with me. Watch where you step, there are still live coals everywhere." She led the way over the chunks of rubble and brought him to a pile of bricks in one corner. "I passed this place as I crossed the city this afternoon. When I saw it was the St. George, I decided to look around a bit." She didn't want to admit that she had been desperate to do something to please him, perhaps report that something on the property had survived. Now she didn't care a fig about pleasing him. She just needed his help.

"I found something," she admitted with a mysterious smile. "When it turned out to be what I thought, I covered it up," she said, proud of her forethought. "Here, help me move the bricks."

He picked one up and pitched it aside. "Ouch. That's still damned hot."

Showing no sympathy, she covered her hands with two handkerchiefs and set to work. With a sigh of resignation, Dylan helped out, working as slowly as a schoolboy at lessons. But after a moment, when he saw what they were uncovering, he began to work faster. Shortly thereafter, all the bricks were moved.

Dylan grinned. "A safe. You found a safe in the building I own. Kathleen, I could kiss you."

*Then do it.* Her cheeks burned with the shame of wanting him. She couldn't believe she still wanted this man who lied with every breath he took, who had told her he loved her, who would have walked away from his marriage without a second thought.

"Can you get into it?" she asked.

"With both eyes closed." He hunkered down beside the heavy safe and touched the hot metal of the dial. "I hope it isn't melted."

"What if—"

"Sh, I'm concentrating." He spun the dial first one way, then the other, his features sharp with concentration.

"Wait," Kathleen said.

Frowning, he stopped fiddling with the dial. "What is it?"

"Before you go on, I think we should come to an agreement."

"What sort of agreement?"

"Well, about how we'll split the money." As they'd crossed the city, she had thought about it long and hard.

"The place is mine and mine alone," he said. "The contents of this safe belong to me."

She said nothing, but everything she asked was in her eyes. She could feel it all there, like unshed tears.

Somehow, she must have touched a sympathetic chord. "Fifty-fifty," he said curtly.

"No," she objected. "You must swear you'll split it three ways."

"Three ways?" He looked offended. "I own the damned place."

"And I found the safe. So. A third for you," she explained patiently. "A third for me and my family. And a third for St. Brendan's."

A scowl darkened his brow. "Why the hell St. Brendan's?"

"You promised, remember?"

"No. Remind me."

"You said you'd reconstruct the steeple."

He laughed. "I only hoped to take up a collection so I could pocket it. Kathleen, you know what my promises are like. They're very fragile. I break them. Happens all the time."

His blunt, frank words hit her like a blow. "Not this time. This is one promise you're keeping."

"Very well," he conceded easily. Too easily.

"If you don't, I'll…" Her voice trailed off. What would she do? She had no power over him. "I'll tell Mr. Costello I'm not your mistress but your wife. Then he'll be so furious that he'll hunt you down and shoot you." She had no idea if Costello would do that, but judging by the look on Dylan's face, it was a very real possibility.

"Three ways," he said angrily. "Have it your way. Now, be very quiet. I need to concentrate."

She stood back and watched him work. It seemed to take forever as he sought every subtle nuance of the workings inside the lock. He had wonderful hands, she thought. They were big, with long fingers, yet they worked with a delicacy that surprised her. Without warning, a memory came back of those hands touching her, skimming over her bare flesh, seeming to detect her inner reaction the same way he read the tiny movements of the lock.

She dabbed at her brow with the handkerchief, dreading the next time she went to confession. Wherever would she begin to recount her transgressions?

They had started, she admitted, long before the night she had donned an heiress's evening gown and jewels. Way back in her childhood, she had coveted a rich girl's fine things. That yearning had only intensified as the years went by.

She had never actually stolen anything from Deborah Sinclair, not anything that could be seen and touched. But she had been a thief nonetheless. Lingering in the schoolroom during lessons, she had stolen the education of a privileged girl. On pretext of helping Deborah with her deportment and dancing, she had filched the graces and refinements of a genteel lady. She had stayed up until the wee hours, night after night, poring over books and magazines, secretly appropriating all the things that made her mistress a woman of privilege. She had learned to distinguish a fish fork from a salad fork. She knew the rules of piquet and understood the nuances of every social ritual from leaving calling cards to the high-class marriage market known as the white ball.

She had allowed herself to forget her place in the world, allowed herself to dream that there was a life for her beyond the workaday world of the West Division. That had been a foolish mistake. If she had stayed tucked into her little niche in life, she never would have known there was something bigger, better, more exciting out there for her.

"Cheer up, dear," Dylan said, breaking in on her thoughts. "I think I've got it."

She cast away her shadowy regrets and squatted down beside him. His face ran with sweat. Though there was nothing left to burn, the building was still as hot as an oven. The heat was a hungry beast, looking for something to devour.

"Ready?" asked Dylan with a gleam in his eye.

"Open it," she urged him.

Using a broken pipe as a lever, he pried open the door.

For a fraction of a second, she saw a fortune before her eyes. In the blink of an eye, she saw stacks of greenbacks loosely bound by paper strips. In the blink of an eye, she saw the salvation of her family.

But before she could blink a third time, it was gone. There was a flash, a whooshing sound and a roar of flames in the belly of the safe. Dylan grabbed her and flung them both backward, away from the small, fierce conflagration. He ripped off his frock coat and tried to beat out the flames, but the fabric caught and his sleeve started to burn.

"Stop," Kathleen cried out. "Stop, you'll burn yourself."

It was over in seconds.

For a very long time, they sat together amid the smoking rubble, dull-eyed and as silent as the burned-out city. Finally Kathleen asked, "What happened?"

"The paper went up the minute the air hit it." He poked his foot at the fragile black leaves. "Amazing. Never saw that coming."

"Obviously not."

Using a piece of brick, he scraped all the charred notes and ash out of the safe. He held up the remains of a fifty-dollar bill, watching the red edge devour itself. Before it went completely out, he took a cheroot from his waistcoat pocket and held the glowing greenback to the tip, lighting it.

"I've always wanted to do that." He sifted through the fragile black flakes and managed to find some coins. But the metal burned his fingers and he dropped most of them. They fell down into the cracks between the bricks.

Kathleen braced herself, expecting him to fly into a rage. Instead, he laughed that wonderful laugh. "Darling, if you bring me any more good luck, I won't need to fear a worse retribution in the afterlife."

Bleak hopelessness washed over Kathleen. Each moment she spent with Dylan, she gained new insights, but they were things she did not want to know. Nothing lasted. Everything could go up in smoke in an instant. Gran always used to say, if something came too easily, it wasn't worth having in the first place. She wondered if that applied to her as well. She had given her entire self to Dylan in a single night.

"Now what?" she asked.

"It's getting dark. We'd better get out of here."

She glanced at the sky, trying to judge whether or not she'd be able to make it home before dark. Home. She pictured herself arriving alone at the house on de Koven Street, bedraggled, defeated, empty-handed. Her family had sent her out to reclaim her husband, and she had failed in every respect. She didn't even know if she had a husband, for he'd hinted at a prior commitment. When her parents found out he was penniless, they would know what a complete failure Kathleen was.

She pushed herself to her feet. "I'd best be going." She couldn't think of what else to say. Farewell? Thank you for the adventure? At a loss, she turned and walked out of the building.

When they reached the street, he puffed on his cheroot, took her hand and said, "Let's go."

"I'm not going anywhere with you."

"And I'm not letting you wander off alone at night." A beguiling smile slid across his face. "The Pullman car's still there."

She balked, digging in her heels. "Never."

"Oh, Kathleen." He swept his arm around her. "Never say never."

# *Thirteen*

Kathleen wasn't certain how she did it, but she managed to sleep like a dead person for a night and half of the next day. Awakening to strong midday sunlight, she sat up in the lavish berth of the Pullman car, rubbed her eyes and wondered how she had slept so soundly.

Moving the Oriental screen that shielded the berth from the rest of the car, she saw no sign of Dylan. At her shrill insistence, he had slept on the fainting couch in the sitting area, and she'd dragged the screen across the alcove of the bed.

Warily she crept out of bed and went to the window, pushing aside the drapes. Linked to other passenger coaches, the palace car sat on a side track near the lake. It appeared to be abandoned and forgotten, surrounded by a wasteland of broken stone and creosote-coated ties on one side, and the mist-covered lake on the other. The sunlight filtering through the lake fog lent a ghostly aura to the scene, and she shivered, wondering what the day would bring. She wanted desperately to know if Deborah and the others were all right, but finding a way to Miss Boylan's seemed impossible.

Next to the lavatory, she found an oval-shaped tub

of water. When she touched it, she drew back her hand in surprise. Warm water. Had Dylan built a fire outside and heated water for her? Impossible. He didn't give a damn for her comfort. Yet he had let her take the berth last night even though she wouldn't let him near it. Now this.

She decided not to wonder about it, and quickly put the screen in place. With a deep shudder of delight she bathed herself, scrubbing her hair thoroughly for the first time since before the fire. She donned a plain blue dress she had found in the luggage. It was beautifully made; from her years of handling Miss Deborah's wardrobe, she recognized the work of a gifted seamstress. She felt guilty putting it on, but couldn't abide the thought of the formal green silk again, so badly burned and hastily mended, and so full of reminders of the night of the fire. Her wedding dress, she thought, holding out the once beautiful gown. Most women went misty-eyed over their wedding dresses. All Kathleen saw was a project. It was going to be hard work, restoring the Worth gown to its former glory.

As she did her hair, using the comb, she wondered what sort of lady belonged aboard this luxurious train car. Pullman cars had been all the rage since George Pullman had won the honor of outfitting the funeral train that brought home the body of the great hero of Illinois, President Lincoln. The best families in the city had decided that the mode of travel was even better suited for the living. Wealthy tycoons and merchants all commissioned their own cars to make rail travel fashionable and comfortable. She imagined herself here, ordering tea and crumpets as the landscape whizzed past through the big picture windows.

Then she stopped herself, scowling away the fantasy. Wishing for things like that had landed her in the fix of her life. Why, oh why, couldn't she have let herself be content with who she was and what she had? Then she never would have met Dylan Kennedy—or whoever he was. She never would have committed the insanity of marrying him in the midst of a disaster. Never would have— She glanced at the unmade bed and brought the thought up short.

"All right, colleen," she muttered to herself, straightening the coverlet and arranging the pillows. "Best see what we're about today."

She went to the door of the salon car and tentatively opened it. There, a few yards down the track, stood Dylan and Bull. An iron kettle suspended over a brazier emitted puffs of steam.

Spying her, Dylan doffed an imaginary hat. "Top o' the morning to you," he said, mimicking her brogue. "And how did milady sleep last night and—" he consulted an imaginary watch "—half the day? Did you enjoy your bath? Do you need more hot water?"

She ignored him. "Hello, Bull. Is your ankle better?"

The big man wore new clothes and shoes. He nodded, sticking out his large foot and rotating it. "Better, thank you."

"Bull was going to hightail it out of town," Dylan said. "But I convinced him to stay a spell."

"Whatever he promised you," Kathleen warned Bull, "don't believe him. He's not to be trusted."

"I don't trust nobody," Bull assured her. "Never have. But I got nowhere else to go."

"Have you a place to stay?"

He jerked his shining bald head at a passenger coach. Like the palace car, it had been taken aside and presumably forgotten. "That'll do for a time." A steam whistle shrilled in the air, and he started toward the terminal. "I'd best be going, see if I can get in line for some grub," he said.

Food camps and makeshift barracks had been set up throughout the city, at Washington Square Park, Madison Street, Harrison Street, Clybourne Avenue and around some of the churches. At the head of the terminal, lines formed as citizens waited for supplies from other cities.

Alone with Dylan, Kathleen could not think of a thing to say. She stood with one foot on the iron stair of the palace car, her hand gripping the figured balustrade. He sent her an easy smile, the same smile that had caught her heart the first moment she'd seen him.

"Are you hungry?" he asked.

"Starved."

He motioned her aboard. Once inside, he took out a bundle containing graham biscuits and four red apples. "This is the best I could do for the moment," he said. "I'm not used to having more than one mouth to feed."

"How kind of you to point that out."

"Who are you calling kind?" he muttered, scowling as he scanned a one-page news sheet. He seemed distracted, probably concentrating on his next swindle, she thought in annoyance.

Without warning, the door opened and a man stepped inside. Dylan swiftly stepped in front of her. "Sir, may I—" Then he strode across the room, his entire demeanor changing as if by magic. A moment ago he had been a calculating trickster. Yet in the blink of an eye, he transformed himself into an earnest, well-heeled Boston gentleman. "Cornelius," he said heartily, "this is a stroke of luck. By God, but it's a fine thing to see a familiar face."

Mr. Cornelius King, who had made his first million, it was rumored, by profiteering during the Civil War, frowned in puzzled fashion. He was short of stature, yet handsome, with shrewd eyes and a well-groomed beard framing his unsmiling mouth. "Have we met?"

"Dylan Francis Kennedy, at your service." Dylan gave his trademark bow. "We met at the Sinclair party some weeks ago."

"Ah, Dylan, of course." King relaxed a little, peeling off his gloves. "I heard nothing but praise for you from my daughters. I apologize for not recognizing you right off."

Kathleen fumed. Had he managed to flirt with every single girl in the city?

"Perfectly understandable," Dylan said. "Under the circumstances, I'd hardly recognize myself if there were an unbroken mirror in the city." He stood aside and drew Kathleen forward. "Miss Kathleen," he said, "I'd like you to meet Mr. Cornelius King."

"How do you do," she said, giving him a slight, but proper, curtsy. Truly, she wanted to fall through the floor and slink away. A dull red blush crept over her. To be caught trespassing on a famous man's property... She knew no rules of decorum for this situation. Yet the man showed no shock at her presence. She knew from her experience belowstairs that the very best social climbers kept mistresses. He probably had one of his own. It shamed her to be viewed in such a light, but she couldn't think what to say. If she claimed to be Dylan's wife, she would be even more humiliated when he denied it. He was no good for her at all, she decided. If she had a shred of pride she would leave right now and never come back.

"I suppose I should ask you," Mr. King said to Dylan, "what you're doing in my palace car."

"I was just about to explain that," Dylan replied smoothly, as if he had been expecting the question. "I found it nearly overrun with squatters. Had the devil of a time getting them to leave." He went on to describe his fictional deeds in very understated but specific detail.

As he spoke, Kathleen marveled at his finesse. It was pure magic, the way this man reinvented himself. One moment he was a cynical con artist, colluding about Lord-knew-what with Bull outside the train car. The next, he played the coolheaded young turk, easily convincing a rich tycoon that he had single-handedly ejected a gang of dangerous looters before they could do any damage to the train car. What a gift it was, to be anyone he chose at the drop of a hat. Yet she found herself wondering who the real Dylan Kennedy was. Did *he* even know, or was he so accustomed to role-playing that he no longer had an identity of his own?

The notion caused a wave of inexpressible sadness to ripple through her, and she grew exasperated with herself. Of all the victims of Chicago's disaster, he should not be the object of her sympathy. But there it was. His gift. He could wrest the desired response from even the most reluctant skeptic. Even from someone who knew he was a swindler and a cheat. And a remorseless breaker of hearts.

She realized she was observing a master at his craft. Within minutes, he had Mr. King eating out of his hand, believing every lie that dropped like honey from his beautifully shaped lips.

"So there you have it," he concluded. "Once I realized your property was at risk, I felt I had no choice but to remain here, on my guard."

"I owe you, Dylan," Mr. King said magnanimously. "You've done me an invaluable service."

"Only too glad to help," Dylan said, deeply modest. "How did you and yours come through the fire, then?"

Mr. King spread his hands, palms up. "My family and I waited out the fire with Lord Kim, up at Lake View, and there they stay. I came to the city to see how the recovery's coming." The sound of cursing and the cracking of a whip drew their attention to the yard outside. On the avenue which ran parallel to the tracks, a muleteer argued with an engine crew. "Another farmer from the prairie," Mr. King remarked, shaking his head. "He has nowhere to sell his grain and will probably end up dumping the entire lot into the lake." Shaking his head, he turned away. "It's a new world, overnight."

"That it is," Dylan agreed.

"Mayor Mason's already convening a Board of Inquiry to investigate the whole thing, though it's pretty clear that it all started in the West Division." He made a fist. "Damned immigrant Irish," he blustered. "They probably caused the fire and are looting the city as we speak."

Kathleen ground her teeth. Suddenly she lost all sympathy for the man on whose property she had been trespassing. She must have made some sound or movement, for he looked at her, then looked closer.

"That dress, ma'am. I believe it belongs to my wife."

"Indeed, sir," she said with melting sincerity. "It was the only way to keep it out of the hands of those disgusting Irish looters."

Dylan slipped his arm around her waist and gazed at her with pure admiration. She realized that she had pleased him by joining his confidence game and by playacting with surprising ease.

"In fact," she went on boldly, "perhaps we should continue to safeguard the train car in your absence. Surely you'd be much more comfortable at your estate in the suburbs, well away from the depraved immigrants, until the city is safe again."

"There's no need, ma'am. I can hire private guards, surely. I would not presume to ask—"

"We insist, don't we, Dylan?" She nudged him in the side.

"Certainly," he said. "We insist."

"It's simply too awful to think of decent folk like yourself suffering through this disaster." She caught herself enjoying this much more than she should. "You'll never find a guard to hire. They're all busy with trivial matters like relief work."

"Very well," he said slowly. "But I can only impose upon you for a day or two, until I find proper help.''

Kathleen sensed that they shouldn't press their luck, but she couldn't help a small suggestion. ''We'll need some things, of course. Supplies and such.''

''I'll see that you get them.''

*And any bills we might incur,* she thought remorselessly.

As Dylan walked outside with Mr. King, she pushed aside her feeling of humiliation. Despite their pretenses, their marriage had been real. Their consummation had been *very* real, unforgettably so. Still, she wished that playing the role of a rich man's mistress did not come so easily to her.

Dylan had no idea why he kept getting involved in Kathleen O'Leary's affairs and schemes. His well-honed sense of self-preservation told him to quietly leave the city, yet here he was, accompanying Kathleen to the West Division, to the home of her family. Like a common servant, he was laden with parcels— a side of bacon and a sack of flour—and they dragged at him like a ball and chain.

Similarly laden, and uncomplaining as a statue of the Virgin Mary, Kathleen walked quietly beside him through the seething city. She managed to look virtuous and pure, an angel of mercy on a quest to succor the unfortunate. She also managed to look imminently desirable, evoking heated memories of the wild bliss of their lovemaking. His body, predictably, reacted to the thought. No more, he told himself sternly. His lust for her must not be permitted to get in the way of expedience.

He intended to abandon her somewhere along the way. He told himself he was better off never seeing her again. True, the marriage had a few well-placed witnesses, but the paperwork was lost, so there was no record to worry about. Within a few hours, Kathleen O'Leary would just be a too pleasant memory of the most disastrous night in Chicago.

Yet when they reached the river, he thought it best to accompany her across to the West Division. And once they arrived there, he thought it foolish to simply drop his parcels and leave them to the foragers darting in and out of the ruins. Each time he saw an opportunity to slip away, happenstance provided him with a reason to stay by her side. Some strange force seemed to be pulling him along with her, like a rogue current that would not let him out of its grasp.

The jewels, he thought to himself. Yes, that was it. That was why he couldn't bring himself to abandon her. She still had the jewels she had worn Sunday night. When he'd questioned her about the diamond-and-emerald necklace, bracelet and earrings, she'd explained that they belonged to her mistress and she had every intention of returning them. He, on the other hand, had every intention of stealing them. He just had to figure out where she had hidden them.

He recognized the tired wreckage of de Koven Street when they reached it. The sagging cottages, some of them burned beyond habitation, others no worse off than they had been prior to the fire, lined both sides of the street. Chickens and goats roamed untended, their owners either having fled or worse. A cow lowed miserably, her udders swollen to the point where they were painful to look at. A man holding a pail kept trying to milk her, but each time he got close, the idiot cow shied away.

Maybe it was the same idiot cow that had started the fire.

"Oh!" Kathleen burst out suddenly. She started marching fast in the direction of her parents' cottage. "How dare they!"

A handful of kids had gathered in the side yard of the O'Leary house, which shared a wall with another dwelling. The kids were shouting and pelting the place with rocks as they chanted, "You started the fi-ire, you started the fi-ire."

Setting down her parcels, Kathleen descended on them like a red plague. "Go on with you, then," she yelled. "I'll see the back of you, or you'll see the back of my hand."

The youngsters froze and stared at her, but they didn't leave. She grabbed the ear of the largest boy. "Perhaps you'd like a visit with Officer Keating, then."

"Ow! Lemme go!" The kid wrenched himself away and fled, the younger ones bringing up the rear.

Dylan couldn't hide his amusement, especially at the heated glare she sent him when she returned for her parcels.

"And what are you laughing at?" she demanded.

"You, my dear. You're ranting." Dylan told himself to leave the supplies on the stoop and hightail it out of town.

But when Mrs. O'Leary spotted him, she gave him a tired smile of welcome and said, "Come in, do. I've got the kettle on for tea."

Against his will, he stepped into the cottage and

stood still, waiting for his eyes to adjust to the dimness. "These are my little ones, Mary and James," Mrs. O'Leary said, gesturing at a grubby pair on the floor in front of the stove. "And those two giant louts having at the parcels are Frank and Connor." She flapped her apron at them. "That'll do, boys," she scolded. "Here Kathleen and Mr. Dylan were good enough to bring us some food, and you're at it without a word of thanks. Shame on you, shame."

"How do, sir," they said, one after another. Frank licked his hand and plastered down a stray lock of hair. The lads were as handsome in their way as Kathleen was beautiful. They had the same deep-red hair and green eyes fringed in long brown lashes. They poked at each other when they thought no one was looking, and grinned broadly, trying to swallow their giggles. "Pleasure to meet you, 'tis," they said.

"I'm sure," Dylan replied, feeling a reluctant approval of these two. Barefoot and clad in rags, they managed to seem full of life and hope despite their dire circumstances. They were about twelve and thirteen, poised at that peculiar spot in life to choose a path and set off.

Choose wisely, he wanted to tell them, because you can't undo some choices. But he didn't say anything. It was none of his business. And besides, he was hardly the one to be giving advice to promising lads.

"I'm so glad to see you back, sir," Mrs. O'Leary said, gratefully unwrapping the parcel of flour and putting it in a tall bin. She made no reference to the way he had left before.

"Likewise," he said noncommittally.

"You needn't 'sir' him, Mam," Kathleen said, sounding annoyed.

"It's just that I remember my manners, I do," Mrs. O'Leary said. "Help me get the goods put up, and then we'll get supper. Your father'll be that pleased to see you, he will."

Mrs. O'Leary and Kathleen busied themselves fixing supper. They worked together at a plank counter, talking in low tones with their heads bent close in conspiratorial fashion. Dylan wasn't certain what they were saying, but he knew that the next time Mrs. O'Leary looked at him, she wouldn't see the tycoon she had thought he was. Wandering outside, he found the lads stacking firewood against the side of the house. While they worked, the little ones gathered bits of charcoal in a rusty bin with a handle.

It occurred to him to help them, but he didn't want them to get the idea that he'd always be around to help. "Laying in for the winter, are you?" he asked.

Frank, the elder by a year or so, nodded, though he didn't pause in his work. "I thought during the fire I'd be happy if I never saw another stick of wood again. But Mam's worried. Winter's coming on, and we've lost all except the house."

The little girl—Mary was her name, he recalled—came over and tugged at his pant leg. She wore several layers of dirt and ash over her porcelain-fine skin, but even so, he could tell she would one day be as lovely as Kathleen. She had a perfect bow of a mouth, large green eyes and a smile that warmed the day. "Mr. Dylan," she said, "is it true you married our Kathleen 'cause you thought she was a rich lady?"

He was unaccustomed to feeling shame, but in this

case, he did. A little. "I married your Kathleen," he said, hunkering down and grinning at the girl, "because we were caught in the middle of the fire and we didn't know what else to do. We were just pretending, though."

She nodded sagely. "I pretended to marry Jackie Slater, but he's not my friend anymore 'cause I had to punch him in the nose."

It must be a family trait, he thought. "Why'd you have to do that?"

She glanced from side to side, then crooked her finger, motioning him to come closer. Then she cupped her small hands around his ear and said, "He tried to look up my dress, he did."

Dylan put his hands on her bony little shoulders. "Did it hurt him, when you punched him in the nose?"

"He bled all over himself and went wailing like a scare-baby to his mam."

"Good. You did the right thing, Mary."

A short while later, a pair of well-dressed men showed up. One of them set a camera on a tripod and aimed the aperture at the O'Leary house. Suspicious, Dylan strode over to them. "Can I ask what you're about?"

"Sure can, mister." One of the men, wearing shirt-sleeves pushed back with cuff bands, pointed at the house. "Charlie Mosher's my name. This is for the *Trib*. Folks'll want a look at the fire starter's house."

"You don't say." Dylan stroked his cheek thoughtfully.

In the yard, the children eyed the strangers with

wary eyes. Mary clung to one of the boys and half
hid behind him.

"So you can just park your camera right here and
take all the pictures you please?" he asked.

"It's a free country." The man in the sleeves took
out a long black cloth while the other opened a box
of plates and chemicals.

"How would you like a picture of Mrs. O'Leary
herself?" Dylan offered.

That got their attention.

"And her cow?" he added.

Within moments they had struck a deal. They
would pay Mrs. O'Leary ten dollars for the sitting.
Now all that remained was to get her to agree.

"Not for all of Saint Appollonia's teeth," she said,
shrinking fearfully from the idea of having her picture
made with the camera. She stood at the window, holding aside the flour sack curtain and peering at the men
from the paper.

"Shame on you for even asking," Kathleen added.

Dylan was experienced enough at this sort of thing
to know what to say next. "Very well. They'll just
get your neighbor to do it for twice the money." He
headed for the door.

"Mrs. McLaughlin? And what's she to do with any
of it?" Mrs. O'Leary demanded.

"No more than you, I imagine." He moved slowly
toward the door. "Not that it matters to the newspaper
reporters."

"Wait," Mrs. O'Leary said just before he left.

"Mam," Kathleen said, "it's exploitation."

"It's ten dollars I don't have," she said.

"I've got to give them an answer," Dylan prodded.

Mrs. O'Leary said nothing. He could feel the dark pressure of her disapproval, and knew Kathleen had told her mother the truth—that he was a penniless schemer who only pretended to be a wealthy tycoon. In the past, he had never paused to consider that his actions might cause trouble or hurt. He simply hadn't cared. Damn Kathleen. Damn her for making him care.

With a quiet sort of dignity, Mrs. O'Leary walked across the yard and spoke with the men. Then she turned to Dylan and Kathleen, hands planted on her hips. "We have a deal," she said. "But what's this you said about a cow, you great fool?"

"A minor detail. Didn't we spy one up the street just a short while ago?" Dylan asked Kathleen.

"It wasn't one of ours," she said.

"We'd just be borrowing it."

"Fine, then go fetch it home."

Dylan kept a poker face. He had absolutely no experience with cows. In some of his burlesque acts, he had used learned pigs and counting horses, but cows were considered too stupid to perform.

"Give me five minutes," he said, undaunted. "Frank and Connor, how about giving me a hand?"

The boys eagerly joined in the hunt for the cow. Anything was preferable to their chores.

"There she is," Dylan called, heading for the middle of the block. The cow stood placidly by a ditch of brackish water. She was a huge thing, bigger than he recalled. She looked considerably calmer than she had earlier. Maybe someone had managed to milk her.

When Dylan and the boys approached, she looked up from drinking out of the ditch. Long strings of moisture streamed from her bovine mouth. She blinked at them slowly.

"Catch hold of her rope, then," Dylan said to the boys.

Connor and Frank poked each other and giggled.

"Well?" he said. "What are you waiting for?"

The boys tried to sober up. One of them circled around the back of the cow while the other caught the frayed rope attached to the halter. "Here you are," he said, holding the end of the rope out to Dylan.

He put up his hands, palms out. "I'll let you lead her home."

"Aw, come on, it was your idea," Connor said, still giggling like an idiot.

"Here, I'll go along behind with a switch." Frank picked up a thin stick and swatted the large, swaying rump.

Dylan shook his head, aware that time was wasting. "Very well. Give me the rope and I'll show you the meaning of easy money."

Easy, he soon found out, was a relative term. It had been easy enough to get the offer from the photographer, and easy enough to convince Mrs. O'Leary to agree to sit for a photograph. However, bringing the cow to the yard was much more of a challenge. When Dylan tugged one way, the stupid beast tugged the other. When he pulled, the thing balked. Then the cow surged ahead, trotting along, and Dylan was almost dragged. Only with the boys herding front and back was he able to steer the animal into position in the yard.

They had managed to find a stool, a pail and a lamp

for props. Kathleen and Mrs. O'Leary were busy putting the older woman's hair neatly under a kerchief. When they heard Dylan come into the yard with the cow, they turned.

Kathleen set her hands on her hips and burst out laughing, and her mother joined her.

Dylan scowled. This was a family of lunatics, to be sure. "What's the matter?"

"I imagine you had some bit of trouble bringing that beast here," Kathleen said.

"As a matter of fact, I did."

"No wonder." She wiped at tears of mirth. "You brought us a bull, Dylan Kennedy."

Still clutching the rope, he whirled around. The boys had disappeared without a trace, but he could hear their laughter somewhere behind the house. Dylan bent down and inspected.

"A bull, eh?" he said. "But I thought that was—"

"There is a difference," Kathleen said.

"How the devil am I supposed to know? I've never seen a bull up close in my life," he said. "Nor a cow, for that matter." He was not used to being the butt of someone else's amusement. "All right then, let's get this picture made."

"With a bull?" Mrs. O'Leary asked.

"It won't matter. Most people don't know the difference." He waved to the photographers. "Gentlemen, we are ready."

Like Dylan, they didn't seem to recognize the bull for what it was, either. With Kathleen feeding handfuls of hay to the creature, it stood placidly enough while Mrs. O'Leary took her place on the stool.

"Go ahead and milk her," Mosher urged. "Just as you were when she kicked the lantern."

Mrs. O'Leary shook her head. "I don't think the poor creature'd take too well to that." Her eyes brimmed with merriment as she rested her hand on the smooth hide.

That was the image they made with the picture. A humble woman and a cow that wasn't really a cow against the backdrop of the weathered siding of the house, with straw strewn upon the ground. In the end they agreed that the image would make a fine picture postcard they could sell for a penny apiece, giving the O'Learys a share in the profits. Dylan did the talking, performing the transaction swiftly and easily, as it was not unlike other deals he had made on the fly. He even managed to sell them the lantern for another ten dollars, convincing them that it would fetch a much better sum as an artifact of the disaster. It never occurred to them to question whether or not this was the exact lamp that had started the fire.

Just before a supper of biscuits with bacon gravy, Patrick O'Leary arrived. Tall and well-built, with brown hair and dark eyes, he inspected Dylan with a keen stare. Dylan could see immediately that he was not a man to be trifled with.

"So you're the one that married my daughter," he said.

"After a fashion," Dylan hedged.

"Without asking my permission." Swift as lightning, O'Leary shoved him up against the wall. "You tricked my poor girl, you did," he accused. "Took her virtue. She could be breeding already, for the love of Christ—"

The possibility of a pregnant Kathleen put the fear of God in Dylan. Or perhaps it was the meaty, drawn-back fist of her father. "Sir, it's a long story—"

"But I'll make short work of you, and all your fancy ways won't save you." He pressed the side of his forearm into Dylan's windpipe. Dylan knew a number of ways to escape, but they all involved fighting dirty. He didn't think kneeing Kathleen's father in the groin was such a good idea. Red-faced from lack of air, he forced out a gurgling sound as his eyes bulged. He pushed at O'Leary's arm, but the burly man was a rock—angry and unwilling to budge.

"Da." Kathleen spoke quietly and put her hand on her father's arm. "It'll be all right, Da. You needn't come to blows."

Dylan was amazed—and gratified—by her timely intervention. But O'Leary only pressed harder, starving Dylan for air.

"He's all red in the face," Mary declared. "Look, Frank! He's gone all red."

"Are you going to kill him, Da?" Connor asked.

"Enough!" Mrs. O'Leary's voice rang with the command of an experienced Irish wife. "You'll not disrupt my peaceful house with your temper, Patrick O'Leary. Let him be. *Now*."

The pressing arm relaxed by inches and finally dropped. Dylan sucked in a deep breath of air. He wondered if anything had been crushed or broken.

"By God I'll have more words with the blighter," O'Leary barked.

"Da—" Kathleen began, but he waved her silent.

"See here, you," O'Leary said. "You'll do right by my daughter."

"Of course, sir." Dylan cleared his throat, which still ached from the assault. He straightened his shoulders and looked O'Leary in the eye. He was experienced at this. He had faced stern, protective fathers before. They liked words of assurance. Of deference. "She'll want for nothing. I'll treat her like a queen."

"Will he?" O'Leary demanded of Kathleen.

When she hesitated, Dylan said, "Didn't I find you shelter in a Pullman car?" he asked. "Didn't we dine on honey and champagne?"

Mrs. O'Leary's weary face lit up. "Is that true, Kathleen?"

"Yes, Mam." She blushed and stared at the floor.

"Honey and champagne," Mary chanted. "Honey and champagne!"

The baby joined in, waving his grubby hands until his mother snatched him up and took him in her lap, laughing softly.

Dylan caught O'Leary's eye. "I kept her safe through the fire," he said. "I didn't let her get hurt."

"Aye," O'Leary conceded. "But if you ever do..." He grasped Dylan's arm, leaned forward and whispered harshly in his ear. It was one of the most creative and violent bodily threats Dylan had ever heard. He felt himself grow pale and his hand strayed protectively to the front of his trousers. O'Leary stepped away, crossing his arms over his thick chest. "Do I make myself clear?"

"Indeed," Dylan said.

O'Leary turned to his elder daughter. "Are you sure, then, colleen?"

"Yes, Da." Kathleen didn't once look at Dylan. He had no idea what she was thinking. "I'm sure."

"He said it was just pretend," Mary piped up.

Both Dylan and Kathleen glared at her.

"Take the boys outside and wash up," Mrs. O'Leary ordered her husband. "Ah, but it's a curse being poor," Mrs. O'Leary said, balancing the baby on her hip as her husband and sons trooped out.

Dylan chucked the baby under the chin. "I've never seen a richer child than this."

Mrs. O'Leary's heart melted; he could see it in her face. And the funny thing was, his comment had been sincere. He had held large fortunes in his hands, but he had never had what this family possessed in abundance.

"Sit down to supper," Mrs. O'Leary said when her husband returned. He took his place at one end of a scarred pine trestle table, and Dylan sat down at the other. Despite the simplicity of the fare, it smelled delicious.

Dylan was about to dig in when Mrs. O'Leary clasped her hands together on the table. Her husband and children followed suit. She bowed her head and said quickly, "For what we are about to receive, may the good Lord our God make us truly thankful. Amen."

The others echoed "Amen" around the table and fell to. Dylan was unexpectedly touched by the O'Learys. He had never had a soul to care about him, to fix him supper and say grace with over a simple meal. He was fascinated by the way the family clung together, bracing themselves in a unified front against the onslaught of hardship. It was a new way to face troubles, one he didn't understand at all. He was used to looking out for himself and no one else.

After supper, Kathleen and Mrs. O'Leary explained about the photograph. Patrick threw a thunderous look at Dylan Kennedy, but his wife intervened. "Winter's coming on, and we've lost nearly all we have. This morning we didn't have five cents to spare. The money will help."

"It's as good as saying you're guilty," he blustered. "What'll you say when you're brought up to make a statement before the Board of Fire?"

She grew pale and reached for his hand. "Patrick, I couldn't."

"You'll have to. I had it from the West Division marshal himself."

She made the sign of the cross and lifted her gaze to heaven. Looking discomfited, Kathleen touched her hand. "You'll be fine, Mam. You did nothing wrong. They can't blame a drought and a windstorm on you, for mercy's sake."

Mrs. O'Leary relaxed a little and forced a smile. "You're a comfort to your Mam, so you are," she said.

They finished eating in silence, and after the washing up, Kathleen took off her borrowed apron. "We must be going," she said.

Going? Dylan scratched his head. He had assumed she would stay here, in the bosom of her family. Yet after he thanked her mother for supper and headed for the door, she came with him.

To Dylan's surprise, O'Leary followed them outside. A twinkle shone in his eye. "I'm giving you a world of trouble, lad," he said gruffly. "And she's worth every last drop of it."

"No doubt about that, sir." Dylan wasn't sure which statement he was agreeing with.

O'Leary gently pressed a kiss to Kathleen's forehead. "*Slainte*, my girl," he whispered.

"Thank you, Da," she said, and the depth of their affection radiated between them. Its glow illuminated a hollow place inside Dylan. Had he ever known that sort of bond? If he had, his heart didn't remember.

"Good night," Kathleen added as her father returned to the house. O'Leary stood on the stoop, solid as a stone as he watched them go.

Dylan walked away, annoyed that she had accompanied him. "Where do you think you're going?" he asked.

She bridled, tossing her head like a proud mare. "That depends. Where are you going?"

He hadn't thought about it much. The safest plan for him would be to skip town and put together a game or two. Once he had a little money, he could start over again, clean and unencumbered. Kathleen was proving harder to shake than a flophouse flea, though.

"I'm going back to the train car. If possible, I'll find a bottle and get roaring drunk."

"Not if I have anything to say about it."

He started walking. "You don't. You should stay here with your family."

"And give them another mouth to feed? No, thank you. They've enough to contend with, what with winter coming on and the barn and wagon gone. They don't need their grown daughter moving back in."

"I have nothing to offer you, Kathleen. Nothing

but trouble.'' He had lied to her father; they both knew that.

She walked fast to match his long strides. ''You'll have to do better than that, boyo.''

''Listen, I did what I could for your family. My own affairs are complicated.'' He thought how impossible it was for him to consider the needs of another person, particularly a person like Kathleen. ''You're better off without me.''

They turned the corner and headed east toward the bridge. At dusk, people still sifted through smoldering piles, already engaged in the arduous task of rebuilding from nothing.

''Maybe I am,'' she agreed. ''Maybe not. But I have no choice. I am married to you.''

''Maybe,'' he said, mimicking her tone. ''Maybe not. There's not a shred of proof, Kathleen.''

''So you've said, but you could be lying about that.''

''How do you know?''

''You lie about everything.''

''Then why the devil would you want to be married to a liar like me?'' He all but tore at his hair in frustration. Damn, she was a persistent, annoying woman.

''Because I didn't know you were a liar Sunday night.'' She lowered her voice. ''I trusted you.''

''That was a mistake. Look, Kathleen. I'm no good. You don't want me. I'm in a hole, and it'll take a big touch to get me out.''

''What do you mean, a big touch?''

''A lot of money.''

She eyed him critically, her gaze probing too deep for comfort.

"What?" he asked, more annoyed than ever.

"You've always run from your problems, haven't you?"

Without thinking, he took her hand to help her over a broken spot in the pavement. "That's what makes them go away." He couldn't help laughing a little at her expression. "It's always worked before."

She kept her hand tucked in the crook of his arm, and despite his mood, he liked the feel of it nestled there. "I don't think it will work this time, Dylan."

"Why the hell not?"

"Because the thing you're really running from is yourself," she said. "One of these days you'll discover that you can't escape who you are."

"You're making no sense at all," he muttered, glaring down at the murky, sluggish river as they crossed the bridge.

"What would it take for you to stay and face up to your problems?" she asked.

He laughed again, bringing the argument full circle. "A big touch."

"Obtained by illicit means, no doubt."

"How else?"

"I have a better idea," she said.

## The Setup

It was beautiful and simple
as all truly great swindles are.

—O. Henry

# *Fourteen*

"How can I possibly give up something so beautiful and precious?" Dylan said earnestly, gazing deep into Kathleen's green eyes.

In the foyer of the building, she hesitated and gazed back at him, briefly moistening her lips with her tongue.

He held his breath. She was weakening, surely. She had come to see reason.

But then she said, "I've been telling you all morning, keeping the jewels is out of the question, and no amount of moon-eyed flattery is going to change my mind." She turned on her heel and crossed the foyer to the stairs. Muttering under his breath, he followed her.

Dylan was not surprised to learn that Arthur Sinclair, one of the foremost businessmen in Chicago, had already reopened his offices in the Lind Block, appropriating space from the Z. M. Hall Grocery. Sinclair's reputation for ruthless and profitable commerce was widely known throughout the city, and he was the sort who would not allow even the holocaust of Sunday night to interfere.

The five-storey building by the river had survived the fire, thanks to an army of dedicated workers who had stayed to battle the embers long after the fire had swept the entire area.

One of those workers was Mr. Milford Plunkett, who sat in the outer office at a desk piled high with messages, papers, account books and parcels. An air of self-importance surrounded him like a thick fog.

When Dylan and Kathleen walked into the office, Plunkett came immediately to his feet, pressing his palms to the desk and trying not to stare at her. But his busily twitching eyebrows gave him away. Dylan told himself he should be used to men's reactions to Kathleen by now. Still, he felt the same savage stirring of jealousy that possessed him every time a pair of male eyes swept over her, or every time a man scrambled to open a door for her or went out of his way to get a look at her up close. She tolerated the attention with a charming mixture of bemusement and befuddlement, which only added to her allure.

It wasn't her fault she was ravishingly beautiful, with her creamy skin and red hair. But it *was* her fault, he thought, that despite her humble background, she carried herself with a certain haughty dignity that challenged and confounded men to the point of distraction.

"Dylan Kennedy," he said, pulling Plunkett's attention away from Kathleen.

Like all good assistants, Plunkett knew the social landscape through which his employer moved, and he instantly recognized the name.

"Mr. Kennedy, of course." The watchful, sharp-featured face relaxed into an expression of deference. "Mr. Sinclair will be relieved to know you survived the fire."

Dylan placed his hand at the small of Kathleen's back, letting Plunkett make whatever he would of her presence. "We should like very much to see Mr. Sinclair." He had no doubt Arthur would receive him. Sinclair was not only the richest man in Chicago. He was also the most socially ambitious. Believing, as all Chicago society did, that Dylan ranked up there with the Old Settlers, Sinclair had been quick to welcome him. Sinclair's only daughter, Deborah, reportedly came with a million-dollar dowry, but she'd already been spoken for by the time Dylan had arrived in Chicago. Just his luck, he thought, cutting a glance at Kathleen, to get stuck with the maid rather than the mistress.

"Sir, I'm terribly sorry, but Mr. Sinclair is not available."

Milford Plunkett's reply startled him. Dylan quickly mulled over the possibilities. Could his ruse have been exposed already?

Costello, he thought. But why would Vince do that? It was to his advantage to help Dylan keep his identity as a member of the elite.

Dylan allowed the man a small, tight smile, while inside, he exulted. He hadn't wanted to come here, anyway. "I see. Well, then, we'd best be going—"

"Mr. Plunkett." Kathleen pushed forward, speaking up for the first time. "I swear, the fire must've charred your brains. It's me. Kathleen. Miss Deborah's maid."

Plunkett gaped at her, then flushed three shades of scarlet. "Sorry, miss," he stammered. "I didn't realize it was you without—" He stopped, clearly aware of no tactful way to say it.

"You mean, without my cap and duster," she said with wry humor.

"Miss Deborah's maid," he said wonderingly. "I scarcely recognized you."

She allowed a tight smile. "That's apparent. I have something of Miss Deborah's. To put in the safe."

He glanced over his shoulder at the door to the inner office. "Would you excuse me for a moment?"

"Of course," she said before Dylan could object again.

He disliked being kept waiting almost as much as he disliked giving back a found fortune. Often when someone "excused himself" it meant one's credentials were being checked or that one was being discussed behind his back. He shot Kathleen a look of fury. "I still say you're out of your mind for doing this."

"I don't expect you to understand honesty."

"I thought you had some grand plan," he said.

"I do. But I refuse to go another moment with something that doesn't belong to me." She put up a hand, touching her bodice, where she hid the jewelry.

"How appropriate," he said, staring unabashedly, "that some of your most delicious attributes are kept in the same place."

"I don't know what you mean," she said, but her blushing cheeks indicated otherwise.

"Your breasts," he said loudly, "and your jewels."

"You're a scoundrel entirely," she hissed, pulling out the necklace. It spilled over the palms of her dainty hands, the sparkle of diamonds and emeralds exaggerated by the sunlight streaming through the window.

He moved close to her, close enough to inhale her flowery scent, to see the velvety smoothness of her cheeks, her throat, her bosom. He couldn't help himself. He brushed his knuckles along her jawline, making a trail southward as a wave of sexual heat passed through him.

"It seems a shame," he whispered, keeping his stare fixed on her, "to leave such a magnificent bosom unadorned."

She gasped, waiting a heartbeat longer than he'd expected before she pulled away. Her outrage was genuine, but so was her barely veiled fascination.

It was still there, the wild attraction that had gripped them both the instant they'd first met. What a strange thing to discover a lust stronger than his lust for the game.

He told himself an honest woman had no value to him. So why did he still want her? When something outlasted its usefulness, he discarded it. That had always been his way. Keeping the jewels in his sight had been his excuse for keeping Kathleen around. Now that she was determined to give them back, he had no reason to stay with her.

Yet in this case, he simply didn't want to let her go. The fool woman made him crazy.

She pretended to take a great interest in the papers that littered Plunkett's desk. Watching her, Dylan realized she wasn't pretending. "What?" he asked.

"Futures contracts," she murmured, then turned to him abruptly. "Oh, dear. I wonder if we're still the only ones who know of that bargeload of grain out at Eden Landing.''

"Is that important?''

She tapped her foot in impatience. "It is critical to my plan, but I need to find out when the grain markets will reopen.''

Milford Plunkett returned with a slip of paper, accompanied by a man wearing an eyepatch and carrying a Colt revolving pistol in a shoulder holster. Dylan recognized the insignia on the man's coat—the open eye and slogan We Never Sleep marked him as a member of the Pinkerton Detective Agency. But the broad-shouldered man's flesh was as weak as any bridegroom's; the minute he saw Kathleen, he turned from watchdog into panting lapdog.

Dylan summoned his best expression of snobbish outrage. Before he could speak, Plunkett began to bow and scrape and apologize. "Just a precaution,'' he explained. "Naturally we are more than grateful, Miss Kathleen.''

"I'm sure you are,'' Dylan said wryly.

Kathleen held out the jewels and tried to launch into the explanation she had agonized over. She'd been terrified of being accused of thievery.

Dylan waved a hand, interrupting her even before she began. She was new at this and didn't understand that you never put yourself at a disadvantage. He took the jewels without looking at them, and shoved them across the desk as if their value made no impression on him at all.

The Pinkerton kept staring at Kathleen, his good eye all but bugged out of his skull. You'd think the fellow had never seen a pretty woman before.

"I'll just put these in the safe." Plunkett consulted the slip of paper, then swung open the thick door. Dylan stared longingly at the stacked boxes, so alluringly anonymous in the dark cave of the safe. Instantly he began to speculate...but Kathleen had been adamant about not stealing from her employer. Elaborately nonchalant, he forced himself to go to the window and look out.

Chicago resembled a field in the aftermath of battle. From his vantage point, he could see block after block of wreck and ruin. He wondered what, if anything, might be found in the hopeless debris. From here, he could see only brick and cut stone, dust and ash, melted matter that was unrecognizable. Yet as his gaze traveled across the sunlit, smoky landscape, he began to notice small pockets of activity. The First Congregational Church, damaged but still standing, disgorged lines of the hungry and homeless in the bright autumn chill. On the road below, General Sheridan's officers directed workers in clearing the roadway and setting up government offices.

In fact, all around the business district workers had begun the chores of rebuilding. Like a drunk putting himself back together the morning after, the city was coming to life. Crudely painted signs announced the reopening of banks and insurance offices. Near the river, men swarmed over a large area, filling wagons with wreckage; the riverfront lot would be the site of the new Board of Trade.

Kathleen swore she knew a way to earn a fortune through legal means. The details still had to be worked out, and achieving success would take tireless labor and patience, two things Dylan had in short sup-

ply. He had no reason to trust her, but she was so
damned entertaining that he found himself willing to
see what she concocted.

Plunkett and Kathleen had concluded their business
under the watchful eye of the Pinkerton. Dylan bade
the men—and, regrettably, the priceless jewels—a
good day. Outside the office, he and Kathleen went
down several flights of stairs to street level. The stair-
well was crowded with hurrying businessmen and
workers. At the bottom, someone had laid planks over
the uneven ruins, creating a narrow walkway. Dylan
placed his hand at the small of Kathleen's back to
help her along.

It was absurd how much he enjoyed even the most
casual touch. She had brought him nothing but trouble
and she represented everything he opposed—need,
poverty, family dependence. She was a liability.
Worse, a liability with relatives. Lots of relatives. Yet
no matter how hard he tried to break free, he could
not seem to keep his distance from her. She plucked
at some forgotten chord of sentimentality deep inside
him, something rich and warm and…vital. He had no
name for what he was feeling, because he had never
felt it before.

Just knowing she was around lifted his spirits. He
had no idea why, because she was such trouble all
the time. Ordinarily, it took a winning game to make
him feel this good. Kathleen O'Leary could impart a
feeling even more powerful simply by breathing the
air.

Perhaps, he thought, he might tell her so. She had
been cold and unresponsive to him last night. Because
he refused to acknowledge their marriage, the con-

founded female refused to let him share the big, comfortable sleeping berth. He had tried to convince her that no piece of legal paper could enhance or diminish her pleasure, but she seemed to believe otherwise.

He couldn't understand it. They had found rapture in that berth. She had elevated mere swiving to something that involved far loftier sensations than the usual fleeting passion. Maybe, in her inexperience, she didn't understand the difference. But Dylan did. Ah, how he did.

Every once in a while he would catch her looking at him, much as he was watching her now, and he'd get the feeling she, too, thought often about those first wild days after the fire. He was almost certain that was what she was thinking, because when he caught her out, she usually acted guilty. He loved the way the tops of her breasts turned pink when she blushed. He loved the way she combed her hair, the way she ate, the way she slept. Clearly he was either falling in love for the first time...or going crazy.

"Stop glaring at me like that," she said, clearly unaware of the dilemma he had considered confessing to her. "It's done. The jewels were not mine."

Her sassy tone of voice quashed the urge to bare his heart. "They never would have been missed," he grumbled, seizing the issue in order to bury the useless sentiment he was feeling. "One would think you've been hoping to regain your post as a chambermaid."

"Lady's maid," she corrected him tartly. "And yes, perhaps I am concerned about employment. It's the way of honest people."

"It's the way of people with no imagination—"

He stopped himself. There, coming along the walkway, looking well-groomed and officious, was Vincent Costello.

Pasting a smile on his face, Dylan wondered if this
day could possibly get any worse. And almost instantly, it did. For even as Costello stepped aside to
let the workers pass, Faith appeared.

Her undisguised delight at seeing Dylan was
matched only by her father's displeasure. She regarded Dylan with guileless gray eyes, saying, "How
are you, Mr. Kennedy? And Miss Kathleen?"

He managed a smile—his usual flashing grin. He
could feel Costello's fury blasting him like a cold
wind, but he ignored it. "Just taking care of business,
Miss Faith. A very small item of business," he added.

"Then you'll forgive our hurry," Costello said,
pushing past them. "We've work to do as well."

His Relief Aid committee was moving their operation to the Lind building. Watching his old partner
in crime, Dylan was struck by the notion that Vincent
Costello had found his true calling. He had spent
years playing the shill to Dylan's act, but this role
seemed to suit him far better. He was made for or-
ganizing and bossing people around; it was apparent
in the way he directed the operation.

"May I help you with that?" Kathleen offered, indicating the wooden box Faith carried. With a smile,
Faith accepted the offer. Within just a few minutes,
the two young women had walked away like a pair
of experienced gossips, their heads bent in conspiratorial fashion.

It was all Dylan could do not to roll his eyes. He

simply did not know Kathleen well enough to figure out what her game was with respect to Faith.

A few moments later, when Faith went inside with her father, a lanky young man approached Kathleen. Immediately the poisonous jealousy started, and Dylan forced himself to stay where he was rather than shoving the interloper out of the way.

The tall man looked familiar. As he bent and gestured, his manner was emphatic; Kathleen was intrigued. Dylan forced himself to stand his ground, not retreating, but not blazing in between them like a jealous lover, either. Later, he promised himself. Later, he would find out what the intimate conversation was about—even if he had to tickle the truth out of her.

After finishing her conversation, she walked toward him with brisk purpose, her lovely face uncharacteristically taut and pale.

"Is something the matter?" he asked, then remembered that he was irritated with her for giving back the jewels. He lowered his brow in a scowl.

"Indeed there is, and we must do something about it."

"So tell me."

She glanced furtively toward the Lind, now a hive of steady activity as businessmen and officials of the government and military moved in. Sensing her need for confidentiality, he led her toward Madison, where they could take the horse car back to the rail yard. As soon as they were alone on the street, she whirled to face him.

"Just what sort of man is this Vincent Costello?" she demanded. "I want to know everything."

Dylan chuckled. "How long do you have?"

"What do you mean?"

"Vince is a complicated fellow. Hard to explain in a few words."

"Then try. It's important."

"He's not an evil man. Not a man who commits senseless violence."

"I asked what he is, not what he isn't."

"I would say that Vince Costello is the greatest opportunist in the state. Maybe in the country. If there is a game going on, you'll always find him at its center. Why do you ask?"

"Because he has already taken advantage of an opportunity," she said. "He has been stealing from the Catholic Relief Fund."

Dylan was not the least bit surprised, though Costello's swiftness impressed even him. He was most startled by the fact that Kathleen had heard about the deal before he had. He grabbed her elbow. "Tell me what you know."

"Ha." She pulled her arm away. 'You're probably in league with him."

"All right. Then don't tell me."

"I won't. I shall tell the police."

The mention of police never failed to put him on his guard. But maybe he knew Kathleen a little better than he thought. He said, "Of course, you must do as you think right. But you'll have to live with the consequences."

"What do you mean by that?"

"Dear, the police have all they can do sorting out the mess Chicago has become and keeping the peace. The mayor's declared marshal law under General

Sheridan. I doubt they would have the time to spare for a petty thief.''

"His theft is not so petty," she said.

"But it's not a matter of life and death. Besides, if Vince is caught stealing something, he's smart enough to buy his way out of trouble.''

"Even if it's a huge amount of money from the fund meant for the homeless of Chicago?''

They came to a large, smoldering ditch, and he lifted her over the gap, his hands spanning her rib cage. Her dress belled out as he swung her around. With an effort, he concentrated on her words.

"How huge?''

She was quiet for a time. Then she stepped back and walked carefully over the littered roadway. They came to an intersection where the horse car waited. Dylan took out two five-cent pieces for the fare.

A number of people milled around, endlessly discussing the fire. A young couple were engaged in an argument. Dylan wouldn't have noticed except that the woman was visibly pregnant. They lacked the fare for both of them, and the husband was trying to convince her that she should beg a free ride, and he would walk. Dylan tossed both nickels to the man, who looked startled, then thanked him profusely.

Uncomfortable with the gratitude, he simply took Kathleen's hand and walked away.

"That was good of you," she commented.

He could not recall the last time someone had called him good. He did not like the sound of it, for it didn't seem to fit him. "At least now we can continue the conversation," he said.

"Ten thousand dollars," she said quietly.

"What?"

"You asked how much he had stolen."

Dylan was staggered by the amount. "How? And how do you know he did it?"

"Barry Lynch told me."

Dylan recalled the lanky young man, and then remembered where he had seen him before. In the rail yard, with Faith amid the wounded.

"He is working as a clerk for the church fund. Mr. Costello is skimming the cream off all the relief monies that come in before sending the balance on to the church auditor."

Dylan gave a low whistle. It was audacious, but typical of Costello. He moved fast, and he didn't worry about such minor details as eternal damnation.

"Now do you understand why we must alert the authorities?"

"Kathleen, he *is* one of the authorities."

"We can't just let him get away with it."

Dylan scarcely heard for his mind had already galloped ahead. The task was obvious. He had to separate the mark from his money. With Vincent Costello, that was not so simple. He knew the ways of a grifter, and he could spot a false enterprise with one eye shut. Still, if he could be made to believe he was the one getting the benefit of a swindle, then he might take the bait.

Suppressing his excitement, Dylan asked, "Do you trust me?"

"No," she said flatly.

He tried another tack. "Would you help me recover the money from Costello?"

"Only if we put it back where it belongs. It's meant for the church."

He would work on that later. For now, it was easier to agree. "What we have to do," he said, "is to convince Costello to spend his ill-gotten gains—"

"On us," she said, flashing him a grin. "Don't look so surprised, boyo. I know how you think." Her eyes sparkled brighter than the emeralds she had so foolishly given up. "This fits in perfectly with my idea—"

"Which you still haven't told me."

She marched ahead, haughty as a queen. "I've been telling you all along. You just haven't been listening." As they approached the rail yard, she said, "You're about to learn an honest trade, Dylan Kennedy. So pay attention."

# *Fifteen*

Dylan paced up and down in the train car while Kathleen tracked his progress with a steady gaze. The Pullman had been moved to an area by the lake known as the boneyard, where derelict or damaged cars were stored. Concerned that Cornelius King would send for his train car before Dylan was ready to give it up, he had decided to move it to a hidden location. Brandishing counterfeit work orders, he had commandeered a crew for the job.

"How is it that you're so familiar with the Chicago Board of Trade, of all things?" he asked.

"I worked for the daughter of Arthur Sinclair," Kathleen said, settling herself on the fringed settee by the window. "Information about the grain trade ran like gossip through that household."

"Why?"

"Because he started out a poor man and made himself richer than God with his trades."

Dylan stopped pacing. "Now I'm listening."

She toyed with a tasseled shade pull. "All right. Picture this. Years ago, farmers would bring their grain to the city, but there was no central place to sell it. Just like the muleteer we saw yesterday. The poor sods had to walk up and down the waterfront looking for the best price for their grain. If there was too much for sale, they wound up dumping their harvest into Lake Michigan.''

''Why? Surely they could get something for the grain.''

''If the price was too low, it wasn't worth the cost of selling it. Before the Board of Trade existed, a farmer might simply decide to cut his losses and go home. Sometimes groups of them would band together and create a shortage by dumping grain. That would drive up the price. Do you follow me?''

''So far.''

''Good. Now, they created a Board of Trade as a centralized grain market. Members buy forward or to-arrive contracts for grain yet to be shipped. That sort of contract is still used, though it's frowned upon.''

She was losing him already, but he wasn't about to admit it. He simply wasn't accustomed to serious business with a woman. ''Does Mr. Sinclair require all his domestics to study grain commerce?'' he asked.

''Of course not. I found it...of interest to me.'' She caught his skeptical expression and said, ''It's not as if I woke up one morning and said, 'Right. Today I shall learn commerce.' But it's something I've always had a knack for. My mother practiced it on the smallest of scales. She would sell tomorrow's milk at today's prices, and have the use of the money until she had to actually make her delivery.''

''So people paid her before they received the milk?''

''Indeed they did. It was a bond of trust. They got a better price by paying in advance, and my mother had a guaranteed sale. It's the same with the farmers and their grain.''

"You sure as hell must've spent a lot of time eavesdropping," he observed.

She dropped the tassel and studied her reflection in the picture window. "A servant is invisible most of the time. Didn't you know that?"

She was right, of course. There was no outright cruelty or intentional slight, but people of privilege tended to regard servants as no more important than a good horse or fine piece of furniture. Ladies and gentlemen who wouldn't dream of revealing themselves to their peers revealed their most intimate secrets in front of the servants.

He studied her profile and the way the light picked out red-gold strands in her hair, wondering how anyone could ever ignore her.

"You were a lady's maid," he reminded her. "Don't tell me you learned all this from gossiping women?"

She sniffed. "You would be surprised to know what women speak of in private. I did spend plenty of time belowstairs with my eyes and ears open. And not just when it came to matters of business."

He tried to picture her in that life, a domestic with a scrubbed face and a white apron, her glorious hair stuffed under a mobcap. Christ, what a waste.

"You probably eavesdropped out of sheer boredom," he said.

Wistfulness softened her face for a moment, and she rested her elbow on the tabletop, setting her chin in the cradle of her hand. "I was never bored. Ever."

Then it struck him. Like it or not, he was coming to know this woman. He was learning what made her happy or sad or excited or frustrated. And he knew why her life as a maid had not bored her. Because it had given her a glimpse into a world she desperately wanted to be a part of.

"You don't sound like any maid I've ever met."

That drew a brief smile from her. "I suppose I was different because I was so curious about everything. I learned to speak French and I practiced it with Miss Deborah, because she was a reluctant scholar. She worked better with me helping her, quizzing her. I learned dancing because she preferred me as a partner over the loudmouthed, clumsy boys the dancing master paired her with. It was she who insisted I accompany her to finishing school. So I suppose, just by being there, I had the same education as Miss Deborah. But without the name and the fortune, it meant nothing."

He sat beside her on the couch, strangely taken by the unfamiliar process of getting to know someone. "Until the night we met."

She winced and shifted away from him. "That was supposed to be a harmless masquerade. I had no idea things would turn out the way they did."

He grinned reassuringly. "You still don't know how things will turn out. That's what makes life so damned interesting."

"Perhaps I don't need for it to be so interesting."

"Then what, Kathleen?" He brushed at a lock of her hair that had strayed from its plait. "What do you need life to be?"

"I don't know anymore," she said. "I used to think it would be so fine to be rich and to have lovely things—"

"Trust me, it is."

"No, I was wrong. In the fire, I saw people who lost everything yet they were content because they and their loved ones survived. I've begun to think that true happiness is made up of something altogether different.''

He grinned. ''But you've always wanted to be rich, haven't you?''

She flushed, and he knew he had hit his mark.

''It's nothing to be ashamed of, Kathleen.''

She stared down at the table. ''I'd be far better off learning to be content with my lot.''

He touched her chin, bringing her gaze back to his. ''You studied finance instead. You learned to speak French and to dance a waltz. It's no sin.''

Still blushing furiously, she pulled away from his touch. ''We were speaking of the grain trade,'' she reminded him. ''You keep distracting me.''

''You're a lot more interesting than grain.''

''Then you haven't been listening. Don't you find it fascinating that a person can buy the future?''

''What do you mean?''

''I've been trying to explain it to you, Dylan.'' She turned toward him, eschewing a ladylike posture and tucking one leg under her. She became bright-eyed, animated. ''You can buy the future. You can buy something that doesn't even exist, and then turn around and sell it at a profit.''

''I wonder why I have never tried it, then. It's a better dodge than I've ever pulled.''

She grinned, and it warmed him to his toes. ''I knew you'd like it.''

''I can't believe it's legal. It sounds like cheating.''

''Then you'll be very good at it.'' Rummaging in a drawer, she found a small tablet of paper and a pencil stub, then returned to the sofa and started making a list. "Now, in order to make a trade, you have to be a member of the Board."

"Who's to say I am not?" He spread his arms grandly. "Hell, who's to say you're not, or Bull Waxman or Father Michael? All the records burned."

"Oh, my," she said, regarding him in a way that reminded him of the first time he had made love to her. "You're catching on fast."

"So I'm a member," he said, going along with it. "Then what?"

"I'm guessing that no one else knows about the grain shipment on the barge *Elyssa*. We could use that knowledge to our advantage."

Dylan felt a stirring that was more than interest. It had a vaguely sexual appeal. He really was feeling strange. He was getting excited about finance.

"As far as Mr. Costello or anyone else knows, there is bound to be a terrible shortage of grain for wheat flour."

"And when something's in short supply, you buy all you can of it, try to corner the market."

"Precisely." She did some figuring on the paper. "Then, when the grain shows up in great abundance, the price will drop dramatically. Those who bought it at a high rate will lose out."

"While those who sold high are the winners."

She nodded vigorously, more curls escaping her braid. "We simply have to get Mr. Costello to take the bait and invest at a high price."

"He's too smart to take anyone's bait," Dylan pointed out.

"Don't underestimate yourself, boyo. You have a profound understanding of greedy, dishonest men. I have a profound understanding of the grain trade. Together we should be able to pull off a...big touch."

Damn. She was a quick study. "I like it when you talk like that," he said with a wink.

"I have been around you entirely too much."

"It won't be for very much longer. As soon as the shipment arrives, we can go our separate ways."

She got up and walked away so quickly that he couldn't judge her reaction. He wasn't even sure what his own reaction was. He ought to be looking forward to his freedom. Instead, freedom was beginning to feel like a penance, for true freedom meant he answered to no one. Cared for no one. Mattered to no one. That never used to bother him before, but it did now.

He observed Kathleen by the opposite window. She stood wrapped in a shawl against the autumn chill, her arms around her middle as the feeble light of the autumn afternoon limned her features. Standing at the broad window, she resembled the sort of subject a fine artist would want to depict. Beautiful, pensive, moody, secretive. Maybe that was the reason she never bored him.

She had an uncanny knack for reading his thoughts, for she turned from the window and set her hands on her hips in a bossy fashion. "Hand me that paper and pencil and then go and find Father Michael and Bull. If we are to recover the stolen money, we have much work to do."

Within a week's time, a huge wooden structure some ninety feet square had been erected at the corner of Washington and Market Streets. Members of the Chicago Board of Trade began to sift through the ashes of their paperwork, trying to recover what records they could. They were not successful, which proved advantageous for Kathleen's plan. Since no records had survived the fire and communication was faulty at best, chaos and uncertainty governed the market.

Bull and Father Michael sat with them in the train car, where the table was littered with paper. "This," she said to Dylan, pushing a printed form across to him, "is your membership to the Board. Now you have trading privileges."

He studied the paper for a moment. "Where did you get this?"

She exchanged a glance with the priest, and both of them flushed. Amateurs at deception, they weren't comfortable with the plan. Yet Father Michael had been outraged to learn that Costello was stealing from the relief fund, and he was determined to serve the greater good, no matter what.

"Never mind that," she said briskly. "Now, here's how a trade works. Give me your hand."

He held it out, and she took it. Why was it, she wondered, that simply touching his hand filled her with warmth? Impatient with herself, she took his wrist and turned it. "Palm outward signals that you're selling. Palm inward is for buying."

"They're just bits of paper," Bull said, frowning.

"They represent bushels of grain."

"What grain?"

"There's a barge load on the lake. It needs only a tug to bring it into port, and we will see to that." She took a deep breath. "But we'll need to buy the contract."

Father Michael lifted his eyes to heaven. "With what? We don't have any money."

"We'll have to raise it. If we succeed, we'll turn one dollar into twenty, fifty, maybe a hundred. But we'll have to work quickly."

"Fast money," Dylan said with a grin. He kept hold of her hand. "That's my specialty."

"We've all got to do our part," Kathleen said.

"And so we shall." Dylan spoke with the confidence of a seasoned cardsharper. "There are four of us. If we work together, we should be able to raise the money in short order."


"Pardon me, sir," Dylan said to the passing gentleman, "but I believe there is something in your hat."

"What's that?" The prosperous-looking gentleman and his female companion stopped walking.

Easing into a familiar role, Dylan helped himself to the gleaming beaver hat and extracted from the crown a fresh rose. He bowed, then handed it to the blushing lady with a flourish. She laughed aloud and held the blossom to her nose.

The man replaced his hat and gave his befuddled thanks.

"No thanks necessary," Dylan said smoothly. "This ten-dollar tip will do." He tossed the coin high in the air and snatched it on its way down.

The mark immediately patted his pocket, then said, "Hey! You nicked that from me."

"Guilty as charged." Dylan winked at the lady, who clearly represented the man's vulnerable spot. "Here you go." He flipped the coin back to the mark, then started to stroll away, counting on her to call him back.

"Oh, give it to him," the lady said. "It's the first laugh I've had since the fire, for heaven's sake."

Nothing like a woman to make a man do her bidding, Dylan thought. As expected, the gentleman tossed him the coin. With a grin and a wink, Dylan moved off in search of his next mark.

"Bless me, Father, for I have sinned," Mrs. Ernestine Gaines said from behind the makeshift confessional screen. Though St. Brendan's steeple had crashed to earth, services had begun again, and Father Michael was hearing Friday confessions in a place that smelled of charred timber and damp stone.

Mrs. Gaines's gaudy jewelry clanked as she pressed her hands together in prayer. Her sharp, expensive perfume fogged the dimness.

"Father," she said, "I am consumed with guilt. I lost nothing in the fire. Not a blessed thing. I cannot decipher what it could mean."

"The meaning is clear, my child. The Heavenly Father meant for you to share your fortune, that you may sup at the table of eternity with him."

Silence, then the clank of a bracelet. She said, "Share."

"Yes, my child."

"How much sharing do you suppose the Lord is looking for?"

"My child, the faithful do not measure God's grace in terms of dollars and cents—"

"How much?" she interrupted.

"Five hundred dollars," he shot at her without hesitation.

"Five hun—"

"And those sapphire earbobs. A small price to pay for peace of mind, ma'am."

Kathleen stood beneath a placard carefully lettered with the words *Temperance Society*, thumping her sign for attention. "Bring those bottles forward," she urged people passing in front of Henckel's Brewery. "The mayor has made a decree to outlaw the sale of liquor in our beleaguered city," she called. "Bring your barrels out," she ordered the brewmaster.

"I was up an entire night trying to keep the barrels from burning," he complained. "I'm not giving them up to you!"

Kathleen sent him a censorious glare. "Very well, keep them and pay a fine for harboring contraband. I believe the amount is fifteen dollars a barrel."

"Fifteen? That's more than I could sell them for!"

But not as much as *I* can sell them for, Kathleen thought, her heart thumping anxiously.

"It's up to you, sir." She gestured at Bull, who waited behind her. "You can take advantage of the manpower I've offered, or risk breaking the law." She frowned. "Now, where was it we passed the civil militia?" she asked Bull. "A block over? Two?"

The brewmaster blanched. "Take it away, then, and good riddance. It's probably ruined from the heat, anyway."

Working swiftly and silently, Bull loaded the untapped beer kegs onto a river barge. Pushing off with a long pole, he bore the cargo away.

Four hundred yards down the river, they sold the entire haul to a saloon owner who had absolutely no knowledge of the mayor's decree.

* * *

"Here," said a man in the crowd gathered at Lake Front Park, tossing an apple to Dylan. "Change that into a pear."

The transformation occurred almost before the mark finished his sentence. It was an old sleight of hand, but the refugees encamped by the lake made appropriate noises of admiration. A crisp new bank note borrowed from the apple man disappeared, then reappeared in the pear. Dylan produced it with a flourish.

The man made a face. "Keep it for a tip," he said. "It's soggy, anyway."

*Chicago Tribune, October 17, 1871.* Beware the Bunco Man. As our embattled city rebuilds after the most famous calamity of its history, tales of selfless acts of heroism mingle with less pleasant stories of knaves and swindlers out to take advantage of the misfortune of others. Sharpers, confidence men and schemers abound in our ruined streets, putting forth false offers to the homeless and helpless. Should a man approach you offering help, make certain his motives are pure before coming to any agreement with him.

In other news, Mr. Cornelius King reports that his private Pullman car, last seen in the Michigan and Illinois yards, has gone missing....

"Do you trust me?" Dylan asked.

"No." Kathleen glared at him. "Why are you constantly asking me that?"

"I keep thinking you'll change your mind."

"What does it matter?"

"In a moment, it will matter," he assured her.

"But—"

"Hush. Time to start the performance."

The crowd, drawn from thirty thousand refugees encamped at Lincoln Park, rustled and settled as Father Michael made the announcement from a stage cobbled together from broken planks and railroad ties.

"And here, in a death-defying act, Horatio Quick will hurl knives at his lovely assistant—"

"Knives?" she hissed. "You said I just have to stand here!"

"It's true. And look pleased. Remember, you feel life most keenly when you are courting death." He pressed close so that she could feel the length of his body. Heat and desire emanated from him even here, now, in front of an inquisitive crowd. "Stand still. That is all you have to do."

"You said nothing about knives."

"Because I knew you'd be a scare-baby and ruin everything, and these people have paid good money for the show. Now hush and tie the blindfold on me, will you?"

"*Blindfold?*"

# *Sixteen*

Vincent Costello was pleased with himself. Damned pleased. It made him proud to be a Catholic, the way the money was rolling in from all points on the map. The faithful took care of their own, he was happy to see.

And he would take care of himself.

Like a king in his realm, he was holding his daily audiences. In the new post, his duties were many and varied. He had to make his reports to the church comptroller and auditor, reckon the expenses of his office and send out letters of pious praise to the generous donors. Then, of course, there were less exalted jobs, such as seeing to the needs of the poor and to the church. St. Brendan's had listed itself in dire want of a steeple, of all things. The faithful flock were clamoring for it to be rebuilt. It had become a symbol of hope for them. Well, they could wait. Vincent had to look out for his own interests.

He wasn't about to fritter away perfectly good money on a steeple while his private fund was still growing. Paper bills and silver certificates were stacked neatly in the new Acme safe installed in his office. All that remained was to decide when enough was enough and then move on.

The trouble was, he liked Chicago. Though he would never admit it, he was glad his hunt for Dylan

Kennedy had led him here. In this town, he was fast discovering, a man could make a name for himself if he knew how to handle money.

Faith was getting on well enough, too. Her misguided affection for Dylan was bothersome, as usual, but Vince couldn't bring himself to reveal him for a scoundrel in his daughter's eyes. The low-bellied thief deserved to get his kneecaps broken and be left to suffer in a ditch somewhere—but Faith would be crushed at the loss. Vince would simply have to bide his time and hope his daughter outgrew her infatuation.

He was doing his best to keep her distracted, ordering her to assist that sniveling clerk—what was his name?—Lynch. Maybe if she had plenty to occupy her, she wouldn't mope around and sigh about Kennedy all the time.

He considered the cash in the safe, and a surge of lust warmed his limbs. He loved money more than women, even. He wasn't happy with the stacks of bills just lying there. He needed to put the cash to use, and he'd already made a place for himself on the Liquor Board and the Board of Trade. He just needed the right opportunity to present itself. He was mulling over his options when an African giant stepped into the office.

Vincent had seen tough fellows before but never one as tough as this. His skin was polished ebony. The breadth of his shoulders blotted out the day. Yet the big man shuffled his feet in a curiously deferential way as he took off his battered hat and held it in front of him.

"Name's Eugene," the man said in a deep bell-toned voice. "Eugene Waxman."

Vincent suppressed a twinge of annoyance. His assistants were supposed to see to individual charity cases. "What can I do for you, Mr. Waxman?"

"I heard tell you got yourself a seat on the Board of Trade."

My, my, thought Vince in surprise. Word certainly traveled fast. "You heard right, young man."

"I come to ask, can you make a transaction for me?"

Vincent perked up. This fellow was far more interesting than a charity case. "Indeed. Perhaps I can. Sit down, Mr. Waxman."

The big man lowered his bulk to a chair. He sat on edge, clearly unused to conducting any sort of business at all.

"I understand your dilemma, Mr. Waxman. Many men won't do business with a man of color," Vincent said bluntly.

"Do you have that problem?"

"Of course not. Money's money."

Waxman took out a soft chamois bag. Holding it reverently, he opened the drawstring and emptied the contents on the desk between them. "There's about a hundred dollars there, sir. All's I got in the world."

Vincent almost felt sorry for the poor lummox. "And you want me to make a trade for you."

"Yes, sir." He rocked back on his heels.

Costello pressed his hands to the surface of the desk. "Mr. Waxman, do you understand how futures trading works?"

"Reckon I do, sir." He held his hat by the brim and kept turning it in circles, as if he were closing a water main. "See, the way I figure it, when there's plenty of grain, it's cheap. And when there's a shortage, the price goes up."

Costello nodded. The big man had at least a rudimentary understanding of the trade. Still, out of fairness he wanted him to comprehend exactly what it was that he risked. Trading was no different from gambling, especially in the hands of an amateur.

"Why now?" he asked. "The new Board's only been open three days."

The hat kept rotating in the big hands. "Well, sir, it's like this." He fixed Costello with an earnest stare. "I heard tell you can turn one dollar into ten when grain's in short supply."

Costello sat straighter in his chair. "What makes you so sure there'll be a shortage?" he asked.

Waxman blinked slowly. He was an odd sort. Huge, lumbering, deliberate. Yet there was a keen precision to his thinking that suggested there was more to him than met the eye. Vince knew when a man was holding back information. He waited, for Waxman appeared to take his time deliberating.

"Well, it's like this, sir. There's been a drought this season—"

"Everyone knows of the drought. The price has been adjusted accordingly."

"But not everybody knows of the shipping report." Waxman spoke very quietly, staring down at the floor.

"The shipping report's not expected until—" Costello stopped. Every hair on the back of his neck seemed to stand on end. He stared at the round cap in Waxman's hands. Gold braid edged the brim, and for the first time he noticed the insignia showing the silhouette of a bird in flight. It was the emblem of the Union Telegraph Company's local branch.

At last Waxman lifted his big, shining head. "The telegraph company likes to use Negro men for couriers, sir. They don't think any of us can read or write."

Costello felt an icy chill clutch at his gut, and his mind came to full alert. This was the same feeling he had when he sat at the poker table and knew he held the winning hand.

The only question now was how much to bet. How much for a full house?

"But the thing is, sir, I can read," Waxman said quietly, matter-of-factly and without pride.

A straight flush, Costello amended. He held very still, but his fingers tingled. He had to restrain himself from diving for the safe.

Ordinarily the Board of Trade received wires directly, but since the fire, price communication had been sporadic and unreliable. Costello forced himself to stay quiet, waiting. Waxman would say what he had come to say in his own good time.

"What I saw, sir," he said in his deep mournful voice, "is that the shipping report is down. There's to be no grain shipped to Chicago because of damage to the yards."

A royal flush, thought Costello.

Cautiously, he said, "It's illegal to act on this information."

"That's why I came to you, sir." Heaving a long, weary sigh, he added, "Reckon I done worse in my life. Reckon you done worse, too."

Costello was about to object when Waxman took a thin folded piece of paper from the brim of his hat.

"Sir," he said, "I got a delivery to make. I can't wait much longer."

Costello swept all the money from the desk and gathered it into a box. When it came to matters of commerce, he considered himself unstoppable. "Tell you what. You leave this with me, and I'll see what I can do."

* * *

The next evening, as the city lay beneath a brooding bank of clouds, Kathleen surveyed the stacks of money they had collected. She could barely move a muscle for soreness. Her nerves were still jangling from the ordeal of having a blind man hurl knives at her. Her sense of ethics suffered each time she thought of those taken in by their games. Being a swindler was hard work, harder still on her conscience.

Glaring at Father Michael, she said, "Why can't you raise funds like a normal priest?"

"My dear, do you know how many bake sales and ice-cream socials it would take to earn this?" He gestured at the counted money. "How many quilt lotteries? Besides, it will all come back to the church."

"One thousand one hundred forty-two dollars," Dylan said.

"And fifty-seven cents," Bull added. At Dylan's surprised look, he said, "I can count. Did you think I couldn't count?"

"The question is," Dylan said, his gaze boring into Kathleen, "is it enough?"

A shiver passed through her, but it was not a shiver of doubt. It was excitement. She aimed a pointed stare at him. "Do you trust me?"

He laughed, and it was the magical laugh that had captivated her from the start. Leaning down, he whispered into her ear, "As much as you've trusted me to stay on the sofa each night."

Her cheeks burned, and she looked up quickly to see if the others had heard. But they were busy looking over the contract drawn up by Barry Lynch, of all people. She had assured Barry that she'd found a way to reclaim the relief fund money.

"I'm getting tired of that sofa," Dylan continued, still whispering in her ear. His warm breath awakened her senses.

She tried to pull away, and it struck her that she was actually enjoying this—the games, the planning, the anticipation. "Go on with you," she whispered back. "We've got work to do."

"Do you have any idea how hard I'd work to—" He dropped his voice even lower. His shameful suggestion made her blush to the roots of her hair. Only the presence of the others stopped her from smacking the smirk off Dylan's face.

Ducking her head to hide her blush, she bade goodnight to Bull and Father Michael and stood at the door while they left.

"Now what?" Dylan asked, walking to her side and pressing close.

She shied away, stepping behind the piecrust table to put some distance between them. "We engage the tug and get ourselves out to Eden Landing with this contract on the grain."

He poured himself a glass of unconsecrated communion wine, thoughtfully provided by Father Michael. "I seem to recall that a train took us there last time. How do you propose we get there tomorrow?"

Her heart sank. "I hadn't thought of that. Do you suppose we could hire a wagon or cart or—"

"Every wagon in the city has been commandeered by the militia."

"We'll walk if we have to," she said stoutly. "It's only twenty miles."

He rolled his eyes. "I'm not the sort to walk twenty miles."

She sniffed and turned away, heading for the berth

behind the screen. "I'm not too proud to walk. But I shall need a full night's rest, so excuse me."

As she undid the bodice of her dress, she sensed, like a phantom warmth, his presence behind her. Looking over her shoulder, she said, "Go away."

Instead, he caressed the nape of her neck with his lips. "Ah, Kathleen. You weren't saying that the first time we—"

"I'm saying it now." She swung back and stared at nothing, hoping her voice didn't betray her hurt. "My bed is for someone who means to stay."

Leaning forward, he kissed her lightly and quickly before she could turn away. "I'll stay with you, sweetheart."

"But for how long?" she asked, struggling to keep her voice even. Even one little kiss from him touched her heart with fire. She feared her own susceptibility to him. "A night? A week?"

"Who knows? Do you really need to know?"

"Yes," she said. "I really need to know."

"Then I don't have an answer for you," he snapped.

She swung away abruptly, pretending she didn't care.

His quick footsteps thudded on the carpeted floor. Then she heard the clink of glass as he finished off the wine, and finally the slam of the door as he left the car altogether.

"Where in heaven's name did you get those?" Kathleen stood in the doorway of the train car, blinking in the dawn light. Dylan stood in the yard, dwarfed by a pair of tall, handsome horses. The sun had just risen, and a deep pinkish gold colored everything the light touched. The hides of the horses appeared bloodred, the surface of the lake a mirror of amber.

An aura surrounded Dylan, and she had to tell herself it was all an illusion. He was a master of disguise. She had seen it again and again. From time to time she herself had been part of whatever fantasy he was trying to create.

But still, she found herself being pulled in by his spell. This morning he resembled a prince from a mythical land, as alluring as a dream. She couldn't keep her heart from skipping a beat or her lips from curving into a wistful smile. She could not stop the memories that pushed into her mind. The way he'd held her and laughed with her. The funny meals they'd made of biscuits and apples. The way his words felt when he whispered into her ear, sending hot shivers all through her. Even now that she knew what he was, the feelings would rise so high in her heart she feared she might float away.

*I miss you,* she thought, studying him in the strange light.

Just for a moment, he tilted his head to one side and frowned, almost as if he'd heard her unspoken words.

Being Dylan, he spoiled the effect the moment he opened his mouth. "Don't just stand there gawking like a beached fish. Get the contract and let's go."

She smoothed her hands down the front of her skirts and assumed an air of annoyance. "Where is the buggy?" she asked.

"There is no buggy. These are not buggy horses, anyway. They'd be insulted if you tried to hitch them to a wagon."

It was then that she noticed the saddles. "I don't ride horseback."

A shadow passed over his face. "Pretend you do. You're good at pretending, Kathleen."

"No better than you are."

He stared at her for a moment, the wavy black hair tumbling down over his brow. "Yes you are, love. Believe me, you are." One of the horses nibbled at his ear. "Are you coming or not?"

"Where did you get the horses?"

"Don't ask questions unless you're sure you want to know the answers."

She stepped down from the car, pulling the door shut behind her. "I haven't the first idea about riding a horse," she muttered. She'd had plenty of experience with Clyde, her mother's dray horse, but sitting on one's back was another matter altogether.

When she drew close to Dylan, she noticed a difference in him. His clothes were rumpled, his cravat hung undone around his neck and his hair was disheveled. She caught a whiff of perfume and whiskey. The air of dissolution felt heavy, oppressive. "Ah, love. I said don't ask."

"I didn't say a word," she said.

"With your eyes," he pointed out. "You asked the question with your eyes."

"You'd best answer with your mouth, because I'm not as clever at reading people as you."

He took a deep breath, as though preparing to jump into cold water. "The owner of the horses is Mrs. Pearl Sacks. I met her at some Old Settler party. She's rich and lonely, and I charmed her." He held up a hand, palm out. "Nothing happened, I swear it. How could I, when all I can dream of is you?"

She scowled. "Enough of your blarney. You probably made her believe the sun rises for her alone and will not set until she commands it."

"Did I harm the old tabby?" he demanded. "Did I do one bit of damage? When I went to her, she was a spry old woman, wishing something—anything—would happen to her. I made her smile, Kathleen. I made her laugh and feel alive. Is that so very wrong?"

"I don't know," she confessed. "I guess it depends on how she survives when she figures out you were lying." She shaded her eyes and regarded the sunlight on the ruined city. "Some lives might be just fine after you've blown through them. Others will burn away to nothing." She wondered about herself. After Dylan was gone, then what? How would she end up?

The one thing she knew for certain was that she would get hurt. Until meeting Dylan, she had never known that betrayal could feel like a physical pain. Her chest squeezed until she winced at the sharpness. Holding in tears became a battle she had rarely fought before, and one she almost lost. Almost.

She stared into that fallen-angel face and forced herself to remember their goal. Too much depended upon their accomplishing it. Nothing could be gained by worrying about what Dylan would do afterward.

"Let's get on with it, then," she said, proud of the steadiness in her voice. "I don't know how the devil to ride a horse without breaking my foolish neck."

"Now there's something I can help you with," he said.

He went down on one knee before her. He probably didn't mean for it to look like a pose of supplication, but it did. He probably didn't try to resemble a storybook cavalier, but it did. And he certainly didn't mean for his touch to take her breath away, but it did.

She prayed that when she put her hand in his, he would not sense her trembling.

"Just set your foot on my knee and swing your leg up and over. You can ride astride, it won't kill you. Like so. She's a good mare," he added. "She's pretty, and does what she's told."

Kathleen pursed her lips as if she'd tasted something sour. "Then you should ride her. She is everything you want in a female."

He laughed as she swung her leg up and over the mare's back. "You're just jealous because you saw her kissing my ear."

She felt awkward and improper, straddling the mare with her skirts bunched up. Dylan did nothing to set her at her ease. In fact, he made it worse by running an insolent hand down her leg, toying with the ruffle of her bloomers.

"Stop that," she snapped. She jerked her leg a little and the mare shied.

Dylan calmed the horse and winked. "I won't tell if you won't." He placed the reins in her hands. "Her name is Petal," he said.

He turned to the other mare, fitting his foot in the stirrup. "And this one is—damn it."

The horse swung her head around and snapped at him. Then, while he still had one foot in the stirrup and one on the ground, she walked forward. Kathleen heard a tearing of cloth.

"Damn it," he said again, muscling his way into the saddle.

"An unusual name for a mare," she commented wryly.

He adjusted the reins, wrestling the horse for control. The mare stepped backward and sideways in a stubborn clumsy dance, but eventually she settled, glared straight ahead and twitched her tail.

"I don't mind a challenge," he said. "Keeps me from getting bored."

There were so many things she could have said to him. Instead, she held her tongue, for this was one time he told the truth. He found a challenge in outsmarting people. In tricking them out of their money. In making women fall in love with him.

Pushing aside the thought, she concentrated on keeping her seat. She felt vulnerable, uncertain, yet determined to succeed. Dylan led the way, walking his horse while Kathleen followed. She experimented with the reins, finding the horse reasonably responsive. When they passed through the outskirts of the city, he urged his horse to a smart trot and then a canter. Kathleen locked her jaw, unwilling to let him know she felt as though she might fall off at any moment. Slowly she grew accustomed to the rhythm, and was surprised to find herself relaxing, almost enjoying the outing.

She watched the sun rise over the blowing prairie grasses and cornfields, and in spite of all her efforts, she could not keep from wondering about the woman who had loaned him the mares. What lies had he told her? What promises had he made?

Watching him furtively, Kathleen wanted so much to ask. But at the same time, she remembered his warning about not wanting to know the answers.

The sweep of morning light over the rippling fields gave a feeling of endless space and possibility to the day. Kathleen took a deep breath and prayed no one had reached the *Elyssa* before them and that the transaction would go smoothly.

At the landing, David Fraser greeted them anxiously. "Mr. Kennedy," he said, a relieved look on his face. "I was hoping I'd see you again."

Dylan grinned. "Didn't I say I'd help you?"

Actually, it was Kathleen who had proposed the deal, but she let it pass.

"I have the cash contract right here." Dylan patted a saddlebag. "And the cash, too, of course."

Fraser couldn't sign fast enough. It was a paltry amount, but sure money in an uncertain time, and Kathleen knew he would gladly take his earnings back to his farm. The deal was concluded in minutes.

"So it's done, then." Dylan inspected the papers and receipt which they would have to present to the clerk of the Board of Trade in order to prove that he actually had something to sell.

"Yes, sir. You now have the futures on the biggest grain barge on Lake Michigan."

"And remember our agreement. There's to be no word of this until the tug comes to haul it to the city. Then you can tell anyone you wish."

Fraser looked so pleased that Kathleen's conscience relaxed. They weren't cheating him, she told herself. Just offering a sure thing while they took all the risk.

As they rode together back toward town, Dylan looked across at her.

"What?" she asked peevishly.

"I just handed that man all our cash."

"That was what we agreed to do."

"For a piece of paper."

"That paper represents a fortune," she assured him. She couldn't resist adding, "Don't you trust me?"

"Ha," he said, and the merriment in his eyes captivated her utterly. "I'll show you trust."

Without warning, he dug in his heels and his mare surged forward in a gallop. Kathleen emitted a shriek of terror as Petal followed. Mingling with the galloping hoofbeats of the horses was Dylan's ringing laughter.

"Hang on, sweetheart," he called, "for the ride of your life."

She clutched the saddle horn helplessly. She felt defenseless, knowing that at any moment she could fall to her death. She had no idea what was keeping her on. And then, as they sailed past the shimmering prairie, something extraordinary happened. She started loving it. The speed, the danger, the rush of wind over her face. Dylan had once said he felt the keenest essence of life when he was courting death.

Now, finally, she knew what he meant. Her heart sang and shattered at the same moment. She knew that, whatever happened from this moment onward, she would be forever changed. It was strangely like making love with him. He had opened her to a new world of sensation. She heard a woman's laughter on the wind and realized it was her own. Dylan whipped a glance back at her and she saw an expression of delight on his face. For two people who disliked and distrusted each other they certainly got along well.

Dressed in sober, conservative fashion, they arrived at the temporary quarters of the Chicago Board of Trade at precisely nine in the morning. The building had been nicknamed The Wigwam for its slapdash appearance, but inside, the atmosphere hummed with brisk business. Dylan resembled a distinguished gentleman, Kathleen his quiet, obedient mistress, patiently batting her eyes in feminine bafflement about finance. But only from a distance. Anyone closer might hear her hissing through her teeth, issuing directives. "Do not do or say anything I haven't told you to do, or you'll spoil the whole thing."

"Bossy woman," he said.

"Huh. If we had to do this your way, I'd be hanging by my teeth from a high wire."

"A great temptation, I must admit."

With falsely cordial smiles and murmured greetings, they entered the boxy wooden structure. They stopped to register their shares with the clerk, who examined their contract. The clerk asked for Dylan's credentials, and he spread his arms in a gesture of futility. "Burned, I fear."

The clerk questioned him no further, for he was clearly weary of trying to verify claims of all the other traders. "You've got a lot to sell there, Mr. Kennedy. Hope you get your price at tomorrow's trading."

That evening, Dylan went off to God-knew-where, moving the scheme forward another step. Kathleen felt agitated and out of sorts, lonely for his presence. The train car was a sort of limbo for her. One thing she had recently discovered about herself was that she enjoyed a sense of permanence. She had discovered other things as well—that money wasn't the answer to her troubles, that, in spite of everything, she was still in love with a swindler.

Working by the light of a single oil lamp, she tidied up the place, scraping bread crumbs into a bin, rinsing out the teapot, folding away a towel or two. Dylan's waistcoat lay in a wad on the chaise, and she picked it up, shaking it out. A small object fluttered to the floor.

With a frown, she set aside the waistcoat and picked it up. A wave of emotion came over her. It was Gran's holy card, something she thought she would never see again. Dylan must have picked it up the night they met. It had probably been forgotten in his pocket all this time.

Suddenly unsteady, she sat down on the fringed chaise. "Ah, Gran," she said. "When I first met him, I thought you had arranged the whole thing." A tremulous smile curved her mouth as she recalled that night when anything, everything, had seemed possible. "But look at us now." She rubbed a thumb over the creased surface of the card, circling the shape of the halo over Saint Bridget's head. "Surely you didn't mean for this to happen. Surely you didn't mean for me to get my foolish heart broken into a million pieces."

She shut her burning eyes. "You always said that love would take me by surprise, Gran. Do you remember that? I used to complain so bitterly that I'd never marry, because I had never met a man I could love. Mam would scold me for the stars in my eyes, but you never did, Gran. Even when Mam nagged me to say yes to Barry Lynch, you patted my hand and told me to keep dreaming, that love would take me by surprise." Her voice shook wildly, and she felt three times a fool sitting there talking to a ghost, but she couldn't stop herself. "You forgot to tell me the rest, Gran. You forgot to tell me how much it hurts."

After that, she couldn't talk anymore. She doubled over and trembled with the effort to keep in the sobs. This hurt was the price she paid for pride. For greed. For being ashamed of who she was and wanting things beyond her reach.

In her misery, she dropped the little picture card. Wiping her face on her sleeve like the crudest of chambermaids, she stooped to pick it up.

Dylan Kennedy got there first, snatching the card.

With a shriek, Kathleen jumped to her feet. "How long have you been standing there?" she demanded.

But she knew the answer from the expression on his face. It was the look of a man facing a firing squad. The look of a man who had heard more than he wanted to hear. "Kathleen—"

She grabbed the card from him. "You should have said something. You should not have sneaked up on me."

"If you're going to bare your soul, you should keep the door locked," he shot back.

She felt more exposed than if she'd been caught buck naked. She knew beyond any doubt that she looked vulnerable. She could not possibly feel any more horrible, but she made herself face him and say, "I wish you had not heard that."

"I wish I hadn't either," he said fervently.

The hot, humiliating tears kept pushing like fire behind her eyes, so she flopped down on the chaise and made no attempt to stop them. No one had ever seen her cry before. She didn't trust Dylan, but she could cry in front of him. She had no idea why that was. "You must be pleased with yourself. I had only one thing in the world worth stealing, and you managed to take it."

"Your virginity?"

"My honor," she blurted out.

"Don't be ridic—"

"I'm not." She spread her arms. "Look at me, Dylan. I haven't a thing in the world. Even the clothes on my back don't belong to me. My family is struggling to survive the winter. The only thing I ever possessed that had any value at all was my honor. And you took it. You stole it."

"Your cleverness, your intelligence are still intact," he pointed out. "I didn't take those. And as for the honor..." He sat down uninvited at the end of the chaise, thrusting a handkerchief into her hand. "That's not the way I recall it. You willingly, eagerly gave yourself to me, Kathleen."

"Because I believed all the lies you told me. I believed you loved me. Because we're married."

"You can't hold me responsible for what you believe."

His twisted logic gave her a headache. She blotted her face with the handkerchief. It smelled of him, and that made her want to cry again, but she wouldn't let herself. "I hold you responsible for lying. For making me love you."

"You don't love me, Kathleen O'Leary, and you never did. Maybe you like feeling wounded. Hell, I don't know. But you can't make up your mind to love someone in just a few hours."

"Since when did you become an expert on matters of the heart?"

"I'm not."

"You could be," she insisted. "All it takes is time, honesty and caring."

"We don't have that," he said. "We never will."

His bald statement shook her. "I understand now," she quietly confessed. "I did a terrible thing, pretending to be an heiress at that cursed party. You are part of my punishment."

He ran a splayed hand through his hair. "Look, I didn't mean to hurt you. I never wanted to hurt you." He shook his head. "I'm sorry. Can we just please— Can we try to get through this thing with Costello? When it's over, we'll go our separate ways. It'll be like none of this ever happened."

She stared at him for a long time. In the amber lamplight, his wavy, glossy hair, his eyes of the purest blue, his face so elegant and fine masked his true character. What an idiot she had been to equate physical perfection with goodness. There was more good in plain, dull Barry Lynch's left elbow than there was in all six well-built feet of Dylan Kennedy.

"How did you get to be so cold?" she asked, genuinely intrigued. "Do you have no heart at all, or did someone steal yours, too, long ago?"

He made a hissing sound as if she had burned him, and just for a moment, anger blazed undisguised in his eyes. "What the hell sort of question is that?"

"It was two questions. And I'm still waiting for an answer."

"I don't have to explain anything to you."

"No, you don't." Intrigued by this chink in his smooth, confident armor, she leaned back on the chaise. "You're too cowardly."

"My earliest memory," he said after a long silence, "is of being in a train station. I was only a little kid at the time. My mother dumped me like a stray cat in a drowning bag."

Kathleen felt a lurch of queasiness. She pictured him as a little boy. He would have been beautiful then, as well, with that coloring and those eyes. "Ah, Dylan, I can't imagine how you must have felt."

"I started fooling around, walking on the backs of the benches in the waiting room, jumping up and down the stairs to pass the time. No one cared what I did so long as I stayed out of their way. There was a fellow with a mouth organ and a little dancing dog. I watched him for a while." He stood up and paced, raking his hand through his hair.

Kathleen cursed her own quick temper. She had

bullied him into dredging up these memories, not realizing the pain that came with them. She wanted to tell him to stop, yet at the same time felt compelled to share his heartbreak.

"Folks would toss him a penny as they passed by," he continued, "and I asked him why they did that. He said people liked things they didn't see every day, like a dancing dog. So I decided to show them something they didn't see every day."

She leaned forward, her heart in her throat. "What did you do?"

"I climbed a steel pole and walked along a beam that stretched across all the platforms. Folks threw pennies to me after that. Turned out I had a talent for doing tricks, dangerous stuff. The sort of thing you're not supposed to let a kid do. But there was no one around to stop me." With his jaw clenched hard, he stared into a distance she could not see. She felt the pain of that child with no mam to scold him and keep him out of danger. He rubbed his hand on his cheeks as if to loosen the tension in his jaw. "I saved up those pennies, got a little more sophisticated with my act and bought a suit of clothes like I'd seen on a rich boy at the train station. That's when I started pretending."

"Pretending what?"

"Whatever I thought folks needed to see or hear. I was on my way to Boston and I'd lost my ticket. I claimed I'd been pickpocketed and needed shelter for the night. People believed whatever I told them. I figured out that if you play your part well enough, people will believe what they want to believe." He hesitated and then said in a flat, harsh voice, "I don't remember my name."

"Oh, Dylan—"

Before she knew what was happening, he pulled her against him and put his face very close to hers so that she could feel the warmth of his breath. "Don't," she said, but he ignored her. He kissed her lightly, briefly, a subtle reminder of the sort of kisses that had made her burn with pleasure.

"I don't have the first idea what love is, Kathleen," he said. "At least I'm honest about that. But I do know there was nothing false about the things we did when we first came to this train car. What we felt was genuine. It's the finest sort of pleasure, Kathleen, and I've missed it."

She struggled in his embrace and tried to resist her own foolish desire. "Well, you'll have to keep on missing it. I'm sorry for your troubles, Dylan, or whatever your name is. I'm sorry you had to come up through the world the way you did, with no family, no one to love you and guide you. But I do have a family, and they taught me what love is, and I'll settle for no less for myself."

He wouldn't release her, but made a trail of little nibbling kisses from her ear to her collarbone, pausing at the side of her neck to suck at the delicate skin there until she gasped. "I can't love you," he said simply. "I don't know how. But I can make you feel things beyond your wildest dreams, Kathleen. You know damned well I can. Because you do the same to me."

She wasn't certain why she stopped protesting. It was as if that part of her common sense flew out the window, leaving nothing but weak, wanting flesh in its place. And in spite of everything, she did want him, and all the things he made her feel, even if she knew in her heart that the shallow, superficial passion was as fleeting as a warm day in autumn.

He undressed her slowly. She had a hundred chances to protest, but she wanted this. Wanted the closeness, the intimacy. The illusion of love. When he carried her to the sleeping berth and sank into her, she cried out in mindless joy.

There was a fierce urgency to his lovemaking, which added to the illusion that he adored and valued her. He was a master of pretense, and like the weakest of gulls, she found herself believing in the tenderness of his caresses, the depth of his kisses, the mindless endearments he whispered in her ear as he gave all his passion to her.

Neither of them spoke afterward, nor made a move to put out the lamp before it sputtered and died on its own, its fuel burned away to nothing. Kathleen lay in the circle of his arms, listening to the steady beat of his pulse. In a small, shadowy corner of her heart, she admitted that his story had moved her. She could do nothing about the lost little boy, abandoned in a train station. But she could hold and touch the man he had become, and hope that some strange magic could reach across the years, take that lost boy by the hand and bring him to a better place.

"You look perfect," Dylan said the next morning. "Absolutely perfect."

Standing on a hastily built walkway near the Board of Trade, Kathleen barely acknowledged his words. They were not a compliment. She had a role to play, and impersonating the perfect tycoon's mistress was part of her act.

"You remember what to say?" she asked.

"We've only gone over it a hundred times. Why are you so nervous?" he inquired.

"I'm not like you, Dylan. I have not spent my life fooling people."

He looked at her for a long moment. "No. You've spent your life fooling yourself."

"What's that supposed to mean?"

"I was just remembering what you were nattering away about last night. I'm damned glad you got that out of your system."

"Got what out of my system?"

"All that nonsense about love."

# The Big Touch

Doubtless the pleasure is as great
Of being cheated as to cheat.

—Samuel Butler

# *Seventeen*

*9:00 a.m.*

Though the slapdash quarters of the Chicago Board of Trade were temporary, the traders observed protocol, opening the day's business with the usual humble plea to God, followed by a frenzy of capitalistic greed. Runners in red caps and jackets circulated through the trading pits, bringing messages from the floor to the posters stationed at large slate boards. Prices were posted in chalk and changed as they rose and fell. Floor traders observed them keenly and made their trades accordingly.

Dylan entered the hive of activity with Kathleen. It was unorthodox for a woman to be present at the Board of Trade, but the occasional female observer would raise only a few eyebrows. After the upheaval of the fire, anything was possible.

"I've always wondered what this would be like," she whispered.

"I suppose you're about to find out. This had better work," he said between his teeth. "It was a hell of a lot of trouble to set up."

She cut a glance at him. "You should love this,

Dylan. It's full of risk and dishonesty. Your specialties."

"If that's supposed to insult me, you've missed your mark," he said, taking her elbow and guiding her along the aisle. But in a dark, private part of his heart, he felt a sinking disappointment. She knew him better than anyone ever had, and that was her opinion of him. Since they'd awakened that morning she had hardly spoken to him. She refused to speak of their lovemaking and refused to repeat the episode. She considered herself no better than the women he manipulated in order to get his way. He supposed he could explain to her what he had done in order to borrow the horses. It wasn't what she thought. For once, nothing had happened, and the irony was, Kathleen wouldn't believe him. He'd only given Mrs. Sacks a few compliments and kisses—in gentlemanly fashion, on the hand. He couldn't help it if the old bag used perfume as if it were rainwater and she was a thirsting crop. He couldn't help it if Kathleen believed the worst when she'd smelled that flowery essence on him.

*Some lives might be just fine after you've blown through them. Others will burn away to nothing.*

Which are you, Kathleen? Will you be fine once I'm gone? He didn't ask it aloud because he was one to abide by his own rule. He never asked a question unless he wanted to know the answer.

She lowered the brim of her bonnet over her brow, probably hoping to appear unobtrusive. But with her blazing-red hair and trim figure, that was unlikely. "Let's go get the trading chits."

"And then what?"

"Then you go down to the pit and wait."

"Wait for the price to rise."

"That's correct. Then you sell."

"Sounds simple enough."

"Just don't sell too soon. Wait until you see me signal. I'll be in the gallery there." She indicated a set of raised wooden bleachers already crowded with farmers and money men, and a few women.

"What will the signal be?"

She laughed, though her mirth had a bitter edge. "Don't you know? I shall drop a hankie like a lady to her champion."

"And how will you know the perfect time to sell?"

"You'll just have to trust me."

After they checked in, he clutched the fistful of trading chits in one hand. With the other he caught her against him, gratified by her surprised gasp, a tantalizing echo of a sound she sometimes made while making love. Before she could get mad, he planted a firm resounding kiss on her mouth. They drew disapproving glares from black-clad businessmen bustling past. Dylan didn't care as he grinned down at her. "For luck," he said.

*9:40 a.m.*

Vincent Costello arrived before the trading began. Shadowed as he often was these days by a nervous, disapproving Barry Lynch, he stopped at the contracts bureau to register. Barry shot a glance at Kathleen, and Dylan held his breath. She had persuaded the clerk to keep mum about the stolen money, assuring him that it would be repaid after today.

Dylan could feel Kathleen's eyes on him, beaming across from the observation gallery. She was a born worrier, that one. She believed that if Costello realized Dylan had come to trade, the swindler would know something was up.

She didn't understand—he wanted Costello to see him. Vince was competitive. Dylan's presence would only make him more aggressive in his transactions. The only secret was that Dylan had come not to buy, but to sell. He turned to Kathleen and gave her a wink. Up in the gallery, amid men clad in black suits or denim trousers, she stood out like a flower, and as it often did, his heart caught at the sight of her.

He couldn't figure out why she meant so much to him. It wasn't just that she was pretty—though she was—because he had been with pretty women before. Yet there was something especially affecting about Kathleen. It wasn't just her slender figure, her red hair, her large clear eyes or the way she smiled. Maybe it was the way she had listened to him speak of the past and the way she wept for the lost boy he had once been. Time and again he willed his heart to free itself from her spell, but he couldn't. Damn the woman. She captivated him, made him want to be with her every day and night without end.

Which was a pity. Because in a very short while he was going to leave her.

Standing at the rail and looking down at him, she had the aspect of an angel, and he knew he was not mistaken. Oh, he had teased and derided her about pretending to be an heiress. He'd tried to convince her that she was as larcenous as he. But he knew it wasn't so. Kathleen O'Leary had a deep core of goodness. She loved her family. She worked hard. She knew what was important in her life.

Dylan pressed his fingers to his mouth and threw

her a kiss. She tried to look disapproving, but instead, a delighted smile played about her mouth. It would be hard to leave this woman. But he would, of course. He simply did not know how to stay.

Besides, he told himself as Costello made his way across the floor, staying in one place was not the paradise it was cracked up to be. He knew that. Within a short time, he and Kathleen would be bickering like children about whether or not she should buy a certain frock or if he should go to a card game on a Sunday or who stole the covers from whom on a cold winter night.

But the trouble was, he liked bickering with her.

Determined not to dwell on it, he went down to the pits.

"What the hell are you doing here?" Costello demanded, thrusting his bulk in Dylan's path.

Dylan gave no indication of his purpose as he greeted his nemesis with a congenial grin. "You know me, Vince. I'm a gambler at heart." For good measure, he tucked a thumb inside his frock coat where he held his sell orders. A knot of traders scurried past, jostling him. He didn't know anyone but Vince here. If they were all like Costello, they were all thieves.

"How'd you get a seat on the Board of Trade?" Costello demanded.

"How did you come up with the cash? You must feel so blessed," Dylan shot back.

"I—"

A long, shrill bell sounded.

Dylan's grin widened. "You'll have to excuse me, Vince. I've got orders."

He knew he'd said the right thing when Costello

broke away and pushed into the midst of the traders and runners. Dylan paused to catch Kathleen's eye one more time. And this time she amazed him. This time *she* threw out the kiss.

## 10:05 a.m.

Kathleen barely glanced at Father Michael as he pushed his way through the rickety bleachers toward her. She was too riveted by the wild spectacle below to do more than give him a brief nod of greeting.

"It's begun, then," the priest said, peering down at the frenetic traders.

She shifted nervously, pressed by the farmer from Peoria who stood next to her. He smelled of hayseed and pipe tobacco, and he'd tried to get friendly with her but she had quickly rebuffed him. She did not want to be distracted. Even if her entire future was not riding on the outcome of the trading today, she would have found the activity fascinating.

Father Michael nudged her. "Does Dylan have the right papers, then?"

"He does, Father." She dropped her voice to a whisper. "There's an entire bargeload of grain on its way, and no one knows about it."

"But he's not selling," the priest objected. "He's just standing there while everyone else is buying like mad."

"He is waiting for my signal." She showed him the handkerchief wadded in her hand. "When I drop this he'll start selling. I'm waiting for Bull to deliver the telegram with the correct price discovery."

"The calculation that there will be an abundant harvest."

"That's correct."

Redcaps and recorders hurried and pushed back and forth across the floor. Relay men shouted price changes from one to another. The activity reminded Kathleen of a bucket brigade. Only instead of water, they were passing along price information.

"Heaven above," Father Michael said. "Look what's happening to the price of wheat."

Kathleen studied the boards in awe. Thanks to Costello's aggressive buying, the price rose steeply and showed no sign of slowing down. Convinced that Costello was on to something, others joined in the bidding frenzy. The price rose at an accelerated rate, and the beating of her heart did likewise. No one noticed that Dylan had not actually bid yet.

"They're going too high," the priest said. "Surely a bushel of wheat isn't worth what they're paying."

"It always happens this way. When a trader sees someone trying to corner the market, he assumes the reason is that there's big money to be made, so he gets in on it."

"So now they're all bidding for the grain."

"That's what is making the price go up."

A recorder frantically wiped and rewrote the price several more times. Kathleen forgot to breathe. She hadn't been so nervous since those knives had come whizzing at her from Dylan's hand.

When? she asked herself. When to sell?

Now she understood the thinking of experienced traders. They kept pushing for another quarter-cent, another half...

Father Michael touched her sleeve. "Perhaps you should drop that handkerchief now, my girl. I can't imagine the price going any hi—"

The recorder raised the price per bushel again.

Father Michael cleared his throat. "Maybe I had just better—"

"Yes," she said, watching Costello gather in chits at a frantic pace.

"—pray," he concluded.

"It's what you're best at, Father."

Then Dylan shot her a look. Urgency and exasperation sharpened his features. He, too, was getting unnerved by the pace of the trading. She glared back at him. As an experienced showman and swindler he ought to understand the importance of timing.

She didn't want just some of the money Costello had stolen from the Catholic Relief Fund. She wanted it all. That meant waiting until the price reached a breath-stealing peak, and then selling off quickly.

Dylan tossed his head like an impatient racehorse. Kathleen smiled. She liked having this power over him. She liked having this control. If she could not have his heart, at least she could have his undivided attention at this critical moment, and even his trust that she would know when the time was right.

It was heady stuff. She almost didn't feel Father Michael nudging her again.

"Isn't that Bull down there, walking toward the telegrapher's desk?"

Kathleen emitted a small, thin gasp. Not yet, she wanted to shout. But Bull was only following the plan. She had been greedy; she had pushed too hard. The hand holding the handkerchief clenched convulsively and then opened. The wisp of fabric, embroidered with a stranger's initials, drifted to the trading floor. The frenzied traders took no note as they trod the fabric underfoot.

Just for a moment, she thought of the night she had dropped Gran's holy card. A man had stepped on it and her life had been changed forever.

"My child," said Father Michael, "you've turned as pale as the grave."

She swallowed hard, darting her gaze from Bull to Dylan to Mr. Costello. "I've had a bad omen, Father."

He didn't bother trying to reassure her. He was Irish. He knew better than to argue with omens.

*10:45 a.m.*

At last the fool woman had made up her mind, thought Dylan as he saw the handkerchief drifting down from the gallery. Finally it was time to do what he had come to do.

Each time he had walked the rope over Niagara Falls, he had been possessed by a keen, focused sense of balance, heightened by the knowledge that one false move would mean certain death. The stunt always exhilarated him, and he was startled to feel that sense now. This was not a matter of life and death, but when he saw the hope on the faces of Kathleen and Father Michael, it felt much more important than that.

He took out his sell orders and held his hand in the air as Kathleen had instructed. A surge of self-confidence welled inside him. This, at least, was his specialty. Convincing people to pay good money for something of no value was what he did best. The current act was no different. He simply had to persuade people to part with their money for an illusion.

There was no convincing necessary. They surged

toward him like flesh-eating fish in a feeding frenzy. Buy order after buy order was thrust at him, and he couldn't gather them in fast enough. Costello was topping everyone's price, smugly certain his private knowledge of the market was enough to trump Dylan's efforts.

Jostled and harassed by the bidders, he felt a keen gratification, gathering in sums far higher than what he had paid for the forward contract. Before his very eyes, a thousand dollars ballooned to ten thousand, then twenty, just as Kathleen had predicted it would.

Yet it was strange. At the core of his thrill in the game was a certain hollowness. An emptiness. Winning was fleeting. Its effects never lasted. He was living proof of that.

And as he gathered in his orders, he felt a twinge of irritation at Kathleen. Damn the woman. She made him think too much. She made him yearn for more than confidence games and sleight of hand. She made him want to seize the very essence of life itself.

Stupid. For him, life was about getting ahead and moving on. That was all he had ever done. That was all he knew.

He became aware of a red-faced recording clerk shouting at him. "You fool! Why the hell are you selling out?"

Dylan was about to trade away the balance of the contract. "Because it's the only thing I can do," he yelled back.

But something, a feeling, an instinct, made him hold on to a fraction of shares. It really only represented about fifty dollars, but he wanted to keep it. He wasn't sure why. In years to come, the chits would remind him of the elaborate scheme he had concocted with Kathleen, he supposed.

With nothing left to sell, his pockets swollen with chits just waiting to be converted into cash, he broke away from the crowd and stood back to let the rest of the trading unfold. There was Bull, right on schedule. Runners rushed forward with the new price discovery report.

And somewhere along the lakeshore, making fast for Chicago, was a bargeload of grain that would take the bottom clean out of the shortage.

*11:05 a.m.*

Rumors rippled through the crowd in the pit like the wind through a field of ripe wheat. Kathleen counted precisely three seconds of sick, disbelieving silence. Then the floor exploded again, shifting from rampant buying to frantic selling.

The recorders resembled men before a firing squad as they posted plummeting prices. Costello desperately tried to unload the grain he had bought at such inflated prices, but could find no buyers. Everyone else was selling, too.

Farmers in the gallery swore and stomped away. Vincent Costello clenched both fists to his chest, raised his face to the ceiling and let out an animal bellow of rage.

And Dylan Kennedy, Kathleen saw with a surge of pride, stood at the barred counter, reckoning his earnings. She sagged back on the bleachers, clutching Father Michael's hand. "It's over," she said. "He got your money back for you, Father."

Yet even as she embraced their victory, she could not stop a welling of sadness. Dylan would leave after this. He had said as much and she could think of no way in the world to stop him.

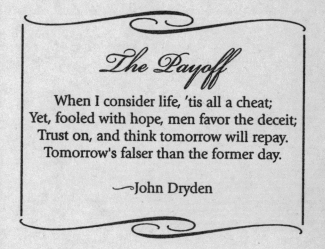

## The Payoff

When I consider life, 'tis all a cheat;
Yet, fooled with hope, men favor the deceit;
Trust on, and think tomorrow will repay.
Tomorrow's falser than the former day.

—John Dryden

# *Eighteen*

On the sandy shore of the lake, Dylan and Bull made a bonfire to chase away the chill of the autumn night. The amber glow cast a wavering circle of soft light over the thick wool blankets they had spread out on the sand. The remains of a meal of roasted chicken, contraband wine and fresh bread lay surrounded by four sprawling forms replete with good food and illicit drink.

Dylan sat with one arm propped behind him and the other around Kathleen. His feet, casually crossed at the ankles, rested on a strongbox containing their earnings in paper cash and coin.

He studied the play of firelight over the box. "You know," he said, "I'm no stranger to a fortune this size. I've seen it before. Why does this one seem so much sweeter than the others?"

Father Michael's beatific smile had been knocked askew by copious amounts of wine, obtained by means he refused to divulge. "'Cause you were doing God's work, my son."

Dylan chuckled and toyed with a silky lock of Kathleen's hair. "Was I?"

"Of course," Kathleen murmured, her voice sleepy with the wine she had imbibed. "Mr. Costello's money was stolen from the church. By earning it back, you restored the church's money.''

"It's not that simple. We made more than that. We doubled the amount that was stolen."

"Only because I made you wait for the right price," she said.

"Only because I convinced Costello there'd be a shortage," Bull said loudly.

"Only because I did such a good job in the trading pit," Dylan chimed in.

"Children, children." Father Michael made a quelling motion with his hands. "Don't poison the sweetness of this victory with pride. Why not concede that the Lord himself delivered good fortune into our unsher—unswerving—undeserving hands?"

"I didn't see the Lord in the trading pit, sweating bullets," Dylan grumbled, taking a swig of wine.

"May God forgive you for your arrogish—arrog— pride." The priest seized the bottle and polished off the wine.

"He will," said Dylan. "That's his job."

"What about the other traders, the honest ones?" Father Michael asked with a troubled frown. "They lost money today, too."

"Hazard of the game," Dylan said easily. "They knew that, and they'll be back to trade another day. Costello was the big loser. He was our mark."

"I feel awful for his daughter," Kathleen remarked. "Imagine, having such a scoundrel for a father."

Dylan couldn't imagine having a father at all. "Faith will be all right. She always is." He didn't mention that he'd had a private conference with Barry Lynch, making certain that Faith would have the means to carry on, no matter what happened to Vince. For years, Dylan had carried a very quiet, protective devotion for Faith in his heart. It didn't mean he wanted to marry her, but he never wished her ill.

Kathleen rested her head on his shoulder. He liked the soft weight of it there. He liked the smell of the soap she used and the gentle rise and fall of her bosom as she relaxed against him.

Bull lit a match and held it to the bowl of his burl pipe. A ripple of smoke swirled around him, and then the night wind snatched it away. "If you had a fortune this big before," he said, "why didn't you hold on to it?"

Dylan stared into the heart of the fire. "I guess I've never been much good at holding on to things."

They sat together in contemplative silence for a time. Some distance up the shore, lights had been strung along Government Pier. The lighthouse emitted its long beam over the restless waters of Lake Michigan. It made a fine sight, particularly with the knowledge that bargeloads of grain were making their way to port.

"Is Mr. Costello a vengeful sort?" Kathleen asked.

"He can do nothing," Dylan lied, lightly caressing her back. "He cannot reveal the source of his capital because it was stolen. And he cannot complain that he was given false price discoveries because that was confidential." Dylan decided not to disclose his prediction as to what Vince might do on a personal level. He was a proud man, harsh and ruthless. During their burlesque days, Dylan's physical condition had mattered, so Vince left him alone. More recently, he had counted on Faith to keep her father's temper in check.

But lately, Faith seemed to be taking more interest in a certain accounting clerk than in Dylan Kennedy.

Now there was nothing to stop Costello from taking revenge. That was yet another reason Dylan had to disappear. Of course, he thought, sliding a glance at Kathleen, it wasn't the only reason.

Father Michael climbed to his feet and patted his middle. "My friends," he announced, trying to hold on to steady dignity, "I must be going. There is mush—much work to be done tomorrow."

He staggered, and Bull got up to help him. "I'll get him back to St. Brendan's."

Dylan reached for the strongbox. Father Michael lifted his hand. "We're too drunk, and it's too dark out, to deal with that now. Bring the money 'round in the morning."

Dylan felt a flash of amazement. He wasn't used to being trusted. Then he saw Bull exchange a glance with Kathleen, and he understood. They bade goodnight all around, and Bull and the priest left. Outside the circle of firelight, the huge man and the drunken priest melted into the velvety night. The waves lapping at the shore filled the ensuing silent void, pierced by the occasional lonely whistle of a train, invisible on the distant prairie.

The sound made him think of all the empty nights to come, and how they would feel even emptier now that he had known a woman like Kathleen.

Without really planning what he would do, he shifted position to face her. He took her lips with his mouth, savoring her softness and the impulse that made her part her lips, maybe in protest, maybe in surprise. He deepened the kiss with pressure and sent a bold suggestion with the motion of his tongue.

She melted into his embrace. He was amazed at how sweetly pliant she was. They had their differences, the two of them, but not when it came to this sort of pleasure. He gave her no chance to protest. They had a mile of empty shoreline and the night was cold, but here in the circle of the fire, it was warm and intimate. He parted the bodice of her dress and drew it down and away from her, then loosened her corset and the shift beneath. Her breasts looked beautiful in the golden light. He put his mouth there, and the heat generated by the intimate contact lit his desire to a fever pitch. She was a magnificent creature, and he lost himself in her, lost all sense of time and space. Nothing existed outside this world of firelight and sensation, of flesh straining for contact and comfort. He loved the taste of her and told her so without words, drawing his tongue over her delicate skin while his hands worked efficiently, divesting her, and then himself, of the encumbering garments that lay between them. He kissed her everywhere, overriding a few halfhearted protests as he turned her this way and that on the blanket. He learned that if he kept hold of her, she never had a chance to escape him, for in truth she didn't want to escape. He warmed her with his hands and mouth and body, discovering the soft shadows and folds of her most secret places.

She tortured him in turn, laughing quietly when he gasped and convulsed with the effort to prolong their lovemaking. She learned his body with an earnest will that drove him mad. She had never been shy with him, not even that first time, and now in the flickering firelight she pressed her advantage. Her small clever hands grasped and caressed, setting him afire. It was a game in which there were no winners or losers, only sensation and the delight of a torment that promised everything.

"God, you are exquisite," he whispered, leaning down to give her the most intimate kiss of all. She shuddered beneath him, and then cried out for him to fill her. He took his time, though her fingers dug into him and her hips lifted toward his. He kissed her lightly, sweetly, lowering himself by inches. "This is how you taste," he whispered, sharing. "You taste like pleasure. You taste like love."

He filled her at last, and moved with a long slow rhythm, still holding back but starting to strain from the effort. When he could wait no longer he poured himself into her, giving everything he had and wishing he had more to offer.

The strange silence of the aftermath went on for long moments. He drew the pile of discarded clothing partially over them and pressed her cheek into the hollow of his chest. He had no idea why he liked holding her as much as he liked making love to her, but he did. It brought a certain rare quiet to his soul.

Finally he confessed it, because he realized he could say anything to her and it wouldn't sound stupid or weak. "When I hold you like this," he whispered, "the whole world seems to stop."

She twisted to her side, propping her chin in her hand to gaze into his face. "I know," she said. "I feel that, too." Taking a deep breath, she said, "I wish—"

"Sh." He touched a finger to her lips. "Don't wish for anything."

"Why not?"

"Then you'll never be disappointed." He didn't want to hear her wishes, because he could not make any of them come true. Besides, she had an uncanny knack for forcing him to make, and keep, promises— something he would rather not do.

She watched him with sympathy and curiosity and confusion. He wanted to explain himself to her but he didn't know how. He didn't know what he was feeling because he had never felt this way before. It was like an illness that wouldn't go away. Love? He had declared love for a woman many a time. It had never occurred to him that *love* was more than just a word to be used like a key in a lock. He suddenly remembered his feelings when the flames were marching toward the courthouse. The fire was something he couldn't control or manipulate or talk his way out of. Loving Kathleen posed the same dilemma.

"You know I have to go away now," he said.

"You don't have to do anything of the sort." She looked him straight in the eye. "You're a good trader, Dylan. You proved that today." She studied him for a long time, seeming to sense the futility of arguing with him. "But it seems you're better at running away."

"I'm not—" He broke off. "There's nothing but trouble for me, and anyone associated with me, if I stay. Costello is probably already looking for me."

"He doesn't scare you. Don't pretend he does." She sat up and hugged her knees to her chest, regarding him with a look as intense as the lighthouse beam. "You claim you are a man who loves risk. But you're afraid of the biggest gamble of all."

Wary, he squinted at her. "And what is that?"

"The risk of giving every part of yourself in a lasting bond. You're good at the shallow gratification of the game, but when it comes to the enduring challenge of love, you're afraid. Because as hard as it is to leave, it's even harder to stay. As much as it hurts to leave, it hurts even more to keep loving me.''

"Who said I loved you?'' he demanded.

Her smile was mysterious and sad. "You said so just now. Not with words, but that's the reason you're leaving. It's the reason you're so scared and the reason you can't stay. So pretend if you like that you won't settle down because you'd get bored. Pretend you have to flee because you've made a powerful enemy. That's a pretty story to tell people and it makes you look manly and interesting as you drift from place to place, game to game. But you and I both know you're running away because you're afraid of staying with me.''

He formed his fists into hard knots, when he actually wanted to clap them over his ears. He didn't need to hear this, damn her. With an effort, he relaxed and spoke with negligent offhandedness. "Very dramatic, but untrue. I don't believe in the kind of love you're talking about. It doesn't exist for me. It never has. No one ever showed me how it's done.''

"Oh, Dylan. You know. You know how it's done. You have to believe you're worth it.''

His mind whirred with confusion. He couldn't be the object of her devotion unless he knew how to return it. And he couldn't return it until he understood what he felt. "I don't know how. I'd only hurt you.''

"You'll hurt me by leaving.'' She slowly dressed herself. As Dylan did the same, he hoped she wouldn't cry, for her tears struck him like bullets from a firing squad. To distract her, he moved to another subject. "What will we do about the money?''

"What do you mean, what will we do? It belongs to the church."

"Only ten thousand of it. The other ten came from the trading."

"But you were trading for the church's money. If not for that, you'd never have the ten thousand."

"Your logic is stunning."

"You promised," she said. "The night of the fire, you promised to rebuild the steeple of St. Brendan's Church. You've earned the money to do it, but you have to give it all, not just half."

"You're serious, aren't you?"

"Serious as a toothache."

"You're the fool of the world, then. With your share of the profits, you could get your family back on its feet. But you're letting it slip through your fingers, all because you believed a liar's promise."

"That's just it, Dylan. I can no longer live a lie. I used to be unhappy with who I was, because I thought I wanted so much more. But at least that poor Irish lass was honest and hardworking. If I have to go back to that life, then so be it."

"But what about the fact that we're married?" Dylan demanded.

"Hah. A fine time for you to bring that up. You've managed to bury all the secrets in the world, Dylan Kennedy. What is one more?" She turned away in a huff. "You are incorrigible. You'll never change."

He watched her until she disappeared into the night. He didn't try to stop her, but for the first time in his life, he hesitated, pondering his options. He realized that he had to choose: riches or Kathleen. He couldn't have both.

* * *

When Kathleen awakened the next day, she knew he was gone for good even before she opened her eyes. There was a certain quality to the air, a quietness and an emptiness, as if all the energy had been sucked out of the room.

She lay unmoving in the berth, deep beneath the feather bed, with her eyes still shut. She tried not to remember the night before but every stinging little ache and warm twinge reminded her of all the ways he had touched her.

She flung her forearm over her eyes, reluctant to let in the light of day. She wondered how he could touch her with such intimacy, how he could whisper words of love in her ear, and then walk out of her life as if she were no more important to him than a horse he had borrowed for an afternoon pleasure ride. He had given her everything she wanted, except the one thing she needed most.

Enough, she told herself, hearing the stern echo of Gran's command in her mind. Enough of the self-pity, colleen.

She wondered what he had done with the money and braced herself for disappointment. Knowing Dylan, he would repay only what the church had lost, and keep the rest for himself. He was an opportunist, after all.

Aching from the wounds of having loved so foolishly, she almost wished they had not made love at the lakeshore. Almost. For her, the experience had been bittersweet; she had known it would be the last time. And she had been wrong ever to think she was unworthy of Dylan's love. She *was* worthy. The reason he had left had nothing to do with her, and everything to do with him.

*My mother dumped me like a stray cat in a drowning bag.* His words whispered through her mind, filling her with pity and understanding. Behind that cocksure, devil-may-care attitude, he believed himself unworthy, unlovable. His own mother had abandoned him. Now, as a grown man, he made certain he was the one to leave. That way, he would never be abandoned again.

With an effort of will, Kathleen flung aside the covers and sat up. Her clothes lay discarded in a heap on a parlor chair. She washed and dressed with great care and control, unwilling to allow herself to shed a single tear. "He was the adventure you always wanted, girleen," she muttered under her breath, sounding exactly like her grandmother. "Don't go having regrets because you made your own dream come true. Most people don't even have that."

She bathed her face with water from the basin and stared into the small oval shaving mirror that hung above the washstand. It was the same face she saw every day—pale skin, green eyes, freckles. She thought getting her heart broken would change her profoundly, but she looked the same on the outside.

She had no belongings to pack. None of this—not the train car, these clothes, these furnishings, this *life*—belonged to her. They were all fleeting, borrowed possessions. She had known that from the start.

She left the rail yard and made her way to Madison. Once aboard the horse car, she leaned an elbow on the rail and watched the city roll slowly by. Though still a wasteland, sad and chill in the autumn morning, Chicago was being rebuilt. Brick by brick, her pulsing life force would be excavated by those who refused to let her die.

Kathleen shut her eyes and let the memories come. She had clung to Dylan's hand and raced through the burning city, knowing from the start that her life would never be the same. She remembered him in all his guises—laughing at danger, then sobered by tragedy, at rare times quiet and pensive. But always, every moment they had been together, he had made her feel as if she were the most important person in the world.

That was why he was so good at his game, she told herself. Because he could make a person feel special and beloved, even when she should know better.

As the car lurched over the bridge, she stared down at the flat gray water, strewn with floating debris. Everyone's life had been changed by the fire. She was not so unique. Like everyone else, she would have to start over.

She had already concluded that she could not go back to being a lady's maid. That had led to her downfall in the first place. Working in a wealthy household had given her a window into a world she could never be a part of. She had sold her soul to belong to that world, and too late had learned the cost was too high.

It was wicked, but, sometimes when she thought back on all that had happened since the fire, she believed it was almost worth the price.

Now it was time to find her proper place in the world and to be content with her lot rather than always craving more. Dylan had taught her that she was smarter and braver than she had ever suspected. He had taught her that she had a foolish heart that could love until it nearly burst with hurt and keep on loving, futilely, even though it was broken.

With her chin held high, she exited the horse car and walked the rest of the way down Clinton Street. There was her parents' home, gray and battered like a ship that had weathered a storm. The little ones played a game of chase in the roadway, while the older boys squatted around a string circle, shooting marbles.

Behind the house, her parents worked together on the barn, raising a new building where the old milking shed had been. Already, four walls and a roof had been framed in. Her mother held a door in place while her father positioned the hinges. Clearly unaware that anyone was watching, Patrick O'Leary put his head around the side of the door and stole a kiss from his wife, who laughed and blushed like a girl.

She was still laughing when Kathleen walked into the yard.

"Mam, Da," she said, "I've come home."

Something in Kathleen's face or voice made her mother set aside her work. "Ah, colleen, what's the matter?" she asked, taking both of Kathleen's hands. "You look as though you've lost your best friend."

The remark rang through Kathleen with stunning truth. She realized she had found the one genuine thing about her and Dylan. In the middle of all their dangerous games and wild adventures he had become the last thing she'd expected. And now that he was gone, she had not just lost the man she loved. She had lost her best friend.

# Nineteen

*April, 1872*

Sir Percival Blake stepped down from the train platform and inspected the newly built terminal. Like all of Chicago, the station wore the spit-polished glory of a phoenix rising from the ashes. After being in a place of ancient monuments and preserved antiques, the newness of Chicago struck him with a restless vibrance and energy he hadn't felt in a very long time.

At the end of the platform, a small slender woman waited for him. She stood with her hands clasped in nervousness as she craned her neck, searching the crowd.

His heart softened at the sight of her, and he was grateful she'd managed to track him down clear across the Atlantic. It was hard to believe she still affected him after all this time. But she did.

Striding forward to greet her, he took her chilly hands in his and bent to kiss her pale smooth cheek.

"Thank you for coming," she said softly. "I didn't know who else to send for."

He squeezed her hand and whistled for a porter to bring his trunk. It was a handsome leather affair from Louis Vuitton, all the rage in Monte Carlo, where he had spent the winter.

Drinking.

Trying to forget.

And failing.

When her wire had come, summoning him for help, he had left immediately. The journey had seemed endless. There were very few people he would cross the ocean and half a continent for, but she was one of them.

"I had no idea this would happen," she said worriedly. "I had no idea my father would react with such a rage, simply because I married Barry Lynch."

So she'd gone and done it. She'd wed the lanky clerk after all. It fit, somehow. The two of them belonged together.

She stopped walking as tears spilled down her face. "Father won't listen to me, Dylan," she said, using a name he had not heard in months. "I don't know what to do."

He took out a clean handkerchief and blotted her cheeks. "It will be all right. I'll speak with your father. He'll come around, my dear."

Faith Costello Lynch sent him a watery, grateful smile. "You must have thought me such a ninny, sending you that hysterical wire," she said. "But I didn't know what else to do. You and Father have had your differences, but he always listens to you."

"I never thought you were a ninny, Faith."

"Not even when I fancied myself in love with you?"

He laughed, but not unkindly. "I thought you were wrong then, but never a ninny."

"What's wrong with loving you?"

"Everything." He had a fleeting thought of Kathleen and it was like an arrow to the heart. Good God, would his feelings for her never mellow? Even now, months after he had walked out of her life, his memories were as harsh as this morning's frost.

"I thought you were a god, but you're mortal like the rest of us," Faith conceded bluntly. "I always saw Barry for exactly who he was, and that was enough." Her mouth formed the beautiful, mysterious smile of a plain woman who knows she is loved. "Father was furious about Barry's role in recovering the church money. Barry stood up to him, though. He is studying to be a lawyer now. Fancy that."

"Tell me what happened," he said, stepping to the edge of the street to hail a hansom cab, "and then we'll figure out what to do."

Faith began talking, and from her very first words, it was clear to Dylan that she belonged heart and soul with poor, but honest, Barry Lynch. Vince was too stupid to see that, so he'd had Lynch arrested on trumped-up charges, blaming the relief fund scandal on him.

"He kept pressuring me to marry rich," Faith continued. "He needed capital to get himself back on his feet. I knew I had to act quickly or I'd be stuck with some horrible wealthy old coot. So I wed Barry in secret."

Dylan grinned. "I'm impressed."

"Thank you, but it doesn't do me a bit of good if the man I love is rotting in jail. Father refuses to understand."

Dylan took her small, gloved hand in his as a cab stopped at the curb. "We'll make him understand, my dear."

"But how?"

He allowed a wink and a smile. "You'll have to trust me."

* * *

By the time Dylan burst into Vincent Costello's office at the Lind, he was spoiling for a fight. How dare Vince stand in the way of true love? Didn't he know how rare it was, how precious? Didn't he believe something might actually be worth more than money?

"You son of a bitch." Costello shot up from the desk and bore down on him. "I figured out your trading trick—"

"You're dreaming, Vince. There was no trick. I got lucky in the futures market, that's all."

"That wasn't luck, damn it. That was a swindle." He drew back his fist. "And here's what I think of it."

Dylan caught Costello's fist before the blow landed. "Look, Vince, don't make me thrash you in front of your daughter."

Costello's face turned beet red with the effort to escape. He made a terrible sound in his throat but failed to stifle a curse that made Faith gasp in shock.

"For once in your life, listen," she said in a commanding tone Dylan had never heard her use before. "Or I swear you'll never see me again, Father."

Costello scowled, but relaxed and stepped back. Dylan slowly released his grip. "The past is over, Vince. Seems to me you'd better be thinking about the future."

"Thanks to you, I'm broke."

"You've got worse problems than that," Dylan pointed out, indicating Faith. "You never wanted her to be miserable before. Why would you go and do a thing like putting her husband in jail?"

"Because she doesn't know her own mind. She'll never be happy with a poor man."

"Really?" Dylan lifted an eyebrow. "Since when was money important to Faith?"

"Since she married a man who's hardly got a pot to piss in."

"That's enough," Faith said. "Father, if you refuse to retract your ridiculous accusations against Barry, I shall never speak to you again."

"Damn it, girl—"

"Let's stop right there," Dylan cut in. "No need to go spouting things you don't mean. Seems to me you and Lynch are in the same boat—both broke. You ought to form a partnership, get back on your feet together."

"Hah." Costello tugged at his moustache. "I'm through with partners."

"You had the wrong one," Dylan admitted.

"Barry's not like Dylan," Faith said, seizing on the idea. "He's—" She stopped short of saying "honest," but Dylan read the thought. He wasn't offended. She simply knew the truth.

"Chicago's ripe with opportunity," Dylan said, though he had no notion of the truth of that statement. "You and your son-in-law should start a new enterprise."

"Like what?" Vince demanded.

"I suppose you're barred from the Board of Trade. But you could set up an exchange for some other commodity. Something that fills an immediate need. What about a butter and egg exchange?"

"Butter?" Costello lifted an eyebrow.

"I have my sources," Dylan lied.

Faith clasped her hands. "What a perfect idea. I

could ask Kathleen to introduce you to her mother.'' She glanced at Dylan and seemed to derive satisfaction from his sudden pallor. ''Kathleen and I have become very good friends,'' she added smugly, then turned to Costello. ''Will you do it, Father?'' she asked. ''Will you?''

Costello's shoulders drooped. ''It might work.''

Dylan's head rang with the sound of Kathleen's name. She was everywhere, no matter how far he traveled or how fast he ran. He'd never escape her.

''And you'll include Barry,'' Faith said to her father.

He hesitated, then nodded.

She let out a long sigh of relief.

Suspicion flared in Dylan. Faith seemed to be having no trouble speaking her mind, he thought. She didn't have to send all the way to Paris for him. Suddenly his mind clouded with dark thoughts.

''Why did you really send for me?'' he asked her. ''If you think I'm going to turn myself in and take the blame—''

''It'd be no more than you deserve,'' Vince blustered.

''Oh, stop it.'' Faith tucked her arm around her father's, and her touch seemed to soothe him. Watching Faith manage him, Dylan realized that maybe she wasn't so helpless after all.

''We have plans to make, then,'' she announced, straightening her bonnet. Then she turned to Dylan. ''I thought you should see the restoration work at the site of St. Brendan's Church, since you are responsible for funding it.'' Then she came forward and stepped up on tiptoe to softly kiss his cheek. ''I'm glad                              you're back. Now go. I think you'll be amazed at what you find there.''

Springtime in Chicago meant far more than budding trees and new flowers. The whole burned district had come back to life with a swift vibrance that lifted his spirits. When the cab reached St. Brendan's, he stepped out without looking down, for his eyes were raised to the sky.

The church had been almost completely restored. The gardens, surrounded by figured wrought iron fences and gates, were ripe with the first flush of the springtime. A new gazebo draped with budding wisteria adorned the chapel garden like a crown.

And high atop the west end of the roof rose a gleaming new steeple.

Inside, the restoration work continued as workmen on scaffolds repaired the plasterwork, glaziers replaced windows and stonemasons mortared chinks in the walls. The smells of fresh varnish and damp plaster mingled with the church scent of frankincense.

Not for the first time, Dylan felt an eerie prescience, like fingertips touching his scalp. Shadowy recollections haunted him each time he entered a church. Images hovering at the edge of his memory resolved into shapes he almost recognized. Long ago he had trained himself not to think about the incident of his childhood that had defined him. He had grown so adept at forgetting that he truly had forgotten, but at moments like this, in church, he began to remember despite his resolve.

''Well, what do you think?'' said a voice with a rolling brogue.

Dylan grinned, stretching out his hand to Father

Michael. Dressed as a carpenter rather than a priest, he looked as fit and healthy as a lumberjack. "It's beautiful."

"Don't forget your part in it," the priest reminded him. "A pity you weren't here to see the work."

Curse the priest. He was as meddlesome as Faith. "I wintered in Monte Carlo, if you must know. Those grain shares I kept back turned out to be pure gold, and I lived like a king."

"It's good to know you're clever about *some* things," Father Michael said. "But even kings get lonely. Come, I'll show you around."

The weird feeling persisted and strengthened as he walked along the aisle, admiring the new pews, side chapels and shrines to those who had perished in the fire. Memories battered at him like wings against a window, and he sensed they were about to break through.

"Sit down," Father Michael said, studying his face. "You've something on your mind."

Dylan sat, but tried his best to dismiss the feeling. "It's probably fatigue from all the travel."

Father Michael leaned down, his voice very soft as he said, "It's more than that. Open your mind, my friend. Unburden your heart."

"I can't stop thinking about Kathleen," he blurted out, appalled by his own admission.

"That's the way love works," the priest said, completely unsurprised. "It's no sin."

"How the hell am I supposed to know what love is? A word. Something I say to a woman to get what I want from her." Panic hissed in his ears. "And why the hell would anyone—" He broke off, angry with himself for what he had almost said.

But Father Michael finished the thought for him. "Why would anyone love you? I suppose because of the worthy person you are."

He moved aside, and Dylan looked up at a colored window, high over the altar. And then the strangest thing happened. He felt himself going toward that round disk of light, to a place that smelled of old stone and incense. He shut his eyes, trying to run from the memory, but that only made it more vivid. Soft, mournful music echoed through his mind. Time rolled away and he was nine years old again, a small boy left in a railway waiting room by a mother who had never come back.

All these years he had refused to understand what had transpired. Now finally, in this searing moment, the truth became clear. She had left him to wait at the station while she sought help, but by the time she had found a church, she must have been too ill to return. Perhaps she'd only had time to send a priest to fetch her son before collapsing. He had been taken to a church that night. He remembered now, remembered his pale mother lying in a pine box while the priest asked him her name, and Dylan had refused to give it. From that moment onward, he had regarded himself as something damaged, something not worth keeping.

"I never knew she was so sick," he whispered, lost in the pain-tinged memories. "I never knew." When he opened his eyes, Father Michael was gone and Dylan's cheeks were wet. He felt drained, but curiously at peace. For the first time in memory, he knew beyond doubt that, long ago, someone had loved him. Her name had been Frances Kennedy. She was lost to him, but the knowledge of her love burned like a fire inside him.

Father Michael returned, looking not at all surprised by Dylan's state. "I believe this belongs to you." He handed him a worn, folded paper. "I saved it from the night of the fire."

Dylan looked down at the battered paper in his hand, studying the ornate document and the signature of Kirby Lane, the court clerk who had died that night with a smile and a woman's name on his lips.

# *Twenty*

Under her homemade dimity dress, Kathleen secretly wore a French garter made of silk and lace. Not the most appropriate article of clothing for doing barn chores, but she had kept the frilly thing, taken from the Pullman car, as a memento of her love affair with Dylan Kennedy. Some lovers gave each other elaborate tokens at their parting, but not Dylan. He had tried his best to leave without a trace. It was silly in the extreme to wear something so fine to do the milking, but no one would know.

Ah, but he had left an indelible memento, she realized, hefting a bucket in each hand. The memories of loving him were forever etched on her heart, her soul. Those images would never ever leave her. She tried not to think about the fact that the most exciting part of her life was over. She tried to take joy in the ordinary and not compare it to the extraordinary time she had spent with Dylan Kennedy.

But he would forever be a memory, she thought with a heavy heart. At least she had a family to give her the patience, the wisdom and the time for her wounds to heal. Now that she was home, working at the dairy, she was learning her place in the world. Her family had moved to Canaryville, east of the

Union Stockyards. She had folded her dreams away
and gone with them.

Finally, she understood that life was about loving
what she had, not coveting something that dangled
out of reach.

Over the hard, busy winter and spring, she had
learned to savor the small joys of everyday living—
a new litter of kittens in the barn, her little sister's
lost tooth, the sound of her parents laughing together
on the front stoop. Things such as these had meant
nothing to her before. Now they provided a source of
contentment and comfort in the wake of her wild affair with Dylan Kennedy.

The price of her newfound wisdom was the pain
of having loved him beyond all reason. She kept waiting for the hurt to go away, but sometimes, on a dazzling April day like this, it seemed even worse.

She finished her chores and went to the kitchen to
give the little ones their morning tea. Her father sat
at the table, a stark white envelope in his hand.

"What's that, Da?" she asked.

"Pegleg Sullivan dropped it off last night." He
held it out to her. "Here. I ain't much for reading."
But the gleam in his eye hinted that he knew what
was in the letter.

Her hand trembled a little as she opened it. The
words blurred, and she had to blink to clear her vision. "It's an invitation, Da. We're all to come to a
dedication of the new steeple at St. Brendan's."

Her father eyed the card. "We don't dare disobey
a summons from the Lord, then, do we, colleen?"

The spire rose over the tops of the trees, stark and
stately in contrast to the puffy clouds riding the lake

wind. Kathleen couldn't stifle a jolt of emotion when she saw the steeple. She recalled Dylan's mad gymnastics the night of the fire, then his rash promise to restore the ruined steeple. He had surprised them all by keeping that promise. When he'd disappeared, he had left every cent of his earnings with the church.

In the shadow of the new steeple, a flower garden bloomed, and parishioners and honored guests milled about. Kathleen stepped through the wrought iron gates, spying a lovely gazebo drenched in sunlight. She bit her lip to hold back tears, for the chapel garden was so like the one she had once described to Dylan that it brought back every moment she had spent with him. Swallowing hard, she called herself a fool for turning so soft and sentimental.

Father Michael appeared, wearing his finest raiments, his young face wreathed in smiles. "A lovely day," he declared, greeting everyone. "A lovely day for a wedding. Right this way, please, there we are...."

Kathleen frowned, turning to her parents. "I had no idea about a wedding," she whispered.

"It's supposed to be a surprise." Bull Waxman's deep voice was round and mellow with good cheer. He wore a new suit of clothes and a shiny top hat, looking dapper as he led the way to rows of white benches. Father Michael had convinced Bull to stay in Chicago, and he worked at the Quimper Shipyards.

She was startled to see Vincent Costello standing beside his daughter Faith and Barry Lynch. It couldn't be their wedding, for they were already married.

Her confusion mounted as she greeted Judge Roth and Mayor Mason, whom she had not seen since the night of the fire. Lucy Hathaway and Phoebe Palmer from Miss Boylan's were there, dewy-eyed and whispering behind their hands. Miss Emma Wade Boylan herself, birdlike and excruciatingly proper, tried to glare the others into silence. Kathleen's former mistress, Deborah Sinclair, had astonished everyone with her marriage to a backwoodsman, and she now lived on a lake island far to the north. So many changes, thought Kathleen with a twinge of wistfulness. Nothing ever stayed the same.

"Pardon me, miss," said a masculine voice behind her, "but I believe there is something in your hat."

Kathleen froze in her tracks as a chill raced up her spine. She told herself to turn and look, but couldn't move. Vaguely she was aware that her family moved past her and took their places in the chapel garden. And then he was there.

Dylan Francis Kennedy—looking even more urbane and handsome than he did in her dreams. With the low, throaty laughter she remembered from their first meeting, he reached beneath the brim of her bonnet and produced a small, shiny object. "Ah, you see. There *was* something in your hat."

She tried to remember how to speak, and finally managed to say, "I—I had no idea you'd be here."

"I was afraid you wouldn't come if you knew."

They stared at each other while the moment filled with birdsong and murmuring voices from the gathering. Without taking his eyes off her face, Dylan lifted her hand and slid on the ring he had "found" in her hat.

"What in heaven's name are you doing?" she whispered, trying not to feel the wild hope in her heart.

"Ah, love. You know." He astonished her further

by dropping down on one knee, eliciting a few female gasps from the crowd. Then the world fell away as Kathleen gazed down at him, into the face she loved so well, into the beautiful blue eyes she had never forgotten. "I have nothing to offer you," Dylan said. "Nothing but this ring, and my heart."

She had wished for riches and fine things, but when he stood and took her in his arms, she knew how wrong she had been.

"That's all I need, Dylan," she said, so full of wonder that she thought she might burst. "It's all I've ever needed, you great fool. Didn't you know that?"

He stood and kissed her, then leaned down and put his mouth very close to her ear. "You'll have to remind me."

Feeling as though she were walking on clouds, she took his hand and walked to the sun-dappled gazebo. There, in the company of friends and family, she renewed the vows she had made to him the night of the fire. Phoebe and Lucy sobbed daintily into embroidered handkerchiefs, while Kathleen's parents bawled happily and lustily, grinning through their tears.

"I love you," Dylan whispered, for her ears only. "I've always loved you." He leaned down and brushed his lips over hers, a featherlight promise of deeper kisses to come.

Kathleen closed her eyes, dizzy with joy. This is it, Gran, she thought. This is my dream.

And in a final miracle that could only be a gift from her dear gran, a dozen white doves, released into the cloudless sky, took flight.

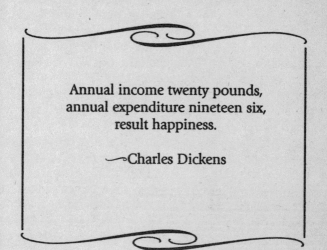

Annual income twenty pounds,
annual expenditure nineteen six,
result happiness.

—Charles Dickens

# *Epilogue*

*April, 1873*

It was an hour before dawn, but Kathleen's baby daughter had no regard for her parents' slumber. Little Bridget Frances Kennedy howled as if pursued by a chariot full of banshees, making more noise at three months of age than the city's new alarm relay system. Kathleen groaned and reached for a pillow to pull over her head. But there was no pillow to be had. Dylan had captured both of them, one for each ear.

She sighed and lit a lamp. "You're a lazy article, you are, Dylan Kennedy," she grumbled, "and your daughter's inherited your impatient, demanding nature." She donned her scuffs and robe. She and Dylan had discussed hiring a nurse and a nanny for little Bridget, but Kathleen couldn't bear the thought of surrendering her baby to the care of another. Certainly it was the way rich folk did things, and at one time, it had been her dream to be rich. Now she understood that she had riches beyond measure, and the most precious gifts had nothing to do with money. It was the lessons she learned in the bosom of her family, not in the employ of the very rich, that stayed with her now. Regardless of fashion, she wanted to be present for every second of her daughter's life. They had shared a heartbeat; now they would share each day to come.

But at four-thirty in the morning, she was open to further discussions about the nurse.

Dylan had given her all that she wanted, and more. He'd kept his seat on the Board of Trade, and had bought her a snug house with a garden, a shed with a milk cow, a few chickens and a horse that went too fast for Kathleen's taste. But there would always be a bit of the daredevil in her husband.

When she walked into the baby's room and saw the dainty limbs flailing, her heart constricted with love. "There, there, girleen," she crooned, crossing the room.

The baby hushed instantly at the sound of her mother's voice. By the time Kathleen had changed her nappy and was seated in the rocking chair, Bridget was smiling and cooing with a charm so delightful that Kathleen couldn't help laughing. "Ah, I love you so, I do," she whispered, putting the baby to her breast. "You are the very best part of me, Bridget Kennedy, and always will be."

Her happiness brought a wave of emotion as it often did since she had become a mother. Bridget drew from her all the aching tenderness of a new mother's heart, and lately she seemed to find a special sentimentality for the beauty of simple things—the bluish sparkle of the stars at midnight, the quiet cooing of her child's voice, the warmth of her husband in bed each night. In the past, the sight of a beautifully crafted piece of jewelry used to move her. Now she wept at the shadows of moonlight on her baby's cheek.

Bridget finished nursing and blinked sleepily at the semidarkness. Kathleen grew hungry as well. Nursing a baby gave her cravings the pregnancy never had. She wanted a glass of warm milk, and was about to put down the baby and go out to the shed when a tall shadow fell across the room.

Her heart lifted when she saw him, her handsome, clever devil of a husband. "Typical man," she scolded softly. "Late as usual."

"You have a talent for troweling on the guilt, Kathleen O'Leary Kennedy," he muttered. "Pillows or not, I can't sleep when I know my two beautiful ladies are awake."

"That was the idea," she said unapologetically.

"Give the little one to me. I'll rock her to sleep and put her to bed."

A toothless smile lit the baby's face when Dylan took her in his large, careful hands. Kathleen let him have the rocker and stood watching them. They were the most wonderful thing she had ever seen, the big man with the tiny baby cradled next to his heart, her little fist batting at his smiling face.

"Are you all right with her, then?" Kathleen asked.

"We're fine, love."

"I was just going to get some warm milk," she said. "Nursing makes me hungry."

"I'll go—"

"Heavens to betsy, no. I can surely fetch a pail of milk on my own, Dylan Kennedy. It's in my blood, after all."

"My point exactly," he said.

She tried not to crack a smile as she lifted her chin

with mock haughtiness. Holding the light in front of
her, she said, "I am off to milk the cow."

"Fine," he said, "but be careful of that lantern,
my love."

# *Author Note*

Dear Reader,

Though no other fire created the sensation of the Great Fire of 1871, there were several more catastrophic blazes in Chicago in the 1870s. However, I'm relieved to report that none of them started in anyone's milking shed.

In *The Firebrand*, Lucy Hathaway loses her fortune but gains a chance to follow her dream of opening a bookshop. Five years after the fire, Lucy unravels the haunting mystery surrounding the child she rescued and adopted. When wealthy banker Randolph Higgins claims to be the little girl's long-lost father, their mutual love for the child brings together the most mismatched couple in town. Will Lucy do battle for her child, or surrender her heart to her enemy?

Please watch for *The Firebrand* in May of 2001.
Until then,
Happy reading,
Susan Wiggs
Box 4469
Rolling Bay WA 98061
SusanWiggs@pobox.com
www.susanwiggs.com

MIRA Books invites you to
turn the page for an exciting preview of

## THE FIREBRAND

Discover adventures and romance with
Kathleen's friend, Lucy Hathaway,
in this unforgettable new historical romance
from Susan Wiggs.
Available in paperback
April 2001

# One

Lucy Hathaway caught herself staring across the room at Mr. Randolph Higgins, pondering the way their public disagreement had led to private thoughts. It was a rare thing to meet a man who made her think. She should not have antagonized him, but she couldn't help herself. He was provocative, and she was easily provoked.

She felt herself edging toward an admission. An admission, followed by a plan of action—for that was Lucy's way. She saw no point in believing in something without acting on that belief.

What she admitted to herself, what she had come to believe, was that she was wildly attracted to Randolph Higgins. It was a first for her. Until tonight, she had never met a man who made her feel the hot electrical sting of attraction. It had to mean something. It had to mean that he was the one.

That was where her plan of action came in. She wanted him for her lover. Now she had to figure out how to get him to want her in the same way.

Seeing no point in dilly-dallying, she marched straight across the room to him. He gave no sign that he had seen her, but when he turned away from the refreshment table, he held two cups of lemonade.

"You," he said, handing her a cup, "are the most annoying creature I have ever met."

"Really?" She took a sip of the sweet-tart lemonade. "I take that as a compliment."

"So you are both annoying and slow-witted," he said.

"You don't really think that." Watching him over the rim of her cup, she explained. Lord, but he was handsome. And in her heart, she felt such a surge of anticipation that she could not govern the wide grin on her face. Because she had found him at last. After a lifetime of believing that she would never meet someone who could arouse her passion, share her dreams, bring her joy, she had finally found him. A man she could admire, perhaps even love.

"Do I amuse you?" he asked, frowning good-naturedly.

"Why would you think that?"

"Because you keep smiling at me even though I have just called you annoying and—"

"Slow-witted," she reminded him.

"Yes," he said. "Rude of me."

"I forgive you." She glanced furtively from side to side. "Mr. Higgins, do you suppose we could go somewhere…a little less public?" Before he could answer, she took his hand and pulled him toward the now-empty lecture room. It was a large salon, its fringed and gilt decor richly overdone. Gaslight sconces glowed gently on the walls, and orange light flickered mysteriously in the windows.

"Miss Hathaway, what is this about?" he asked, carefully taking his hand from hers.

"I wanted to speak to you in private," she said.

Her heart raced. This was a simple matter, she told herself. Men and women arranged trysts all the time.

"Very well." He propped his hip on the back of a chair, the pose so negligently masculine that she nearly forgot her purpose. "I'm listening."

"Did you enjoy the lecture tonight, Mr. Higgins?"

"Honestly?"

"Honestly."

"It was a crashing bore."

Her heart sank. Clearly he didn't share her fascination. She pulled in a deep breath. "I see. Well, then—"

"—until a certain young lady began to speak her mind," he added. "Then I found it truly interesting."

"Interesting?"

"Yes."

"And...provocative?"

"Most definitely."

"Did you think it was...stimulating?"

He laughed aloud. "Now that you mention it."

Her spirits soared. "Oh, I am glad, Mr. Higgins. So glad indeed. May I call you Randolph?"

"Actually, my friends call me Rand."

She most definitely wanted to be his friend. "Very well, Rand. And you must call me Lucy."

"This is a very odd conversation, Lucy."

"I agree. And I haven't even made my point yet."

"Perhaps you should do so, then."

"Make my point."

"Yes."

Ye gods, she was afraid. But she wanted him so much. "Well, it's like this, Mr.—Rand. Earlier when I spoke of passionate feelings, I was referring to you."

His face went dead white. His mouth moved, but no sound came out.

"You see," she rushed on, "I have always wanted to have a lover. I never did encounter a man I wanted to spend my life with, and if I took a lover I would simply have no need of a husband."

"Lucky you." Some of the color and arrogance returned to his handsome face.

She could sense suppressed laughter beneath his wry comment. "But I wouldn't want an affair just for the sake of having one. I was waiting to meet the right man." She looked him square in the eye. "And I've found you at last."

The humor left his expression. "Lucy." He spoke very low, and the timbre of his voice passed over her like a caress.

"Yes?"

"My dear, you are a most attractive girl."

She clasped her hands, thoroughly enchanted. "Do you think so?"

"Indeed I do."

"That is wonderful. No one has ever thought me attractive before." She was babbling, but she couldn't help herself. "My mother says I am too dark and intense, and far too outspoken, and that I—"

"Lucy." He grasped her upper arms.

She nearly melted, but held herself upright, await-ing his kiss. She had never been kissed by a man before. When she was younger, Cornelius Cotton had kissed her, but she later found out his older brother had paid him to do it, so that didn't count. This was going to be different. Her first honest-to-goodness kiss from the handsomest man ever created.

Late at night, she and the other young ladies of

Miss Boylan's would stay up after lights-out, speculating about all the ways a man might touch a woman. One thing she remembered was to close her eyes before a kiss. It seemed a shame to close them when he was so wonderful to look at, but she wanted to do this right. She shut her eyes.

"Lucy," he said again, an edge of desperation in his voice. "Lucy, look at me."

She readily opened her eyes. What a glorious face he had, so alive with character and robust health and touching sincerity. So filled with sensual promise, with his lips curved into a smile, the way his eyes were filled with...pity? Could that be pity she saw in his eyes? Surely not.

"Rand—"

"Wait." Ever so gently, he touched a finger to her lips to silence her.

She nearly burned from his caress, but he quickly took his finger away.

"Lucy," he said, "before you say any more, there's something I must tell you—"

"Randolph!" a voice called shrilly from the doorway. "There you are, Randolph. I've been looking all over for you."

Lucy turned to the back of the salon. The dry windstorm that had been swirling through the city all evening battered at the windows. There, in the doorway, stood the most stunning woman she had ever seen. Petite, blond and willowy, she held her lithe body in the shape of a question mark, clad in a magnificent gown with a flounced bustle. In a rustle of perfumed silk, she moved toward them, hand outstretched toward Rand.

"I've found you at last," the gorgeous blond woman said, her words an ironic echo of Lucy's.

Rand's pallor quickly changed to dull red as he bowed over her hand. "Miss Lucy Hathaway," he said, straightening up and stepping out of the way, "I'd like you to meet Diana Higgins." He slipped an arm around the other woman's slender waist. "My wife."

*From seduction in the royal sheikhdom to
high adventure in the hot Arabian desert comes a
breathtaking love story by international bestselling author*

# DIANA PALMER

## LORD OF THE DESERT

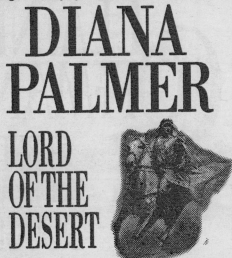

Gretchen Brannon was completely out of her element when she
aligned herself with Sheikh Philippe Sabon, the formidable ruler
of Qawi. They came from different worlds, but he made her aware
of her own courage. She, in turn, aroused his sleeping senses like
no other woman could.

But now that Gretchen's heart belongs to the Lord of the Desert,
she's become the target for vengeance by the sheikh's most
diabolical enemy. In a final showdown that will pit good against
evil, can love and destiny triumph...?

**"The dialogue is charming, the characters likable
and the sex sizzling..."**
**—*Publishers Weekly* on *Once in Paris***

*On sale October 2000 wherever paperbacks are sold!*

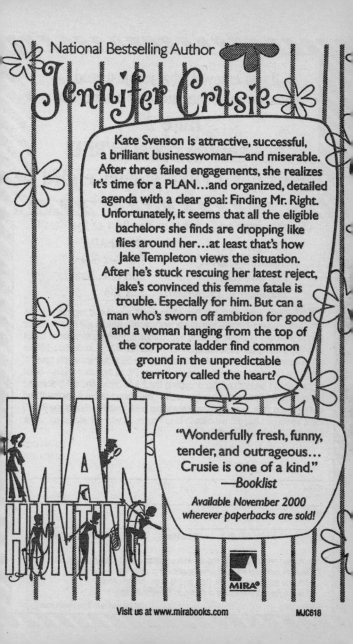

If you enjoyed what you just read,
then we've got an offer you can't resist!

# Take 2 bestselling novels FREE!
# Plus get a FREE surprise gift!

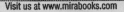

New York Times Bestselling Author

# DEBBIE MACOMBER

### Return To Promise

The town of Promise, Texas, is a good place
to raise a family and spend the rest of your days with
the person you love.

Cal Patterson and his wife, Jane, certainly thought so.
But after months of emotional upheaval brought on
by doubts about their marriage, the two separate,
and Jane takes their children to California.

Cal is now forced to confront what he really wants
in his life, what he *needs*. Jane is confronting the same
questions.... How seriously does Cal take his marriage
vows? And how important is Promise to Jane? Is there
hope for a reconciliation—in time for Christmas?

"Popular romance writer Macomber has a gift for
evoking the emotions that are at the heart of
the genre's popularity."
—*Publishers Weekly*

*On sale October 2000
wherever hardcovers are sold!*

## SUSAN WIGGS

| | | | | |
|---|---|---|---|---|
| 66592 | THE HOSTAGE | ___ | $6.50 U.S. | ___ $7.99 CAN. |
| 66534 | THE HORSEMASTER'S DAUGHTER | | | |
| | | ___ | $5.99 U.S. | ___ $6.99 CAN |
| 66459 | THE DRIFTER | ___ | $5.99 U.S. | ___ $6.99 CAN. |
| 66449 | THAT SUMMER PLACE | ___ | $6.99 U.S. | ___ $7.99 CAN. |
| 66301 | THE LIGHTKEEPER | ___ | $5.99 U.S. | ___ $6.99 CAN. |

*(limited quantities available)*

TOTAL AMOUNT                                     $_____
POSTAGE & HANDLING                          $_____
($1.00 for one book; 50¢ for each additional)
APPLICABLE TAXES*                              $_____
TOTAL PAYABLE                                     $_____
(check or money order—please do not send cash)

To order, complete this form and send it, along with a check or money order for the total above, payable to MIRA Books®, to: **In the U.S.:** 3010 Walden Avenue, P.O. Box 9077, Buffalo, NY 14269-9077; **In Canada:** P.O. Box 636, Fort Erie, Ontario L2A 5X3.

Name:_____
Address:_____ City:_____
State/Prov.:_____ Zip/Postal Code:_____
Account Number (if applicable):_____
075 CSAS

*New York residents remit applicable sales taxes.
 Canadian residents remit applicable GST and provincial taxes.

**MIRA®**